NAVAL
HISTORY OF
WORLD WAR II

Jane's

NAVAL
HISTORY OF
WORLD WAR II

Bernard Ireland

HarperCollinsPublishers

In the USA for information address:
HarperCollins*Publishers* Inc.
10 East 53rd Street
New York
NY 10022

In the UK for information address:
HarperCollins*Publishers*
77-85 Fulham Palace Road
Hammersmith
London W6 8JB

First Published in Great Britain by HarperCollins*Publishers* 1998

1 3 5 7 9 10 8 6 4 2

ISBN 0 00 472143 8

Colour artwork by Tony Gibbons. Cutaway illustrations and profiles
of Graf Zeppelin, Gascogne, Tosa and Sovietksy Soyuz ©Tony
Gibbons. Other artwork ©Aerospace Publishing
Computer graphics: Richard Burgess

Design: Rod Teasdale

Colour reproduction by Colorscan
Printed in Great Britain by The Bath Press

Contents

Foreword

The maritime aspects of World War II were complex, and many accounts are likewise long and detailed, often burying essentials in a mass of peripherals. In order to concentrate on what mattered, the Author has here identified five major areas which, in his opinion, were decisive to the final outcome. To win or lose in any of these was to win or lose the overall struggle.

Through concentrating on a small number of specific areas, it has been possible to include a degree of background to set matters in context and to chart progress with a minimum of discontinuity in either chronology or geography.

The Author would like to acknowledge the continuing support of Ian Drury, who identified and procured the illustrations and artwork. He would also like to thank his wife, who, as ever, was landed with the task of converting a mass of corrected longhand into a readable typescript.

Bernard Ireland
Fareham, 1998

Fred T Jane and *Fighting Ships*

*J*ane's Fighting Ships is one of the world's most famous titles, yet many must have wondered just who was this androgynous naval expert. He himself joked about his own name, once signing a sketch 'Fred Mary-Ann'. Fred T Jane, as he was really known, was born on 6 August 1865, the son of a Church of England clergyman. He grew up during a period of rapid technological change that profoundly affected the two worlds he inhabited: journalism, and the Royal Navy. New printing processes, and more general literacy created a wider reading public, taking a more active interest in defence matters, partly inspired by the spectacular pace of naval and military change, and partly by the international instability this brought with it.

Fred T Jane, however, grew up in the peace of Cornwall, and Devon, where his father held various benefices. He attended Exeter School as a day boy, where it cannot be said he shone academically, describing himself later as an awful thickhead. He did better on the football pitch, being recognised as a plucky and straight running half-back, apt to get too near the scrimmage through over-eagerness: an observation often borne out in later life. Significantly Jane was also responsible for the *Toby*, an alternative school magazine which enjoyed much success for its illustrations, and total disregard for veracity, or the law of libel.

Unable to enter the Royal Navy for health reasons, Jane went to London, where he occupied an attic above 41 Gray's Inn Road, scraping a living by pictorial journalism. This was poorly paid work, and recognition came slowly. Jane's chance came in July 1890 with a cruise on board HMS *Northampton*, an elderly ironclad, to cover that summer's naval manoeuvres for the *Pictorial World*. Over the next two months a flood of sketches appeared over his name. These were something quite out of the ordinary. Not only did Jane's ships lie in the water as ships really do, but he drew everything that happened, by day or night, starting in Tor Bay with what became Jane's trademark: a display of electric searchlights.

Jane's participation in these annual events allowed him to extend a portfolio of warship sketches dating back to an album he started at school. Inspired by the Royal Navy's bombardment of Alexandria in 1882, 'Ironclads of the World' gradually began to merit its ambitious title. Fred T Jane became an accepted authority on foreign warships as well as British. When the Russian fleet visited Toulon to seal the Franco-Russian Entente, or a Spanish cruiser was wrecked off Gibraltar it was Jane who sketched the occasion for the *Illustrated London News*. So remarkable was his ability to conjure up

warships he had never seen, that for years Jane was believed to have taken part in the Chilean Civil War of 1891, on the strength of his illustration of the torpedo attack on the *Blanco Encalada*, a Chilean cruiser. Only after Fred's death did his brother reveal that the sketch was made in Devon. In 1897 Fred T Jane used the expertise he had developed to produce a revolutionary new warship directory, to be known as *All The World's Fighting Ships*, the engraved blocks for which, laid end to end, stretched some 400 feet.

The frequent naval scares that followed the development of steam warships fed upon ignorance of the true state of the strategic balance between the leading naval powers, particularly Great Britain and France. Journalists, novelists, and politicians exploited public fears, deliberately exaggerating the strengths, and weaknesses of both sides for their own commercial or political advantage. In the 1880s Lord Brassey, still a significant name in defence publishing, began to publish the *Naval Annual*, tabulating many of the world's warships. However, as a directory of warships it was not entirely successful. Illustrations appeared separately from ships' specifications, and gave little idea of their true

appearance. The format of the data tables varied, making it impossible to compare British and foreign warships, or armoured ships with unarmoured. Some information was misleading. Original trial speeds appeared for ships which were notoriously immobile, for example the Turkish fleet which never left the Bosphorus. Ordnance was described in terms of calibre, or weight of shot, which was unhelpful when modern 6-inch quick-firers rivalled older 10-inch guns with a slow rate of fire, and low muzzle energy.

Fighting Ships addressed all these shortcomings. Jane's contacts among the Royal Navy's engineering branch ensured he quoted only the latest speeds. Illustrations appeared next to the standard set of data provided for all ships. Jane insisted on documenting the most obscure auxiliary warships, 'on the same principle that a dictionary includes words on account of the mere fact of their existence'. He classified guns alphabetically, according to their muzzle energy, so their performance could easily be compared. Conversely he classified armour by its ability to keep shells out. Thus "A" class guns, such as the 12-inch guns of the Royal Sovereign class battleships of 1891-92, could penetrate "a" class

armour out to 4000 yards, then the tactical range for heavy naval guns. "A" class guns also included older 16-inch and 13.5-inch weapons, whose heavier rounds made up for their lower velocity.

Although the level of detail varied over the years, Jane never forgot the needs of the man on the bridge, in a hurry to identify another ship on the horizon. It was for him that Jane provided his most striking innovation. The first issue of *Fighting Ships* included a visual index of ship silhouettes to assist recognition. *The Naval Warrant Officer's Journal*, the mouthpiece of the professional 'bone and muscle of the service', recognised the value of this, recommending that the new directory should be in every chart-house, within reach of the signal-man and officer on watch.

The same journal in 1902 described *Fighting Ships* as, 'more indispensable than ever', and made a plea for the Admiralty to place a copy within reach of all naval personnel. Although ships did acquire copies, officialdom never took Jane seriously. To some extent this was due to his irreverent sense of humour, that found an outlet in outrageous practical jokes, most notoriously the kidnapping of a Labour MP in 1909. Jane infuriated

the Navy League by suggesting that if they really wanted to help modernise the Navy, they would do well to throw Nelson overboard. When the 1903 *Fighting Ships* carried an article describing a revolutionary fast battleship, armed exclusively with 12-inch guns, the proposal was derided as more suitable for the pages of HG Wells than a serious naval publication. The Admiralty, however, was already considering such a ship, the *Dreadnought*, justifying the claim of a later editor of *Fighting Ships* that, 'Never before had Jane so clearly attained his ambition of making *Fighting Ships* the mirror of naval progress'.

Jane's lack of official favour was clearly demonstrated by the failure to use his talents during the First World War. Unlike modern defence experts, he profited little from the opportunity to play the pundit. Perhaps his views were not to the taste of a jingoistic public who regarded the war as a football match, with ships sunk instead of goals scored. Jutland and its aftermath vindicated Jane's unfashionable prediction that the war would end without a decisive Trafalgar-style victory over the German battle fleet, but he did not live to comment on the battle. He had undertaken an exhausting lecture

Above: Fred T Jane developed a highly detailed naval wargame which enabled military and civilian players to evaluate the comparative strengths and weaknesses of the world's warships.

tour, from Plymouth to Dundee, to defend the conduct of the naval war, and in October 1915 was soaked to the skin driving from Portsmouth to Cheltenham in his open topped racing car. He caught a chill. The following March Fred T Jane died alone in his apartment in Southsea, apparently of heart failure brought on by influenza. Fortunately he had made careful arrangements for the continued publication of *Fighting Ships* which, alone among its rivals, continued to appear throughout the war.

Richard Brooks

Chapter 1 – The War against Commerce

In time of war, the United Kingdom's island situation is, at once, its strength and its weakness. With insufficient natural resources to support a relatively large population, the nation is dependent upon overseas trade. Until the dissolution of its empire, following World War II, its economy was inextricably bound to shipping. Countless vessels brought in raw materials and cheaply-produced foodstuffs, returning with the finished goods by which the nation earned its living. Passenger liners rotated the vast numbers of administrators and military personnel engaged in the functioning of the empire. A substantial fishing fleet provided a further cheap and staple commodity, supporting numerous communities. Small wonder, therefore, that the business of building, repairing, managing, manning, insuring and chartering of shipping occupied a huge sector of the British workforce.

History had shown, however, that such a dependence on seaborne traffic could be exploited by an adversary with maritime capability. Quite modest forces, suitably deployed, could cause loss and disruption quite disproportionate to their strength.

Germany's determined campaigns against commerce during two world wars were based on historical precedent. Military defeat in itself would not necessarily bring the United Kingdom to sue for peace. The Royal Navy still possessed the world's greatest battle fleet, guaranteeing the home islands against invasion. But the destruction of seaborne trade would starve the population and cut off materials for the continuance of war. During World War I, therefore, the Germans mounted a focussed and sustained onslaught with the aim of forcing a conclusion. It is worth considering this campaign in a little detail, for it provided many models for World War II.

Reckoning ocean-going ships as those of 1600 gross registered tons (grt) capacity and above, in August 1914 the British controlled 4068 vessels, aggregating some 17.5 million grt. Underpinning these was the world's largest shipbuilding capacity and the wealth to purchase foreign tonnage. Even discounting the defensive measures with which the British would safeguard their assets, the Germans were faced with a considerable task. This was undertaken by both surface and submarine attack. As these were not coordinated, they need to be considered separately.

Surface Raiders

These included both regular warships and auxiliary cruisers. Regular warships were restricted to those already serving on distant stations at the outbreak of war. German diplomatic activities had established a network of foreign-based nationals and sympathisers who could organise limited support. However, without the docking and maintenance facilities necessary for the upkeep of complex modern warships, it was apparent

During September 1941 when this convoy crossed the Atlantic, another 30 German U-boats put to sea. In World War I the U-boats had sunk some 5,000 Allied ships, a total of over 12 million tons of shipping. Despite this, the Royal Navy devoted little effort to anti-submarine measures between the wars and at the start of World War II, British ASW forces were quite inadequate to the task. Paradoxically, the German navy concentrated on surface ship construction in the 1930s and had only a modest submarine force available by 1939.

Right: Orion, Conqueror, Monarch and *Thunderer,* dreadnoughts of the Grand Fleet's 3rd battle squadron. Before 1914 it had been assumed that the battleships guaranteed Britain's control of the seas. But the U-boat changed everything.

from the outset that such raiders could enjoy only a brief career in foreign waters.

Disappearing from her pre-war Caribbean station, the *Karlsruhe* operated briefly and successfully around the focal points off Brazil. Evading capture by several hunting warships, she destroyed sixteen merchantmen of nearly 73,000 grt before falling victim to a mystery internal explosion.

Operating in the Bay of Bengal, the *Emden* was equally successful until over-confidence led to an attack on the important communications centre of the Cocos Keelings. Responding promptly to a distress call, the Australian cruiser *Sydney* caught and destroyed the raider in the act. In contrast, the *Königsberg*, having destroyed one merchantman and a small British cruiser, sought sanctuary in the labyrinthine Rufiji delta. There she was blockaded and, eventually, destroyed by a vengeful Royal Navy.

The first German auxiliary cruisers in action included merchantmen armed locally on distant stations. Armed by the *Karlsruhe*, for instance, the *Kronprinz Wilhelm* went on to destroy eleven Allied steamships, totalling about 54,000 grt. Two merchantmen armed at Germany's isolated Chinese naval station at Tsingtau had little luck: *Prinz Eitel Friedrich* and *Cormoran* led a hand-to-mouth existence until mechanical decrepitude obliged them to seek internment.

A disastrous choice for conversion was the large passenger liner *Kaiser Wilhelm der Grosse*. While her 22.5-knot speed enabled her to out-run most regular cruisers, her coal consumption was prodigious, leading to early apprehension.

Later auxiliary cruisers were selected more subtly. Merchantmen of unremarkable appearance, their armament was both comprehensive and well concealed. Most successful was the *Möwe*, which carried five medium-calibre guns, two torpedoes and a large load of mines, one of which accounted for the British battleship *King Edward VII*. Her anonymity allowed her to make

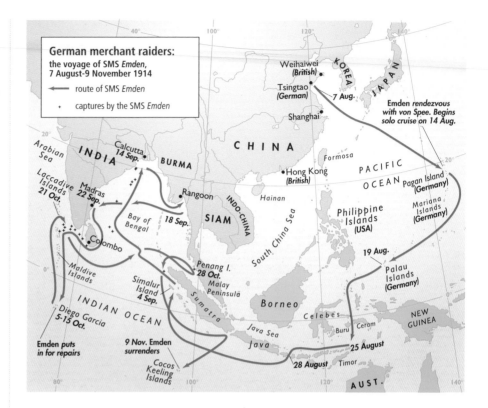

two extended cruises, totalling over six months, and surviving. Her 36 sinkings, aggregating 173,000 grt, were all independently-routed ships. This successful conversion was matched by that of the *Wolf*, even more heavily armed and carrying a small seaplane to extend her horizon. She made a 15-month cruise between November 1916 and February 1918. Ships sunk directly and by her minefields totalled twenty, of 114,000 grt.

The Germans had hit upon the most successful formula for an auxiliary cruiser, a good quality merchantman with no distinctive features but with reliable machinery capable of being maintained with a

Above: When war broke out in 1914 Germany had a cruiser squadron based in China. The *Emden* was detached to raid into the Indian Ocean where she sank 17 Allied merchant ships in three months.

comprehensive on-board workshop. Far more effective and cost-efficient than regular warships, their accomplishments were still only a small proportion of the total roll of losses. Their greatest contribution was in the disruption that they caused to trade, and in the disproportionate resources that needed to be employed by the Allies in an effort to track them down.

Above: The German East Asiatic squadron was intercepted off the Falkland islands by a British squadron including two battlecruisers. Here *Inflexible* rescues survivors from the *Gneisenau*. There were no survivors from von Spee's flagship *Scharnhorst*.

Left: The *Nurnberg* seen in Chilean waters after von Spee's squadron sank the British cruisers *Monmouth* and *Good Hope* with all hands at the battle of Coronel. Although it took a large number of Allied warships to track down the German surface raiders, it did not weaken the naval blockade of Germany.

Right: U-35 and U-42 in the Mediterranean where the former set an as yet unbeaten record total of merchant ships sunk, under the command of Arnauld de la Pérrière. He was to have taken command of the U-boat force in the Mediterranean in World War II but was killed in a plane crash on his way to Rome in 1941.

Submarines

As early as 1908 a senior, and far-sighted, German naval officer called for the creation of a substantial submarine fleet 'to sink a large number of English (sic) merchant ships (which) would be much more significant than defeating the opponent in a naval battle'. Prewar exercises had demonstrated the capacity of early U-boats to cruise safely to the Scottish coast and remain on station for several days. Few visualised their full potential, but it was calculated that 70 boats would be required just for coastal defence and operations in the North Sea. However, Admiral von Tirpitz, masterminding the construction of a battle fleet for the Kaiser, had little time for submarines. Their development was poorly funded.

International law, enshrined in the Hague Conventions, permitted warships to be sunk without warning. Attacks on merchant ships, however, were subject to the so-called Prize rules. The identity of a non-combatant had first to be established, together with the nature, destination and end-user of her cargo. In the case of her destruction, the crew were to be permitted orderly abandonment, with consideration for their safety in open boats. For submarines, these conditions were near-impossible to recognise. Their strength lay in their invisibility, compromised when surfaced. They had no space for survivors and no spare provisions for them.

Once brought into the war by Germany's invasion of Belgium, Great Britain declared a blockade of Germany. The definition of what constituted conditional and absolute contraband was continuously widened by the British. By German law, this amounted to waging war on the civilian population. By way of retaliation, restrictions on U-Boat operations were lifted from February 1915, overcoming political reservations about offending neutral powers. A further argument was, that by defensively-arming their merchantmen, the British had made it impossible for the Prize rules to be observed. Submarine operations had also assumed a new importance once the first wave of surface raiders had been eliminated, by April 1915.

As British coastal shipping included enormous numbers of colliers and ocean-going vessels moving

Above left: The German navy was commanded by Admiral Erich Raeder from 1933-43. Raeder served as Admiral Hipper's chief-of-staff during World War I, and had written the volumes of the official history dealing with the exploits of the commerce raiders. He devoted considerable effort to new surface raiders in World War II.

Above: Britain introduced convoys at the start of World War II, but immediately discovered that there were not enough escorts to protect them. Worse, pre-war assumptions about the effectiveness of Asdic (sonar) proved over-optimistic.

between ports, the Germans found it worthwhile to build classes of submarine tailored for inshore use. These were the torpedo-armed 'UB' series, and the 'UC' minelayers. The British policy of minelaying in open waters, albeit publically announced, was also deemed by the Germans to warrant the retaliation. The Germans began the indiscriminate mining of British coastal waters.

Within the 'War Zone', declared by the German Admiralty, all shipping, Allied or neutral, was liable to

attack without warning. The south-west approaches, in particular, teemed with traffic, proceeding independently. British warships patrolled ceaselessly but were completely ineffective against submerged submarines.

At first, losses were relatively light: insufficient to alarm the British, but enough to attract international condemnation of sinkings that involved high loss of life. The United States protested vigorously when, on 7 May 1915, the White Star liner *Lusitania* was sunk. Of 1198 fatalities, 128 were American citizens. Although the US protest was disregarded, the destruction of the same company's *Arabic* on 19 August brought an unequivocal warning. The German government re-imposed restrictions on U-boat operations. The submarines were shifted more to the Mediterranean, rich with targets but with less chance of offending American interests.

Right: The crew of a British minesweeper fire rifles at a mine. Minelaying caused considerable disruption to Allied convoys in both wars, although minesweeping and other counter-measures meant that less than 10 per cent of losses were inflicted by mines.

By the end of 1915 the Allies had lost 1.1 million grt, but steady acquisition of hulls had actually increased the total available. Nevertheless, there was a developing shortfall in tonnage due to the quantity supporting overseas military campaigns. The ominous statistic was that three-quarters of the losses had been caused by U-boats, while only 25 of these had been sunk. Of these, only one had been destroyed by direct offensive action while it was submerged.

Throughout 1916 restrictions placed on submarine operation caused friction between the German Navy and the German political leadership. Despite this, the rapidly increasing U-boat fleet inflicted losses approaching 200,000 grt per month by the year's end.

In December 1916, Admiral von Holtzendorff, the Chief of the German Naval Staff, issued a memorandum based on the carefully-reasoned arguments of a group of shipping experts. It was estimated that the U-boat force could sink 630,000 grt monthly if all restrictions were lifted. Such a rate, it was calculated, would 'terrorise' up to 40 percent of neutral tonnage from assisting in British trade. The consequent dearth of merchant shipping would force Britain to sue for peace within five months. War with the United States would be a high-risk consequence but could be accepted as, by definition, insufficient shipping would be available to enable the Americans to intervene decisively. Neither could the Allies build replacement tonnage fast enough to compensate for the losses.

After protracted agonising, the Kaiser gave his assent to lift restrictions from February 1917. The effect was immediate, with losses soaring to one-third, then half, a million grt monthly. Only resolute action by the British kept the neutrals trading.

Introduction of convoys

Admiral Jellicoe relinquished command of the British Grand Fleet in December 1916. As First Sea Lord one of his first actions was to set up a new Anti-submarine Division at the Admiralty. As existing protective measures were ineffective, the principle of convoy was again examined.

Although employed throughout the age of sail, convoy was widely considered to have been made obsolete by the introduction of steam power. It was argued that unacceptable delays would be incurred in the assembly of convoys. They would be limited to the speed of the slowest ship, and have to travel to dispersal points remote from actual destinations. To masters unaccustomed to steaming in close company, the risk of collision appeared enormous. It was also argued that the assembly of a great mass of shipping would present a U-boat skipper with an unmissable target. Finally, to a Royal Navy inculcated with an attacking spirit, protecting convoys was seen as 'defensive'. Chasing U-boats with hunting groups–although shown already to be futile–was considered 'offensive'.

Nevertheless, there were already some convoys in operation. Trades with the Netherlands (for foodstuffs) and France (with coal) were conducted in convoy because the continuous stream of ships could not be adequately covered by standing patrols. Nobody understood the correct ratio of warships to escorted

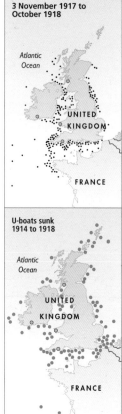

Submarine warfare, 1916-18
- ocean convoy assembly point
- location of merchant vessel sinkings
- U-boat lost

1 September 1916 to January 1917 (restricted warfare)

Atlantic Ocean

UNITED KINGDOM

FRANCE

2 February to October 1917

Atlantic Ocean

UNITED KINGDOM

FRANCE

3 November 1917 to October 1918

Atlantic Ocean

UNITED KINGDOM

FRANCE

U-boats sunk 1914 to 1918

Atlantic Ocean

UNITED KINGDOM

FRANCE

Left: From 1914-18 the U-boats sank most of their victims by surface gun action, picking off lone ships near the British and French coasts. Once convoys were introduced, losses fell off to about 1 per cent.

Right: The majority of the Royal Navy's pre-war destroyers were designed for fleet duties rather than ASW. Flotilla leader *Inglefield*, seen here in March 1942, was eventually lost to a German HS 293 guided bomb in 1944.

Below: Named after the heroic commander of the East Asiatic squadron in 1914, the *Graf Spee* was one of three heavy cruisers ordered by the *Reichsmarine* in the 1920s. The first (*Deutschland*) was launched in 1931. With enormous endurance and six 11 in (280 mm) guns, these raiders were optimized for commerce raiding.

Above: Exeter led the 6 in gun cruisers *Ajax* and *Achilles* to a timely victory over the *Graf Spee* in December 1939. Although the German raider caused great disruption, its modest tally of sinkings was poor exchange for its destruction.

Right: Fearing that the *Tirpitz* would raid the Atlantic convoys, in 1942 the British raided St. Nazaire, the only dry dock in France long enough to take the giant battleship. Packed with explosives, HMS *Cambeltown* rammed the gates. She exploded shortly after this photo was taken.

merchantmen, but best-informed opinion was one-for-one: clearly impossible to apply if trans-Atlantic crossings were convoyed.

Exasperated by the futility of his repeated warnings, President Wilson declared war on Germany on 6 April 1917. Any British hopes that this would somehow make available a host of anti-submarine (A/S) escorts were dashed.

Fortunately, the Anti-submarine Division took a reasoned look at the statistics prepared regularly by the Admiralty. These were found to include cross-channel packets, coasters and colliers, grossly inflating arrival figures. Superficial examination made convoy organisation appear to be impossible. The huge total had a second undesirable effect: it made the number of ships

Left: The battleship *Hood* took part in the hunts for successive German raiders until she intercepted the *Bismarck* in May 1941. She exploded and sank with the loss of all but 3 of the 1,419 men on board.

sunk in transit appear to be a small percentage. Refining the figures to include only relevant ocean-going ships, the Division discovered that the number actually requiring convoy was less than 10 percent of that generally assumed. The re-assessment demonstrated also that losses were concentrated in this, the most vital, sector.

Establishment of a convoy system followed quickly. Although the then Prime Minister, Lloyd George, claimed personal credit, it is obvious that the requisite action had preceded political intervention.

The Royal Navy believed that a convoy network would rob the Grand Fleet of so many destroyers that its

free operation would be jeopardised. However, reasoned analysis showed that better use could be made of what was available. Currently, this was 350 destroyers and the first 60 of the huge new construction programme of A/S sloops. These were being built to mercantile standard to simplify design and to reduce building times.

Where convoy was instituted, it was an immediate success, reducing overall losses to some 1.1 percent. Sinkings elsewhere, however, were still very high, notably in the Mediterranean. Available tonnage, in fact, continued to decrease, month on month, until February 1918, reaching its nadir at about 14.4 million grt.

Left: Tirpitz was almost ready to accompany her sistership *Bismarck* in May 1941. Instead, she was deployed to Norway to menace the Allied convoys to Russia. Although never succeeding in intercepting one, the threat of her presence drove Admiral Pound to order convoy PQ17 to scatter, with disastrous results.

Right: Renown (right) and *Duke of York* providing heavy cover for an Arctic convoy. *Renown* attacked *Scharnhorst* and *Gneisenau* off Norway in 1940, but it was *Duke of York* that finally sank the former in a gun action in December 1943.

Below: Heavily armoured and with ten 14 in (355 mm) guns, the *Duke of York* was one of four King George V class battleships, the most modern capital ships in the Royal Navy. On paper, they were equal to the *Bismarck* but their main armament was prone to stoppages.

The merchant fleet at war

Allied mercantile capacity proved inadequate for war due to the enormous demands of the services, not least a still-predominantly coal-fired navy. Space was quickly saved by the limitation of non-essential imports, although exports were maintained as far as was possible. Centralised control made for more efficient use of shipping although the inevitable delays caused by a convoy system reduced capacity by a considerable amount, some studies suggesting up to 30 percent. Confiscated enemy-flag vessels were allocated to British companies for their manning and management. Strict contraband control was an incessant cause of friction with neutral owners; their assistance was, nonetheless, essential, and guaranteed by the high profits associated with high risk.

Manpower was a problem. Large-scale enlistment robbed the docks, shipbuilders and ship repairers of their best personnel, resulting in slower turn-rounds and supply of new tonnage.

From 1916 steps were taken to accelerate merchant ship construction. Machinery was standardized, all 'frills' were eliminated, and the interchangeability of sections and sources of supply ensured. Of four major designs, 148 hulls were ordered, of which 106 had been completed by the armistice. They represented 427,000 gross tons, with a carrying capacity of some 678,000 deadweight tons. Introduced earlier, such standardisation would have made a considerable contribution but, in fairness, no-one could have foreseen the catastrophic scale of loss inflicted by the submarines.

Including a large number of fishing vessels, over 7.8 million grt of British shipping was lost to enemy action during World War I. Nearly half the casualties occured during the crisis year of 1917. Significantly, U-boats claimed 6.6 million grt. Mines (0.7 million grt) and surface raiders (0.4 million grt) were minor irritations by comparison.

Merchant shipping between the wars

Boosted by the needs of allies, then by active participation in the war, the US mercantile marine expanded more than fourfold, totalling nearly 10 million grt by the end of 1918. Further momentum took the total wearing the Old Glory to an unsustainable 12.5 million grt by 1920.

Reduced to 14.4 million grt by the armistice, British-flagged shipping recovered to 18.1 million grt by June 1920, assisted by a share of the 3.2 million grt of ex-enemy shipping confiscated as reparations at the war's end.

The natural resilience of the industry saw it recover more quickly than the commerce that it served. Over-capacity was soon evident. Protectionism and subsidies reduced the available freight in the cross-trades from which many companies earned their keep, and British shipping saw its previous pre-eminent position being relentlessly eroded. As world industry turned to oil-based energy, exports of British coal plummeted.

Barely recovered from the effects of the war, the developed economies were struck by an unprecedented recession. By 1932 over 3.5 million grt of British shipping was laid up. Shipbuilding yards, that had launched over two million grt annually before and after the war, were now producing a tenth of that total. Many yards, together with the companies that they served, went out of business or diversified into other trades. Although matters improved from 1934, British shipping now competed in a different world, and market share declined inexorably. Within 20 years it shrank from about half the world total to less than one third.

As war loomed again in the late 1930s, British shipping was less able than in 1914 to serve the nation's needs. Much of its reduced capacity was now represented by tankers. Dry-cargo vessels had grown appreciably in size, so there were fewer of them. The loss of any one being the more serious. Differing trades meant that most British owners built ships characteristic of their companies. Unlike the Americans, they did not think in terms of standard ships, and no plans existed to build them. With the ending of the slump and the commencement of re-armament, yards were, in any case, more interested in bidding for lucrative warship contracts.

Artificially inflated by the availability of cheap, war-built tonnage, the American merchant fleet had suffered even more than the British during the depression. However while the British government left its industry to secure its own salvation, the US government took positive action to stimulate recovery. One crucial problem was that it cost at least 60 percent more to build a ship in the USA than in a European yard.

In 1936 Congress passed the Merchant Marine Act, the consequences of which were far-reaching. In establishing the US Maritime Commission, it sought to reverse the decline in the shipping industry, which had received nearly $1 billion in subsidies over the previous 17 years, in an abortive attempt to make it competitive. In 1937 a new and better-focussed programme was launched, aimed to re-vitalise the industry to the extent where it would build 50 new ships annually for the ensuing ten years. Old, uneconomic tonnage was to be traded-in against new hulls. Three standard freighter and one fast tanker design were offered, adaptable to owners' requirements. With first orders being placed in 1938, the industry was brought up to speed at a critical juncture.

Below: Still on fire after a torpedo hit, an American freighter is towed to safety by the Dutch tug *Zwarte Zee* in 1943. The tug had saved 22 merchant ships since 1940.

German re-armament

The re-emergence of Germany as a world power is well chronicled. Reduced by defeat, and stripped by onerous demands for reparation, the nation descended into a state of seething resentment in the 1920s. Many lost their life savings, while a tiny minority became wealthy. Against a background of rising unemployment, economic instability, strikes and political violence, stable government became impossible. National Socialism prospered through promising an end to it. Elected democratically, Hitler and his party took a tight grip on the state which, over the following few years,

Left: Anti-submarine lookouts aboard the old British carrier *Argus* in 1942. She served as an aircraft ferry, shipping aircraft to Russia and Malta and surviving several U-boat attacks in the process.

Below: 34 year-old *Ritterkreuz* winner, Gerhard Bigalk, returns to port after sinking the carrier *Audacity* in December 1941. He was lost with his crew in July 1942 when *U-751* was bombed and sunk by a Whitley and a Lancaster.

U-3 was a Type IIA coastal boat, the first type of submarine built by the German navy after World War I. In 1939 *U-3* sank two small coasters in the North Sea under the command of future 'Ace' Joachim Schepke. *U-3* was the first command of two other *Ritterkreuz* winners later in the war. Assigned to the 21st flotilla at Pillau from July 1940 to April 1944, *U-3* was stricken that August and scrapped in 1945.

Type II data (Type IID)

Displacement:	314 tons surfaced
	364 tons submerged
Dimensions:	43.95 m (144 ft 2 in) x 4.87 m
	(16 ft) x 3.9 m (12 ft 9 in)
Diving depth:	150 m (492 ft)
Propulsion:	diesels delivering 700 hp and
	electric motors delivering
	410 hp to two shafts
Speed:	13 knots surfaced; 7.5 knots dived
Endurance:	6,500 km (4,040 miles) at 12 knots
	surfaced or 105 km (65 miles)
	submerged at 4 knots
Armament:	3 x 533 mm (21 in) torpedo tubes
	with 6 torpedoes
Crew:	25

crossed the invisible divide that took it into dictatorship.

The Treaty of Versailles had imposed strict limitations on the size and content of the Germany Navy. Existing ships could be replaced only at a specific age; 'armoured ships' and cruisers could displace no more than 10,000 and 6,000 tons respectively. No submarines were permitted. These and other conditions were widely circumvented by the Germans, aided by the relaxed attitude of the Allied Control Commission.

When Admiral Raeder took over as C-in-C, German Navy in 1928, he inherited a system, established by his predecessors, of 'Black Funds', for progressing secret armed forces projects.

There was little secret about the *Deutschland*, first of a planned five 'armoured ships', whose awkward label quickly saw them christened 'pocket battleships' by the foreign technical press. Although they were very much circumscribed by the 10,000-ton limit, all of the eventual three units exceeded it. Designed to give a

Below: The U-boat campaign in the Atlantic was belatedly supported by a small force of *Luftwaffe* FW 200 Condors, but co-ordination between the air force and the U-boats fell far short of Admiral Dönitz's hopes.

'big-ship' appearance, to counter any acceptance that the Navy was being reduced to a coastal force, they were meant to be able to fight any adversary that they could not outrun, battlecruisers excepted. Their all-diesel propulsion system was meant to save on both volume and weight. In these respects, it failed, but was

Right: Because Germany attacked neutral countries that owned large merchant fleets, such as Norway and the Netherlands, the quantity of shipping under British control actually increased from 17.5 million tons to over 20 million between 1939 and 1941. This Norwegian tanker is one of 193 tankers joining the Allies during this period.

Below: The 'four stacker' destroyer *St. Albans* (formerly USS *Thomas*) was transferred to the Royal Navy in September 1940. In 1944 she was handed to the Russians and served with the Northern Fleet as the *Dostoinyi* until 1949.

successful in conferring enormous range and maintainability: prerequisites for commerce raiding.

Submarines were a different matter. To keep U-boat design teams together, front companies were set up in the Netherlands, offering design expertise and the overseeing of construction and commissioning. Contracts from Spain, Turkey and Finland enabled prototype U-boats to be legitimately built and evaluated by proxy.

Aware that it could no longer influence events in Germany, the United Kingdom concluded a bilateral naval agreement in 1935. The major concession was to accept a 100:35 tonnage ratio in all principal classes of warship. To the amazement of the world, submarines were allowed up to 45 percent of the Royal Navy total, and up to parity if the Germans felt that circumstances warranted it. The Germans had, in any case, already torn up the rule book. Designs for 250-, 500- and 750-ton submarines had been thoroughly developed. In defiance of Versailles, the first dozen 250-ton Type IIs were nearly complete and, in September 1935, the first flotilla was commissioned under Captain Karl Dönitz, a capable and experienced U-boat commander from World War I.

Despite the unlikelihood of a maritime war with the United Kingdom as long as the agreed tonnage ratios were maintained, Dönitz planned for just that event. Believing in the soundness of *guerre de course*, and that earlier U-boats had failed because they worked on an individual basis, he developed group tactics to facilitate the discovery of a convoy, holding it and overwhelming it. He looked upon the 500-tonner as an ideal submarine and, suitably improved, this became the Type VII: workhorse of the service. Within the tonnage ceiling then adhered to, Dönitz preferred to have more Type

Right: The Hunt class destroyer *Aldenham* helped sink *U-587* in March 1943. The Type VIIC boat was surprised on the surface near a troop convoy and depth-charged by four escorts without apparent results—but was lost with all hands. *Aldenham* was mined and sunk in December 1944.

Left: The Italian navy lost more submarines in World War II than the US Navy. From 1940 32 Italian boats were transferred to Bordeaux to operate in the Atlantic and half were lost by 1943. The *Brin*, seen here, served in the Mediterranean and surrendered in 1943, serving on as an ASW training target.

Right: The Flower class corvette *Starwort* seen in April 1942, five months before she sank *U-660* (illustrated on p46) during Operation Torch. She took over from *Lotus* which had already made three attacks, and took off the U-boat's crew after it surfaced and surrendered.

VIIs rather than smaller numbers of the 750-ton Type IX favoured by the High Command. The latter pushed also for a 2000-ton U-cruiser, which Dönitz resisted strongly, but the resulting disagreements led to an inconsistent construction programme. By 1939 Germany had only 63 operational submarines, a formidable enough figure but one which included two flotillas of low-endurance Type IIs.

As Hitler's quite unacceptable actions led once again to the spectre of war in Europe, the British and French discussed a joint naval policy. The French were still soured by the bilateral 1935 Anglo-German agreement and close harmony was a distant prospect. However, they accepted that, in the event of hostilities, the Mediterranean would be a French responsibility; and that some of their heavy units would be made available for Atlantic trade protection .

Only in May 1938 did Hitler advise Raeder that war with Britain was possible. Even then, it was not seen as imminent. As naval parity was never likely, the British

Above: The 20 mm Oerlikon cannon was widely employed in the anti-aircraft role, particularly aboard merchantmen on the Arctic and Malta convoys where the greatest danger came from German air attack.

Above: A Type VII U-boat seen from the tower of another U-boat off Norway. Hitler ordered extra U-boats to Norway to guard against an Allied invasion and an increasing proportion of U-boats were based there to attack the Arctic convoys, especially after the effective withdrawal from the Atlantic in 1944.

merchant marine was again identified as the target whose destruction would be decisive. On this basis, a naval expansion programme, the so-called 'Z-plan', was drawn up. This initially called for six 50,000-ton battleships, up to twelve 20,000-ton cruisers or a smaller number of 30,000-ton battlecruisers, four 20,000-ton aircraft carriers, a 'large number' of light cruisers and nearly 250 U-boats. The mix was based on the premise that surface raiding groups working against convoys would be powerful enough to oblige the Royal Navy to

provide task groups for their defence. These would thus be exposed to action with superior forces and submarines. The latter would be organised in 23 flotillas: 22 operational and one training.

The Z-plan would take a decade to implement, but the *Führer* decreed that it would be completed in six years, i.e. by 1945. For its part, the Navy recognised that construction on this scale could only result in another naval race, and a disastrously premature war. Priority was given to battleships and U-boats, with the

completion of the submarine programme advanced to 1943.

In April 1939 the German Navy's worst fears were realised. Hitler abrogated the naval agreement with Britain; although as late as July 1939 Raeder was still being assured by his leader that 'in no circumstances' would there be war. Just six weeks later, hostilities commenced. The U-boat arm had just 46 boats ready for action. Less than half of these were of a size that could be used in the Atlantic.

The battle of the Atlantic

Learning from World War I, the British had stockpiled medium-calibre guns from warships long scrapped. Defensive arming of merchantmen started immediately but, as the fleet included about 3,000 ocean-going ships and over 1,000 coasters, the task of fitting weapons and training gunners was both immense and protracted. Defensive arming was initially limited to low-angle weapons, protection against air attack was a secondary consideration.

The Admiralty assumed control of British-registered shipping on 26 August, a week before general hostilities commenced. It exercised control through its Trade Division, represented world-wide. Day-to-day marine affairs were the responsibility of a new Ministry of Shipping, later to become a limb of the Ministry of War Transport. Stringent rationing was instituted to reduce demands on import space, in order to release tonnage for military purposes.

Convoy was quickly introduced, its organisation and the provision of escorts being the responsibility of the

Right: The 'flush decker' HMS *Roxburgh* (ex-USS *Foote*) seen in Hampton Roads, September 1942. She took part in the sinking of the Type IXB *U-65* in April 1941 and was another of the destroyers transferred to Russia in 1944.

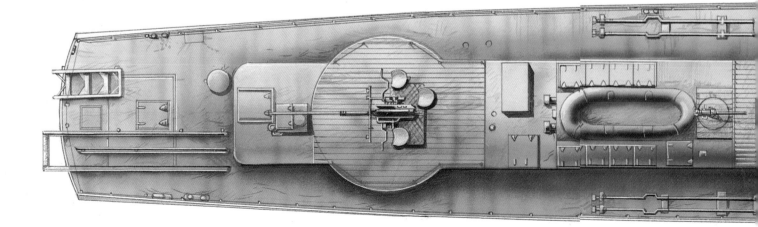

Trade Division. Among the first convoys were those along the British east coast. Such movements contained many laden deep-sea ships, proceeding between ports. Offshore shoals, suitably reinforced by defensive minefields, afforded some protection from seaward, but left narrow and tortuous inshore routes. Convoys became dangerously attenuated and difficult to protect. As the route was well within German aircraft range, quick response fighter cover and anti-aircraft (A/A) escorts were a continual requirement.

The route was also vulnerable to enemy minelaying. Bold nocturnal forays by German destroyers added to the total deposited by the smaller U-boats. Aircraft could not lay with the same precision, and one result was the gift of a pair of magnetic mines, that had been causing a major nuisance. Their recovery and dissection enabled a comprehensive programme of wiping, de-perming and de-gaussing countermeasures to be initiated.

Mining caused a continuous drain of casualties. Ships were often not sunk but suffered extensive shock damage that tied up months of capacity for a repair yard. Mine countermeasures demanded huge resources, in a task that was never-ending. During the first seven months of war, the so-called 'phoney' phase, 129 British, Allied and neutral ships, totalling over 400,000 grt, were lost.

Further irritation was caused by German 'S'-boats,

S-26 class

Displacement:	115 tons full load
Dimensions:	34.95 m (114 ft 8 in) x 5.1 m (16 ft 8 in) x 1.4 m (4 ft 7 in)
Propulsion:	three diesels delivering 6,000 hp to three shafts
Speed:	39.5 knots
Endurance:	1,390 km (864 miles) at 35 knots
Armament:	2 x 533 mm (21 in) torpedo tubes with four torpedoes; 2 x 20 mm cannon
Crew:	up to 21

Below and right: Known to the British as the 'E-boat', the German *Schnellboot* or *S-boot* was designed to prey on coastal shipping, and proved so effective that the shipping lane off the English east coast became known as 'E-boat Alley'. In addition to their exploits in the North Sea, these torpedo craft operated in the Baltic, Mediterranean and Black Seas. One of their most devastating attacks took place off Dorset when they got in amongst an amphibious landing exercise and massacred the landing craft.

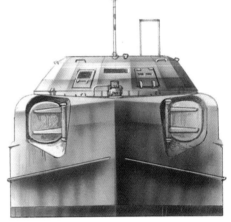

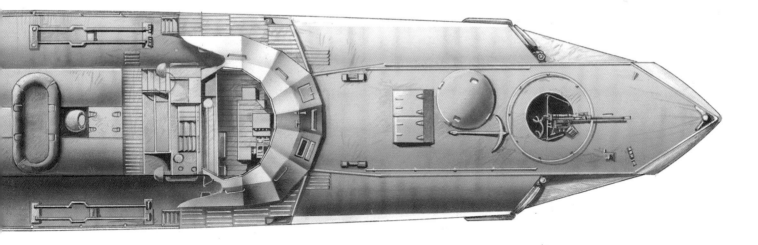

The British employed 13 armed merchantmen to patrol the Iceland-Faeroes gap and the Denmark Strait in 1939. The ex P&O liner *Rawalpindi* (Captain Edward Kennedy) ran into *Scharnhorst* and *Gneisenau* in November and was sunk after a valiant fight against impossible odds. The German commander, Admiral Marschall stopped both his battleships to pick up 27 survivors.

inexplicably known to the British 'E'-boats. Their combination of high speed and shallow draft allowed them to stage sudden and unexpected gun and torpedo attacks. The 'S'-boats too, were involved in minelaying. Although rarely more than a nuisance, they posed a threat that demanded powerful convoy escort.

From the outset, U-boats accounted for more mercantile losses than all other factors combined. But until April 1941, when series production added significantly to the capability of Dönitz's force, sinkings by German surface raiders attracted greater significance than perhaps they warranted.

German surface raiders– the warships

Following earlier experience, 26 merchantmen had been selected for conversion once hostilities had commenced. As noted above, Raeder's Z-plan had envisaged using heavy units against convoys to cause the Royal Navy to expose its own in a defence role. Despite only limited progress on the plan, this policy was still pursued. Two 'pocket battleships', *Deutschland* and *Admiral Graf Spee*, were readied on their Atlantic stations before the outbreak of hostilities. Both proved their concept by making extensive cruises, although mechanical problems obliged the *Deutschland* to return in mid-November with only two sinkings to her credit.

Like her, the *Graf Spee* operated against independents and had accumulated a total of nine captures, about 50,000 grt, before being brought to action off the River Plate in the December. Her subsequent scuttling was a severe psychological blow to the German Navy but, once again, brought home the problems of facing a regular warship when employed

Above: Lt Cdr Aubrey, RN, commanding the Shoreham class sloop *Fowey* in 1941. The *Fowey* damaged *U-55* with an accurate depth-charge attack in January 1940 and, joined by three destroyers and an RAF Sunderland, hunted and sank the U-boat after it was forced to the surface.

Right: This convoy is seen south of Newfoundland in July 1942, under the protective umbrella of maritime aircraft based in North America. To the east lay the 'Atlantic gap', the central part of the ocean beyond the range of Allied aircraft, where the U-boats were at their most dangerous. RAF Bomber Command resisted pressure to divert four-engine aircraft to the battle of the Atlantic, insisting that it could destroy U-boats more effectively by attacking their bases and factories.

Rawalpindi

Displacement: ....16,697 tons

Dimensions: ....167 m (547 ft 9 in) x 21.7 m
(71 ft 4 in) x 8.6 m (28 ft 4 in)

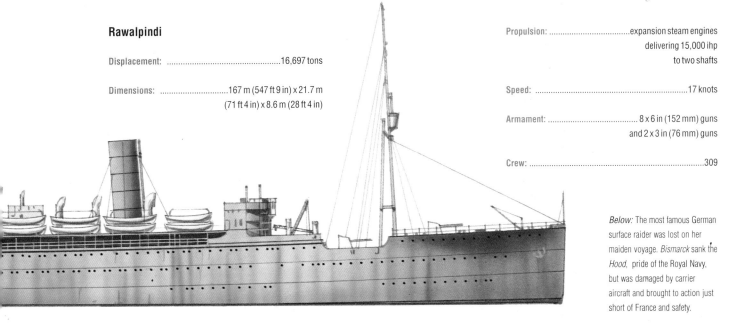

Propulsion: ....expansion steam engines
delivering 15,000 ihp
to two shafts

Speed: ....17 knots

Armament: ....8 x 6 in (152 mm) guns
and 2 x 3 in (76 mm) guns

Crew: 309

Below: The most famous German surface raider was lost on her maiden voyage. *Bismarck* sank the *Hood,* pride of the Royal Navy, but was damaged by carrier aircraft and brought to action just short of France and safety.

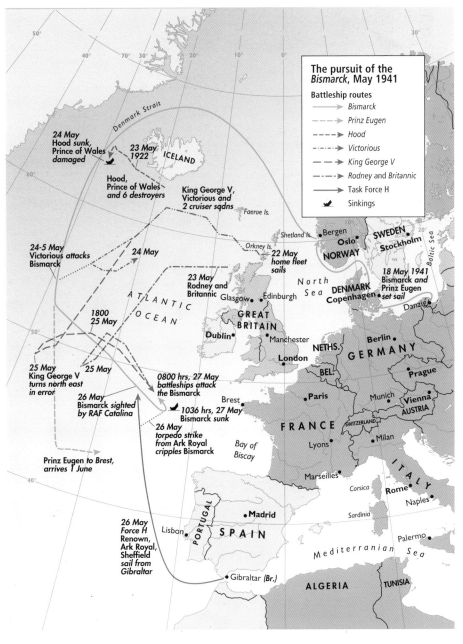

The pursuit of the *Bismarck*, May 1941

Battleship routes

- *Bismarck*
- *Prinz Eugen*
- *Hood*
- *Victorious*
- *King George V*
- *Rodney and Britannic*
- Task Force H
- Sinkings

The heavy cruiser *Prinz Eugen* as seen at Bergen, April 1941. Her sistership *Hipper* made several raids into the North Atlantic, but *Prinz Eugen*'s only appearance there was during her famous sortie with the battleship *Bismarck*. Damaged by the RAF while in Brest, she spent the rest of her war in the Baltic after the 'Channel Dash' back to Germany in 1942.

far afield for raiding. Although her value far exceeded that of the ships that she had destroyed, she had exercised the system of pre-positioning supply ships–and taught the British how essential it was to find and sink them–and had again demonstrated the hugely disruptive potential of the surface raider.

Most successful of the trio was the *Admiral Scheer*, whose five-month cruise starting in October 1940 netted 16 ships of over 100,000 grt. Her score should have been far greater, as she had encountered a 37-ship convoy protected by only a single armed merchant cruiser, the AMC *Jervis Bay*. Instead of ignoring the armed liner and going for the convoy, the *Scheer* was drawn into a gunnery duel which, although desperately one-sided, gave the convoy time to scatter, so that only five ships were subsequently lost.

Fortunately, the British had little alternative use for the unmodernised battleships of the Queen Elizabeth and 'R' classes. In the absence of the planned German 'super battleships', their presence with ocean convoys was decisive, as no raider could risk damage from their heavy projectiles. Their deterrence value was well illustrated during the cruise of the *Scharnhorst* and *Gneisenau*, early in 1941, when three escorted convoys were encountered. Each of these was covered by a single old battleship which, although slower, had heavier-calibre guns and superior protection. The convoys went unmolested. On three other occasions, however, the Germans came across groups of unprotected merchantmen from recently-dispersed

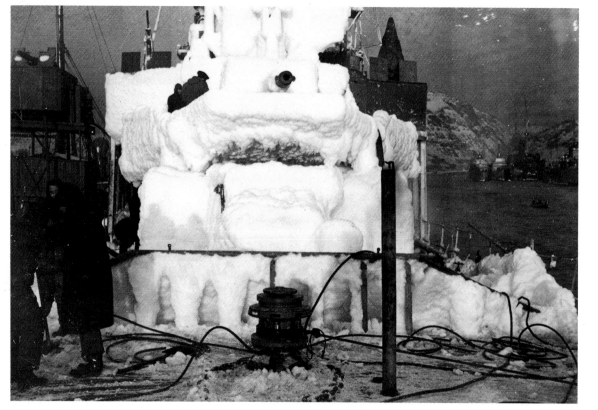

Left: Looking aft from the forecastle of the modified 'W' class destroyer, *Witch*. She took part in the defence of convoy ON115 against the 6 U-boats of Group *Wolf* in August 1942. The mainly Canadian escort was very active, driving off the 'Ace' Topp in *U-552* and damaging another U-boat until reaching safety in the fog banks off Newfoundland.

Right: A German wartime view from a U-boat on patrol. The U-boats had no radar and relied on their lookouts to locate the targets. They did have hydrophones (passive sonar) which could detect a convoy at over 70 miles, but they provided the bearing only and could not be used when the U-boat was making a fast passage on the surface.

Hipper class

Displacement:	18,400 tons full load
Dimensions:	210.4 m (690 ft 4 in) x 21.9 m (71 ft 10 in) x 7.9 m (25 ft 10 in)
Propulsion:	turbines delivering 132,000 shp to three shafts
Speed:	33 knots
Armour belt:	80 mm (3.1 in)
Armament:	8 x 203 mm (8 in) guns; 12 x 105 mm (4.1 in) guns; 12 x 37 mm guns; 24 x 20 mm guns and 12 x 533 mm (21 in) torpedo tubes
Aircraft:	two
Crew:	1,450

Class: *Hipper, Prinz Eugen, Blücher.*

convoys. These accounted for all but one of the 22 ships of 226,000 grt destroyed during the cruise.

The first foray, in May 1941, by the new battleship *Bismarck* and the heavy cruiser *Prinz Eugen*, provided a combination that would have been a match for any British battleship escort. But it was a disaster for the Germans. Despite the momentous sinking of the battle cruiser *Hood*, the *Bismarck* was intercepeted and destroyed without sinking a single merchant ship.

German surface raiders– disguised merchantships

By the time the Bismarck was lost, the German auxiliary cruisers were in operation. These were no mere armed merchant ships. Their carefully-modified topsides concealed up to six 15 cm (5.9 inch) guns and four or six 21 inch torpedo tubes. All had hidden anti-aircraft weapons and a pair of Arado floatplanes in an after hold. Up to 420 mines could be stowed, for sowing in small batches at focal points world-wide. With adequate self-maintenance workshops and auxiliary bunker capacity, they were capable of extended cruises.

The first such, *Atlantis*, sailed in March 1940. By the end of June, a further four were at sea, joined by four more by early 1941. They preyed on the many independents to be found beyond the convoy network that functioned in the area of the main submarine war. They thus operated commonly in the Central Atlantic, the Indian Ocean and Australasian waters, striking suddenly and moving on.

Countering them were older cruisers and AMCs on distant deployments. Their success against either the raiders or the German supply ships depending upon good intelligence or promptly-despatched distress calls from molested ships. Even when apprehended, a raider was not always destroyed. The *Thor*, for instance,

fought British AMCs on three separate occasions, sinking one of them, before going on to destroy 23 ships of over 150,000 grt. She was eventually destroyed in then-neutral Japan after an explosion and fire suffered while refitting. Having taken nearly 70,000 grt of prizes, the *Kormoran* was intercepted off the Australian west coast by the regular cruiser *Sydney*. Disguised, and claiming to be neutral, she had the cruiser hold fire long enough to effect surprise. In a furious exchange of gunfire and torpedoes, both ships were eventually sunk.

Only nine auxiliary raiders actually undertook cruises. Just two survived. While undeniably, a disruptive nuisance, they were never a statistically significant threat: their 830,000 grt bag being spread over three years. By the end of 1942, they were largely accounted for, and it was to the U-boat that Germany once again turned for a decisive result.

As we have seen, Rear-Admiral Dönitz began operations with an inadequate submarine force. With the premature outbreak of hostilities, the Z-plan was abandoned. Work stopped on all capital ships except the two Bismarck class, and the shipyard capacity thus released was directed toward an increase of U-boat production from the originally-planned nine units monthly to 29. Implementation, however, was slowed

Komet

Displacement:	7,500 tons
Dimensions:	115 m (377 ft 4 in) x 15.3 m (50 ft 1 in) x 6.5 m (21 ft 4 in)
Propulsion:	two diesel engines delivering 3,900 bhp to one shaft
Speed:	16 knots
Armament:	6 x 150 mm (5.9 in) guns; 1 x 60 mm gun; 2 x 37 mm guns; 4 x 20 mm guns; 2 x 533 mm (21 in) torpedo tubes; 270 mines; one LS minelaying boat with 30 mines
Aircraft:	2 x Arado Ar 196
Crew:	270

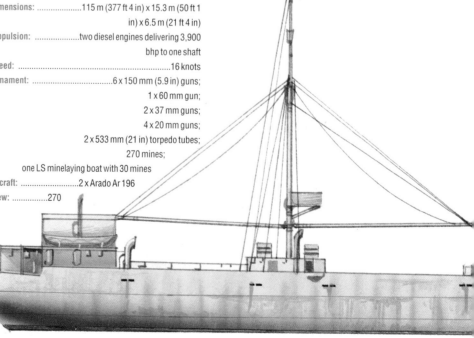

Left: Troop convoys AT 15 and NA 8 carrying US troops to Iceland and Northern Ireland, seen at Halifax on 3 May 1942. Note how the liner *Aquitania* dwarfs the battleship *New York*. The escort also included the heavy cruiser *Brooklyn* and the British CVE *Avenger*. Only one U-boat saw this amazing target, but *U-576* was out of torpedoes.

Right: The Isles class admiralty trawlers carried up to 30 depth-charges and, in the case of the *Gairsay* seen here, a single 12-pdr gun. The *Gairsay* was sunk in 1944 by an explosive motor boat.

by Hitler, who had plans for the military defeat of France. This, he felt, would shock the British into seeking an accommodation. Only when this proved not to be the case was U-boat construction given the highest priority, by which time ten precious months had been lost. Dönitz' initial strength of 39 operational boats proved to be a total unattainable again until mid-1941, as losses and wastage outstripped production. Truly, the Allies (at this stage effectively the British alone) were granted a providential spell in which to organise an efficient convoy system and to initiate crash programmes for its escorts.

The convoy system

Convoys fell into two major categories. Some, outside the scope of this narrative, were 'operational', typically comprising large passenger liners engaged on trooping duties, or selected merchantmen gathered for missions such as the re-provisioning of Malta. The common factor was the heavy naval escort. Most convoys, however, ran to a regular cycle for the protection of commercial shipping.

The principal convoy routes were functioning before the war was a month old. Along the British east coast

The German raider *Komet* was converted in 1937 and sailed from Norway in July 1940. Her 510 day voyage began by passing north of Russia (with Soviet assistance) to enter the Pacific, then into the Indian Ocean and around Cape Horn to reach Hamburg in November 1941. She sailed again in October 1942, risking passage down the Channel escorted by four torpedo boats. Ambushed by British destroyers and MTBs, she blew up after a torpedo hit. There were no survivors.

ran the already-mentioned cycle between the Thames Estuary and the Firth of Forth (coded FN northward and FS southward). Between the United Kingdom and Gibraltar ran the HG/OG convoys, mostly with traffic to and from the Mediterranean. Shipping from the east coast of South America and from Southern Africa usually connected with the SL/OS convoys that used Freetown, in Sierra Leone, as a southern terminal. By far the most significant, however, were the North Atlantic movements, without which Britain could not have sustained its lone resistance to a rampant Germany.

Halifax, Nova Scotia, supplemented by Sydney, Cape Breton, were the western limits of fast OB (later ON) and slow (ONS) westbound movements, and fast (HX) and slow (SC) eastbound. These were shifted to New York from the end of August 1942. In theory, convoys of less than nine knots were 'slow' but, in practice, seven knots was nearer the average. It was around these cycles that the Battle of the Atlantic was primarily fought. This battle had to be won, as the United Kingdom represented the only practical springboard from which Europe could eventually be liberated.

Convoys had two primary functions. Firstly, to lower loss rates in merchantmen: a given number of ships in a group were far less 'visible' to searching U-boats than the same number scattered over the ocean. Secondly, to increase loss rates in U-boats: the 'honey pot' effect of a convoy brought submarines to the A/S forces which, consequently, did not have to waste time in fruitless search. While this simple philosophy ultimately proved successful, it took time to implement. Convoys initially were far from the floating citadels that planners intended, and thousands of good ships were to be lost before defences finally got the upper hand.

Slow convoys did not zigzag but, like faster movements, were still routed evasively. Crossings were thus typically of 3000 to 3500 sea miles, so that a slow convoy might make a 20-day passage and a fast one, 15. With sailings at weekly intervals, half a dozen loaded eastbound convoys might be at sea at any one time, together with others of westbound 'empties'. Occasionally, varying speeds and routing brought them

into fairly close proximity but, in general, the immensity of the ocean conferred a good chance of remaining undetected for at least a major part of the crossing.

Although small relative to the vastness of the Atlantic, a convoy was still large in absolute terms. Normal deep-sea formation was rectangular, with a long frontage. Numbers of ships grew with time but could occupy nine to eleven parallel columns with three to five ships in each. The precision of its formation was greatly weather-dependent, and adequate spacing was required to accommodate the waywardness of individual vessels. A rectangular convoy of, say, 45 ships might stretch 8000 yards across its diagonal. Its escorts needed to be placed about 3000 yards further out to intercept submarines beyond effective torpedo range. The periphery to be held by the escorts was, thus, of a flattened elliptical shape, some 14,000 yards (or nearly seven sea miles) along it major axis. Its length would be of the order of 60,000 yards, or 30 sea miles.

At first, the number and type of escorts was determined by availability rather than being derived from a scientifically-devised relationship. One certain statistic was that there were never enough. In reasonable conditions, at convoy speeds, an escort's Asdic (Sonar) set could be effective to about 2500 yards. Average North Atlantic weather halved that. As early sets were inoperable over the 200-degree arc from ten degrees forward of either beam, the escort commander often had problems in placing his ships to the best advantage. He might have only four units, the resulting yawning gaps being covered by continuous speed changes.

Below: In June 1940 *Verity* became the first British destroyer to be fitted with ASW radar, the 1.5 m wavelength Type 286M. Together with the radar-equipped *Wolverine* she attacked a U-boat on 7 March 1941 which may have been *U-47* (Prien) which was never heard of again after that day.

Right: A troop convoy of liners escorted by one of the British Revenge, or 'R' class 15 in gun battleships and a Sunderland flying boat. Fast liners often made independent voyages, relying on high cruising speed to avoid U-boat attack.

The protective ring was further weakened by distractions. Having forced a submarine down, or gained a solid contact, an A/S ship's commander wanted to go for a kill. But a corvette might have only an eight knot speed advantage over a convoy, so that a two-hour prosecution of a contact would require a further two hours to catch up. During its four-hour absence, much could happen, and a high-speed overtaking run made huge demands on fuel, reducing the escort's endurance. As many early corvettes were coal fired, replenishment at sea (RAS) was not possible.

Some convoys were eventually accompanied by small, dedicated rescue ships but escorts were still often delayed by assisting damaged and straggling vessels, and were embarrassed by large numbers of survivors. Unaccustomed to the violence of war, crews or parts of crews were occasionally panicked into premature abandonment, thus occupying an escort vessel in rescue, standing by, putting the personnel back aboard and nursing the casualty back to the main group.

Escorts were fortunate if granted 48 hours between trips, and even this involved the crew in essential maintenance, storing, etc. At the outset, surface escort was provided only as far as 12½ degrees West, not a hundred miles beyond Ireland's west coast. Beyond this point, its charges proceeded in company for a period before dispersing, while the escort met and accompanied the next eastbound movement. By October 1940, better organisation and more warships allowed escort to be extended as far as 19 degrees West.

From the outset the Royal Canadian Navy (RCN) gave unstinting support. Starting with a handful of destroyers, which provided local escort as far as 53½ degrees West (short of the eastern tip of Newfoundland) the service expanded steadily to a sizeable force of, mainly, homebuilt A/S vessels. Between the limits covered by British and Canadian escorts yawned a 2,000 mile gap. It was in this gap that the Atlantic war was fought and decided and although, by July 1941, some measure of surface escort could often be provided all the way, the all-important long-range air cover was critically slow to materialise.

German naval strategy

The London Naval Treaties of the 1930s had also resulted in the adoption of a protocol that governed the future conduct of submarine warfare. Generally reiterating the earlier Prize Rules, it was adopted and ratified by the treaty signatories and, subsequently, by every state with pretensions to maritime interests, including Germany. Having failed to have submarines banned completely, the United Kingdom again put its trust in international law. As the British Government could hardly be accused of naivety, this had to be a triumph of political expediency over hard-won experience.

All too aware of the inadequacy of their fleet in the face of the combined naval strength of the United Kingdom and France, the new German Supreme Command issued its first directive on 31 August 1939. It stated unequivocally: 'The Navy will concentrate on commerce destruction, directed especially against England (sic)'. Earlier experience had shown that, in

The Type VII was the workhorse of the U-boat arm with 568 boats commissioned during World War II and some still under construction at the end of the conflict. Later Type VIIs were cleared to dive to 200 m (656 ft) and some survived emergency dives to 300 m (984 ft).

Type VIIC U-boat *U-617*

1 Bow torpedo tubes
2 Hydroplane
3 Hydroplane guard
4 Inner hull
5 Outer casing
6 Forward torpedo compartment
7 Crew quarters

8 Saddle tank
9 Battery compartment
10 88 mm gun
11 Fin
12 Bridge
13 Search and attack periscopes
14 Radio direction finder
15 Quadruple 20 mm AA gun
16 Magnetic Compass housing
17 Conning tower
18 Boat air inlet

19 Diesel air inlet
20 Snorkel
21 Main fuel tank
22 Radio room
23 Control room
24 Firing control panels
25 Auxiliary pump controls
26 Fuel and diving tanks
27 Casing to fuel tank
28 Senior ratings' quarters
29 Compensating tanks
30 Engine room controls

31 Diesel engine room
32 1400 hp diesel engine
33 Diesel exhaust coupling
34 Main frame
35 Motor room
36 Motor room controls
37 750 hp electric motors
38 Reduction gear
39 Prop shaft casing
40 Aft torpedo tube
41 Propeller
42 Hydroplane
43 Hydroplane guard
44 Rudders

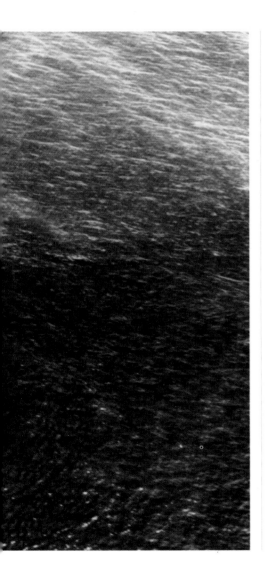

order to be effective, this required unrestricted submarine warfare. In spite of their desire to avoid inflaming neutral opinion, neither Raeder nor Dönitz could really have had any intention of abiding by the rules, although this charge was not easy to prove at the Nuremberg trials in 1946.

Once again, routine British measures made it easier for the enemy to drop any pretext of observing restrictions. From the outbreak of war British merchant ships were defensively armed and instructed to ram, if possible, any surfaced hostile submarine. They were darkened and sailed in convoys under armed escort and told, when molested, to report their position by radio. Within a month the Germans lifted all restrictions on submarines operating in the North Sea and, by mid-October 1939, this zone was extended to 20 degrees West, well beyond the then limit of Western Approaches escorts. From 17 November, only passenger liners were exempted from attack without warning, unless identified as hostile. However, all this counted for little: on the very first day of the war, the liner *Athenia* was torpedoed and sunk on the grounds that she was blacked-out and zigzagging. The German High Command supported the U-boat commander's decision, but this early example of *schreklichheit*–frightfulness was hugely damaging to its standing.

Dönitz believed that convoys should be attacked by the greatest possible number of U-boats in order to overwhelm the defences . Tactical command by a senior commander on the spot he rejected as impractical. He

Left: A tanker sinking at Jupiter inlet, Florida on 4 March 1942 during the U-boat offensive against the US east coast. U-boat skippers did not like operating in such shallow water, but the plethora of targets and absence of escorts enabled several to run up large scores.

preferred his headquarters–to a large degree himself–to direct operations up to the point of attack, after which commanders would work independently. This strategy involved the garnering of intelligence from every available source but, as for the Allies, the necessary allocation of long range maritime aircraft was tardy. Given the necessary ingredients, Dönitz' methods proved highly effective. Its weakness lay in the volume of radio traffic that it generated.

Recognising that U-boats had failed against convoys in 1917 because they worked individually, Dönitz developed group tactics, both theoretically and in exercises, from 1935. By September 1939 the basics of 'wolf-pack' operation had been identified. U-boats in an area would be contacted to form a named attack group. This would form a line of search, remaining stationary or advancing on an ordered bearing. The first U-boat to locate the target had the primary duty but to transmit a sighting report, rather than attacking. Maintaining contact with the convoy, it transmitted its speed, course and position at frequent intervals. Only when a sufficient number of boats had been homed-in would the go-ahead for an attack be given.

British developments in Asdic between the wars were well publicised, with two unfortunate effects. Firstly, and against all practical evidence, there grew in the Royal Navy a general belief that the submarine no longer posed a practical threat. Secondly, Dönitz, a seasoned ex-submariner, realised that the late World War I tactic of attacking on the surface at night would go far toward offsetting Asdic's advantages. Surprisingly, he committed this hypothesis to print in 1939, in the open press. More incredibly, its significance seems to have gone unremarked by the British.

There were too few U-boats to engage in group tactics at the start of the war. Nonetheless, despite a

Type IXB

Displacement:	1,051 tons surfaced
	1,178 tons submerged
Dimensions:	76.6 m (251 ft) x 6.8 m
	(22 ft 4 in) x 4.7 m (15 ft 5 in)
Diving depth:	230m (754 ft)
Propulsion:	two diesels delivering 2,200 bhp
	and electric motors delivering
	500 shp to two shafts
Speed:	18.2 knots surfaced;
	7.3 knots dived

Endurance:	25,000 km (15,535 miles) at
	10 knots surfaced or 115 km
	(71.5 miles) submerged at 4 knots
Armament:	1 x 105 mm (4.1 in) gun; 1 x 37 mm
	gun; 1 x 20 mm gun;
	6 x 533 mm torpedo tubes
	and 22 torpedoes.
Crew:	48-56

The Type IXB boat *U-106* made eight war patrols before her loss in August 1943, bombed by two Sunderlands off Cape Ortegal. Like all 14 Type IXBs, *U-106* was very successful, sinking 21 Allied ships for a total of 131,803 tons.

crisis caused by defective torpedoes, U-boats had sunk 300 ships of some 1.1 million grt by June 1940. This was the climactic month of Dunkirk, the collapse of France and Italy's entry into the war as Germany's ally.

The British again mined the Dover Strait, obliging U-boats to curtail their time on station through having to take the long, northabout route. After the armistice, the Germans took over French facilities on the Biscay coast. Early in the July the first U-boat was serviced at Lorient and, by the end of August, Dönitz and his headquarters were French-based. Shorter and safer transits increased his effective strength by nearly 25 per cent, compensating for the fact that U-boat numbers were still falling, reaching an all-time low of just 22 boats in January 1941. Thereafter, the force increased rapidly as series production came on stream. Within a year, over 90 boats were available.

Finding that France's defeat would not make the United Kingdom sue for peace, Hitler declared a total blockade from mid-August. Even neutral shipping was to be sunk on sight within the war zone. The first squadrons of Focke-Wulf FW.200 Kondor aircraft were sent to Western France, their duties maritime reconnaissance and attacking single merchantmen. For the next year, until its mass transfer to the Russian front, the Luftwaffe also disrupted British ports by large scale and regular attack.

Expanding the merchant fleets

Strange-to-relate, the overrunning of Western Europe actually benefited Britain. Norway and the Netherlands and, to some extent, Denmark, possessed disproportionately-large merchant fleets. Some 75 percent escaped capture and the United Kingdom entered into complex charter agreements with governments-in-exile.

Even as the British merchant marine was occupied greatly in the shipping of Lend-Lease materiel from the United States, so it was to the United States that Britain turned to redress the steady, and worsening, haemorrhage of its strength. The US Maritime

The U-boat Aces

The top six U-boat skippers accounted for 1.2 million tons of Allied shipping between them. They were feted by the High Command and the Nazi regime, and the *Ritterkreuz* became a customary reward for high-scorers, leading to some inflation of scores. Few of the medal-winners survived the war.

Otto Kretchmer — 263,682
Wolfgang Luth — 228,429
Victor Schutze — 212,036
Erich Topp — 184,244
Herbert Schultze — 179,165
Heinrich Lehmann-Willenbroch — 174,326

Gross registered tonnage (GRT)

Commission's objective of building 50 new ships annually had got off to an uncertain start, with a high proportion of the tonnage remaining in Government ownership, and being chartered-out to owners with an option for later purchase.

In June 1940 Congress approved a $4 billion dollar programme to double the size of the United States Navy. Creation of this 'two-ocean' navy would take time and, in one ocean at least, time could be purchased by keeping Britain in the fight. British yards were choked with war-damaged ships needing urgent repair. Replacement tonnage, in the form of standard designs, was sought from the United States, but the British found themselves competing with the US Navy. Lacking sufficient Pacific bases, the US fleet required large numbers of auxiliaries to ensure self-sufficiency in the event of war with Japan.

Late in 1940 a British mission toured facilities in

both Canada and the United States. It brought with it the design of a simple, reciprocating-engined freighter, capable of shifting 10,000 deadweight tons at eleven knots. While the Americans demurred, their own, more complex, standards were already encountering bottlenecks in steam turbine manufacture. The sheer size of the British requirement, initially 6000,000 grt., persuaded the Americans to open new facilities, with orders for 60 ships, with a further 26 hulls from Canadian yards.

Thus began the programmes that ran eventually to

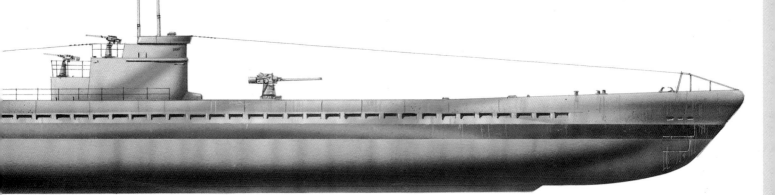

Left: An American merchant ship hoists in a 5 in gun for anti-submarine protection in March 1942. Manned by hastily-trained Navy gunners, these were rather a token armament, but a lucky hit could stop a U-boat from diving again.

Known as 'flush deckers' or 'four pipers', the Wickes and Clemson classes of destroyer were built for the US Navy at the end of World War I. Fifty were supplied to the British in 1940. *Churchill* seen here (ex USS *Herndon*) served as an escort in the Atlantic, administering a severe depth-charging to Kentrat's *U-74* in May 1941. Handed over to Russia in 1944, she became the *Deyatelnyi* and was sunk off Kola in January 1945 by the Type VIIC *U-997*.

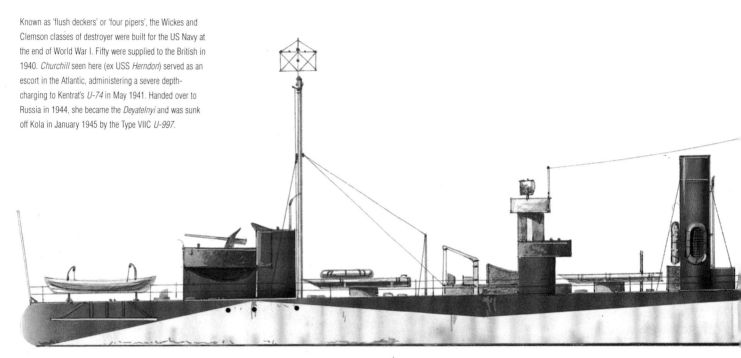

over 2700 'Liberty' ships, 530 of the faster 'Victory' derivatives, 525 T2 tankers and several hundred Canadian-built 'Forts', 'Oceans' and 'Parks'. The Americans were adept at modifying traditional construction techniques to the faster method of welding, and assembling ships from pre-fabricated modules rather than the usual riveted plate-on-frame structure. This colossal undertaking did not win the war, but certainly prevented it from being lost. In crude terms, the Allies managed to build ships faster than the enemy could sink them.

In 1941 this was still in the future. To improve coverage of the convoy routes, and to circumvent any move by the enemy, Iceland and the Faeroes were garrisoned, and both air and naval facilities commenced.

Propelled by a sympathetic President Roosevelt, the United States adopted a 'short of war' policy. Neutrality patrols had, theoretically, prevented the Atlantic war from spilling over longitude 60 degrees West. Creation of a new Atlantic Fleet marked the beginning of a more active involvement. Bases were established on leased territory in Bermuda, Newfoundland and Greenland. Fifty old 'four-piper' destroyers and ten long-range coastguard cutters were transferred to the British flag. Utilising bases in Iceland and at St. John's, in the extreme east of Newfoundland, it was now possible to provide surface escort all the way. Canadian escort groups were responsible to meridian 35 degrees West, the so-called MOMP, or Mid-Ocean Meeting Point. From here to longitude 18 degrees West (the Eastern Ocean Meeting Point), coverage was by Iceland-based British groups, which then handed over to Western Approaches escorts.

Above and right: Workmen in the New York Navy Yard installing a .50 cal (12.7 mm) machine gun aboard a merchant ship. This was often the only protection the ships had against German air attack in the Arctic Ocean.

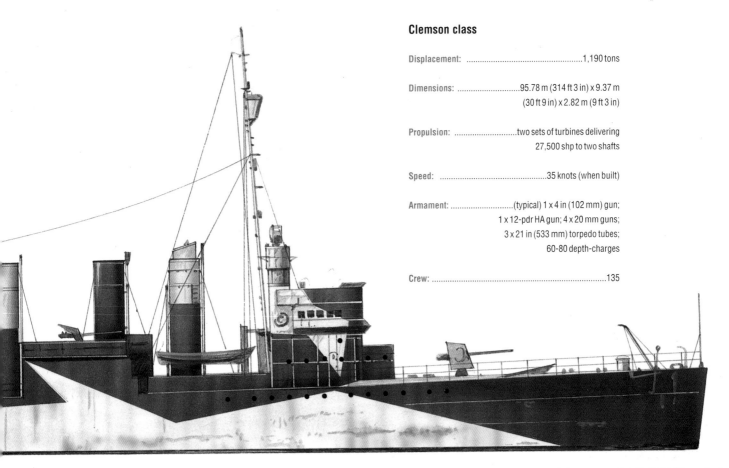

Clemson class

Displacement: ....1,190 tons

Dimensions: ....95.78 m (314 ft 3 in) x 9.37 m
(30 ft 9 in) x 2.82 m (9 ft 3 in)

Propulsion: ....two sets of turbines delivering
27,500 shp to two shafts

Speed: ....35 knots (when built)

Armament: ....(typical) 1 x 4 in (102 mm) gun;
1 x 12-pdr HA gun; 4 x 20 mm guns;
3 x 21 in (533 mm) torpedo tubes;
60-80 depth-charges

Crew: 135

Loading a Liberty ship

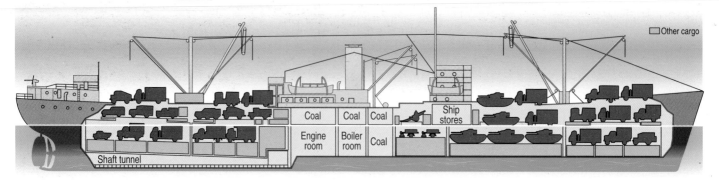

Above: SS *Fort Halkett* (10,384 dead weight tons) as loaded at Swansea in February 1943. She carried a mixed cargo to the Allied forces ashore in Tunisia, including artillery tractors, Churchill tanks, universal (Bren Gun) carriers, lubricating oil, ammunition, camouflage netting, explosives, scout cars, water tanks, wireless trucks and stores for the Royal Engineers.

There remained a huge gap in air coverage. The only aircraft with the necessary endurance was the specially-modified very long range (VLR) Consolidated PB4Y Liberator. Production rate was very slow and most available aircraft were immediately sent to the Pacific. Britain's inability to use bases in the Irish Republic exacerbated the air gap problem at a time when the Gibraltar and Sierra Leone convoy routes were also under determined submarine attack.

The U-boats' 'happy time'

The air gap allowed U-boats to operate on the surface virtually unhindered. Night attacks were followed by a highspeed surfaced 'end-around'. After this, its air and batteries replenished, the submarine could attack again on the following night. Rendezvous with specially-modified Type IX supply boats replenished fuel, torpedoes and food. Endurance was thus limited by that of the crew, or the boat's mechanical reliability.

This was the heyday of the U-boat 'ace', who accounted for 70 percent of losses by surfacing boldly at night within the escort screen. With their Asdic useless and the necessary surface radar only just entering service, the escorts could only do their best with illuminants and gunfire. The three most successful commanders, Kretschmer, Luth and Topp, between them sank 121 ships totalling 687,000 grt.

On his belated entry into the war, Mussolini offered to assist the Germans with a submarine force. Well below strength, Dönitz, readily agreed, but was rapidly disenchanted. The temperament of the Italians seemed little-suited to convoy attacks, while cooperation proved virtually impossible. Their boats and their training left much to be desired. Within a year, Dönitz had banished them to the Central Atlantic and the Caribbean. Their contribution was, however, useful, totalling 106 merchantment of 564,000 grt. In view of their generally poor press, it is worth remembering that the most successful non-German submarine of World War II was the Italian *Enrico Tazzoli*, credited with 17 ships of over 120,000grt. Sixteen Italian boats, half those deployed from their Bordeaux base, were lost in action.

Left: U-660 seen from HMS *Starwort* just after she blew to the surface and surrendered. The boat was badly damaged by depth-charges and sank shortly after this photo was taken.

Right: The 8,800 ton tanker *Dixie Arrow* was torpedoed by *U-71* (Flaschenberg) off Cape Hatteras on 26 March 1942. Of the 33 men on board 22 were saved by prompt rescue work. Walter Flaschenberg made one of the most successful attacks on the US coast that spring, sinking 39,000 tons of shipping.

British counter-measures

Although patchy and subject to fluctuation, the results of Allied countermeasures were definitely showing improvement by the second half of 1941. The first six months of the year had seen losses to U-boats of 263 ships of 1.45 million grt; in the latter half of the year this was reduced to 169 of 720,000 grt. Convoys were routed further northward to take advantage of Iceland-based air cover. While this added to the length of the voyage it also kept more beyond the range of the FW.200s, whose sinkings were more than halved.

As with many long-term trends, there was no single reason for the improvement. Early U-boat aces were eventually lost, while the rapid expansion of the U-boat fleet (to about 240 boats by the end of 1941) diluted existing talent. The number and effectiveness of British A/S forces was increasing markedly. The Royal Navy also began to specifically target German supply ships and supply submarines. So successful was this ploy that the Germans endlessly suspected betrayal or compromisation of codes.

Encyphered German communications traffic was indeed being read by the British. The means stemmed from several sources, but notably from the capture of the *U-570* and the rapid clearance of material from the *U-110* before she sank. Both coups remained top secret and were unsuspected by the Germans. Very high level intelligence was known as Ultra, and had to be used with extreme circumspection to avoid the enemy suspecting its existence.

The passage of convoy HG.76, which sailed from Gibraltar for the United Kingdom on 14 December 1941, proved to be something of a watershed. Its 32 ships were unusually well protected by twelve escorts (mostly comprising the escort group of the redoubtable Captain Frederick ('Johnny') Walker) and the prototype escort carrier *Audacity*. The latter carried only six Martlet fighters, but these downed two FW.200s, kept the remainder at arm's length and located surfaced submarines. Dönitz zeroed-in nine U-boats, later reinforced by a further three. A four-day battle resulted in five submarines being sunk for the loss of only two merchantmen. The hard-worked escort lost the ex-American 'four-piper' *Stanley* and the *Audacity* herself, which had been singled out but, for Dönitz, the outcome was a distinct reverse.

Left: Another victim of 'Drum Beat': the 8,100 ton British tanker *Empire Gem* sinks off Cape Hatteras on 24 January 1942. She was one of five ships sunk by Richard Zapp in *U-66*. He earned a public thanks from Admiral Dönitz and later won the *Ritterkreuz*.

Right: Gentian was part of the escort of convoy SC67 in February 1942. On the morning of the 11th she discovered a raft with eight survivors from the Canadian corvette *Spikenard* which had been torpedoed during the night, but no trace of the rest of the crew was found.

U-boats off the US coast

For all its significance, this convoy battle was overshadowed by events elsewhere. Japan's assault on Pearl Harbor on 7 December had surprised Hitler as much as anybody else. More surprisingly, the *Führer*, already embroiled in war with the Soviet Union since the previous June, then declared against the United States.

America's eastern seaboard, from the St. Lawrence to the Caribbean, teemed with shipping, much of it tankers from the Gulf, the Dutch 'ABC' islands and Venezuela. No plan existed for its protection. There were no convoys, few aircraft and fewer A/S escorts.

Dönitz had long badgered to be allowed to respond to the 'short-of-war' policy. On 9 December, two days before his leader declared war, he proposed the immediate despatch of a dozen long-range Type IXs which, in any case, had been found to be insufficiently agile for anti-convoy operation. Only five were allowed to be sent, joined later by smaller Type VIIs.

To maximise the effect of the campaign, U-boat commanders had to await a joint go-ahead. As this was not signalled until 13 January 1942, the American authorities had had at least five weeks to profit by others' experience. That they did not remains inexplicable, but the short-term result was a massacre. Bottomed during the day, the U-boats surfaced and moved to the inshore shipping lanes by night. Merchantmen, proceeding in fully-lit peacetime conditions, were sunk in scores. As the Americans slowly responded, Dönitz shifted the centre of gravity of the assault to keep them off-balance. Even the hard-pressed Royal Navy loaned what it could to assist, but not until April 1942 were the enemy being forced back into deeper waters.

At no stage in this so-called 'Paukenschlag' campaign were more than a dozen U-boats on the US coast, their endurance extended by supply submarines. The loss rate for merchantmen, previously reducing, mushroomed. Over each of the first seven months of 1942 they averaged nearly 100 ships of 500,000 grt. Fortunately, although this was a tremendous fillip to German morale, it could not disguise the fact that, out in the Atlantic, the long-term trend was still moving in favour of the defences. While, in the first half of the year, Dönitz's operational strength increased from 91 to 140 boats, his losses were 32.

Defeat of the U-boats

The air-gap was slowly closing, with convoys increasingly able to count on the presence of a VLR Liberator. Just one aircraft could make attackers dive, causing them to lose touch while, on transit, they often provided warning of U-boats concentrating ahead of a convoy, whose course would be changed to evade them.

Some 25 escort groups now operated within the Western Approaches Command. Over 50 ocean escorts were Newfoundland-based. Many were new frigates–longer legged, better armed and less brutally uncomfortable for their crews than the corvettes.

A significant development at the turn of 1943 was the formation of the first five support groups. Operational analysis had shown that the Home Fleet could spare a few destroyers to contribute. A first escort carrier (CVE) was also allocated. Support groups had a roving commission to join any convoy under threat and their appearance coincided with the period of greatest crisis in the Atlantic.

During the spring of 1943, operational U-boat strength had risen to a record 240. Their deployment owed much to the activities of the German radio intelligence service, which eavesdropped the daily British situation report. As this transmission was largely a digest of decoded U-boat reports, and relevant Ultra input, it illustrates the degree to which 'behind-the-scenes' activities influenced the overall outcome.

March 1943 saw the climactic convoy action in which the slow SC.122 was closed by the fast HX.229 and targeted jointly by over 40 U-boats, organised in three groups. Twenty-one ships of 141,000 grt. were lost, all in the air gap. The escort strength was about normal but was overwhelmed by the scale of the onslaught. For all the efforts by the defences, just one U-boat was sunk, and that by a Sunderland flying boat, whose operational radius was considerably less than a VLR Liberator's 800 miles.

In this dreadful month Dönitz came nearest to meeting his objective. In the first 20 days his boats sank about 100 merchantmen, aggregating over 500,000 grt. Of this total, 65 were destroyed in the North Atlantic. That most were in convoy flew against all statistical evidence, but caused voices question again the convoy concept. However, the German advantage was reversed just as quickly. During the last eleven days of March, Atlantic losses dropped to 17. Rapid Allied reaction had seen the number of VLR aircraft available increased to 30, while all support groups were active.

Dönitz's analysts were misled by the spectacular, but singular, success of the SC.122/HX.229 action and by persistent over-claiming by returning U-boat commanders, among whom competition was strong. In fact, since the second quarter of 1942, sinkings had been declining, while U-boat losses were increasing. Early in 1942, some 220,000 grt had been sunk for each submarine loss; by May 1943 the exchange rate had dropped to just 5,500 grt. If Dönitz required any other statistic to convince him that his campaign was faltering, it was that of Allied newbuildings. In July 1943 more standard-built merchant tonnage was completed than the sum total of losses from all causes. And construction rates were still accelerating.

During May 1943 Dönitz's men suffered some sharp reverses. When the slow convoy ONS.5 was threatened by 41 submarines, the convoy escort was reinforced by first one, then two, support groups. A two-day battle, fought out in a spring storm in ice-strewn waters, saw seven U-boats destroyed, for the loss of twelve merchantmen. Within days, 36 boats were re-directed at the fast HX.237 and slow SC.129. Here, the tally was five submarines for five freighters. A week later, Dönitz set 17 submarines on to SC.130. VLR Liberator support was rapidly reinforced, teaming with the escorts to destroy six U-boats, in one of which Admiral Dönitz lost his own son. The convoy was unscathed.

In April and May 1943, 56 U-boats were sunk, an unacceptable rate which caused their temporary withdrawal for a re-evaluation of the campaign.

Left: In August 1943 a Liberator of 200 Sqn RAF attacked the Type VIIC *U-468* on the surface off West Africa. The U-boat's gunners hit the Liberator, setting it on fire, but Flying Officer Lloyd Trigg continued with his bombing run. The depth-charges hit and sank the U-boat, but the Liberator crashed into the sea, killing all aboard. Here, one of the seven survivors of the U-boat, found in a dinghy by HMS *Clarkia* is landed at Freetown. Their description of the Liberator's heroic attack led the authorities to award Trigg a posthumous VC.

Right: The crew of the Type VIIC *U-593* (Kelbing) surrendered to an Anglo-American escort force off Bizerta in December 1943 after a seven hour duel. *U-593* sank the Hunt class destroyer *Tynedale*, triggering an intensive search. Kelbing torpedoed and sank a second destroyer, HMS *Holcombe* but was detected on sonar by USS *Wainright* which delivered an accurate depth-charge attack supported by HMS *Calpe.*

Dönitz's reasons for carrying on were that the scale of resources devoted by the Allies to A/S warfare, if re-directed, would cause major problems elsewhere. He knew that revolutionary types of submarine and torpedo were in the stages of final development. The former would be able to remain submerged in the presence of continuous air cover, yet still have the speed to work around convoys.

Acoustic torpedoes, introduced in September 1943, were designed to cripple escorts but, although they proved a nuisance, an antidote was quickly produced. The main hazard to the U-boat remained the aircraft, whose coverage was extended from October 1943 by an agreement with the neutral Portuguese for the use of airfields in the Azores.

By then Battle of Atlantic had effectively been decided. In the months of September and October alone, 2,468 ships were convoyed across. For sinking just nine of their number, 25 U-boats were destroyed. Atlantic convoys were now typically of 80 ships or more. The main reason was that their periphery increased only approximately as the square of the number of ships comprising the convoy and, therefore, it was more economical in escorts.

Losses from the saturation 'Bay offensive', combined with powerful convoy defences, engendered a growing attitude of despair in U-boat commanders, who no longer pressed home their attacks in the face of air support.

Following the Normandy landings of June 1944, the Allied advance obliged the Biscay submarine bases to be evacuated. By the end of September, all surviving U-boats had been transferred to Norway. This, and the clearance of remaining re-supply submarines in a carefully-coordinated and continuing operation, effectively signalled the end of the long struggle for the Atlantic sea lanes.

Innovatory technology had proved to be of doubtful value or too late. Schnorchel-equipped submarines were, indeed, able to remain submerged for long periods but this resulted in a conventional boat having its usual 60-100-day endurance reduced to an average 37 days, and its duration on actual operations from 40 to nine. Only with the high submerged speed, Schnorchel-equipped 'Elektroboote' (Types XXI and XXIII) would all requirements have been met, but the first of these formidable craft entered service during, literally, the closing days of hostilities.

Cold statistics cannot begin to paint an adequate picture of the pain and wastage occasioned, for the second time in a generation, by the German U-boat arm. Estimates differ, but the total loss in Allied and neutral merchant ships was in the region of 5,200 vessels of nearly 22 million gross tons capacity. Approximately two-thirds of this toll was claimed by submarine attack. In terms of individual tragedy, an estimated 63,000 personnel met their deaths, rather more than twice the number lost in the submarines encompassing their destruction.

Right: 'Z' Zebra makes RAF Coastal Command's last wartime patrol on 4 June 1945. Although aircraft accounted for a handful of U-boat losses in the first 18 months of the war, they became the deadliest enemy of the submariners, sinking the majority of U-boats lost from 1942 onwards.

Chapter 2 – The War against the U-boat

Anti-submarine warfare in World War I

Anti-submarine warfare during 1914-18 was something entirely new, tackled by the Royal Navy with tenacious persistence rather than with the help of science. In the previous chapter we have seen that the three most successful U-boat commanders of World War II were credited with a joint total of 687,000 grt of merchantmen sunk. This highly damaging total pales beside that of the three top skippers of the earlier war, who destroyed 1.08 million grt. Worse, the 20 top commanders are all credited with scores in excess of 130,000 grt.

Their success was due simply to not being sunk themselves. Submarine flotillas were based on the main arenas of the North Sea and the Mediterranean, so that multiple cruises were possible. Such was the inefficacy of counter-measures that the top scorers made up to 24 cruises. Defensive measures slowly caught up. During 1915 and 1916 respectively, only 20 and 22 submarines were sunk. In 1917 and 1918 the totals reached 65 and 72.

Important lessons can be drawn. It takes a considerable time to build and to train an effective A/S force. Nations that fail to invest sufficiently in defence during peacetime will be punished severely in time of war. While it was the re-introduction of the principle of convoy that arrested the haemorrhage of mercantile loss in World War I, it was the eventual application of science to A/S warfare that enabled submarines to be actually sunk.

From the outbreak of war in 1914, the Admiralty scientists had experimented with hydrophones for submarine detection., It was soon discovered that extraneous water noise quickly swamped any useful

US Coast Guard Cutter *John C. Spencer* depthcharging the Type IXC U-boat *U-175*, 17 April 1943. The U-boat eventually surfaced and tried to fight it out with the *Spencer* and another CG cutter, *Duane*. *U-175's* commander was killed by a direct hit on the conning tower and the crew abandoned the boat.

signal. If used only at low speeds, hydrophones could be deployed from surface ships. Multiple units, with matched characteristics could indicate the approximate direction of the submarine. Although the French and Americans also devoted considerable resources to the problem, the British retained their lead, putting into production a towed, streamlined 'fish' housing a uni-directional microphone. This could be rotated and, by listening for the loudest signal, it gave a directional accuracy of about ten degrees with, of course, no indication of range.

Sensing a submerged target was one thing; attacking it successfully was quite another. Although by 1918, hydrophone contact with U-boats was common, Admiralty records credit only four sinkings resulting solely from the equipment i.e. without visual sightings. The depth charge was trialled in a primitive form as

Right: HMS *Vanity* was one of the 'V' class destroyers built at the end of World War I and pressed into service as escorts in World War II. Re-armed for an AA role with four 4 in guns, she carried 30-40 depth charges.

early as 1911 but was issued to the fleet only in 1916. In 1917 the D-type charge was simply a drum of 300 pounds (136 kg) of TNT, detonated by a hydrostatic switch that could be pre-set in increments of 50 feet (15.2 m) down to 200 feet (61 m). It was normally fatal if it exploded within 30 feet (9.1 m) of a submerged submarine, and the chances of success were greatly improved by dropping a simultaneous 'pattern' of charges.

Before the end of hostilities, two further elements had been introduced. Both would eventually have a profound effect against the U-boat threat. The first of these was air power. 'Power' seems hardly the correct term for the ad hoc organisations that sought to exploit the potential of flight. However, ceaseless improvisation by enthusiastic pioneers on both sides made it work. By 1916, useful payloads had increased to the point where

offensive bombing was possible.

In August 1916 Austro-Hungarian naval aircraft raided the Venice arsenal and put the British submarine *B-10* on the bottom. A month later, and more significantly, their flying boats spotted the French boat *Foucault* submerged in the Adriatic and disrupted her primitive depth and trim control by accurate bombing. Forced to the surface, she was then sunk by other aircraft.

Well ahead of their time were the British experiments in dunking hydrophones from airships or landed floatplanes. Only the fragility of the equipment caused ultimate disappointment. By the close of hostilities the British had assembled some 560 aircraft of various types in their war against enemy submarines. While only one U-boat was probably sunk outright and four more in combination with surface craft, U-boat

Above: The US Navy had so few ASW vessels in commission in 1942 that 25 'Flower' class corvettes were transferred from the British and Canadian navies. *Begonia*, seen here, became USS *Impulse*.

Left: A typically weathered 'Flower' class corvette, *Convolvulus* seen in September 1941. She has twin depth-charge racks aft and the two depth-charge projectors on either beam: a total fit of 40 DCs.

Right: Direction finding equipment and intelligence from 'Ultra' gave the Royal Navy an increasingly accurate view of where the U-boats were. In early 1943 this was sometimes used to fight convoys through the 'wolf packs' rather than re-routing the shipping.

The Type II Hunt class destroyer *Badsworth* comes alongside her depot ship. Carrying no torpedoes, the Type IIs were optimized to fight aircraft and submarines: armament included four high-angle 4 in guns and up to 60 depth-charges. *Badsworth* survived the war to be transferred to the Royal Norwegian Navy in 1946.

commanders were already reporting on their freedom of movement being inhibited by constant air patrols.

During the eighteen months or so that a fully-integrated convoy system was in operation, only 257 ships were lost out of the 84,000 escorted. This represented a loss rate of only 0.3 percent. Of these, only two losses occurred while the surface escort was supplemented by aircraft.

The second new element was the use of intelligence. By design, this attracted no attention, but assembled a mass of information from a wide variety of sources to provide a mosaic of data. This was continuously updated and provided the basis for conclusions to be drawn and decisions made.

Hydrophones function through diaphragms being vibrated by incoming acoustic energy. They work equally well in a reverse mode, the diaphragm emitting energy if excited by an adjacent oscillator. In water, as in air, a small proportion of energy encountering a solid object is reflected as an echo, and a suitably sensitive hydrophone, tuned to its frequency, can detect it.

Experiments with such transmitter/receiver combinations were pursued in both Great Britain and the United States. Despite the confusion of a continuous flow of energy and its poor directionality, the Americans claimed in 1917 to have detected a submerged submarine at a range of 1000 yards from a craft moving at 15 knots.

For accurate sound ranging, however, a sharp pulse of emitted energy was required. Gases exploded in a chamber worked well but the associated gear was hopelessly cumbersome. It was the French that produced the answer in piezo-electricity. If certain pure crystals are stressed mechanically, they emit a transient electrical charge. Reverse the process and electrical stimulation will cause them to vibrate. Outputs are tiny, but the French already had a suitable high-frequency valve amplifier to produce a useful signal. They shared their findings with the British, who quickly produced a prototype apparatus for evaluation afloat. Sited in a suitably streamlined and retractable dome, it proved able to detect a submerged target at upwards of 2,500 yards (about 2,300 m) in good conditions. It is worth noting that even by 1939, this performance was little improved, and the average range at which U-boats were detected during World War II was only half this.

Deliveries of the new sets were too late to be of use before the armistice and, with the coming of peace, the allies inevitably cut funding and released personnel. From July 1918 the British referred to the apparatus as 'ASDIC', and graded its details highly confidential. The acronym is generally thought to be derived from 'Anti-Submarine Detection Investigation Committee' but, mysteriously, there is no written evidence that such a body ever existed.

ASW tactics between the wars

The first destroyer asdic sets were issued in the Royal Navy in 1922, trials and exercises uncovering the problems which remain problems today. Deep water contains unpredictable layers of differing temperature and salinity, while pressure increases linearly with depth.

All these factors have the effect of distorting or

Above: Hibiscus was one of 35 'Flower' class corvettes built by Harland and Wolff. She was transferred to the US Navy in 1942 as the USS *Spry*.

bending asdic transmissions, and varying the propagational speed of sound. Cold, deep water could produce 'convergence zones', at which targets could be detected at abnormal ranges. However, these were associated with complementary shadow zones, from which sound energy never returned. In shallow water an asdic operator, straining to separate a tiny useful signal from a background of extraneous and ship-induced noise, would be further hindered by multi-pathing: acoustic energy scattered on contacting the seabed.

It was discovered that while the water noise associated with a ship's speed was a significant factor, so too was the relatively unfamiliar phenomenon of cavitation. More attention was thus paid to optimising flow around a hull and its appendages, avoiding discontinuities and, particularly, designing propellers for optimum performance within specific speed bands.

The 'business end' of early asdics was cranked around by hand, enabling the operator to listen on a specific bearing or to search in azimuth. Improvements saw it motor-driven and connected to the ship's gyro repeater, to keep it on a constant bearing despite a ship's

manoeuvring. Developing instrumentation techniques allowed range and bearing to be displayed remotely, for the benefit of bridge personnel.

A high number of spurious contacts were inevitably detected. There was another difficulty too: in the final approach for a depth charge attack, pulse and echo became virtually coincident and the all-important change of bearing difficult to detect. These problems resulted in solutions that were to be fully exploited only very much later. One was the ahead-firing 3.5-inch stick bomb thrower, which could range a half-mile to a submerged target still in the asdic beam. Development was abandoned in 1934 by withdrawal of funding. Another technique was for one destroyer to continuously 'illuminate' a target with asdic, while giving directions to a second which actually carried out the attack.

By the early 1930s the remaining escorts built during World War I were judged to be no longer effective and new classes were introduced. Asdic was only just being made available for smaller ships which, defying historical lesson, were equipped more with an eye for anti-aircraft defence and minesweeping than for A/S work. It was assumed that the low submerged speed of submarines would allow them to attack convoys only from within a well-defined sector forward of the beam, and the theory and tactics of escort cover were based on

this faulty supposition.

The Spanish Civil War (1936-9) provided the first opportunity to evaluate asdic under near-wartime conditions. British warships were serving on the neutrality patrols, one of whose functions was to muzzle Italian submarines which, masquerading as Spanish, were attacking shipping in defiance of international law. When one near-missed the destroyer *Havock* with a torpedo in August 1937 she, in turn, was pursued and depthcharged by several British ships, but escaped damage because asdic contacts could not be held.

As a handful of German U-boats were also present in the war zone, the British Admiralty established an Operational Intelligence Centre to track their progress, assess available data and to promulgate information to relevant parties. Direction-finding (D/F) stations were set up in support and the whole organisation was worked-up at an opportune time, providing the basis for rapid expansion when the European War broke shortly afterwards. It was to prove of inestimable value, particularly the Submarine Tracking Facility.

With the founding of the unified Royal Air Force in 1918, the Royal Navy lost direct control of its air element. The often-acrimonious, twenty-year political battle to regain it is not the business of this narrative, but the pre-eminent British position in naval aviation

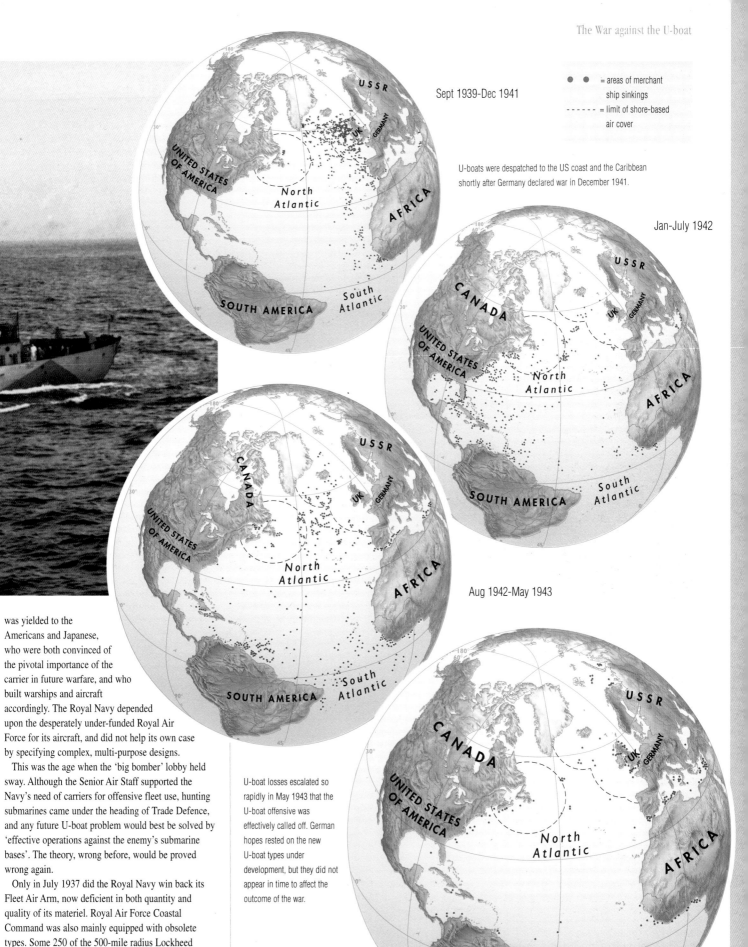

Sept 1939-Dec 1941

● ● = areas of merchant
ship sinkings
----- = limit of shore-based
air cover

U-boats were despatched to the US coast and the Caribbean
shortly after Germany declared war in December 1941.

Jan-July 1942

Aug 1942-May 1943

U-boat losses escalated so
rapidly in May 1943 that the
U-boat offensive was
effectively called off. German
hopes rested on the new
U-boat types under
development, but they did not
appear in time to affect the
outcome of the war.

June 1943-May 1945

was yielded to the
Americans and Japanese,
who were both convinced of
the pivotal importance of the
carrier in future warfare, and who
built warships and aircraft
accordingly. The Royal Navy depended
upon the desperately under-funded Royal Air
Force for its aircraft, and did not help its own case
by specifying complex, multi-purpose designs.

This was the age when the 'big bomber' lobby held
sway. Although the Senior Air Staff supported the
Navy's need of carriers for offensive fleet use, hunting
submarines came under the heading of Trade Defence,
and any future U-boat problem would best be solved by
'effective operations against the enemy's submarine
bases'. The theory, wrong before, would be proved
wrong again.

Only in July 1937 did the Royal Navy win back its
Fleet Air Arm, now deficient in both quantity and
quality of its materiel. Royal Air Force Coastal
Command was also mainly equipped with obsolete
types. Some 250 of the 500-mile radius Lockheed
Hudsons were on order from the USA, but by
September 1939, only one squadron had been
converted. The excellent new Shorts Sunderland flying

boat was also in production, but only two squadrons had been so equipped. Of strike aircraft, Coastal Command was effectively devoid.

Thus, with a new war looming, the Royal Navy had inadequate aviation support, while being dangerously over-confident in the capabilities of asdic.

Preparations for war

In view of the inadequacies of the Royal Navy (and, indeed, the French, although this soon ceased to be an issue) it was fortunate that Hitler's policies forced the German fleet into a conflict for which it, too, was ill-prepared. The much-criticised 45 percent submarine quota allowed under the terms of the abrogated Naval Agreement would have represented about 72 U-boats of the sizes required. In reality there were still only 56, of which 30 were 250-ton Type IIs, designed for North Sea and coastal operations. Eighteen were 500-ton Type VIIs, the 'workhorse' Atlantic submarine, and the remainder a mix of long-range Type Is and Type IXs.

That the high proportion of 46 boats were operationally ready reflects the personal ability of Dönitz. Typically Germanic, with a strong sense of duty and discipline tempered by heavy sentiment, the

Admiral broke with traditional attitudes. Sailing often with training boats, he encouraged informality between officers and men, who would need to live, cheek-by-jowl, in acute discomfort for weeks on end. While the force was small, he knew his men and, often, their families on a personal basis. As it grew, he devoted what time he could spare for face-to-face contact, addressing crews, conducting de-briefings, awarding honours and, ever more frequently, penning letters of condolence. His qualities of leadership formed the cement that bound the U-boat arm in both victory and, eventually, bitter defeat.

Days before the commencement of hostilities, the

Like Britain and France, Germany toyed with the idea of long-range submarine cruisers equipped for surface action. The Type XI designed in 1937 had four 127mm guns in two turrets and six torpedo tubes, and was to have carried an Arado Ar 231 autogyro. With a crew of about 110, almost double the complement of a Type IX, these giant 3000 ton submarines (*U-112-115*) were laid down in 1939 but the contracts were cancelled on the outbreak of war.

Type IXC

Displacement	1,120 tons surfaced; 1,232 tons dived
Dimensions	76.76 m (251.6 ft) x 6.76 m (22.1 ft) x 4.4 m (15.5 ft)
Diving depth	230 m
Powerplant	diesel engines delivering 4,400 hp and electric motors delivering 1,000 hp to two shafts
Speed	18.2 knots surfaced or 7.3 knots submerged
Range:	25,000 km (15,535 miles) surfaced at 10 knots; 115 km (71.5 miles) submerged at 4 knots
Armament:	one 105 mm gun, one 37 mm and one 20 mm AA gun, six 21 in (533 mm) torpedo tubes with 22 torpedoes.
Crew:	48-56

Type IX U-boat

1   Hydroplanes
2   Rudder
3   Propeller
4   Aft torpedo room

The Type IX was intended for long range operations on the assumption (proved wrong) that the workhorse Type VII lacked the range to operate in the mid-Atlantic. Armed with a 105 mm gun and carrying 50 per cent more torpedoes, the Type IX's only disadvantage was its slower diving time.

Right: The defeat of France in 1940 transformed the U-boat campaign. Based on the French Atlantic coast instead of Germany, U-boats could spend far longer on patrol and even the Type VIIs could reach as far as the US east coast. The concrete shelters built to protect the submarines from air attack proved impervious to bombing.

5 Crew space	14 Engine room	23 Search and attack periscopes	32 Battery compartment
6 Steering compartment	15 Oil sump	24 Bridge	33 Captain's cabin
7 Access hatch to torpedo room	16 Machine room/auxiliary pumps	25 Compass housing	34 Officers' mess
8 Motor room	17 Double hull	26 88 mm gun	35 Officers' quarters
9 Motor room controls	18 37 mm gun	27 Control centre	36 Galley
10 1,000 hp electric motors	19 Fin	28 Fuel tanks	37 Senior ratings' quarters
11 Trim tank	20 Conning tower	29 Main frame	38 Gun support
12 Reduction gear	21 Snorkel	30 Loading tubes	39 Upper casing
13 2,200 hp diesel engine	22 20 mm gun	31 Ammunition stowage	40 Free flooding vents

41 Control, communication, electric tubing
42 Anchor windlass
43 Crew sleeping area
44 Forward torpedo room
45 Torpedo tubes
46 533 mm torpedo
47 Spare torpedo stowage
48 Motor control to hydroplanes
49 Torpedo tube covers
50 Wire cutter

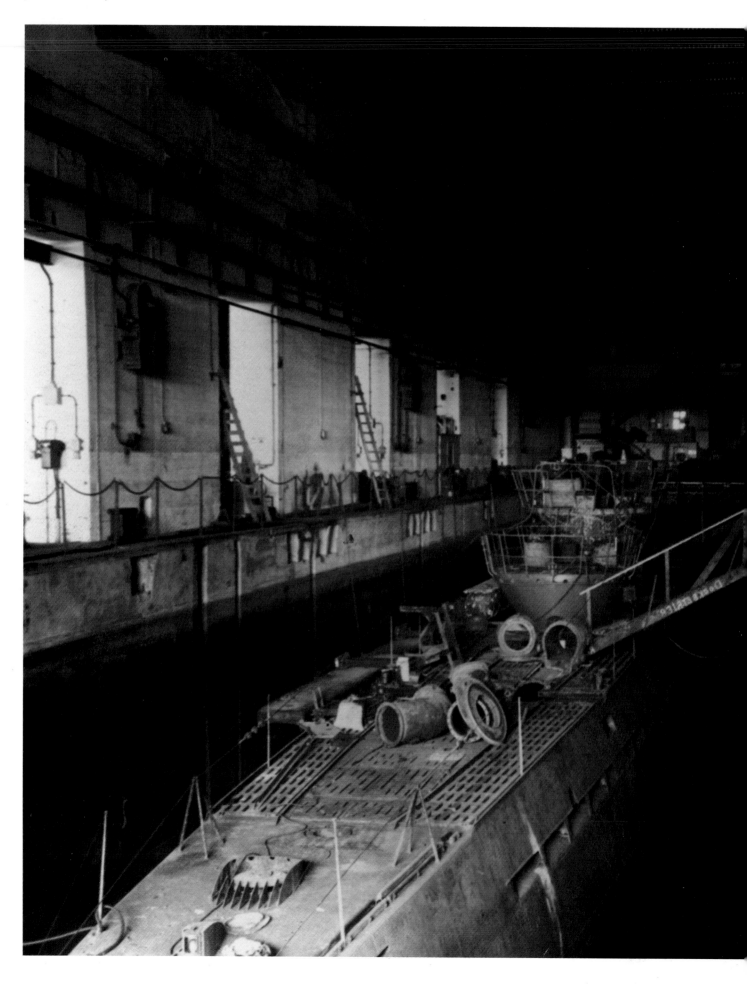

available U-boat force was already deployed, in the Baltic, the North Sea and in the Western Approaches to the United Kingdom. As the *Führer* still hoped for rapprochement with the British and French, German U-boats were bound strictly by the 1930 Submarine Protocol. This limited them to attacking only identified troopships, auxiliary warships, and commercial ships in convoys protected by warships.

To defeat Dönitz's men, the Royal Navy had 176 destroyers, but over 60 of them dated from World War I. As Fleet duties demanded the more modern flotillas, only the older units were available as escorts. Although excellent in their day, they were now considered small, with low standards of habitability. Their range, never large, was decreased further by the necessity to run their high-powered machinery at low speeds for extended periods. Some had a boiler space stripped to provide

eventually, the introduction of '*Kurier*', which sent messages by burst transmission.

The Germans had high confidence in the security of their naval Enigma encypherment, persistently underestimating the abilities of their enemies to defeat it. Building on work commenced during the Spanish Civil War, the British extended their shore-based network of direction-finding (D/F) stations around the North Atlantic periphery. It would be a while before such gear could be miniaturised to the extent that it could be fitted in the escorts themselves.

Every scrap of data, gleaned from whatever source, found it way to the Submarine Tracking Room of the Admiralty's Operational Intelligence Centre. Working around the clock the centre's teams rapidly became adept at assessing Dönitz's dispositions and, quite often, his intentions.

extra bunkerage and accommodation. A few had their obsolete low-angle armament replaced by dual-purpose weapons of lighter calibre. All were deficient in depth charge capacity. To support them, a significant programme of corvettes and A/S trawlers had been initiated, but it would be some time before these appeared in useful numbers.

In the course of World War I, possibly 50 U-boats were sunk on mines and 19 by British submarines. The latter total had been sufficiently encouraging for the British to design and built the specialist R-class A/S submarines. Completed late in the war, these had a submerged sprint speed of 15 knots but, 30 years ahead of their time, they were soon scrapped and, like so many innovative concepts, this was put on ice.

Profiting from experience, submarines of 1939 were significantly quieter than their predecessors, hence less detectable by passive hydrophone techniques. Dönitz's centralised command system generated a huge volume of radio traffic, but the duration of messages was reduced by the extensive use of coded 'shorthand' and,

Left: This Type IX U-boat seen inside the U-boat pens at St. Nazaire was captured by the Allies in May 1945 after a 110 day patrol to Japanese waters.

Above: Admiral Dönitz awards iron crosses to some of his U-boat men. Both his sons were killed in action while serving with the German navy in World War II.

Early days

For the first few weeks of World War II, most U-boat commanders observed the prize rules scrupulously. However, all British ships had been instructed to transmit a submarine warning ('SSS') if attacked and, when destroyers or aircraft responded rapidly, there were some close calls. As early as 23 September 1939, the Germans lifted restrictions on ships using their radios. By the 30th, all restrictions had been lifted in the North Sea and, on 4th October, as far as longitude 15 degrees West.

The aircraft carrier was still a weapon untried by war. Eventually, it would be an effective killer of submarines

Left: Springbank was an auxiliary AA ship, a 5155 ton merchantship equipped with eight 4 in guns and a Hurricane fighter. Four U-boats attacked homeward bound Gibraltar convoy 73 on 26 September 1941, sinking her during the night.

Above: The Canadian *St. Croix* was one of the 50 US destroyers (ex-*Williams*) transferred to the RN and RCN in 1940. Escorting convoy ON113 on 24 July 1941 she sank *U-90* with three patterns of depth-charges.

but, early in the war, lacking techniques, suitable aircraft, intelligence and weapons, it was not. Nonetheless, the Royal Navy's offensive doctrine saw two of its priceless carriers employed on U-boat sweeps.

Responding to an SSS signal the *Ark Royal*'s aircraft found and attacked a surfaced submarine. Two were brought down by the detonation of their own A/S bombs, released from low level and fused to explode on contact. The carrier's escorting destroyers later succeeded in gaining asdic contact but their depth charges only shook their quarry. Control difficulties forced the boat, a Type VII, down to a new record depth of 144 metres, a useful discovery for the U-boat crews.

During these operations the *Ark Royal* was attacked by a second U-boat, whose torpedoes were fitted with magnetic pistols. These were designed to detonate

beneath a target's keel but, like their British counterparts, were giving much trouble, in this case exploding prematurely. A destroyer counter attack blew the culprit to the surface and destruction.

The *Ark Royal*'s narrow escape carried a clear warning, yet on the following day, the *Courageous* was still engaged on similar operations. Presenting the *U-29* with an unmissable target, she was sunk by two of a salvo of three torpedoes. Her loss was a severe blow to the Royal Navy, which promptly released fleet carriers from A/S work.

Coastal Command aircraft had a first priority of reconnoitering the North Sea exits against breakouts by German heavy naval units; submarines were a second priority. Bomber Command aircraft, too, were forbidden to attack surfaced submarines as they were classed as

secondary targets. In either case was voiced the extraordinary doubt that aerial navigation was accurate enough to guarantee that a sighting was not that of a friendly boat, working in a designated area.

Dönitz made his first attempt at a group attack in October 1939. Of six U-boats involved, one was sunk on the new Dover Strait minefield while taking a short cut. The remaining five rendezvoused satisfactorily, but lost one of their number when attempting to sink an independent. Two boats contacted the target convoy, sank six ships but lost another U-boat in so doing. Although the remaining three U-boats were re-directed onto a second convoy, from which they sank three more merchantmen, the loss of half of their attacking strength was a severe blow. The Dover Strait was soon prohibited to U-boat transit. The above two sinkings were to fleet destroyers, with well-trained asdic operators, but such ships could seldom be spared for convoy escort duties in the future.

Just prior to this first pack exercise, Gunther Prien penetrated the Scapa Flow defences in *U-47* and, in a fine feat of arms, sank the battleship *Royal Oak* at her berth. The sinking, nonetheless, produced a considerable bonus for the British in the shape of two of the new German wakeless electric torpedoes which, missing the target, grounded without exploding. They were equipped with the unreliable magnetic pistol, but their

Above: The survivors from a Focke-Wulf FW.200 Condor are rescued by British sailors. Dönitz had high hopes of co-ordinating U-boat and air attacks against the convoys, but such operations were dogged by poor liaison between the Luftwaffe and Kriegsmarine.

characteristics, along with those of recovered magnetic mines, allowed the British to further refine degaussing methods to reduce the weapons' effectiveness.

Torpedoes continued to give the Germans major problems, failures in the magnetic pistols being compounded by unreliable depth keeping. Foreshadowing American experience some two years later, at least a quarter of all war shots were computed as duds. As targets escaped, and submarines were heavily counterattacked, and crew morale suffered badly. Dönitz initiated a thorough programme to isolate and resolve the problem, which did not prove easy.

A second attempt at pack operation was made in November 1939. Only three U-boats could be mustered but the attack exhibited what was to become a familiar pattern–initial sighting, tracking and reporting, reinforcement and repeated attacks. Over three days, six ships were sunk for no loss. One new type VII, however, launched a four-torpedo salvo of which three exploded prematurely and one was dud. Its position revealed, the boat underwent a thorough depth-charging that sent her down to an unprecedented depth of 170 metres. This survival was invaluable, for an interrogated prisoner had recently revealed that British depth charges had a maximum setting of about 150 metres.

By April 1940 the U-boat war was obviously not going entirely Dönitz' way. Nearly one million gross tons, over half of it neutral, had been destroyed, but only eight new boats had joined against the loss of eighteen. One casualty, the first to an unaided aircraft, but in shallow water, was salvaged and repaired.

To cover the invasion of Norway in April 1940 Dönitz

Above: Two ratings from *Wild Goose* try on the escape apparatus used by U-boat crew. *Wild Goose* was in Walker's 2nd Support Group, accounting for at least three U-boats herself and taking part in the destruction of another six.

was obliged to withdraw 42 U-boats from the war against commerce. Their experiences were grim. The high latitudes and generally strong level of natural field strength made magnetic pistols yet more unreliable. Mixing salvoes with contact weapons did not help due to the depth problems. Sinking warships freely manoeuvring at sea proved a very different matter to

pursuing merchantmen. The nature of the campaign did, however, involve British and French warships operating in the fjords at low speed, or even anchoring. Many ships survived because of dud torpedoes; several U-boats survived because the shallow, confined conditions defeated asdic equipment. Short spring nights and frequent aircraft interruption prevented the U-boats from

replenishing completely either their batteries or their air.

Although the Allied campaign proved to be a military failure, the U-boats' efforts to prevent it were ineffective. Their total strength of 52 could ill afford the four that were lost, while mercantile losses during March and April were halved.

Shortly afterwards, the Germans captured the British submarine *Seal*. The simple, robust design of her torpedoes' contact pistols was used as the basis for an improvement of the Germans', which were unnecessarily complex. However, it was to be late in 1941 before the depth-keeping problem was solved. Following lengthy submergence, the internal pressure of a U-boat inevitably increased. Faulty seals within the torpedoes allowed this pressure to be transferred to their atmospheric reference chambers. As depth keeping was hydrostatically referenced to this datum, the weapons automatically ran deep.

1940 and the fall of France

Following the occupation of Norway and the Low Countries, Dönitz resumed the Atlantic war in full force. Patrols in the southern North Sea and off the British coast were already becoming hazardous, and the little Type IIs were withdrawn to the Baltic for the urgent task of training new crews. With an average operational strength of only 33, of which just 14 could be expected to be at sea at any one time, the force received a considerable fillip by the collapse of France in June 1940. Porting facilities became available along the Biscay coast, shortening distances to operational areas, whilst reducing the risk from patrols and mines.

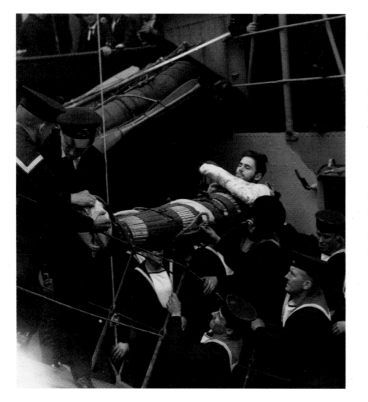

Above: Another Black Swan class sloop of Walker's 2nd SG, *Woodpecker* sank *U-119* and participated in several other sinkings before succumbing to a U-boat torpedo in February 1944.

Left: Wild Goose lands an injured survivor from one of her U-boat kills. The sloop's last success occured in March 1945 when she took part in the destruction of the Type VII *U-863* in the English Channel.

Existing French facilities could also be used for repairs and maintenance. Therefore, although the average number of operational boats continued to fall, 16 could now be expected to be found at sea. Virtually all operational restrictions had been lifted by July 1940.

A new programme was commenced, geared to the production of 29 new boats monthly from mid-1942. An assumed loss rate of 10 percent was not, in fact, incurred until Spring 1943. While the Type IIs were curtailed at 50 hulls, the Types VII and IX were to be in production for most of the war. As the accompanying data shows, however, they were considerably improved over this period.

Quite small increases in dimensions significantly increased displacement, i.e. volume. Extra fuel and stores could thus be accommodated for extending endurance. The sheer length of a torpedo, however, prevented an increase in number stowed, which remained virtually constant at 14 for a Type VII and 22 for a later Type IX. As salvo firing of three or four at a single target was common, it will be apparent how

Above: Commander F.J. Walker's sloop *Starling* led the 2nd SG on its sweep through Biscay in early 1944, an operation that destroyed six U-boats and contributed to the sinking of five more. Walker had commanded the Royal Navy's anti-submarine school before the war, and had been passed over for promotion, yet few individuals made such a contribution to victory in the Atlantic.

Left: A Martin Maryland photo-reconnaissance aircraft of No 771 Sqn RAF. German naval bases were continually monitored by the RAF which mounted such heavy attacks on Brest that the battlecruisers *Scharnhorst* and *Gneisenau* were obliged to withdraw to Germany.

Left: No. 204 Squadron flew its Sunderland I flying boats from the Gambia, patrolling the South Atlantic in the summer of 1941. With a range of over 2,500 miles, the Sunderland provided vital air support to convoys in mid-ocean, forcing the U-boats to dive where they often lost contact with their prey.

Right: The *Rapana* was one of the improvised aircraft carriers converted from merchant hulls by the British in 1942. The obsolesence of the Fleet Arm Arm's Swordfish then proved a blessing in diguise: few other aircraft could have operated from a flight deck just 126 m long on a ship capable of no more than 12 knots.

necessary was re-supply to prevent premature return from patrol. Endurance much depended upon crew size which, in this pre-automation age, also remained virtually constant. With little scope for the improvement of hull forms on existing dimensions, designers could not greatly increase speed without large increases in installed power, although an extra knot or so was gained on the surface by the introduction of diesel turbocharging.

With the entry of the Italians into the war in June 1940, the Royal Navy, in the absence of the French,

needed to build up the strength of its Mediterranean Fleet. The abortive Norwegian campaign and the French evacuation had also left it with many ships undergoing repair at a time when Dönitz's U-boat force was increasing its effort. During the three months May-July 1940 his boats sank about 535,000 grt for the loss of only four U-boats.

To offset the advantage of the U-boats' French bases, the British extended continuous convoy escort to longitude 17 degrees West, improved to 19 West in October 1940. Although the scale of escort was light, it

began to give problems to earlier boats with their restricted bunker capacity. Attacks on dispersed convoys were also now against international law, in being beyond the declared war zone.

The period from July to October was known to the U-boat crews as the 'Happy Time', with convoys, once detected, virtually defenceless. From September, President Roosevelt made available the first of 50 old 'four-piper' destroyers. Although far from ideal for Atlantic conditions, the Royal Navy received them gratefully.

Less willing cooperation was, however, apparent between the German services. To facilitate pack tactics, Dönitz required long range air reconnaissance, but only pleas to the very top wrested a squadron of FW.200 aircraft. *Reichsmarshall* Göring was suspicious of the foundation of a 'private' air force. Their value was not disputed but they were rarely available when required. Only in January 1941 did Dönitz manage to obtain the Führer's sanction for direct control of these aircraft.

With growing numbers of escorts requiring working-up, the British established a specialist facility at

Tobermory. Each new ship underwent a punishing one-month training before graduating to an escort group, where she would be subjected to further group training. Commanding and senior officers also attended the tactical school, set up at the Liverpool headquarters of Admiral Sir Percy Noble, C-in-C Western Approaches.

By 1941, it was possible to form escort groups of reasonable strength, although they were often a strange amalgam of British, or ex-American destroyers, corvettes and Admiralty trawlers. It was policy to keep groups together once they worked effectively as a team.

Even when under-strength they were very rarely diluted with new ships.

To the year's end Dönitz' men had destroyed some 340 ships, totalling about 1.7 million grt. The normally-reserved admiral followed the flamboyant Göring's lead in instituting the *Ritterkreuz* award for the highest-scoring 'aces'. This encouraged over-claiming which, inflated even further by the Germans' overheated propaganda machine, caused the High Command to badly over-estimate their success.

The truth, however, was bad enough. Slow convoy

Left: The merchant aircraft carrier *Audacity* started life as a German merchantman, the *Hannover,* but was captured in 1940. Her airgroup contributed to the successful defence of convoy HG76 until *U-751* sank her, earning its commander Gerhard Bigalk the Knight's Cross.

Right: The merchant carrier *Ancylus* was another tanker converted to carry aircraft. Remarkably, all 19 MACs survived to return to merchant service once the escort carriers became available.

SC.7 was attacked by eight U-boats simultaneously in October 1940. In a surfaced night action barely 200 miles from the North Irish coast, the convoy lost 20 ships. It was unfortunate in its adversaries including four aces, Kretschmer, Schepke, Endrass and Frauenheim, whose speciality was just this form of attack. Those still with torpedoes left after the massacre rendezvoused with a fifth expert skipper, Prien, and were vectored onto a second convoy HX.79, which lost 14 ships.

The British worked frantically to develop countermeasures to this form of attack which should, with hindsight, have been anticipated as it had been used previously at the latter end of World War I and had been described in Dönitz' own writings in 1939.

An unspectacular, but invaluable, advance was the introduction of reliable radio telephony (known to the Americans as TBS, or Talk Between Ships), which allowed all escorts to be in contact en clair. The senior officer of the escort thus had a clear idea of events in the various sectors in his command, allowing him to deploy his forces accordingly.

At night a surfaced U-boat offered only a small profile, glimpsed fleetingly, if at all. Asdic, in any case swamped by convoy noise, was virtually useless against it. An improved illuminant, 'Snowflake', was introduced but lit both friend and foe indiscriminately. What was required was a suitable radar. This had been under intense development but did not enter service until early in 1941.

An unexpected bonus from the Germans' capture of HMS *Seal* was their recovery of charts showing estimated U-boat dispositions in the Atlantic. These were based on British and French D/F intercepts from shore stations. Knowing their boats' exact positions at the times indicated, the Germans were gratified to find very considerable errors, usually so great that the

estimate would have been useless to any hunter. Direction-finding was thus devalued in German estimation. Dönitz continued to exert tight control through radio link, while the British strove to miniaturise a D/F set for operational use aboard escorts.

From mid-1940 the Germans became aware that U-boats were often being actively hunted only one or two hours after having made a transmission. Compromised cyphers or just chance sightings were the preferred reason accepted by the Germans when, in fact, it resulted from good intercepts from a rapidly improving shore-based D/F network. Only in 1942 did High

Above: Seen here addressing the crew of HMS *Wild Goose*, Captain Walker trained and led the most effective ASW group of the war. The strain of spending day after day on the bridge contributed to his premature death in 1944 from cerebral thrombosis.

Left: One of the 90 Short Sunderland Is in service with RAF Coastal Command from 1939. The beam positions, equipped with Vickers 'K' guns were replaced by a power-operated dorsal turret on the Mk II.

Frequency Direction Finding (H/F D/F, or 'Huff Duff') get into the escorts. Operating at short ranges, it gave an accurate bearing on a transmitting submarine. Two simultaneous bearings from a pair of escorts gave range in addition.

Pack tactics were reliant upon the shadower being able to keep touch until sufficient forces had been assembled. A single U-boat, betrayed by her tracking reports, might be kept down by the escort until she lost touch but a long-range maritime aircraft was a different problem. The psychological effect of a 'snooper', slowly circling a convoy beyond gun range, was considerable. Dönitz railed constantly about the availability and reliability of the FW.200, a militarised civilian aircraft, but their presence was hated by convoy crews as it inevitably preceded a submarine attack. To make the most of their range they flew from their Bordeaux base along a great arc to the west of the British Isles, landing at Stavanger in Norway. Weather permitting, they would return on the following day.

Since the mid-1930s, the British Admiralty had prepared plans for the conversion of diesel-engined passenger liners into auxiliary aircraft carriers for the purpose of trade protection. In the event, few went ahead owing to the perennial shortage of troopships. A first response to the FW.200 was, therefore, the Catapult-Armed Merchantman, or CAM ship. Only 35 were completed of a planned 250, because of their limitations and a shortage of catapults. Retaining Red Ensign status, the ships carried full cargoes. The

catapult was mounted on the forecastle, aircraft in position. Once launched it could not be recovered, flying on to an airfield ashore if within range, or ditching alongside a friendly ship if not. Early, and thus expendable, marks of Hurricane fighter were most common. In practice, because of the risk to the pilot, captains were reluctant to launch unless a kill was virtually certain. Thus, of about 170 round trips recorded by CAM ships, only eight launches are recorded, resulting in six FW.200s destroyed and others damaged or driven off. Although the material results of the programme were thus meagre, the deterrent effect on the snoopers was considerable, reducing the quality

Above: Kptlt. Götz Baur took command of the new Type VII *U-660* in January 1942. Operating from La Spezia, *U-660* was detected attempting a daylight submerged attack off Oran on 12 November 1942. After 90 minutes' depth-charging from two escorts, Baur surfaced and scuttled the boat, he and his crew surviving to surrender.

Below: Wren picks up survivors from *U-608* in the Bay of Biscay where the U-boat had been detected underwater by an RAF B-24 Liberator on 10 August 1944. Depth-charges from the aircraft and the 2nd SG led her commander to surface and scuttle the boat at 04.00 the next day.

of their reconnaissance data.

Aircraft, with their speed and observation, were also the answer to the shadowing U-boat, which needed to be surfaced in order to maintain contact with the convoy. CAM ships here were of little value, as continuous patrols were required, properly serviced and armed. For this, there was no substitute for a flight deck. Conversely, aircraft from such a deck would take care of both airborne and submarine shadowing.

The answer remained the Auxiliary Aircraft Carrier, a hull built to ordinary mercantile standard topped of with a flight deck and equipped with the most basic facilities that would do the job. Both the British and Americans reached this conclusion at about the same time, and apparently independently. The American prototype (USS *Long Island*, CVE-1) actually commissioned about three weeks before the British equivalent, in July 1941, but as the United States was still neutral it was HMS *Audacity* that was first proved operationally. Her life was short and violent, and her capacity was just six aircraft, but she triumphantly demonstrated the value of the concept.

As described in greater detail in chapter 5, a huge CVE programme was initiated but, for various reasons, initial deliveries were disappointingly slow. As a stopgap, the British improvised the Merchant Aircraft Carrier, or MAC ship; tankers or bulk grain ships which could still load a full cargo (handled by pumping) with a flight deck above.

Following their precedent with the troublesome Flanders flotillas in World War I, the Germans quickly commenced the construction of bombproof pens for U-boats based in Biscay ports. During the building process these were highly vulnerable to bombing, but priorities for the Royal Air Force still lay in Germany itself. Once complete, the pens offered near 100 percent protection

Above: Inspecting the depth-charges aboard USS *Greer*, June 1943. One of the 'flush deckers' retained by the US Navy, USS *Greer* was attacked by *U-652* after 'pinging' the boat with sonar in September 1941, three months before Germany declared war on the USA.

Right: USS *Atherton* depth-charges the Type IXC *U-853* off Long Island on the evening of 5 May 1945. Voluntarily or not, the U-boat lay on the bottom in shallow water, where it was attacked for over 12 hours before wreckage came to the surface. There were no survivors.

to submarines within and huge retrospective bombing attacks caused little damage, but wide devastation in the surrounding French conurbations. Even the U-boat crews remained untroubled. Between patrols, they were billeted in resorts down the coast for rest and recreation.

The campaign intensifies

As 1941 progressed Dönitz steadily increased his strength, despite wrangling in the High Command over priority for materials, and the need for ever more training boats. As designs were improving, the Admiral was able to move operations ever further into the Atlantic, although at the cost of shorter operational duration. The Royal Navy's escort strength was, meanwhile, expanding at a rate of only six to eight corvettes per month, although increasingly assisted by the Canadian-built contribution, which had begun in November 1940. Also, with the obvious abandonment of German intentions to invade the United Kingdom, the Home Fleet was able to release a useful number of older destroyers.

Severe and rising shipping losses led the sympathetic

President Roosevelt to offer American naval escort from the eastern seaboard to meridian 22 degrees West. Still neutral, his pretext was the protection of American-flagged ships but, from September 1941, this was extended to all flags. The decision meant that Western Approaches escorts could operate more efficiently, no longer having to divert to Iceland to refuel. Methods for refuelling at sea (RAS) were being developed, but it would be mid-1942 before it became a general procedure.

The escort mainstay, the Flower-class corvette, had been conceived as a coastal escort. Its modest size and simple design enabled it to be built in many small yards. For Atlantic use, however, it proved too small, too slow and lacking in endurance. Its antics kept its crew permanently wet and fatigued, greatly affecting their efficiency. In 1940, therefore, the Admiralty ordered the first group of a new and larger type, which came to be known as a 'frigate'. Some 5 percent longer, they were also four knots faster, more seakindly and able to ship more weaponry. Named after British rivers, they had also twice the endurance and proved to be formidable adversaries for the U-boats.

In the Spring of 1941 both escorts and Coastal

Command aircraft began to receive shortwave radar capable of detecting surfaced U-boats. Like asdic, however, it had the limitation for aircraft that the target was lost during the final run-in. The answer was the Leigh Light, named for its inventor. Used first in Vickers Wellingtons it comprised a standard naval 24-inch projector, housed ventrally in a retractable 'dustbin' and controlled precisely by the standard hydraulic servo system used for gun turrets.

Having located a surfaced target at night, the aircraft would throttle back to 'quiet' speed, weapons readied. About one mile from target, the beam would be snapped on, its bearing and vertical angle given by radar data. Before the bedazzled U-boat crew could respond, they would be recipients of a clutch of shallow-set depth charges. Like other good British ideas, however, and to the endless bewilderment of the Americans, the Leigh Light was subjected to 18 months of development before it entered service. It was June 1942 before the

Right: U-175 seen from the USGC *Spencer* after their gun duel in April 1943. The crew member by the conning tower disappeared moments after this picture was taken. Coast Guardsmen boarded U-175 but it sank before any secret equipment could be seized.

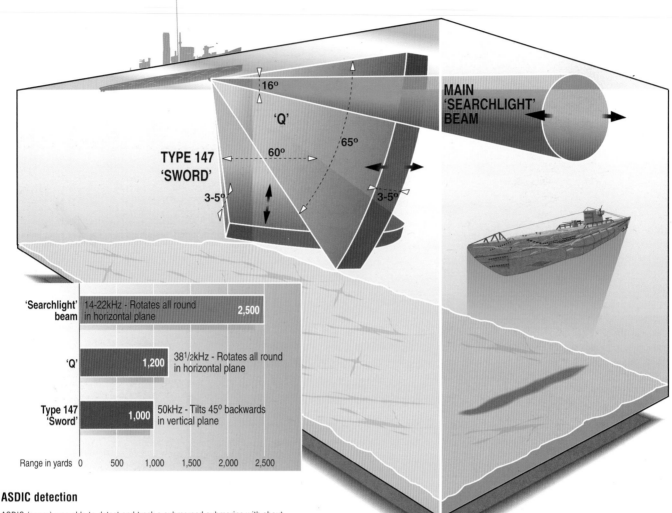

MAIN 'SEARCHLIGHT' BEAM

'Q'

16°

65°

TYPE 147 'SWORD'

60°

3-5°

3-5°

		Range in yards				
'Searchlight' beam	14-22kHz - Rotates all round in horizontal plane	**2,500**				
'Q'	**1,200**	38½kHz - Rotates all round in horizontal plane				
Type 147 'Sword'	**1,000**	50kHz - Tilts 45° backwards in vertical plane				

Range in yards 0   500   1,000   1,500   2,000   2,500

ASDIC detection

ASDIC (sonar) was able to detect and track a submerged submarine with about 2,000 yards in good conditions. However, the escort had to slow down for the system to operate properly, and until the development of the contact-fuzed 'Hedgehog', the escort always lost contact just before making its depth-charge attack.

In April 1941 the U-boat Command carefully examined its radio procedures and introduced new cyphers. There was increasing evidence that convoys were being routed around submarine concentrations and that the subjects themselves were being found more easily. Dönitz's force, recovering from an all-time low strength of only 22 operational boats, had 25 available when, in March, five were lost. Three were commanded by 'aces', Prien, Schepke and Kretschmer. Their loss affected Dönitz deeply and he suspected a new British development. In fact, the escorts involved were the typical mix of Flowers and elderly V and W-class destroyers, fortunately in strength sufficient to be able to devote time to track their convoys' assailants. What Dönitz thought to be something new and sinister was really a result of the growing strength and expertise of the escort forces.

Worse was to come. Lemp, sinker of the *Athenia*, made a submerged daylight attack on slow convoy OB.318 in May 1941. In company with Schnee in *U-201*, he quickly hit four ships but, concentrating on a further shot, Lemp was overrun by a Flower class

Above: Some of the survivors of *U-175* seen from the USGC *Spencer*. If a crippled U-boat could manage to surface, its crew had a reasonable chance of escape, but few men emerged from submarines unable to come up.

corvette, the *Aubretia*, which blew him to the surface with a shallow pattern of depth charges. Following standard practice, Lemp's crew set scuttling charges and abandoned. However, his *U-110* was reluctant to sink and was taken in tow by the British, who had time to strip it of anything that looked useful. While the boat eventually foundered, the German High command never discovered that her yield had included a naval Enigma machine and all relevant signal codes. The find, kept top secret, was to greatly influence the struggle against the U-boats.

This same month saw the first transatlantic convoy, HX.129, given continuous surface escort, provided in turn by Newfoundland, Iceland and Western Approaches-based groups. Within two months, the vulnerable Freetown route was likewise covered.

The theory that the U-boat problem could be solved by bombing their bases and building yards was meanwhile proved unsound. Prime Minister Churchill's ringing 'Battle of the Atlantic' directive in March 1941 had given Bomber Command this task as a priority, but by the end of the year, of 66 German submarines destroyed, not one loss could be attributed to strategic bombing or minelaying by aircraft. Coastal Command's score of one U-boat sunk by aircraft alone was little better when, in August 1941, it had an extraordinary stroke of good fortune.

Eighty miles south of Iceland, the new *U-570* was operating. Her crew was unusually inexperienced and, without sufficient checking beforehand, the skipper surfaced directly beneath a patrolling Hudson. A prompt release of four, shallow-set depth charges caused sufficient damage to prevent her diving to safety. As the aircraft radioed for assistance the German crew panicked. Believing their boat to be sinking they wished to abandon but, having nowhere to go, signalled their desire to surrender. Further aircraft dissuaded them from changing their mind until surface ships arrived. The crew was duly removed and the U-boat was towed to Iceland for emergency repairs and then to the United Kingdom where, refitted, she entered naval service as HMS *Graph*. All confidential material had been destroyed by her crew and, as the capture could not be kept secret, it was made into a major publicity exercise. Her main contribution was to yield performance characteristics for the Type VIIC.

More numerous escorts allowed the totally inadequate Armed Merchant Cruisers (AMC) to be withdrawn. U-boat skippers tasked with penetrating convoy screens began to report on the increasing quality and aggressiveness of the defence. In August 1941, Dönitz changed policy by ordering his boats to go first for the escorts if opportunity offered, in an effort to make them more cautious. The weapon for the purpose was the G7 *Zaunkönig* acoustic torpedo. Still in the final stage of development, and often unreliable, many were released for use in the autumn.

Displaced in Bomber Command by the new generation of four-engined aircraft, Armstrong-Whitworth Whitleys and Vickers Wellingtons were transferred to Coastal Command to support the Hudsons and Sunderlands. A further useful newcomer was the attractively ungainly Consolidated PBY Catalina flying boat/amphibian, of which later versions had an

The ASDIC system

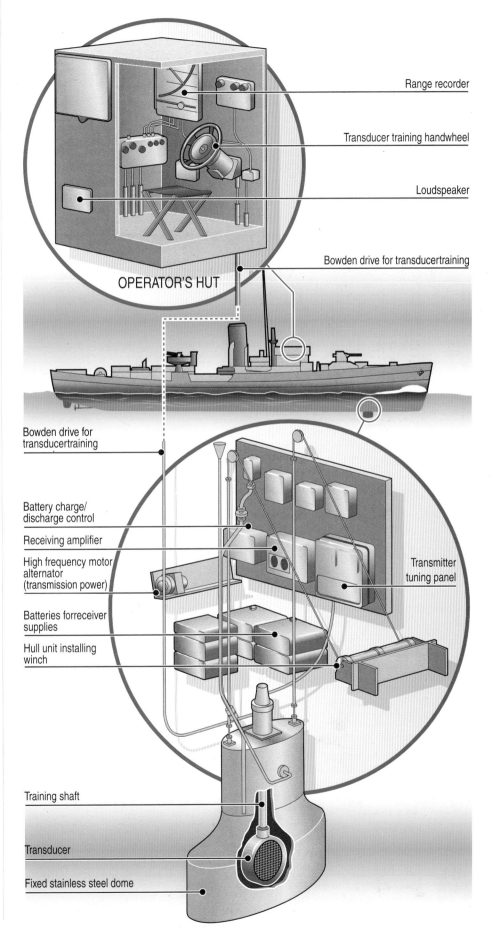

Range recorder

Transducer training handwheel

Loudspeaker

OPERATOR'S HUT

Bowden drive for transducertraining

Bowden drive for transducertraining

Battery charge/discharge control

Receiving amplifier

High frequency motor alternator (transmission power)

Batteries forreceiver supplies

Hull unit installing winch

Transmitter tuning panel

Training shaft

Transducer

Fixed stainless steel dome

Above: Five officers and 25 ratings survived from *U-175* to be picked up by the US Coastguard. Of the 13 casualties, most were caused by a direct hit on the conning tower.

such that he could put five ships into hunting her. The corvette *Penstemon* obtained a firm contact and, as her early asdic could give no indication of depth, released a ten-charge pattern set variously for depths from 150 to 400 feet (47-122m). Damaged, the *U-131* surfaced, only to be strafed by *Audacity*'s aircraft, abandoned and sunk by gunfire.

The following morning the *U-434* was destroyed in much the same way, having just arrived from refuelling in the supposedly-neutral Spanish port of Vigo. Sharing credit for the latter kill was the old four-piper *Stanley* which, in the pre-dawn darkness of the next day, sighted another. Also just sailed from Vigo, the *U-574* dived and turned the tables with a quick shot which, hitting the destroyer, caused her to disintegrate in a massive explosion. Walker exacted a rapid revenge, his own sloop, *Stork*, bringing her up within 15 minutes.

A single freighter was then sunk by one of the three U-boats still in contact. Dönitz quickly despatched three more, with orders to sink the *Audacity* first. With good reason, for the carrier's handful of fighters had just downed two FW.200s and driven off a third, damaged. They were also harassing those U-boats still in contact.

The U-boats closed in for a classic group attack on the night of 21/22nd. A second merchantman was sunk, but the use of Snowflake illuminants also silhouetted the *Audacity*, which was destroyed by a three-shot salvo from the *U-571*. Her skipper was the ace Endrass but, in attacking on the surface, he was spotted by the sloop

boat/amphibian, of which later versions had an endurance of approaching 3,000 miles.

Patrols were intensified over the Bay of Biscay to harry U-boats moving to and from their bases. Most of the aircraft involved carried ASV radar and a clutch of depth charges, but success was slow in coming. For their part, the Germans' attitude to radar had more than a hint of ambivalence. Pre-war experiments had not been over-successful, and had convinced scientists that an airborne radar could never have the definition to detect a target as small as a surfaced U-boat, yet any unexplained incident was invariably ascribed to their opponents' use of it. To improve their search technique in the face of intensified defences, U-boats required a surface search radar set, but development was very slow.

Suddenly switched to the Strait of Gibraltar, ASV-equipped aircraft enjoyed a succession of encounters with submarines transiting on the surface at night. Two were destroyed and three so damaged as to abort their patrols.

During December 1941, the fateful month of Pearl Harbor, there was a watershed battle around the Gibraltar convoy HG.76. Its 32 ships had an unusually powerful escort in the prototype escort carrier *Audacity*, three destroyers, four sloops and nine corvettes. The core of the screen was drawn from Captain Frederick Walker's 36th Escort Group, the Navy's best.

The first U-boat, *U-127*, seeking to locate the convoy for its group, was detected on the surface by the advanced destroyer screen. It dived but fell victim to a straightforward, asdic-guided attack with depth charges. Within 48 hours, nonetheless, FW.200 reconnaissance had zeroed-in four more U-boats. One was sighted by a Martlet fighter from the *Audacity*. Walker's strength was

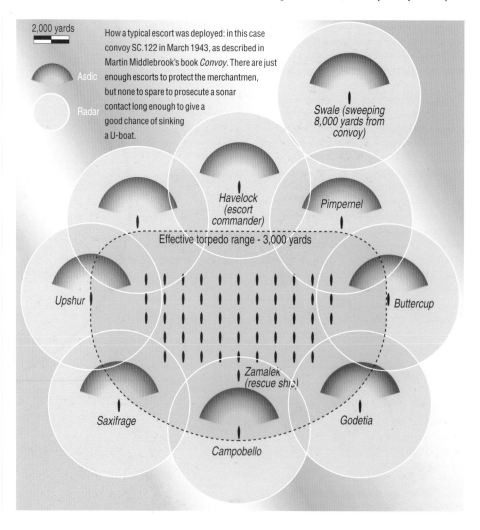

2,000 yards

Asdic

Radar

How a typical escort was deployed: in this case convoy SC.122 in March 1943, as described in Martin Middlebrook's book *Convoy*. There are just enough escorts to protect the merchantmen, but none to spare to prosecute a sonar contact long enough to give a good chance of sinking a U-boat.

Swale (sweeping 8,000 yards from convoy)

Havelock (escort commander)

Pimpernel

Effective torpedo range - 3,000 yards

Upshur

Buttercup

Zamalek (rescue ship)

Saxifrage

Godetia

Campobello

Above: The long-delayed arrival of VLR Liberators extended air coverage across the North Atlantic, severely hampering U-boat operations. Portugal was eventually persuaded to allow the Allies to operate aircraft from the Azores: in this case Liberator MkVIs from No. 220 Squadron Coastal Command.

Below: US VLR aircraft operated from Britain: this PB4Y-1 is seen over the Bay of Biscay in the summer of 1943. Caught so often on the surface, some U-boats received extra AA weapons and attempted to fight it out with the Allied bombers.

Deptford. As he dived, his boat was crushed by two shallow-set patterns of depth charges.

Once the convoy neared British waters, Dönitz gave up. His men had destroyed the *Audacity* and *Stanley* to be sure but only two of the all-important freighters. The cost of three submarines was too high.

The action around HG.76 well illustrated the general situation in the U-boat war. Stronger, more experienced escorts gave attackers a hard time. Radar was making the standard surfaced night attack hazardous. The presence of a small carrier kept submarines down and liable to lose contact.

Across the Atlantic, Dönitz had opened the devastating *Paukenschlag* offensive. It petered out in six months, however, as lessons learned elsewhere at so high a cost were applied. In the face of a convoy system and a rapidly-increasing number of shore-based aircraft, the U-boats moved further offshore and south to the Gulf and the Caribbean.

Aircraft versus U-boats

Leigh Light Wellingtons, which had entered service so slowly, were also improved with a radio altimeter: a rapid-response instrument giving the all-important absolute height on the attacking run. They also received a newly-designed airdropped depth-charge which would explode directly beneath a surfaced U-boat. On 5 July 1942 a Wellington, piloted appropriately by a volunteer American pilot, recorded the first Leigh Light sinking, disposing of the *U-502* west of La Rochelle.

Losing the protective cloak of darkness had a powerful psychological effect on U-boat skippers, whose reports alarmed Dönitz. Unaware of just how slender British

resources actually were, he ordered his boats to transit the Bay on the surface in daylight. This disastrous decision resulted in almost daily sightings, and the sinking of four more submarines by 3 September.

Tardily, the Germans turned to the development of a radar search receiver, to indicate to a skipper that he was under radar illumination. The lack of urgency was the more surprising as a repaired ASV set from a crashed British aircraft had long been trialled in a Luftwaffe FW.200.

The search receiver, known as 'Metox', from one of the French firms that manufactured it, was a crude affair: the antenna had to be erected by hand each time the boat surfaced. Initially in very short supply, Metox units were transferred from outward-to-inward-bound boats. Occasionally, submarine were ordered to group around a single Metox-equipped boat for protection. The equipment was also counter-productive: it frequently picked up extraneous signals that may, or may not, have indicated an ASV aircraft. Skippers invariably opted for prudence and dived, thus wasting time.

Under the 'Biscay Cross', as the antenna became known, the Germans regained some of the initiative, again traversing the Bay on the surface, usually at night. Allied air patrols by day were also increasingly harassed by long-range, fighter versions of the Junkers Ju-88. The British responded with escorts of Bristol Beaufighters or de Havilland Mosquitoes.

In September 1942 the *U-156* sank the British liner *Laconia* near the Cape Verde Islands. Too late, the skipper discovered his victim to be transporting 1,800 Italian prisoners of war. Also aboard were 160 Poles and 700 British crew, military personnel and dependants, including 80 women and children. He quickly assembled three other U-boats of his group and

broadcast en clair for Vichy French assistance from West Africa and that no vessel engaged in this act of mercy would be attacked. Before French ships arrived Liberators with American markings had carried out three attacks on the surfaced and encumbered U-boats, each of which was clearly marked with ad hoc Red Cross flags and towing lifeboats.

Incensed by what he considered a breach of faith, Dönitz issued what came to be known as the 'Laconia Order'. Henceforth, the safety of the U-boat was to be paramount and, with the exception of Commanding Officers and Chief Engineers (useful for interrogation) survivors were not to be rescued. A final rejoinder was 'Be severe'. At his subsequent trial at Nuremberg Dönitz was found guilty on this count since, although he had not, as many alleged, ordered the killing of survivors, his order was in clear contravention of the 1936 Submarine Protocol, to which Germany was party. U-boats, if they could not assist survivors, should not sink their ships in the first place.

Other than in the Mediterranean or the Western Approaches, operations involved U-boats in lengthy transits, which limited their time on station. Re-supply ships were based in the Canary Islands by the good offices of a friendly neutral Spain. When firm

Above: US Coastguards load a Mk.6 depth-charge onto a 'Y' projector. Note the depth settings (in feet) marked around the fuze. The U-boat crews discovered that their submarines could dive deeper than early war Allied depth-charges.

Right: The thunderous detonation of a depth-charge seen from a US submarine chaser in 1944. The standard US Mk7 contained a 272 kg (600 lb) explosive charge and sank at 2.7 metres per second to a depth of 91 m. Later types could be set to depths of up to 305 m: deep enough to sink any U-boat.

diplomatic action by the Allies ended the practice, specially-equipped vessels were scattered at pre-arranged rendezvous in the deep ocean. Based on Ultra intelligence, a British sweep of June 1941 caught nine within three weeks. As Germany's auxiliary cruisers also relied on these vessels, the operation was doubly valuable.

The need for specialist submarines had already been foreseen, resulting in the short and portly Type XIV. Each could stow 430 tons of fuel oil, 45 tons of dry stores and four reload torpedoes. Of 24 units projected, only ten were actually completed. Each could refuel up to a dozen Type VIIs or five Type IXs and, known as

'*milch-cows*', made possible the *Paukenschlag* offensive. As larger numbers of U-boats were directed onto specific convoys, it became practice to tail the action with a Type XIV. This practice was halted by the closing of the Atlantic 'airgap' and, especially targeted, all ten Type XIVs were sunk.

To survive the attentions of aircraft, U-boats gradually augmented their anti-aircraft (A/A) armament. Their 88 mm or 105 mm deck guns, now rarely used, were landed in favour dual-purpose 37 mm weapons. Performance deteriorated as the tower became festooned with various combinations of 20 mm and 13.2 mm weapons, with attendant platforms and armour plate. Several submarines were destined for conversion to 'flak boats', for escort of their colleagues across the hazardous waters of the Bay of Biscay. The experience of the first in the face of aggressive air attack saw the programme abandoned. Any submarine electing to fight it out on the surface could find itself under fire from salvoes of 30 kg underwing rockets or even 57 mm guns which, mounted in the nose of modified Mosquitoes, fired six-pounder ammunition. Just one puncture in a pressure hull would prevent diving, and an inability to dive was now invariably fatal.

Technological improvements

Escorts could still use hydrophones to listen passively for submarines, as opposed to detecting them 'actively' by asdic. To make U-boats quieter, their machinery was increasingly resiliently-mounted to de-couple vibration from the hull. Propellers were also designed to reduce cavitation over the range of speeds usually employed.

Aerated rubber coatings were introduced for hulls. These were designed to absorb asdic pulses rather than reflect them, sharply reducing echo strength. Decoys could be released, emitting bubble clouds that gave false asdic returns; these were being refined to imitate actual U-boat characteristics.

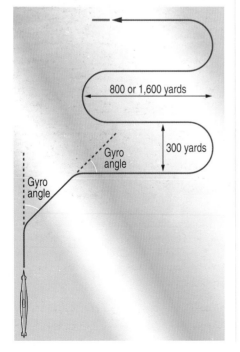

While the magnetic pistol still caused problems, new types of torpedo were entering service. To avoid the need to approach convoys closely, the so-called FAT would run for a pre-set straight course before embarking on a series of loop manoeuvres to increase its chances of a hit. For the estimate of the initial range, U-boats acquired a modified Luftwaffe radar. High-speed torpedoes, with hydrogen peroxide engines, were also under development.

As Metox had considerably offset the advantage of ASV II, the Allies concentrated on a new, centimetric set. This, ASV III, was available late in 1942 but it enjoyed lower priority than the H2S radar then being

Left: The Germans developed the *zaunkönig* torpedo which followed a pre-set zig-zag pattern, increasing its chance of hitting a ship in a convoy. U-boats firing them were supposed to warn other U-boats to stand off while the torpedo was active.

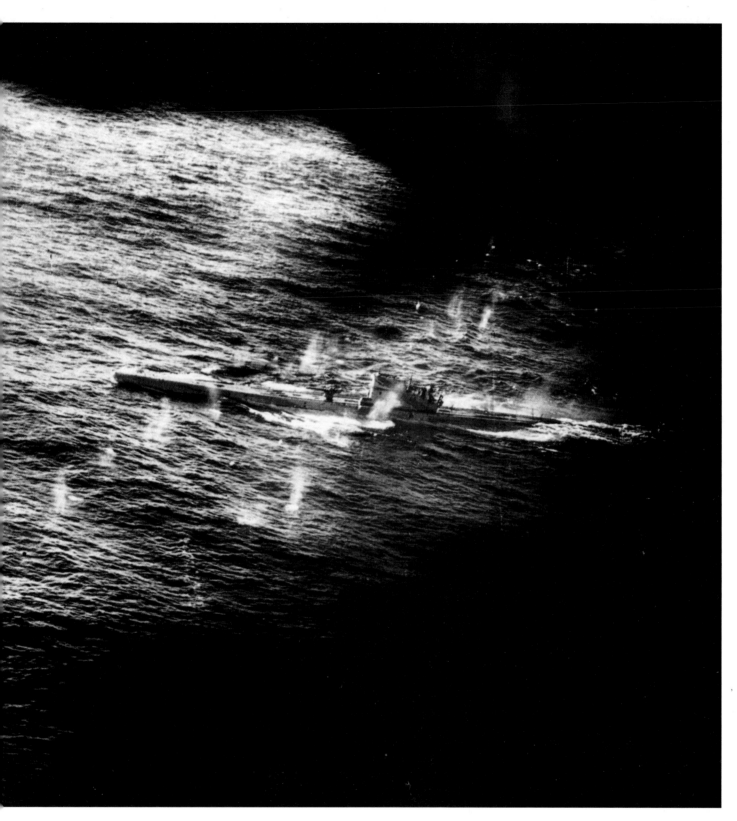

produced for RAF Bomber Command. American-built sets, destined for VLR Liberators, were therefore acquired for Coastal Command early in 1943. To Metox, tuned to a longer wavelength, ASV III was invisible.

It was in the early months of 1943 that the U-boat war peaked. Dönitz could deploy over 200 operational boats, with as many again training or working up. About 70 new boats were being completed each quarter. However,

German statistics showed that average results per patrol were steadily diminishing, as was the life expectancy of the boats themselves. On the other hand, meagre individual results were offset by sheer numbers. Overall shipping losses, Allied and neutral, fluctuated about an average of 400,000 grt monthly.

The apostles of strategic bombing were given their heads in the spring of 1943. Nearly 7,000 sorties were flown against the Biscay bases and German U-boat

Above: A U-boat caught on the surface by an aircraft. To stay up and fight risked damage that could prevent the boat submerging, so a crash dive (in under 20 seconds) was the usual reaction. From 1944 the introduction of air-dropped acoustic homing torpedoes made this equally dangerous.

assembly facilities. Some 19,000 tons of bombs were dropped, for the loss of 266 aircraft. Protected by several metres of concrete, not a single U-boat was damaged.

Above: Bowmanville was one of 12 Castle class corvettes operated by the Canadians. Their main weapon was the squid anti-submarine mortar, fitted in a super-firing zareba abaft the 4 in gun turret. Note the pale North Atlantic camouflage scheme.

Research in the United States was aimed at the eventual sinking of submarines by refined scientific means–detection by airborne magnetic anomaly detectors (MAD), tracking by disposable air-dropped sonobuoys, and destruction by homing torpedoes. Success, however, came only late in the war. In the absence of an efficient surface search radar, the Germans were experimenting with tethered helicopters, both electrically-and wind-powered, to extend a submarine's horizon. In the presence of air patrols, the measure was hazardous, as it hopelessly increased diving time.

As the Atlantic war climaxed, there were changes at the top on both sides. Dönitz succeeded Raeder in overall command of the German Navy. Although retaining his interest in the U-boat arm, his attentions were greatly diverted elsewhere. In Liverpool, meanwhile, Admiral Sir Max Horton had replaced Admiral Noble as C-in-C, Western Approaches. A career submariner, he brought a formidable talent to bear on the latter phase of defeating the U-boat.

With the introduction of ASV III, submarine losses climbed steeply: 25 were destroyed by aircraft between February and April 1943, then 21 in May alone. There is no doubt that its slow entry into service saved scores of U-boats.

In the February, the Germans recovered an intact H2S unit from a crashed British bomber and immediately commenced development of a countermeasure, a search receiver dubbed 'Naxos'. But it proved difficult to perfect and the early units, which went to sea at the end of 1943, were so short in effective range that the boat

Above: Midnight in the Bay of Biscay, 26 February 1944: U-91 is caught in HMS Gore's searchlights. After two hours of depth-charging, Kptlt. Hungerhausen surfaced, and after a brief gun action, the boat was sunk. Sixteen U-boat men were rescued, 35 went down with the boat.

had a bare minute in which to respond. Only in May 1944 did an effective receiver ('Tunis') enter service, capable of detecting both ASV III and the American SCR 517 but, by this time, the U-boat had lost the initiative.

The steeply-rising loss rate from March convinced the Germans that Metox was to blame, emitting radiation on which Allied aircraft homed. Considerable effort, therefore, was wasted on the design and production of a low-radiation variant ('Wanze'), diverting resources from 'Tunis', the proper remedy.

The weapons that beat the U-boat

By April 1943, the U-boat arm was definitely in decline. Losses were running at 30 percent of boats commissioned, while their average success rate was only about 20 percent of what had been the norm two

Above and above right: the schnorkel device in lowered and raised positions respectively aboard the Type IX/C40 *U-889*. This boat commissioned in August 1944 and survived to surrender off Nova Scotia on 15 May 1945.

Below: the crew of a Sunderland shot down over the Bay of Biscay by a Junkers Ju-88 are rescued after a 24 hour search by HMS *Starling*, August 1943.

years earlier. In vain did the *Führer* authorise a programme of 40 new boats monthly: labour and materials were insufficient to build them, as were trained personnel to man them. New boats were going to sea with unrectified faults that would have been quite unacceptable shortly before.

This was, nevertheless, a time of quite horrifying loss to merchant shipping. To improve the number of long-range maritime aircraft, Boeing B-17 Fortresses and ex-Bomber Command Handley-Page Halifaxes were drafted in, but the ideal platform, the modified Liberator, was mostly being taken by the US Navy for use in the Pacific. This was at a time when the Atlantic airgap was still being referred to by the Germans at the 'Black Pit'. It took personal intervention from the President to re-define priorities and procure more for operations in this theatre.

Escort carriers (CVE) were now coming forward in numbers but were proving to be very useful to regular naval operations, leaving few for A/S work. The British version of the American Grumman F-4 Wildcat fighter, the Martlet, was an admirable performer against U-boats, but lacked the performance to deal with later marks of Ju-88. Suitable types were under development in the Fairey Firefly and Firebrand but, for the moment, and despite their relative fragility, navalised Supermarine Spitfires and Hawker Hurricanes were the alternative.

The British Admiralty's intention had been to integrate CVEs with the convoy escort, but their views

Type XXI U-boat cutaway key

1   Rudder
2   Hydroplane
3   Rudder steering gear
4   Screws
5   Trim tank
6   Hydroplane motor
7   Outer casing
8   Main pressure hull
9   Escape hatch
10 Generating room

Below: The Type XXI employed a massive array of batteries to achieve a higher underwater speed than some Allied escorts could manage on the surface. Able to achieve firing solutions by sonar alone, and equipped with homing torpedoes, it would have been a formidable opponent, but construction standards were badly affected by the Allied strategic bombing campaign and few of the Type XXIs in service by 1945 were capable of realizing their theoretical performance.

17	Diesel electric engines	23	Escape hatch to rear of fin	33	Ammunition room
18	Crew quarters	24	Twin 37 mm guns	34	Radio room
19	Battery room	25	Radio aerial	35	Fresh water
20	Fin	26	Snorkel	36	Captain's quarters
21	Conning tower	27	Search and attack periscopes		
22	Access to 37 mm gun position				

37 Mess area
38 Spare torpedo stowage
39 Torpedo room
40 Torpedo tubes
41 Torpedo tube covers

28 Radio direction finder
29 Galley
30 Control room
31 Control panel
32 Air flasks

11 Electric motors
12 Generating room control area
13 Reduction gear
14 Fuel
15 Main frame
16 Engine room

were modified by the effectiveness of the American system. Here, a single CVE and six escorts normally comprised an A/S group, working independently on the basis of good intelligence or being diverted as a support group to cover a threatened convoy.

The Anglo-Canadian escort force now included about 185 Flower class corvettes and 50 River class, but a huge boost was imminent with the coming on stream of the huge American destroyer-escort (DE) programmes. Designed to a joint specification, the DEs were well received. Lively, but dry in a seaway, they had covered access from forward to aft, a blessing to a hard-pressed crew. The British actually ordered 520 DEs but, due to urgent American requirements, received only 78.

When attacked by a frigate, a U-boat skipper usually went deep to give the ship a three-dimensioned problem. Early U-boats could manage to dive to a recommended 180 metres and later marks could manage 300 metres. The penalty was some 250 tons of extra stiffening and plate thickness, which inevitably forced up displacement to compensate. What the A/S frigate required was an asdic with depth-finding capability, and an ahead-firing weapon to nail a target while it was still fixed by the asdic beam.

The Royal Navy staff requirement for asdics called for their being able to measure target depth down to 1200 feet (366 m), later revised to 1300 feet (396 m). It was achieved by adding to the main transducer stack a so-called 'Q' attachment, producing a narrow, wedge-shaped beam that could be angled downward. With the emphasis now fully three-dimensional, scientific minds became much occupied with the associated problem of beam shaping and the effects on the beam of water layers of varying temperatures.

As the Americans were still trailing in this field, the British supplied them with sets until the end of the war, when their QD4 entered service. The first British unit was tested at sea in May 1943 and was found to be able to hold a deep target down to a range of about 750 metres. An ahead-throwing weapon was thus required with at least this range.

Although, officially, work on such a device had been curtailed in the early 1930s, informal scientific interest had persisted, enabling experiments, as early as 1940 to determine the relative merit of a few large or many small depth bombs. Because of its comparative simplicity, the latter option was first adopted. Known as 'Hedgehog', the weapon comprised a frame in which 24 bombs could be loaded onto spring-loaded spigots. The latter were angled so as to project the bombs into a circular pattern some 130 feet (c. 40 m) in diameter. The bombs contained 20, later 30, pounds (9.1/13.6 kg) of explosive and detonated only on achieving a direct hit on the target.

Rushed to sea from September 1941, Hedgehog was at first a disappointment, due to deficient training and poor maintenance under stress of war. Nonetheless, its success rate through 1943 (although judged on fewer samples) was about 8.3 percent of attacks, against conventional depth charges' 4.5 percent. During 1944

Left: The Allied strategic bombing offensive inflicted severe disruption on German industry, and slowed the construction of the new Type XXI submarines. These Type XXIs were captured in the early stages of assembly at Bremen in 1945.

Right: The Type XXI *U-2518* commissioned in November 1944 and joined the 11th flotilla in Norway in April 1945. It never made a war patrol and was transferred to the French navy and commissioned as the *Roland Morillot*, serving until 1967.

Below: The Type XVII was an experimental coastal submarine powered by the Walter closed-cycle propulsion system. Only three (*U-1405-7*) were completed by the end of the war, and all were scuttled on 5 May. *U-1407* was later raised and operated by the Royal Navy as the *Meteorite*.

Type XVII

Displacement	312 tons surfaced; 337 tons submerged
Dimensions	41.05 m (136 ft) x 3.4 m (11 ft) x 4.3 m (14 ft)
Propulsion	surfaced diesel delivering 210 hp; submerged Walter closed cycle system delivering 2,500 hp or electric motor delivering 77.5 hp
Speed	9 knots surfaced; 21.5 knots dived
Range	3000 miles at 8 knots surfaced; 123 miles submerged on Walter engine or 46 miles on electric motor
Armament	two 21 in (533 mm) torpedo tubes with four torpedoes
Crew	19

the weapon really came into its own with 21.5 percent success against 7.1 percent by depth-charges. Note that conventional depth charges had also achieved a 60 percent improvement, possibly because of the introduction of Torpex, an explosive two-thirds more powerful than TNT.

Hedgehog was adopted widely by the US Navy, sometimes split and mounted to flank the superstructure. As some American ships were excessively tender, a lightweight version ('Mousetrap') was also developed. Because they exploded only on contact, Hedgehog bombs did not need a rapid, last-minute depth setting neither, in the event of an unsuccessful attack, did they cause an asdic 'white-out' that could prevent the target being re-acquired.

Disquiet was voiced over reports of German submarines being able to dive ever deeper, and a pre-war concept for a heavy, three-barrelled mortar was thus resurrected. The 'Squid', as it was known, was better stabilised against ship movement and could lob its three bombs to nearly 300 metres. Each contained 200 pounds (91 kg) of another new explosive, Minol. Larger frigates took a 'Double Squid', which laid two patterns over a similar area, but at different depths. Electronics had

Type XXI

Displacement	....1,621 tons surfaced; 1,819 tons dived	Speed	.....................................surfaced 15.5 knots, dived 16 knots or 3.5 knots on creeping motors
Dimensions	.....................................76.7 m x 8.0 m x 6.32 m	Range	............................17,895 miles surfaced or 325 knots dived at 6 knots
Diving depth	....280 m	Armament	........................Four 30 mm or 20 mm AA guns, six 21 in (533 mm) torpedo tubes
Propulsion	................................surfaced diesels delivering 4000 hp; submerged electric motors delivering 5,000 hp or low power motors delivering 226 hp		and 23 torpedoes
		Crew	57

It is a commonplace that the Type XXI would have tipped the balance in the Atlantic had it arrived in 1943, but then if a few squadrons of four-engine bombers had been given to Coastal Command earlier the war would have been equally different. With its high underwater speed, sonar and rapid reloading system, the Type XXI represented a significant advance. Its powerful battery system needed only a few hours charging (via schnorkel) every couple of days, so it could remain submerged throughout a patrol.

Left: U-858 surrendered at Portsmouth, New Hampshire on 14 May 1945. For a late war U-boat, *U-858* was unusual: a Type IXC/40, it was commissioned by *Kptlt.* Bode in September 1943 and he and his crew survived the two most dangerous years of the submarine war. *U-858* had no confirmed sinkings.

Below: It fell to a Type XXIII coastal submarine to make the last U-boat attack of the war, sinking two merchantmen in the Firth of Forth on 7 May 1945. These small boats could crash dive in 10 seconds and presented a tiny silhouette on the surface but they were intended for submerged patrols. Six were operational before the end of the war.

Type XXIII

Displacement	....................232 tons surfaced; 256 tons dived
Dimensions	.....................................34.1 m x 3.0 m x 3.75 m
Diving depth	....180 m
Propulsion	......................surfaced diesel delivering 580 hp, submerged electric motor delivering 500 hp or electric motor delivering 35 hp
Speed	.....................................10 knots surfaced; 12.5 knots submerged or 2.5 knots on creeping motors
Range	...................................1,550 miles or 202 miles submerged at 4 knots
Armament	....Two 21 in (533 mm) torpedoes. No reloads
Crew	14

advanced to the point where loaded Squid bombs could be fused automatically from incoming asdic data.

Squid entered service in mid-1944, by which time acoustic torpedoes had also become common. The American Mark 24 was contemporary with the German *Zaunkönig*, and the capture of the *U-505* in June 1944 enabled comparisons to be made. Designed to withstand an air-drop from a VLR Liberator, a Mark 24 (known as 'Fido', or 'Wandering Annie') traded speed, only 12 knots, for endurance and silence.

During July and August 1944 CVE-based groups appeared in numbers. Their A/S aircraft worked successfully in pairs. If a U-boat was caught on the surface, it was depth-charged. If it dived quickly, a homing torpedo would be dropped near the swirl left by its submergence.

British pre-war interest in acoustically-homed torpedoes had been retarded by lack of a staff requirement. Wartime research advanced weapons to prototype test stage but quantity production was not commenced until after the war. Much useful research data was, however, freely communicated to the Americans.

Even by mid-1943 it was obvious that Dönitz's submarines had not only failed to defeat the convoys but actually faced extinction themselves. One encounter in five saw a U-boat sunk. While ever more U-boats were in service, the lack of skilled labour and materials for their maintenance saw seatime drop from 60 to only 40 percent. The airgap had been closed by CVEs and VLR Liberators and it was obvious that, to survive, a U-boat would need to remain continuously submerged. To have any hope of successfully attacking a convoy, it would require a high and sustained underwater speed.

Advanced submarine technology

Since 1933 work had progressed slowly on propulsion systems that could function without the need of atmospheric oxygen. There were two main types: Walter's high-speed turbine system which used hydrogen peroxide ('Ingolin') as an oxygen source; and a slow-speed boat using a closed-circuit diesel, which required stored oxygen and catalysts. While prototype boats were demonstrated, the systems were too complex and/or hazardous for mass production. The requirement for a high underwater speed in the Walter boats had, however, instigated research into improved hulls, research that was to prove of great value.

During the Spring of 1943 Walter brought to Dönitz's notice the concept of an air induction mast. Such a fitting would allow a boat to cruise at 5 or 6 knots on diesels while submerged. In crossing the Bay she would thus present a very small radar target while also being able to keep batteries topped up. Such an idea was not new; it had been patented by the Dutch and fitted before the war to some of their large 'overseas' boats.

Dubbed '*Schnorchel*' (or 'Snort' in Allied parlance), a prototype was tested at sea in September 1943. Conversion kits for existing U-boats were put into emergency production, but it was June 1944 before the first half-dozen snort-fitted boats went operational. The introduction was timely, for conventional boats sent to interdict the Normandy landings had suffered badly: nine were sunk and eleven damaged to the extent that their patrols had to be abandoned.

In calm conditions, contemporary radars or even a keen naked eye could detect the head of a snort mast at about four miles, but even a small breaking sea would defeat both. Its presence was, however, sometimes betrayed by a trailing exhaust cloud.

It had already been acknowledged by the German High Command that, even if current production targets of 27 new U-boats per month were to be met, their objectives would not. The Allied defences were now technologically advanced, demanding a similar German approach. With a crisis imminent there was no time to wait for the Walter boats.

Dönitz called a conference at his headquarters (relocated to Paris after the British commando raid on St. Nazaire in March l942). The Navy's construction branch suggested a short-term compromise, with the combination of a 'high-speed' hull and snort with a propulsion system based on proven electrical technology. By deepening the amidships section to a figure eight (i.e. '8') configuration, three times the usual number of cells could be accommodated. Dönitz demurred at the projected 1600-ton surface displacement but agreed when offered also a diminutive version, which would be able to penetrate the now 'no-go' British coastal waters.

In June 1943, preliminary calculations demonstrated the vast improvement that might be expected. Designated Type XXI, it would achieve a submerged speed of 18 knots for 90 minutes, or 12-14 knots for ten hours. Current boats could manage a best 5-6 knots for 45 minutes, the Type XXI could sustain 6 knots for 60 hours! Furthermore, it could then recharge by snorting, without the need to surface.

Previous construction programmes had been controlled by the Navy but, to accelerate this one, responsibility for the '*Elektroboote*' was transferred to Albert Speer's Ministry of Arms and Munitions. Speer set up a Shipbuilding Commission, which had powers to co-opt expert opinion from any likely source. In July 1943 Dönitz agreed a new building programme, also the revolutionary appointment of Otto Merker as supremo.

Merker was an industrialist from the heavy road vehicle industry but quickly produced proposals for reducing building times by one third. Following American methods for constructing standard ships, submarines would be assembled in dedicated facilities, using pre-fabricated and already fitted-out sections shipped in from scattered sources.

In August 1943 all contracts for earlier boats were cancelled, except for 80 hulls already well advanced.

Merker's de-centralisation scheme was designed to minimise the effects of Allied bombing, but had a weakness in that the huge sections could be transported only by water. Allied intelligence was quick to note the resulting importance of the German inland waterway system. Instead of wasting bombs on the seven metres of concrete that now roofed the assembly halls, raids concentrated on particularly vulnerable sections of the canals. Only four firms could contribute the huge number of electrical cells required. These, too were targeted.

Despite this, Merker completed 60 Type XXIs by the end of 1944 and had launched 30 more. Of the Type XXIII diminutive type, 31 were commissioned and a further 23 afloat. Getting them battleworthy was another problem. Long a quiet backwater, ideal for training and working-up, the Baltic was now extensively mined and subject to sweeps by Allied A/S aircraft. While only a handful of boats were destroyed, training schedules were continually disrupted. In consequence, the first Type XXIII went operational only in February 1945, and the first Type XXI in April.

With its fourteen crew, the little Type XXIII surpassed expectations by being able to remain at sea for a month. Eight boats conducted patrols in British coastal waters. Fast, manoeuvrable and quiet, they succeeded in sinking a handful of ships but their weakness lay in their having only two torpedo tubes, without reloads. No re-supply was possible, a situation that obtained even in the Atlantic, where the last of the U-tankers and supply ships were being remorselessly hunted down.

Left: Two Type XXIs visible in Hamburg, May 1945. Many of the U-boat crews scuttled their boats rather than surrender them. A notorious handful elected to escape, *U-997* making its celebrated submerged passage to Argentina, rather than give up.

Above: Incomplete Type XXIs in Bremen, 1945. US analysis of captured Type XXIs revealed serious shortcomings: inferior materials and poor workmanship resulting from the Allied bombing campaign.

The end of the U-boat campaign

Pack attacks had been abandoned early in 1944 as no longer practicable. By September 1944 Allied advances in France saw the Biscay bases abandoned and surviving U-boats transferred to Norway. In March 1945 the first submerged, snort-equipped boat was destroyed by aircraft using a combination of sonobuoys and homing torpedo. As Germany teetered toward total collapse, she had lost both the production and technology battles.

In total 1,153 U-boats of all sea-going types were completed, while a further 1,394 had been ordered. Only 154 were actually surrendered at the capitulation in May 1945, 218 more having been scuttled in a final act of defiance.

Over the long campaign they had sunk, besides the enormous total of commercial tonnage, some 175 Allied warships and auxiliaries, a number which made the achievements of the surface fleet appear almost insignificant.

Allied A/S forces destroyed or captured 636 U-boats at sea. Air attack, unfortunately only late in the war, disposed of 63 more in bases and shipyards. Accidents, mines and unknown causes accounted for a further 82. Of the 40,000 personnel that manned the boats, no less than 28,000 were lost.

Chapter 3 – The American Submarine War against Japan

Over 6,000 miles from the American West Coast, the Philippine Islands came under United States control in 1898, following the brief war with Spain. Japan, only recently opened to Western influence, had already trounced a decadent China in 1894-5. In 1905 she went on to beat Russia decisively, emerging as the major military and naval power in the Far East. Japanese expansionism was set to continue: the Japanese home islands supported a relatively dense population, but had few natural resources.

Reluctant landlords of the Philippines, which proved a financial liability, the Americans began to plan for what they regarded as the inevitable day when the Japanese would seek to seize by force the resources that they required. Even by 1911 it was hypothesised that the Philippines and other major island groups would be taken to provide a safeguard for her flanks as Japan embarked on expansionist adventures on the Asiatic mainland.

Matters were complicated by the settlements following World War I. Relatively minimal involvement in the Allied cause, won Japan a mandate over a vast area of Micronesia. The myriad islands enfiladed any reasonable route by which an American expeditionary force could advance to recover the Philippines. The Washington treaties included clauses which forbade any fortification of the islands. But the same clauses worked against American interests by preventing the development of the island of Guam as a Western Pacific bastion. That function would need to be assumed by Hawaii. Guam was some 1,500 miles from the Philippines: Pearl Harbor on Hawaii was 4,800 miles away.

In 1941, the major component of the United States Fleet in the Pacific was stationed at Pearl Harbor, a base still in the throes of expansion. The most forward element was Admiral Thomas C. Hart's Asiatic Fleet, based at Manila. Its tasks were to safeguard American interests in the region and to maintain relationships with the other colonial powers. Of no great size, the Asiatic fleet's responsibility in the event of a Japanese military invasion was mainly to support the army. As the islands were considered ultimately indefensible, the major ships would gradually need to fall back to work with those of the British and Dutch to resist further enemy expansion.

When the blow fell, in December 1941, Admiral Hart's three cruisers and nine destroyers were well scattered. At the bases on Manila Bay lay mostly small fry: minesweepers and China gunboats. Hart had 30 of the Navy's 51 Pacific-based submarines, only two of which were detached. Of these, six were old 'S'-boats, 850/1,090 tonners (i.e. 850 tons surfaced displacement, 1,090 submerged) launched in 1919-21 and really fit only for training; for tropical conditions, their standards of habitability were abysmal. Another six were of the 'P'-class, varying in detail but averaging 1,320/1,980 tons. These dated from 1935-6. The remainder were new 'S'-class boats, built 1937-9 and displacing up to 1,475/2,340 tons. Organised in five divisions, the boats had only recently arrived from Hawaii, in line with a general plan by General Douglas MacArthur to contest the islands in the event of invasion. American submarines were considerably larger than German U-boats, reflecting the vastly greater area over which they would have to work.

Below: The US Navy's fleet submarines were substantially larger than the German Type IX U-boats (1,500 tons compared to 1,100 tons) and had superior fire control systems, air conditioning and radar. However, like the U-boats, they experienced prolonged difficulties with their torpedoes which frequently malfunctioned.

Above: One of 12 Tambor class submarines, USS *Tautog* made 13 war patrols under three different skippers and sank 26 Japanese ships for a total of 72,600 tons, making her the most successful US submarine of the war.

Below: Nautilus (V6) and *Narwhal* (V5) were the largest submarines in US service until the nuclear boats of the 1950s. Designed in the 1920s as long range submarine minelayers, they were regarded as too slow and cumbersome for combat patrols by 1942 and were mainly used for landing special forces units. *Nautilus* sank the crippled Japanese aircraft carrier *Soryu* at Midway.

The Defensive Phase

Following their assault on Pearl Harbor, the Japanese virtually wiped out American air power in the Philippines, most of it on the ground. Manila and its environs were then systematically bombed, virtually without opposition. On 10 December 1941 the submarine base at Cavite Navy Yard was laid waste, but only one boat, *Sealion*, was destroyed as most of the remainder and their three valuable tenders (depôt ships) had been dispersed. A major blow was the loss of half the stock of torpedoes.

On this same day, Captain John Wilkes was appointed Commander Submarines Asiatic Fleet. His ship, the tender *Canopus*, remained berthed in Manila as the only remaining support for the submarine force but, as the port was being bombed on a daily basis he, his staff, and some key facilities were dispersed ashore.

On 10 and 12 December, the Japanese made a series of landings which left the Americans in the Philippines as baffled as their allies elsewhere. The probing, encircling and advancing enemy appeared unstoppable and, by the 27th, MacArthur and his remaining forces

had abandoned the capital and retired into the stronghold of the Bataan peninsula. Without the aerial reconnaissance upon which their training had made them reliant, the submarines had achieved little to prevent Japanese freedom of movement by water and, by the last day of the year, the now-damaged *Canopus* and her remaining charges had been withdrawn.

At Pearl Harbor, the transfers to Manila had left the submarine force depleted. Rear-Admiral Thomas Withers, Commander Submarines Pacific Fleet, was left with 21 boats but no less than eleven of these were in the United States for repairs and modernisation. His effective command thus comprised four 'one-offs' of doubtful value and six new 'T'-class boats, 1,475/2,370 tonners of the type that were to provide the basis for wartime standard designs.

Like all senior American submariners, Withers had taken a professional interest in the manner in which Admiral Dönitz had been operating over the previous two years. Centralised control and 'wolf-packing' were not liked–American boats would operate individually and under strict radio silence. In addition, like their Japanese counterparts, American skippers were trained to regard warships as their primary targets.

Narwhal

Displacement:	2,730 tons surfaced
	3,900 tons submerged
Dimensions:	112.9 m (370.5 ft) x 10.13 m
	(33.25 ft) x 4.8 m (15.75 ft)
Diving depth:	350 ft (106 m)
Propulsion:	combination drive with four diesels
	delivering 5,400 hp and two
	electric motors delivering
	2,540 hp to two shafts
Speed:	17 knots surfaced; 8 knots dived
Endurance:	33,354 km (20,725 miles) at 10
	knots surfaced and 93 km (58 miles)
	at 5 knots submerged
Armament:	2 x 6 in (152 mm) guns and six 21
	in (533 mm) torpedo tubes with
	36 torpedoes; later 10 tubes
	and 40 torpedoes
Crew:	89

Left: Church service in the after torpedo room of the Balao class boat *Bullhead* during her first war patrol, early 1945. Lost on 6 August 1945, the day Hiroshima was destroyed by an atomic bomb, USS *Bullhead* was the last of the US submarine fleet's 52 wartime casualties.

In the run-up to real war Withers wanted to accustom his crews to two-month patrols. Boats which, under leisurely 'normal' routine, rarely dived beyond periscope depth, found themselves suddenly exercised to the safe operational limits for their pressure hulls, and cruising for six weeks.

The great error made during the Japanese assault on Pearl Harbor had been their lack of attention to facilities ashore. The American submarine base was unscathed. Washington immediately ordered unrestricted submarine operation, all Japanese shipping being assumed to be supporting the military effort.

Boats were ordered to exercise caution on early patrols as the enemy's capability was little known. The result was too much time spent on passage submerged. Instructions to conserve torpedoes, following insufficient peacetime firing practice, saw most shots wasted. And from the outset fears were expressed about the reliability of US torpedoes.

It was not even known for certain whether Japanese destroyers were equipped with sonar (as the Americans called Asdic). The *Plunger*, an early arrival, quickly settled the question. She had not advertised her presence, but was roughed up by a Japanese destroyer that not only had sonar, but knew how to use it, accompanied by copious depth-charging.

American submarines were fitted with the early SD air search radar outfit, whose omni-directional antenna was extended before surfacing. Many skippers believed that it acted as a beacon as well as a detector, but there is no evidence that pre-issue trials were undertaken to evaluate any such shortcoming. The set was later joined by the SJ surface search outfit, its early introduction contrasting with Dönitz's lukewarm enthusiasm for similarly equipping his U-boats.

From the outset, the Americans were quick to adapt the experience of their foreign peers to their own use. Like the British, they rapidly established a comprehensive, intelligence-based system to show an up-to-the-minute estimate of enemy dispositions and intentions. Japanese transmissions were already being monitored around the clock and usually decyphered.

Admiral Dönitz believed that submarine crews, returned from an exacting patrol, deserved the best of treatment. They were billeted in fine hotel accommodation, well removed from the base where their boat was being serviced. It was a procedure followed by the Americans too.

In 1941 a good proportion of American submarine skippers were of comparatively high age. They were naturally cautious, drawing criticism for over-high torpedo consumption and the tendency to favour submerged night attack. They were urged to follow German practice.

From the outset, a successful patrol resulted in a skipper receiving a high decoration, the Navy Cross. As early promotion usually followed, this resulted in persistent over-claiming. Over the whole campaign the

Right: Seen through the periscope of the Balao class boat *Aspro*, another Japanese merchant ship slips below the waves. Once the US submarines obtained reliable torpedoes, sinkings increased rapidly and the Japanese belatedly devoted some energy to anti-submarine measures.

force was credited with about 4,000 Japanese ships sunk, when post-war analysis indicated about 1,300. German experience was much the same with awards of the *Ritterkreuz*.

Of Manila's 28 surviving boats, 22 had attempted to stem the enemy invasion of the Philippines. Seasonal bad weather and a lack of aggressiveness produced disappointing results, compounded by numerous dud torpedoes. The *Sargo*, for instance, wasted 13 in six separate attacks. As some targets had been virtually unmissable, her skipper suspected the secret new magnetic exploder, which also appeared to detonate the weapon prematurely. He had them de-activated in favour of contact pistols but when these, too, produced no result, reported that the weapons were running deep. For 96 torpedoes fired at the invaders, only three

Above: This photo was taken inside the control room of the *Wahoo* while under depth-charge attack at 300 ft. *Wahoo's* skipper 'Mush' Morton won the Navy Cross after his second war patrol but the boat was lost with all hands in October 1943.

freighters were sunk.

As the whole force withdrew to Surabaya in Java, early in January 1942, it knew that it had failed badly and that there were many lessons to be learned. A relaxed attitude to essential maintenance needed to be addressed. With the Japanese assault developing along predictable lines, submarines had not been deployed at critical points in good time. Pre-war training had been neither realistic nor sufficiently demanding. Although the bombing of Cavite Navy Yard was inevitable, no attempt had been made to disperse either submarines

Below: The 'Sen Toku' (special submarine) or I-400 class built by the Japanese navy was almost twice the size of USS *Nautilus*. These giant boats were a pet project of Admiral Yamamoto who wanted to bomb the locks of the Panama canal using seaplanes launched from submarines. Three were launched in 1944, one converted to serve as a fuel tanker. Their intended mission never took place.

spares or torpedoes beforehand. Finally, and inexplicably, the tender *Canopus*, with her fine facilities and highly trained crew, was scuttled off Corregidor rather than take her chance at escaping.

The remaining pair of tenders, *Otus* and *Holland*, arrived safely in the north Australian port of Darwin. Also in the region were naval units from Australia herself, the United Kingdom and the Netherlands. Together they could muster a force substantial enough to deal with any of the multiheaded Japanese probes, but two months of persistent defeats had accustomed them to retreat. Despair and dispute permeated down from the top. Admiral Hart, temporarily headquartered in Java, was involved in political problems and was succeeded by the Dutch Vice Admiral Helfrich.

The general hope was that the enemy advance might be held at the so-called Malay Barrier: the chain of islands extending from Sumatra to New Guinea. By the end of January 1942, for the loss of two of their

number, the Asiatic Fleet submarines had sunk just six enemy transports, although targets were plentiful. Defective peacetime procedures were as nothing compared with the plague of faulty torpedoes. As target after target escaped, skippers reported angrily. The Bureau of Ordnance (BuOrd) disclaimed responsibility, despatching 'experts' who castigated naval practice rather than their torpedoes which, in any case, were in too short supply to expend in practical tests.

The Japanese advance flowed with bewildering ease from one island and one strategic point to the next. Each move was made by sea, often with scant naval cover but usually under the protection of land-based aircraft. Where the latter was not possible, carrier aircraft were made available.

As the Asiatic Fleet boats were still operating out of Surabaya, where they shared inadequate facilities with 16 Dutch submarines, Wilkes moved his two tenders back from Darwin to Tjilatjap, on the more remote

I-400 class

Displacement:	5,223 tons surfaced
	6,650 tons submerged
Dimensions:	121.9 m (400 ft) x 12 m
	(39 ft 4 in) x 7 m (23 ft)
Diving depth:	100 m (328 ft)
Propulsion:	diesel engines delivering 7,750 hp
	and electric motors delivering
	2,400 hp to two shafts
Speed:	19 knots surfaced and
	7 knots dived
Range:	7,000 km (4,350 miles)
	at 14 knots surfaced and
	110 km (68 miles) at 3 knots
Armament:	one 140 mm (5.5 in) gun, 10 25
	mm AA guns, 3 Aichi M6A1
	aircraft, 8 533 mm (21 in) torpedo
	tubes and 20 torpedoes
Crew:	140

south coast. They arrived on 7 February 1942, but this accomplished little, for the 'barrier' was already under attack.

On 15 February Singapore surrendered. Timor, a bare 300 miles from Australian soil, was taken and Darwin itself repeatedly bombed. Most of the remaining Allied surface units had been lost at the Battle of the Java Sea, where their ad hoc squadron was despatched in detail by numerically inferior enemy forces.

The Japanese seemed to be everywhere. Allied reconnaissance and intelligence operations had broken down, so that the submarines, for the most part, cruised hopefully rather than effectively. Their total score of twelve enemy freighters, totalling 50,000 gross registered tons (grt) made no mark on the enemy advance. Having been unable to sink a single enemy ship in the eventual invasion of Java itself, Captain Wilkes pulled out. His tenders moved to Fremantle and Albany in south-west Australia and his own title of Comsubsaf (Commander Submarines Asiatic Fleet) ceased to have relevance.

By early April the Japanese had occupied the Malay Barrier and, until finally checked in New Guinea and the Solomons, they threatened to invade both India and Australia. Naval forces to resist such attacks were totally inadequate and, for all its limitations, Wilkes' submarine force remained the sole practical means of striking back.

Its degree of combat readiness had been shockingly low. Starting with 73 boats, the Pacific force was larger

Above: Admiral Charles A Lockwood, commander of the US Pacific Fleet submarine force, seen at Pearl Harbor after being awarded the Legion of Merit medal by Admiral Nimitz, February 1944.

Right: Launched in December 1918, *S-33* was one of 64 obsolete 'S' class submarines in the US Navy in 1941. Most were used for training, as they lacked the range and habitability for Pacific operations, but several saw action off the Philippines during the Japanese invasion.

Below: Launched in June 1941, USS *Drum* was the first of 72 Gato class submarines to be commissioned, and one of the few to be preserved today. This view through her periscope was taken in the summer of 1945.

than that operated by the Germans yet, with no shortage of targets, had sunk less than a quarter of the tonnage in the same period. This total, 300,000 grt, represented less than Japan (a major maritime power in her own right) had acquired in the course of her conquests.

As Wilkes set up shop in Fremantle, some 1,800 miles from the nearest Japanese, it was time to take stock and report to Admiral Ernest J. King, who held the joint offices of CinC, US Navy and Chief of Naval Operations (CNO).

There was much to do. In 136 separate attacks to date, American submarines had fired about 300 torpedoes. Although 36 targets had been claimed as sunk, the total was actually only ten. The submarines themselves had problems. The United States had little tradition in diesel engine construction, and one particular type, the HOR, proved to be highly unreliable. A fleet boat contained 77 personnel, living cheek-by-jowl and, for extended patrols in the tropics, air-conditioning, refrigerator plant and plenty of evaporator capacity were essential for avoidance of tropical complaints and poor morale. The 'pre-war' profile of fleet boats was also too conspicuous and needed to be considerably reduced.

Pre-war Allied contempt for the Japanese fleet was quickly replaced by respect for its skill and hard-fighting qualities. Trained in unrealistic peacetime practices, American skippers had to readjust quickly.

Left: The traditional skull and crossbones flag flown by British submarines graces the *Tally Ho* which sank the Japanese cruiser *Kuma* off the Malacca strait in January 1944. On his next patrol Lt.Cdr Bennington sank a German U-boat operating from Penang.

Many could not, and were relieved. Admiral King made the controversial decision to leave Wilkes' force based in Australia rather than transfer it to Hawaii. Its operational area among the main island groups was never as productive as waters around the enemy's home islands, while transit times were long. As a result, Pearl Harbor boats were able to undertake consistently better patrols.

Until regular resistance in the Philippines ceased with the fall of the island fortress of Corregidor on 6 May 1942, submarines from the commands of both Wilkes and Withers made nocturnal visits in its support. This contact allowed skippers to meet briefly, discovering that their frustrations and problems were common to both groups.

To complicate the command structure further, a new force came into being on 15 April with the arrival in Brisbane of Captain Ralph Christie, with the tender *Griffin* and half-a-dozen later 'S'-boats. This force was augmented by the transfer of Wilkes' five remaining S-class submarines, Christie being tasked with assisting in the defence of Australia itself.

Both Wilkes and Christie came under the operational command of General Douglas MacArthur who, as Supreme Commander Southwest Pacific, was headquartered in Melbourne. Withers, relieved at Pearl Harbor in May 1942 by Rear Admiral Robert H. English, was part of the command of Admiral Chester W. Nimitz, an ex-submariner who was now C-in-C, Pacific Fleet.

Like their Asiatic Fleet colleagues, the Pacific Fleet boats began hesitantly. Operating from Hawaii into the Mandates and Japanese home waters, they made 17 patrols in the first three months of 1942. At a time when a bare dozen U-boats disposed of over one million grt. off the Eastern Seaboard, Withers' boats sank just 15 ships, totalling about 53,000 grt. Over the ensuing two months matters improved only marginally before the bulk of the force was diverted in preparatory moves for what was to be the strategically important battle of

Midway. However, this was to be a battle for the carriers. The 19 American submarines deployed to intercept the enemy forces failed through a blend of indifferent attack techniques, torpedo malfunction and confusing instructions from Pearl Harbor. The experience of the skipper of the *Nautilus* summed it up. Encountering the disabled and blazing wreck of the Japanese carrier *Kaga*, he attempted to finish it off with a four torpedo spread. One failed to leave the tube, two missed and one was observed by Japanese survivors to hit the ship and disintegrate without exploding.

USS *Tambor* came across a secondary Japanese force. The sight of her periscope induced frantic manoeuvring, which resulted in two heavy cruisers coming into collision. But it was left to carrier aircraft to sink one and to badly damage the other.

The battle of Midway was a major feat of arms for the US Navy and its intelligence organisation. But for the submarine service, it resulted only in mutual recrimination between English and his skippers. A major staff reorganisation followed, several skippers were relieved and younger officers appointed instead. No longer regarded as under imminent threat, Midway island also became home to the tender *Fulton*. One thousand miles west of Hawaii, the ship offered repair and refuelling facilities that considerably enhanced operational durations.

The Submarine Programme

Following the catastrophic turn of events in Europe in 1940, Congress had approved two rapid increases in strength for the US Navy. In June and July its submarine force alone was permitted an expansion of 91,000 tons, corresponding to about 60 units of the then-current 1,475 tons displacement. Because President Roosevelt had declared a state of limited national emergency, it was possible to streamline building procedures and to introduce more yards to the

intricacies of submarine construction.

To the choice builders of Portsmouth Navy Yard and the Connecticut-based Electric Boat Company were added Mare Island Navy Yard in California, Cramps at Philadelphia and the Manitowoc Yard in Wisconsin. Expertise was thus spread between both public and private sectors, while retaining the element of competition.

Electric Boat created a new facility for constructing hulls, which were then transferred to the home yard for fitting out. Throughput expanded from three to 21 boats at a time, which also brought about a significant decrease in unit price. Surprisingly, the company took an average of ten months to launch a hull, and three more to fit it out, although the overall record for one boat was 317 days. Of 115 submarines ordered from Electric Boat, 82 were completed.

Manitowoc was sited on a confined river which ran into the fresh waters of Lake Michigan. This limitation, and the severe northern winters to which the area was subject, encouraged the yard to be innovative in building pre-fabricated sections and moving them around for assembly, the completed hulls being launched sideways. Following trials on the lake, each completed boat then required its tophamper to be removed prior to being transferred by barge down the Mississippi River system to New Orleans. Here, it was finally re-assembled and checked out before proceeding to the Pacific via Panama. Effectively a subsidiary of Electric Boat, Manitowoc started from scratch and completed 28 of the 47 submarines ordered. Its best time was under 300 days, roughly the same as that of Portsmouth. Cramp's average was rather higher, the yard having difficulty in attracting skilled labour in competition with other yards in the area.

By the end of the war, the submarine service enjoyed an excellent four-tier support organisation. Thirteen specialised tenders and two shore facilities provided support at 'the sharp end'. Routine repair and refit was handled at Pearl Harbor, while really badly-damaged boats were sent back to Portsmouth. Mare Island, in addition to having twelve submarines under construction at any one time, specialised in full overhauls.

The design of the twelve-strong Tambor class, ordered in 1939-40, provided the basis for the 'war standards'. These 1,425/2,370 tonners included all experience to date, adopting a six-tube battery forward and four aft. A weakness of grouping the four main diesel-generator units together in one large space was quickly corrected by the addition of a further watertight bulkhead, a measure that cost a further five feet (1.52 m) in length. The first boat of this type, *Gato*, lent her name to a very extensive class of 77 submarines.

To expedite construction, design was strictly frozen, although minor differences still existed between builders. Hulls were of ordinary rolled mild steel plate. In shipbuilding parlance '40-pound plate' (i.e. plate weighing 40 pounds per square foot) was one inch in thickness, so Gato's 27½-pound plate approximated to eleven-sixteenths of an inch (17.5 mm). This gave a safe operating depth of 300 feet (91.5 m). It was discovered, however, that many fittings considered necessary in peacetime could be dispensed with. This, unusually, resulted in a more-than-adequate ballast margin, which was turned to good use by beefing-up the pressure hull.

Although, at this point, the United States was not yet at war, European experience pointed to the advantages of deeper diving. Succeeding classes therefore adopted 35-pound plate of about seven-eighths of an inch (22.2 mm) and up-graded to a high-tensile quality. As no extra weight was involved, the size and shape of these later boats (known as the Balao class) showed no change, although they were rated to dive to 400 feet (121.9 m) operationally, or 450 feet (137.2 m) in extremis. Both classes, however, were rated conservatively. In emergencies, some boats dived to almost double their safe depth–and lived to tell the tale.

One hundred and nineteen Balao class submarines were completed and, of 137 further contracts, 80 were converted to the further refined Tench class. The end of hostilities saw contracts for 57 Balaos and 55 Tenches cancelled.

Because success in the Atlantic was crucial to the outcome of the war, the Germans were driven to technical innovation to improve U-boat design. To the Americans, as indeed to the British, submarines were but one weapon of an array designed to debilitate and defeat an enemy on a broad front. Their submarines

Below: USS *Salmon* took part in an attack on a Japanese convoy in October 1944 but her torpedoes broached the surface and an accurate depth-charge attack ensued. Badly damaged, she sank past 600 ft (over twice her designed depth) before control was restored.

reflected this. Simple, rugged designs were chosen to facilitate series production. Improvements were low-key and gradual, enhancing habitability and endurance, stealth and survivability, and the quality of sensors.

Japanese naval planning– and lack of same

Japan went to war primarily to secure the supply of raw materials that she lacked. The empire Japan acquired in the amazingly adroit campaign starting in December 1941 was referred-to as the 'Greater South-east Asia Co-prosperity Sphere'. In reality it amounted to no more than Japanese access to such materials under the superficial banner of overthrowing western colonial rule.

During 1940, the last full year before hostilities, Japan imported over 22 million tons of bulk and finished materials, foodstuffs and scrap for re-processing. To this total could be added about 1.2 million tons of oil products. All of this was, obviously, transported by ship. Most processing was undertaken on the Japanese home islands so that shipping was required not only for initial import but for subsequent re-distribution. The new empire comprised a multitude of islands, mostly with garrisons that required to be supported and supplied. A large and efficient mercantile marine was thus as essential to Japan as it was to the United Kingdom, and just as vulnerable to sustained attack.

Strangely, despite the British experience of World War I, neither the Americans nor the Japanese had really grasped the significance of this. Successive up-datings of the American Plan Orange concentrated on sweeping movements of fleets and armies across the broad

compass of the Pacific. The Japanese thought in terms of short war and took few precautions. Their assumption was that the United States would not go to war to assist colonial powers in the recovery of territory, or to regain their own protectorates of Guam and the Philippines, which were financial liabilities. The nation would accept a status quo, public opinion prohibiting a war over 6,000 miles distant. But for Pearl Harbor, history might well have shown this assumption to be correct.

By 1940, Japan's conduct in China brought about trade embargoes by a still-neutral United States and the warring colonial powers in Europe, of which France and the Netherlands were, themselves, occupied by Germany. Japan was experiencing shortages before she opened hostilities in the Far East in December 1941. Large scale shipping movements were immediately evident, replenishing diminished stockpiles, and an early wartime mission for US submarines was to chart and assess their major routes.

In terms of volume, the most important Japanese sea land was that linking the home islands, across the Yellow Sea, with Korea and Manchuria and thence, via the East China Sea, with Formosa (Taiwan). A trunk route was also established between the major islands of the Dutch East Indies, to Singapore and French Indo-China, thence along the coast of mainland China and through the Formosa Strait to Japan. Over its 3,000-mile length passed a continuous flow of oil, rubber, aluminium and iron ores, coal and rice. A 2,000-mile direct route also connected the larger, more easterly islands with Japan. Important Japanese fleet bases established at Truk, in the Carolines, and in the strategically-important Marianas, also generated a great deal of traffic. While all of these routes could be interdicted by sea, the Japanese did have the great

Tench class

Displacement: ....1,570 tons surfaced; 2,415 tons submerged

Dimensions: ....95 m (311 ft 8 in) x 8.31 m (27 ft 3 in) x 4.65 m (15 ft 3 in)

Diving depth: ....400 ft (122 m)

Propulsion: ....four diesel engines delivering 5,400 hp and two electric motors delivering 2,740 hp to two shafts

Speed: ....20 knots surfaced and 9 knots submerged

Endurance: ....21,316 km (13,245 miles) at 10 knots surfaced and 204 km (127 miles) at 4 knots

Armament: ....one or two 127 mm (5 in) guns and 10 533 mm (21 in) torpedo tubes with 28 torpedoes

Crew: 81

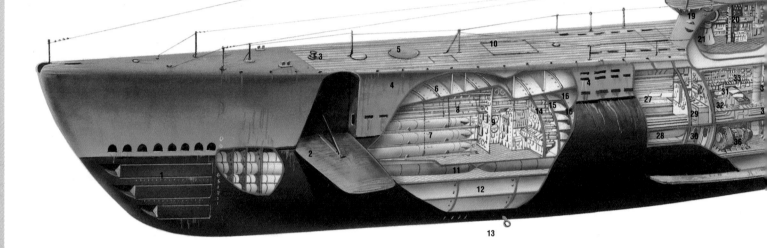

potential advantage of being able to mount near-continuous air cover from airfields on both mainland Asia and the numerous islands that flanked the routes.

In 1941 Japan ranked third in the world's maritime powers, yet 33% of her foreign trade was carried by other flags. Her total of 6.3 million grt. of home-flag shipping was quickly supplemented by 0.57 million grt. captured or salvaged. However, army and naval requisitions took up 3.8 million grt, leaving the bare three million considered the minimum to sustain the needs of the population and to transport essential materials to and from the new empire.

For some years, Japanese mercantile shipbuilding had been reduced in order to leave the yards free to

concentrate on naval construction. As it was assumed that any war would be of short duration, no plans existed for emergency or standard merchant ship programmes: a policy of salvage and repair was deemed sufficient. As warships assumed priority for yard capacity, however, merchant ships had refits postponed; and increasing numbers experienced breakdown, were laid up for essential repair or were lost by natural hazard following mechanical problems. During 1942 Japan built just 250,000 grt. of merchant shipping. Although this figure was tripled in 1943 and doubled again in 1944, it was to prove insufficient.

Despite obvious shortfall in tonnage, no single authority existed in Japan to manage the merchant fleet

efficiently. Ships frequently made long ballast voyages when they could usefully have diverted with a cargo. Focused solely on offensive military operations, the state's ruling officers assumed that enemy submarines would, like their own, be directed to sinking warships. A corollary of this assumption was that a convoy system, with its attendant delays, was unnecessary. Mass production of 'defensive' escorts need not detract from 'offensive' warship programmes.

Japanese unwillingness to face facts is demonstrated by the persistent underinvestment in ASW forces. In December 1941 the Japanese navy had some 200 eclectic units with no overall ASW organisation. By August 1944, with merchant ship losses causing a deep

Below: The Japanese I-15 class were large cruiser submarines also designed for long range patrols in the Pacific. Built to carry a small floatplane, they accounted for the US carrier *Wasp* and some 400,000 tons of Allied merchant shipping, but 19 out of 20 were sunk in action.

USS Cero (Gato/Balao class)

1 Bow torpedo tubes
2 Hydroplanes
3 Capstan
4 Outer casing
5 Escape hatch cover
6 Pressure hull
7 Torpedo room
8 Crew space
9 Control panels
10 Torpedo loading hatch
11 Spare torpedo stowage
12 Trim tanks
13 Sonar
14 Piping
15 Main frame
16 Saddle tank
17 20 mm Oerlikon
18 Bridge
19 Fin
20 Conning tower
21 Compass
22 Search and attack periscopes
23 Lookout platform
24 SJ radar

Below: The first Gato class submarines were completed just before Pearl Harbor and bore the brunt of the US submarine offensive. After 72 units had been built, the improved Tench class was introduced, constructed with new HT steels that increased the official diving depth to 400 ft (122 m) although this was regularly exceeded. An incredible total of 256 Tench class was ordered and 122 completed by the end of the war. The Gato/Tench class suffered 29 losses.

25 SD radar
26 Conning tower casing
27 Officers' mess
28 Compressed air flasks
29 Office
30 Fresh water tank
31 Control centre
32 Diving station
33 Indication board
34 Periscope tubes
35 Computer
36 Pump room
37 Fuel tank
38 Wireless room
39 Galley
40 Pyrotechnic stowage space
41 Small arms magazine
42 5 in gun magazine
43 Handling room
44 Crew mess
45 Battery room
46 Crew compartment
47 5 in gun
48 Bilge keel
49 Machine room
50 Diesel engines
51 Main ballast tanks
52 Engine room controls
53 Motor room
54 Electric motors
55 Motor room control area
56 Aft torpedo room
57 Rudder

Below: The Gato class submarine USS *Sea Dog* seen off Guam, preparing for her last war patrol in May 1945. By this time there were 160 American submarines operating in the Japanese sea lanes, enough for two to collide underwater! A new mission for the submarines was the rescue of downed aircrew after the B-29 raids began against the Japanese home islands.

crisis, this total had increased by hardly a third. Only in November 1943 had a convoy system been initiated, together with a crash construction programme for utility frigates, by which time it was hopelessly late.

The US Submarine offensive

At about the time of Midway, American submarine command in the Pacific faced a further upheaval. John Wilkes, whose Fremantle-based fleet boats were at low pitch and achieving little, was relieved by Rear Admiral Charles A. Lockwood, whose seniority saw him heading up all naval forces in western Australia, loosely organised as Task Force 51 (TF51). Lockwood's buoyant nature was the tonic that the jaded, demoralised force needed. Yet just two months later, its severest critic, Admiral English, died in an air crash and Lockwood was transferred to replace him as Comsubpac. Ralph Christie, appointed Rear Admiral, then took over in Australia, as Comsubsowespac.

The enervating period of musical chairs did not stop there. To tackle the technical problems besetting torpedoes, and to improve production rates, a new supremo was necessary. Christie, a torpedo specialist, was selected, moving back to the United States in December 1942, his place being taken by 'Jimmy' Fife.

Between the Commander of the Australian-based submarines and General MacArthur was Vice Admiral Leary. His was replaced by Vice Admiral Carpender, whose personal relationship with Lockwood was poor. One of Leary's actions had been to create the beginnings of a forward base. To interdict Japanese shipping linking the Dutch East Indies with the home islands, submarines needed to operate in the South China Sea, some 3,000 miles from Fremantle. Darwin, the preferred choice for reducing this distance, was within bombing range of enemy occupied Timor. The tender *Pelias* was thus sent 750 miles up the coast to

establish a base at Exmouth Gulf. This inhospitable place, however, offered such appalling weather and geographical isolation that the project, which would add two days to a submarine's patrol time, was slow to mature.

One of Lockwood's first actions was to thoroughly investigate the torpedo problem. On one hand, BuOrd was adamant that skippers were blaming faulty torpedoes for their poor shooting; on the other, the skippers were citing case after case where the weapons were seen to run true, but without result. As the standard Mark XIV torpedo was fitted with a magnetic as well as a contact pistol ('exploder'), their reports implied that the weapons were running very deep. After six months, in which BuOrd had refused to consider the possibility of a design fault, Lockwood initiated practical tests in which instrumented warshots were fired at a submerged taut fishing net. Holes in the net demonstrated that the weapons were running consistently eleven feet (3.35 m) deeper than set. BuOrd's response was to scorn the trials procedure. Lockwood took their comments into account and tried again, with identical results. As the report had attracted the attention of the CNO himself, BuOrd stirred itself. Tests showed that the depth-keeping mechanism (like that of the Germans two years previously) was of faulty design.

This still did not solve the problem of premature explosions, torpedoes frequently detonated either some 300 metres from the point of firing or just short of the target. Despite magnetic detonation being much more lethal to a target ship than contact detonation, Admiral Nitmitz was obliged to order that magnetic exploders be deactivated. Like the Germans and the British before them, the Americans had discovered that any mechanism sensitive enough to be activated by the limited magnetic field of the target would respond also to variations in terrestrial magnetism.

Unbelievably, torpedoes continued to give problems. Matters came to a head when USS *Tinosa* stopped the

19,000-ton whale factory ship *Tonan Maru* with a spread of six torpedoes. The big ship showed no sign of sinking so, in perfect conditions, and with no opposition, the *Tinosa's* skipper spent over an hour firing carefully aimed shots to finish her off. Each weapon was carefully checked before firing. Hydrophones detected a hit in every case, but none exploded. In all, eleven shots of fifteen were duds. Retaining one torpedo for later examination, the *Tinosa's* irate skipper stormed back to Pearl Harbor.

Admiral Lockwood set up further trials, with torpedoes being fired at vertical Hawaiian cliffs. Results were variable, but dissection of recovered, unexploded rounds indicated a malfunction of the actual firing mechanism. This was confirmed by dropping unarmed weapons vertically from a crane onto steel plate. Good square hits deformed the pin, so that no detonation could occur. On the other hand, oblique strikes worked in about half the cases. Local ordnance experts ditched the finely engineered BuOrd pistol in favour of a robust and simpler design produced in their own workshops. Finally, after 21 months of heartbreaking frustration, American submarines had torpedoes which could be relied upon.

Ironically, development was well advanced on an electric torpedo. Although slower and with shorter

Below: Launched in March 1944, *Momo* was the second of 18 Matsu class destroyer escorts ordered by the Japanese navy. They were heavily armed for their size and shipped 36 depth-charges. The *Momo* was torpedoed and sunk by a US submarine in December 1944.

Right: While German U-boats reduced and finally dispensed with their gun armament, US submarines increased the size and number of their deck guns as large targets became scarce. The 5 in (127 mm) gun aboard *Sea Dog* would make short work of small coastal craft in the South China Sea.

range, it was quieter and left no telltale wake. BuOrd had not succeeded in perfecting a satisfactory weapon, but the German G7e could now be used as an exemplar. The Paukenschlag campaign had been conducted so close inshore that several of these weapons had been recovered after running aground on beaches. Under the CNO's direction, development went to private industry rather than BuOrd but, nonetheless, encountered difficulties. It eventually entered service early in 1944 as the Mark XVIII, and was used for daylight operations, with the faster Mark XIV being used at night.

With American submarines subject to geographical division and a complex command structure, their direction lacked the single-mindedness of Admiral Dönitz. The Fremantle-based fleet boats covered the Philippines, Singapore and the Indo-China coast but, in 1942, were too few in numbers to pose a major threat. From Brisbane, the elderly 'S'-boats were tasked primarily in hindering the Japanese defence of the Solomons. With no air conditioning, their interior temperatures rose routinely to 120 degrees Fahrenheit

(49 degrees C), with humidity so high that electrical gear failed and decks puddled. Their wasted hulls were in no condition to resist a severe depth-charging, yet their major targets were the crack enemy destroyers that maintained the 'Tokyo Express'. Four skippers from eleven were relieved, officially for lack of productivity but, in reality, largely from the exhaustion resulting from keeping their boats operational.

The major Japanese fleet bases at Palau and Truk were well removed from the Solomons, so that powerful forces were forward-based at Rabaul and Kavieng. As Halsey's offensive to recover the islands got into its stride, enemy targets abounded but, generally, were beyond the capacity of the 'S'-boats to catch. Despite one or two successes (notably the sinking of the heavy cruiser *Kako*) the veterans were withdrawn for training duties by the end of 1942, and replaced by fleet boats from Fremantle and Pearl Harbor. As their priorities had been warships rather than merchantmen they had contributed little to the build-up of the blockade of Japan.

Establishing a close blockade of the Japanese home

islands was the major task of the Hawaii-based boats. Initially, these could detect little pattern or regularity in Japanese movements which, until production was restarted in the conquered territories, were concerned mainly with the consolidation of the new Japanese empire. Nimitz's general strategy was to cover certain key areas and routes but, with a shortage of boats, this was made difficult by diversions for 'special operations' - minelaying, intelligence gathering, or the insertion and evacuation of personnel. Topping-up fuel at Midway extended patrols by up to eight days. Patrols averaged some 48 days of which 32 might be spent in transit.

Despite the lack of time on station, and the faulty torpedoes, these submarines (including a handful of Dutch and British boats working the area to the west of the Malay peninsula) sank nearly 650,000 grt. of enemy shipping during 1942. From all causes, over 1.1 million grt had been sunk, although more than half of this had been offset by captured tonnage.

A surprising statistic is the rate of torpedo consumption, which steadily increased as the war progressed. During 1942 American submarines

USS Salmon 1942

1 Propeller guard
2 Hydroplanes
3 Rudder
4 Screws
5 Aft torpedo room

expended an average of 9.6 torpedoes per merchantman sunk. In 1943 this rose to 13.5. After an improvement to 11.6 in 1944, the average rose to a staggering 20.3 in 1945. For the first three of these years about 30 percent of targets attacked were sunk but, in 1945, this dropped to below 20 percent. The figures indicate a gradual recovery from the initial dearth of torpedoes, the greater readiness of new and younger skippers to fire large spreads, and their later difficulty in the face of improving Japanese defences.

Intelligence staff had a tough time attempting to judge what actually happened from the reports of returning skippers. An instance is the patrol report from the *Gudgeon*, one of 17 boats covering the enemy's fleet base at Truk in the autumn of 1942. The *Gudgeon's* first encounter was with a small patrol craft, which she missed with three torpedoes. A few days later she was stalking a small tanker convoy by night when a vigilant destroyer forced her down, followed by a brief depth-charging. Another night attack, on a single escorted freighter, followed. *Gudgeon's* skipper, William S. Stovall, thought that he hit with two torpedoes from three. A daytime submerged attack followed on a single, unescorted merchantman, again with two hits out of three claimed. Stovall's next encounter was with two cargo ships, escorted by a pair of destroyers and with air cover. Three torpedoes hit the first ship and two the second, whereupon *Gudgeon* endured a sequence of

about 60 depth charges. Stovall was credited with destroying four ships, totalling about 35,000 grt, on one of the most productive patrols to date. Postwar records shown, however, that his total score was a single ship of under 5,000 grt. Even greater disparities are evident with the two patrols made by the *Grampus* off Guadalcanal at the height of the Japanese campaign. Many skippers sighted little but, on the first patrol

alone, John R. Craig reported 44 cruisers and 79 destroyers. Following six attacks he was credited with the sinking of a destroyer and the damaging of another. During his highly active second patrol he sighted 41 ships, recording attacks on four freighters, a destroyer and a submarine. He was credited with three freighters, totalling 24,000 grt. Japanese records, post-war, failed to substantiate any of these successes.

Right: USS *Bullhead* investigates a Chinese junk in early 1945. By this time, US submarines had sunk over 1,000 Japanese merchant ships, cutting off the supply of raw materials to Japanese industry.

6	Crew space	16	Fin	26	Control centre	36	Main frame
7	Outer casing	17	Conning tower	27	Diving controls	37	Hydrophones
8	Trim tank	18	SJ radar	28	Navigation area	38	Torpedoes
9	Electric motors	19	SD radar	29	Pump room	39	Forward torpedo room
10	Electric motor room	20	Search and attack periscopes	30	Fresh water	40	Ballast tank
11	Electric motor control centre	21	Bridge	31	Double hull	41	Capstan
12	Engine room	22	Fuel	32	Officers' mess	42	Additional bow-mounted torpedo tubes
13	Diesel engines	23	Galley	33	Officers' quarters		(only fitted for a short period)
14	Engine room control centre	24	Radio room	34	Air flasks	43	Torpedo tube covers
15	3 in (76 mm) gun	25	Stores	35	Battery room	44	Bilge keel

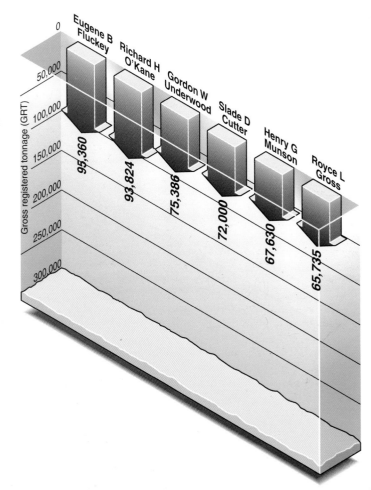

S class

Displacement:	854 tons surfaced and 1,065 tons submerged
Dimensions:	66.83 m (219 ft 3 in) x 6.3 m (20 ft 8 in) x 4.72 m (15 ft 6 in)
Diving depth:	200 ft (61 m)
Propulsion:	two diesel engines delivering 1,200 hp and two electric motors delivering 1,500 hp to two shafts
Speed:	14.5 knots surfaced and 11 knots dived
Endurance:	9,270 km (5,760 miles) surfaced at 10 knots
Armament:	one 4 in (102 mm) or one 3 in (76 mm) gun and four or five 21 in (533 mm) torpedo tubes and 12 torpedoes
Crew:	42

Only from November 1942 did available Japanese tonnage start to diminish in actual terms. The decline was aggravated by the backlog of ships awaiting repair and maintenance. In total this amounted to some 800,000 grt., which remained fairly constant throughout the war. Expressed as a percentage of that available, however, it increased spectacularly from some 14 percent in 1942 to 42 percent at the close of hostilities.

At the end of the 1942 there was a dearth of American torpedoes and submarines were often despatched with a part load of mines, which could be substituted for torpedoes at a rate of two to one. Although small fields could thus be laid with great precision, Lockwood always viewed the activity as a misuse of his force. Within months, the torpedo situation improved and the increasing availability of long range aircraft made this mode of laying the preferred option. Minelaying caused a trickle of casualties, rather than a flood. But it caused regular disruption to Japanese shipping movements and forced the Japanese to devote new efforts to counter-measures.

Over the whole of 1942 American submarines conducted 350 patrols: virtually a departure each day. The High Command must have been highly satisfied with the 274 enemy ships claimed as sunk, whose aggregate tonnage of 1.6 million grt. far outstripped any replacement programme. In reality, the total of 180 ships of 725,000 grt. had reduced the Japanese fleet by only 1.8 percent with negligible effect on the flow of raw materials. Of seven American boats lost in 1942, only three were to enemy ASW forces, and two of these are not confirmed.

US Submarine Aces

Right: The top scoring American submarine commanders could not match those run up by the U-boat 'aces', but Japanese merchant ships were generally smaller than those in Allied Atlantic convoys, and there were fewer of them. The record tonnage sunk by one US submarine was just over 100,000 grt (USS *Flasher*) while USS *Tautog* sank the most ships (73 of over 500 grt). Second top-scoring sub skipper 'Dick' O'Kane was lucky to survive the accidental torpedoing of his own boat (*Tang*) and subsequent capture by the Japanese.

Analysis showed that, although Pearl Harbor-based boats accounted for less than one patrol in six (54 out of 350), the fact that they operated in more productive Japanese home waters saw them sinking over 40 percent of the total loss to the enemy. The enormous problems involved in mounting a sustained campaign from Australia were probably worth it in terms of disruption to the enemy but the boats were spread thinly and spent long periods in transit.

As the submarine service expanded, and older and under-aggressive skippers were relieved, new names began to emerge. One such was Dudley 'Mush' Morton, who took over the USS *Wahoo*. With Guadalcanal regained, the Brisbane submarine force was reduced, and the seven boats transferred back to Hawaii mostly made war patrols en route. Morton, who had been quickly accepted by his crew, but who horrified them with his casual boldness, penetrated the deep Wewak anchorage in New Guinea with no proper chart. Finding an enemy destroyer getting under weigh, he pioneered the 'down-the-throat' shot, keeping his periscope exposed as a lure. Missing with four torpedoes as the ship approached, he destroyed it with a fifth at under half a mile range.

En route to Palau, the *Wahoo* encountered a four-ship convoy. Firing seven torpedoes, Morton hit two freighters and a troopship. Surfacing later he found one freighter had gone and the other still under weigh. The trooper was stopped. A single further torpedo proved to be a dud but a second finished the ship. Morton ignored the two surviving ships, turning his guns on the thousands of swimming survivors. 'After about one hour. . .we destroyed all the boats and most of the troops' he recorded laconically. Setting off after the two escaping

Above: In May 1944 USS *England* entered the record books by sinking 6 Japanese submarines in 12 days. The boats were part of a Japanese patrol line waiting to attack US warships in the battle of the Philippine Sea. The first victim, *I-16* was a 3000 ton submarine actually larger than the *England*.

ships he expended his seven remaining torpedoes in destroying the freighter and hitting a tanker twice.

Although Morton's credit of five ships, totalling 31,900 grt., was trimmed postwar to three of 11,300 grt. his reputation was made. The lack of official comment on the contentious issue of massacring survivors may be interpreted either as official acquiescence or an unwillingness to censure a hero that the service so badly needed.

Morton was then given the task of exploring the as-yet untapped potential of the dangerously shallow Yellow Sea. With no obvious ASW measures in place,

he operated freely, claiming a bag of eight ships, totalling 36,700 grt (actually nine ships of 20,000 grt). He was already far and away the most successful American skipper to date. Three further ships were sunk on a trailblazing patrol to the Kuriles. Dud torpedoes allowed three more targets to escape and Morton's furious denunciation of the weapons was highly influential in having the problem tackled, for he and his fire-control team were considered the best.

A further pioneering patrol, to the Sea of Japan, was dogged by torpedo trouble. From nine targets, seven were missed, one was hit by a dud and the final one was missed by a torpedo that first broached and then ran erratically. It was a period when skippers and crews were exposed to every danger but with little hope of success.

Aggressive as ever, Morton requested another mission to the Sea of Japan. It was *Wahoo's* seventh war patrol and she disappeared without trace, believed to have been destroyed by aircraft in the Strait of La Perouse. Postwar records show that he had destroyed a further four ships, making a confirmed total of 19, totalling 55,000 grt. His legacy was to create an example that the service had lacked. Also, in his first wardroom, he had, as Executive Officer, Richard 'Dick' O'Kane and, as a junior hand, George W. Grider.

In a fast-expanding force, both men went on to create their own records, in the *Tang* and *Flasher* respectively. Grider proved to be the only American skipper to sink over 100,000 grt of shipping as verified by Japanese records postwar.

Left: Similar to the US 'S' class, the Japanese L3 class were built in the early 1920s. Only three were completed and served throughout World War II as training boats until stricken in May 1945.

Below: The Ha 201 class (Type STS) were similar in concept to the German Type XXIII: a streamlined coastal boat with improved underwater performance. Fitted with radar and a schnorkel device, they were intended to help stop the Allied invasion but only 10 were completed by the end of the war, none early enough to become operational.

As larger numbers of American submarines began to make an impact on shipping in Japanese home waters, ASW measures were reviewed. As with most things Japanese, the results were unusual. An outer 'trip-line' of radio-equipped fishing vessels was maintained at up to 600 miles east of the home islands, causing a nuisance to submarines transiting on the surface. An inner cordon, of more ad hoc craft (usually referred to by US observers as 'sampans'), was stiffened with a few regular ASW ships and covered the approaches to ports. These vessels could quickly summon aircraft and further surface ships. Although American skippers scorned these defences, they needed to take them seriously as the seven submarines lost in 1942 increased to seventeen in 1943.

Several sweeps, designed to 'roll up' the lines, failed

Below: The giant *I-402* had been converted to a submersible fuel tanker for supplying Japanese garrisons on isolated islands in the Pacific. The hanger could accomodate up to three floatplanes. Note the raised schnorkel abaft the tower.

because the patrol craft were too small to torpedo, and difficult to sink by gunfire from the unsteady platform offered by a submarine. They were also well armed and resolutely defended. Such probes quickly resulted in reinforcement and the submarine having to break off the action and, in turn, becoming the hunted. Regular ASW escorts generally lacked radar until later in the war but they used sonar effectively. As Japanese coastal waters are mostly shallow, the escort's task was the easier.

In November 1943, with the monthly loss rate averaging 100,000 grt., the Japanese created a formal escort command and a convoy system. To minimise delays to shipping they ran many small groups, which was an error because it spread the few escorts too thinly.

With the Allies' re-taking of the Solomons chain and their westward advance along the north coast of New Guinea, it became possible to forward base submarines, and to offer limited refits, at Milne Bay. Also in New Guinea, this facility saved 2,400 miles on a round trip from Brisbane. As the enemy responded vigorously to any attempt to put him on the defensive, movements of

Ha 201

Displacement:	377 tons surfaced and 440 tons submerged
Dimensions:	53 m (174 ft) x 4 m (13 ft) x 3.4 m (11 ft)
Diving depth:	350 ft
Propulsion:	one diesel engine delivering 400 hp and one electric motor delivering 1,250 hp to one shaft
Speed:	10.5 knots surfaced and 13 knots dived
Range:	5,600 km (3,480 miles) at 10 knots surfaced or 185 km (115 miles) at 2 knots submerged
Armament:	two 533 mm (21 in) torpedo tubes and four torpedoes
Crew:	22

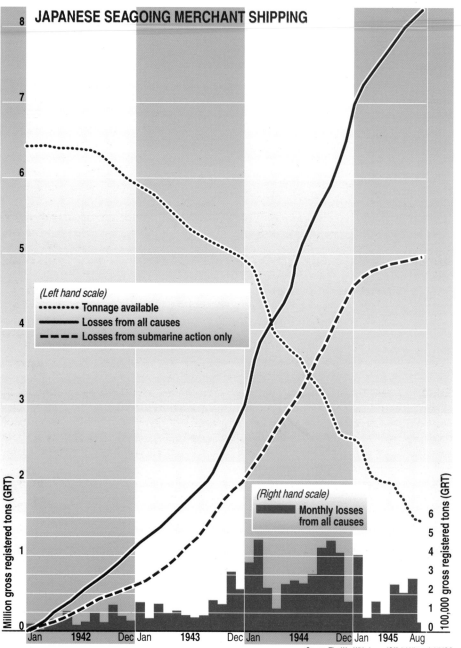

JAPANESE SEAGOING MERCHANT SHIPPING

(Left hand scale)
- ●●●●●●●● Tonnage available
- ——— Losses from all causes
- – – – Losses from submarine action only

(Right hand scale)
- ■ Monthly losses from all causes

Million gross registered tons (GRT)

100,000 gross registered tons (GRT)

Jan **1942** Dec Jan **1943** Dec Jan **1944** Dec Jan **1945** Aug

Source: The War With Japan (Official History). HMSO

Left: US submarines accounted for the majority of Japanese shipping losses in World War II, effectively wiping out the Japanese merchant fleet by mid-1945. The Japanese navy was eventually immobilized for lack of fuel and the Japanese war economy came to a virtual standstill.

Right: The speed with which the US Navy expanded its submarine fleet was not matched by the Japanese forces, which continued to disregard the danger until it was too late.

limited to finding them targets, indicated by the now-continuous flow of Ultra information. German-style tight control was abhorred because of the inevitable radio traffic that it generated.

Once vectored, a pack would adopt a line of search, spaced at useful radar range of about six miles. Radar could be used freely as it was known that the then technologically-backward Japanese had no search receiver, such as the German Metox. The plan was that the boat first contacting a convoy would trail it, using the short-range radio telephone to zero-in its colleagues. Having attacked, each would drop back in turn to a tracking position, both to guarantee that the group would not lose contact and to be able to deal with stragglers or damaged ships.

The first three-boat group–'wolf-pack' seems an over-statement–left Pearl Harbor in October 1943. Sailing with it was a four-ring captain as divisional officer. Charles B. 'Swede' Momsen had been a major force behind the introduction of group tactics, but his presence was not universally appreciated by the fiercely independent skippers. Guided by 'Ultras' from Hawaii, the group operated between Formosa and the home islands. Communication problems seemed insuperable. Two boats, *Shad* and *Grayback*, made individual attacks on separate convoys, followed by *Grayback* sinking an independent in a solo attack. The closest thing to a group operation came when the same two boats fired on a third, four-ship, convoy, only to succeed in torpedoing the same ship. Although claimed results were higher, this pioneer pack sank just three ships, totalling 23,500 grt. As if to prove the point, *Grayback* went on to make an 'orthodox' solo patrol, with confirmed destruction of three freighters and a destroyer.

Undaunted, Lockwood despatched a second group to the Marianas. Again, 'Ultras' were indispensable but inter-boat communications were poor. First to encounter a convoy, USS *Harder* fired off a complete outfit of torpedoes to sink three ships totalling barely 15,000 grt. With no torpedoes remaining, and experiencing repeated engine failures, the *Harder* dropped out. USS *Pargo* latched onto a new convoy, her radar emissions guiding in the *Snook*. Again, a prodigious number of torpedoes were expended in accounting for four ships of 16,500 tons. Although Lockwood rated these early operations a success, individual skippers remained far from convinced. There was still some way to go.

Over the last four months of 1943, submarines accounted for about 700,000 grt. of Japanese shipping. Although this was moderate in comparison with losses in the European theatre, the enemy's rate of replacement was far lower and a growing proportion of his remaining fleet awaited repair. More American

troops and materiel guaranteed a high level of shipping activity, justifying the arrival of a further submarine squadron and its tender. It was at this juncture that the first experiments were made with pairing submarines in joint attacks. They failed because skippers were steeped in self-sufficiency, suspicious of any procedure that involved increased radio traffic.

The idea was, in fact, not new in the US Navy, Lockwood recorded how 'section attacks' had been exercised during the 1920s. Night section attacks were also practised, but both failed for the same reasons–poor communications and risk of what today would be termed 'blue-on-blue' encounters. Before his posting to the Pacific however, Lockwood had been American Naval Attaché in London and had seen at first hand the merits and demerits of Dönitz's methods. As, by 1943, surface-search radar was linked to the Plan Position Indicator (PPI), submarines could work to a common

display, which could be discussed in real time over a short-range, high-frequency radio telephone.

Wargames were devised for skippers and their fire-control teams, using the black and white chequered dance floor of the Pearl Harbor Officers' Mess. These were extended to dummy attacks on incoming friendly convoys. Such exercises proved that group attack was possible without mutual interference, and confirmed yet again the value of aerial reconnaissance.

The American technological lead was also extended to the provision of frequency-modulated sonar (FMS). This had been developed on the rather vague premise of indicating nearby solid objects, but proved ideal for the detection of moored mines, a silent hazard that was posing ever more of a problem as submarines began to penetrate remote corners.

American 'wolf-packs' would be kept small, usually to three boats. Pearl Harbor's involvement would be

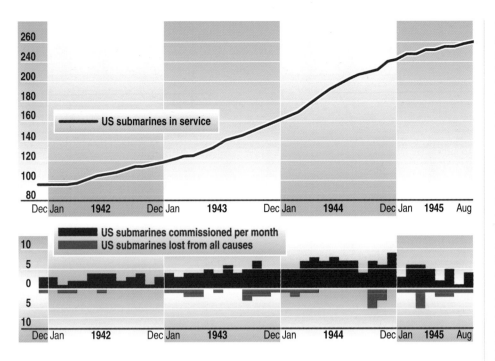

US submarines in service

US submarines commissioned per month
US submarines lost from all causes

tankers had suffered comparatively few losses. Their cellular structure and complex pumping arrangements make them difficult to sink. Unless sailing with slack tanks, in which case the ullage space above a cargo fills with explosive vapour, a tanker with a load of crude oil is difficult to ignite. Unfortunately for the Japanese crews, they often shipped Indonesian crude oil which is very light and highly inflammable.

Attracted by intelligence on the growing Japanese oil shortage, US planners elevated tankers in the priority list. 'Ultras' directed submarines at their convoys and losses were averaging about 60,000 grt. monthly by the end of 1943. (It should be noted that, in the shipping world, tankers are normally reckoned by deadweight tonnage (dwt) rather than gross registered tonnage (grt). A figure of 60,000 grt. would equate to a more realistic 85,000 dwt.). Through new construction and the conversion of dry cargo ships, the Japanese maintained their tanker tonnage almost to the end of 1944. However, imports were never more than half the pre-war average, Japan conducting its war effort with ever-diminishing strategic reserves. Early in 1944 the Japanese transferred the bulk of the Combined Fleet to Singapore in order to site it close to oil sources. Through being tied to a specific base it surrendered some freedom of movement.

Oil tanker losses had been minimised earlier by the remoteness of their main routes. But American submarines were increasing rapidly in numbers. Seven to nine were commissioning each month, except in the depths of winter, when this reduced to about four.

submarines were also being lost, probably due to increasing boldness on the part of their skippers rather than a general improvement in the performance of the average Japanese escort.

Japanese radar, where fitted, was not very effective. Growing Allied experience with underwater acoustics already influenced how a convoy and its escort were disposed, but the Japanese still lacked this appreciation. They placed great emphasis on Magnetic Anomaly Detection (MAD), with aircraft especially fitted to detect the mass of submerged metal that was a submarine. Flying low ahead of a convoy they could

obtain only a transient twitch on their instruments as they passed directly over a target. At aircraft speed, there would be insufficient time to mark the point accurately, but the mere warning of a submarine's presence would enable an escort to take appropriate action. With the then-current state of technology it is doubtful if MAD was ever as effective as the Japanese claimed.

Although submarines were set targets in order of priority, such priorities could best be observed in practice only through choice of patrol area. Supplies of oil were always rated highly but, until the end of 1943,

Below: An emergency building programme enabled the Japanese to maintain the strength of their tanker fleet, but half their dry cargo ships were sunk during 1944. Here another ship takes its final plunge, seen from a US submarine at the end of 1943.

Greater strength and forward basing facilitated a blitz on tanker traffic. By continuing to station a considerable proportion of their battle fleet on the strategic base of Truk, the Japanese had to maintain a long and vulnerable tanker-rich route to service it. Paradoxically, the Japanese had been so ill-prepared for war that there were cases of urgently-needed tankers laying idle, full of oil, in ports that had inadequate storage facilities.

By the close of 1943 US forces had begun their great island-hopping progress across the Pacific, with the Gilberts secured and the Marshalls soon to be assaulted. Because older and war-damaged submarines were reduced to training duties, the number of patrols had remained fairly constant but, sinking 340 ships aggregating over 1.5 million grt capacity, these had been twice as productive. The reasons for improvement were various. All major Japanese routes were now discovered. Younger and bolder skippers, often under 30 years of age, had replaced the older and more cautious. With torpedo problems at last solved, there was a fair chance of sinking a target. The Japanese were now losing tonnage at a far higher rate than it could be replaced. Bulk imported commodities had reduced by some 18 percent on the year. But, if 1943 was the year when the submarine service began to make its mark, 1944 was when it wrote it large.

Seventeen American boats had been lost to all causes during 1943, a total which was to increase to nineteen in 1944. At least two were able to prove their toughness by surviving severe depth-charging. Off Kyushu, USS *Salmon* (Lt. Cdr. Harley K. Nauman), grouped with the *Trigger* and *Sterlet*, savaged a large tanker that,

unusually, was escorted by four frigates. Already minus its after end, the tanker was hit twice more by the *Salmon*. Located by the escorts, this 'thin-skinned' boat suffered a rapid, four-pattern counter attack that sent her out of control to below 500 feet (152 m). Depth charges and over-pressure left the hull distorted and leaking. Nauman surfaced quickly, with a 15-degree list. It was night but, as the crew fought to correct the worst of the damage, the *Salmon* was spotted by the escorts. One was actually fought off by superior firepower but a second was evaded only through the intervention of a rain squall. Although the crew brought the boat home, she was declared a constructive total loss and reduced to training duties.

Just a fortnight later, USS *Halibut* (Lt. Cdr. Ignatius J. 'Pete' Galatin) attacked a four-ship convoy. She was one of a six-boat pack, formed from two groups. Detected by an aircraft, the *Halibut* was subjected to a brief but devastatingly accurate combination attack by aircraft and escorts. With hull plates dished and leaking, and major systems inoperative, the *Halibut* limped to Saipan for emergency repair but, like the *Salmon*, she had to be retired.

At their peak strength American boats were organised in 117 packs, of which 64 were Pearl Harbor based (SUBPAC) and the remainder administered from Australia (SUBSOWESPAC). In contrast to German groupings, which could be temporarily composed of 40 or more boats, the Americans persisted with permanent trios. Where German groups had predictably Teutonic codenames, such as *Mordbrenner*, *Reisswolf* and *Schlagetod*, American culture was equally well

Above: A *Kaiten I* suicide submarine is launched from a Japanese light cruiser. In reality a converted torpedo, the *Kaiten* travelled at 30 knots but the operators could barely see out and very few managed to hit their targets.

expressed by such as 'Blair's Blasters', 'Clarey's Crushers' and 'Wilkin's Wildcats'.

As the number of packs increased, territories shrank and cooperation between adjacent groups became more common. Two such were those of L.t Cdr. Gordon W. Underwood in *Spadefish*, leading *Peto* and *Sunfish*, and Lt. Cdr. Charles E. Loughlin in *Queenfish*, with *Barb* and *Picuda*. Operating in typically loose fashion, they had an initial success when *Queenfish* evaded three escorts to sink two small cargo ships with a six-torpedo spread. Within hours Loughlin expended a further six to put down another small cargo ship, missing a nearby tanker. *Barb* then encountered an independent, a large modern cargo carrier which succumbed to three hits from six. In very poor weather conditions, *Queenfish*, *Barb* and *Peto* latched on to a twelve-ship convoy with six escorts, but were able to account for only two ships for the expenditure of 25 torpedoes.

MacArthur's steady advance was threatening the Philippines, which the Japanese were reinforcing. An Ultra intercept placed the US submarines into the path of a convoy that was carrying a complete Japanese army division, aircraft and fuel. Evading the powerful escort, *Queenfish* destroyed a freighter laden with crated aircraft with a four-torpedo salvo. *Barb* loosed her remaining seven weapons fruitlessly at the auxiliary carrier *Jinyo* and a freighter, following which she broke off. On the following evening, the five remaining boats put together a group attack which disposed of two troop transports and three freighters before *Spadefish* finally nailed the *Jinyo* with six torpedoes. Individually, the boats then went on to sink four more merchantmen. The two packs had not only destroyed a total of 17 ships, an escort carrier and a frigate, but had considerably weakened the defences of the Philippines.

During 1944 Japan faced inevitable defeat. Nimitz's central Pacific advance took the Marianas, a critical acquisition which allowed heavy bombers to be used against Japan for the first time. As raids involved a 3,000-mile round trip, fighter cover could not be provided. The Boeing B-29s had to fly at maximum altitude, sacrificing much of their bombload for extra fuel. Many still became casualties, and submarines acquired a new task of 'lifeguarding', spaced along the flight path to rescue aviators from aircraft that had been obliged to ditch on the long passage home.

Except for those months when submarines were diverted in numbers to support major operations, Japanese mercantile losses exceeded 200,000 grt. Faced with oil starvation, they gave priority to maintaining tanker capacity. This was to the detriment of dry cargo and passenger shipping, the total of which declined over the year by about two million grt. Roving submarines also severely punished the Imperial Japanese Navy during 1944, sinking a battle cruiser, seven carriers and nine cruisers.

As the noose on Japan tightened, carrier aircraft began to poach increasingly on what had been exclusively the submariners' patch. China-based reconnaissance aircraft had been valuable in reporting some remotely-routed convoys and by the close of 1944, such aircraft were flying from the Philippines as well. Japanese shipping hugged the coast, hopping from

Above: British X-craft midget submarines attacked two Japanese cruisers in the Johore strait in July 1945, sinking *Takao* and earning two VCs in the process. Other X-craft cut the underwater telephone lines between Singapore, Hong Kong and Tokyo.

Below: It fell to USS *Torsk*, seen here in 1952, to sink the last Japanese 'maru' of the war, the day before the surrender. Japan had lost 4.8 million tons of shipping and most of its remaining merchant vessels were either laid up for repair or trapped in distant ports.

sanctuary to sanctuary in shallow waters. Far-ranging aircraft hit anything that moved and American submarine skippers quickly learned to dive when aircraft appeared on the radar plot.

The Japanese over-compensated on tanker tonnage, creating more capacity than they were able to use in the face of such stiff opposition. With staple commodities in desperately short supply, they began to convert shipping back for dry cargo. Early in 1945 they experienced two convoy disasters, losing 17 from 20 ships in one, and nine from ten in the other.

Convoys ceased running from Singapore in March 1945 and the South China Sea was effectively abandoned. As Japan had gone to war for the primary purpose of ensuring her supplies of raw materials, this was of fundamental significance.

As 1945 ran its course, sinkings fell off dramatically. Such tonnage as still ran carried small parcels of essentials for a population whose morale was sapped as

rations were cut, and cut again. The state was surviving rather than waging war and, when B-29s turned to sowing the harbours with mines, the blockade was complete. Nuclear weapons, when they came, only hastened the High Command to accept the inevitable.

The principle of convoy, that had twice saved the British from defeat, failed the Japanese, whose relentlessly 'offensive' ethos prevented them from giving 'defensive' issues such as the protection of merchant shipping the priorities that they deserved. At the Surrender, in August 1945, over 1.6 million tons grt still remained but, of this, nearly one million awaited repair and much of the remainder was marooned in distant ports.

From being the only means by which the United States could strike back at a rampant Japan, submarines had progressed to becoming the weapon of terrible retribution. Their sinking of nearly 4.8 million grt was probably the greatest single contribution to their enemy's defeat. From all causes, 52 boats were lost, the smallest number of all five main combatants. Individual tonnages retrospectively confirmed for 'aces' were much lower than those for the German Navy, reflecting the generally larger size of ships operated by the Allies.

Chapter 4 – Amphibious Warfare

If the end of the Dunkirk operation in June 1940 closed the gates of western Europe to the British, their ejection from Crete in May 1941 marked a total exclusion. Nevertheless, at a time when the national mind was focused mainly on survival, Prime Minister Churchill, was bombarding the Chief of the Imperial General Staff with minutes enquiring after progress on specialised flat-bottomed craft capable of putting troops and vehicles ashore on an enemy coast. The Premier's primary objective was the discomfiture of the enemy through raiding, but his ultimate aim was nothing less than the liberation of Europe itself. Whether by crossing the English Channel or the wide Mediterranean, an entirely new form of warfare would be required.

Such slim resources as could be spared were devoted to the study of problems posed by Combined Operations, the insertion of forces over defended shores, sustaining them and, where necessary, recovering them.

This effort proved to be doubly valuable when, in December 1941, Japan unleashed her long-threatened campaign in the Pacific. Within four months she had acquired a sprawling island empire including, as predicted by successive American war plans, the territories of the Philippines and Guam. An enraged United States required nothing less than the total defeat of the Japanese. However, the route to the enemy's home islands across the vast Western Pacific was studded with island groups on which the Japanese established strong garrisons and air bases. By the Spring of 1942, the USA found itself with much the same problem as the British, albeit on a larger scale.

German and Japanese victories in the early years of World War II meant that Allied victory depended on amphibious warfare. Hitler's 'Atlantic Wall' defences would have to be broken if western Europe was to be liberated. The defeat of Japan's island empire demanded a new generation of specialist warships and tactics. Here US troops from the 31st infantry division wade ashore from LCIs (Landing Craft Infantry) at Morotai island in the Moluccas, September 1944.

The pioneers of amphibious operations

Developments in the 1920s and 1930s were overshadowed by the bitter experience of Gallipoli, a prime example of the courage and sacrifice of the many being squandered by the shortcomings of the senior few. That operation was widely regarded as proof that an assault over a defended beach was not possible. To more far-sighted observers, it provided a yardstick against which future activities would be measured. The commanders of the separate forces involved in an amphibious assault clearly required a common objective, together with fallback strategies agreed beforehand. The strengths and weaknesses of the defence needed to be assessed in advance, and adequate and appropriate forces assembled to meet them. Everything had to be placed where required; it was simply not enough to dump personnel and equipment onto a beach and expect things to be sorted out under fire. Finally, surprise should be sought and the initiative, once gained, should not be lost.

Above: British attitudes to amphibious warfare were haunted by the spectre of Gallipoli. Attempts to force the straits by warships led to heavy losses including the French battleship *Bouvet* seen sinking here. Landing ground troops led only to bloody stalemate.

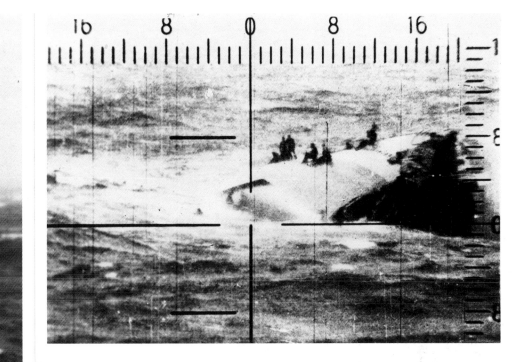

Pre-war American amphibious operations

During World War I the US Marine Corps was vastly expanded, and its prescribed function of base defence extended to that of acting as elite infantry. The distinction between it and the army thus became somewhat indistinct and, in the savage defence cuts that followed the war, its continued existence appeared doubtful. Designated the Marine Corps Expeditionary Force in 1921, it still lacked a clearly defined role.

Japan's reward for its participation in World War I included a mandate over huge areas of the Western Pacific. US war planners anticipated an eventual conflict of interests, and studies commenced for a war plan against the expanded Japanese Empire.

Serving on the marine staff at this time was one Lieutenant-Colonel Earl H. Ellis, an eccentric Lawrence of Arabia-type figure. He had an exceptional talent for studying an opponent's situation and arriving quickly at a solution for his defeat. Ellis's grasp of a situation extended from the tactical to the strategic but, on a personal level, his behaviour was rather bizarre. Even before World War I, he suspected Japan's ultimate intentions, and wrote theses on the likely American requirement to seize islands in Micronesia, which were under German control until 1915.

Posing as a company representative, Ellis travelled widely about the mandates, an odyssey apparently sanctioned from the very top. Before his mysterious death in the Carolines in 1923 he submitted a series of plans and recommendations to the then Commandant of the Marine Corps, Major-General John A. Lejeune. The latter effectively re-invented the Corps, convincing Congress that it should exist not merely to defend bases but to spearhead the eventual trans-Pacific advance. From that point in 1921 the terms 'Marine Corps' and 'amphibious warfare' became virtually synonymous.

Although clauses in the Washington Treaties had

Left: The doomed destroyer *Glowworm* seen from the heavy cruiser *Hipper* during their one-sided duel off Norway during the German invasion. After firing all his torpedoes and with few guns left, *Glowworm* turned to ram her opponent.

Above: Some of *Glowworm*'s survivors seen from *Hipper*, clinging to her upturned hull. Lt. Commander Roope was awarded a posthumous VC after the details of the action were learned after the war.

expressly forbidden any fortification of western Pacific islands, Japan turned them into a virtual exclusion zone, increasing American apprehensions. For years, the Marine Corps directed its tight funding primarily towards developing techniques and equipment in a series of small-scale exercise landings in the Caribbean. These were sufficiently valuable to have the marines' amphibious assault role adopted, in 1927, as part of national military policy.

The Corps was divided into East and West Expeditionary Forces, ostensibly attached to the Atlantic and Pacific Fleets respectively, but it was very busy quelling unrest in the Caribbean, and protecting US interests in war-torn China. In 1933 a re-organisation resulted in the establishment of the Fleet Marine Force, with Atlantic and Pacific elements each of about brigade strength. Each included what might be termed a rifle regiment, supported by light artillery and ancillary units—engineers, medical personnel and signallers. The latter were trained in ship-to-shore procedures. Enhancing their self-sufficient status, the brigades added light tanks and aircraft, the pilots of which developed the arts of precision dive-bombing and close support for their colleagues on the ground.

A specialist equipment board was established which, appraised by Ellis's prescient reports, began development of a tracked landing vehicle for the negotiation of the offshore reefs that surrounded all likely Pacific objectives.

Above: The German navy's most spectacular loss during the invasion of Norway. The heavy cruiser *Blücher* was torpedoed and sunk by a Norwegian torpedo battery in Oslofjord. Astern of her, *Lützow* had her forward turret knocked out by a shore battery.

The year 1935 was significant in seeing not only the first major amphibious exercise conducted at fleet level but also the publication of the Tentative Landing Operations Manual. This, to be regularly up-dated, set out a basic doctrine for a new style of warfare. The manual was important in identifying the major components of a successful operation. These were:-

1. Organisation and Command

The complete formation, termed the Naval Attack Force, would comprise two elements, the assault group of the Fleet Marine Force and the Naval Support Group, which was charged with tasks such as escort and fire support. The commander of each subordinate element would report directly to the Attack Force commander until, the assault phase complete and the beachhead secure, the Marine Force Commander would assume tactical independence. From this point he would be responsible to the area commander.

2. Naval Gunfire Support

The defences had to be softened-up before the troops went ashore, and naval gunfire would continue to provide support during the landings. Exercises showed the need for forward observer parties to be put ashore with the first wave to direct naval gunfire at centres of resistance, enemy heavy weapons or to deal with counter-attacks. This meant calling down fire dangerously close to

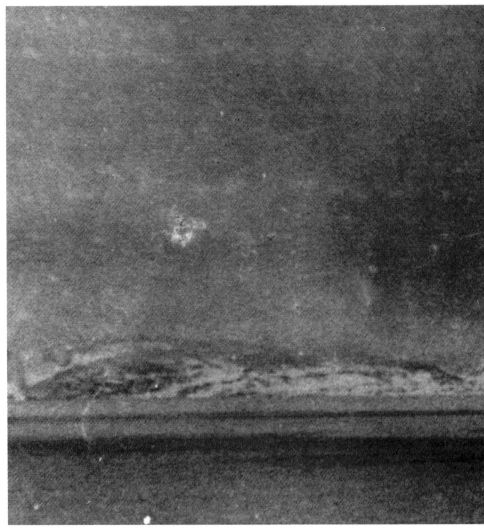

Left: Norway was a disaster for the German destroyer squadrons, with ten destroyers sunk at Narvik. The *Erich Giese* is seen here on fire and abandoned after 21 hits from the battleship *Warspite* and the destroyer *Bedouin*.

Above: A British destroyer at Narvik after the actions of 10 and 12 April. The aggressive British counterstroke sank half the German destroyer force, but was celebrated by the *Kriegsmarine* as a heroic defeat against heavy odds.

friendly forces, so marine officers were trained for the purpose, paired with naval liaison officers afloat. Robust communications equipment was essential. Account needed to be taken of the high velocity of naval gunfire: the corresponding flat trajectories at short range meant naval guns were unsuited to engaging targets on reverse slopes.

3. Close Air Support

Essentially an extension of naval gunfire support, aircraft required pinpoint guidance if a close-quarters situation existed on the ground. Fully understanding the difficulties below, Marine pilots were found to be the best. Once again, the need for reliable communications was highlighted. The long-legged Pacific campaign often outstripped the range of existing land-based air cover and initially, Marine Corps pilots were not trained to work from carrier decks. This had to be addressed.

4. Ship-to-shore movement

While the manual recognised the critical importance of the speedy and efficient transfer of men and equipment from ocean-going ships to a defended shore, but a practical solution had yet to be found. Up to thirteen soldiers could be landed in

the high-speed, 32-foot (9.75m) Higgins, or Eureka, boat which could be stacked, dory-fashion , aboard the parent vessel. Early versions of the aforementioned Landing Vehicle, Tracked (LVT) were also being evaluated. Using its tracks both for waterborne propulsion and for progress ashore, the LVT could lumber over offshore reefs and beyond the beach to the treeline, where it would drop off its 20 troops in greater safety. Known as 'Alligators', the LVTs became identified with the Marine Corps, giving individuals the nickname of 'Gators'. While an LVT could carry cargo in lieu of personnel, it was ill-suited to the purpose, and the Americans quickly adapted where possible to British-designed landing craft already being built in the USA for the British.

5. Logistics

The manual recommended that a single transport should be capable of lifting a battalion-strength assault unit, complete with equipment. 'Combat loading' required gear to be stowed so that it came off in order of priority. As this involved stowage of heavy equipment high in the ship it invariably drew the wrath of responsible chief officers. Improvised

Above: Naval brigades had been landed to take part in almost every British colonial war in the 19th century. In 1914 the Royal Navy improvised a division of ground troops to defend the Belgian port of Antwerp, and naval troops would remain on the western front until 1918.

Right: An armoured train operated by the Royal Navy defending Antwerp in 1914. The Royal Naval Air Service also provided ground forces in the shape of a squadron of armoured cars.

vessels abounded until the introduction of the specialised Attack Transport (AP).

6. Securing the beachhead

Until the beachhead was sufficiently well established to support and defend itself, it would be dependent upon forces afloat for fire support and continuous logistic support. The substantial quantities of supplies required a naval organisation to deliver them to the beach and an army/marine equivalent to distribute them. This necessitated dedicated personnel, trained to co-operate under fire. Practice modified this to the shore party

commander exercising control, with a naval beachmaster reporting to him.

With the benefit of experience to date, the Tentative Manual re-emerged in 1937 as the Landing Operations Doctrine, the 'bible' which provided the guidance for World War II operations. By 1940 the United States had not only enunciated the principles of amphibious warfare but had also exercised them as rigorously as peacetime funding allowed. The 27-month grace period between September 1939 and December 1941 allowed a substantial build-up from very slender beginnings, albeit in competition with many other major programmes.

British developments.

Over centuries of administering and policing an empire the British had had to transport military expeditions to hotspots on many occasions. The first body of British marines thus dated from the seventeenth-century Dutch Wars. Its subsequent strength fluctuated with the fortunes of the Royal Navy. Marines served either as infantry or gunners. During the period of the Pax Britannica bluejackets, too, were trained in military skills and a battleship would be expected to be able to field a self contained naval brigade of about 400 men.

Naval brigades had a long and proud history of interventions ashore.

A full Naval Division, comprising one brigade of marines and two of seamen, was raised before World War I. All reservists, their function was 'Home Defence, or for any special purpose, such as the seizure of an advanced naval base'. Their employment might thus have paralleled that envisaged for the US Marine Corps, except that in 1914 they were subsumed into the under-strength British Expeditionary Force in France.

Gallipoli, where the Naval Division was well represented, was the first major amphibious operation of modern times, but World War I also furnished examples

of that other type of combined operation, the raid. Zeebrugge was a fine example of what is something of a British speciality. Raids differ from expeditions in that their objectives are limited and, once they are achieved, the force is withdrawn.

That controversial genius, Admiral Sir John ('Jacky') Fisher, as First Sea Lord, advocated landing an army on the coast of Pomerania, just 80 miles from Berlin. By-passing the stalemated Western Front, this bold operation would have driven straight for the capital and an early termination of the war. Too radical for the military establishment of the time, the plan was stillborn. However, Fisher had already recognised the requirement for specialised craft. Built at his behest were the shallow-draught super-cruisers of the Courageous class, 'tin-clads' with 15-inch guns for close fire support, and a succession of flat-bottomed craft for putting troops over the beach. These, officially termed X-and Y- type motor lighters, were known, unofficially, as 'Beetles'.

Looking to repair the damage of Gallipoli, the British sought to improve their organisation through post-war exercises. Interestingly, in light of American preoccupation with Japanese intentions, the 1924 exercise simulated a Japanese attempt to seize Singapore. A requirement was soon identified for troop carriers, modified to be able to put their men ashore by means of assault craft slung under their own davits. Also highlighted was the need for specialist craft capable of putting men and vehicles directly over the beach.

An inter-departmental committee was established, drawing its members from all three services and the-then Board of Trade. Its brief was to consider the designs and numbers of landing craft necessary to put ashore personnel and armoured vehicles onto a defended coast, and to define such experimental programmes as were required to support their production.

Within two years the first Motor Landing Craft (MLC 1) was produced. Of 16 tons lightweight it exhibited the features that were later to become standard, including forward ramp and double hull. The waterjet propulsion, stipulated for silent running, proved to be underpowered, while the completely flat bottom required the addition of fore-and-aft curvature ('rocker') to assist refloating.

By 1929 the Committee had gone on to specify and procure the prototype MLC 10, an enlarged version capable of transporting a 12-ton vehicle over 250 miles.

Ten of these, to slightly varying specifications, were built and enabled much useful exercising during the 1930s. Having proved its worth, the Committee was superseded by an Inter-Services Training and Development Centre in 1938. This produced the Assault Landing Craft (ALC), weighing under ten tons for slinging under standard davits, yet capable of accommodating a fully-equipped infantry platoon. Quantity production of the ALC began in 1940.

A major failing of the Norwegian campaign of 1940 was the resolute manner in which the service commanders went their own ways. This disasterous campaign also involved the loss of most of the assault craft so far built.

It will be noted how, during the interwar years, the Americans had developed the doctrines for amphibious warfare while the British, fortuitously, had concentrated on the associated specialised craft.

One topic to which the Americans had paid scant attention was the ocean passage that could precede a landing. The British identified two major categories, i.e. 'landing craft' for ship-to-shore movement and also short open-sea passages, and 'landing ships' capable of ocean voyages but, in general, too large to 'take the beach'. The clear distinction between these categories would eventually become blurred.

By September 1939 both the Americans and the British had developed individual doctrines (if not necessarily the means) for the conduct of amphibious warfare. The British preferred surprise, with an emphasis on night assault. Probably assuming that a long Pacific approach was certain to be detected beforehand, the Americans opted for daylight landing following a pre-assault bombardment. They were well ahead of British practice in appreciating the value of close air support, if necessary mounted from carrier decks.

Japanese and German amphibious warfare

Although expertise in amphibious warfare was to be dominated by the two major allies, other forces were not without capability. Japan's military adventures during the 1930s required power projection over considerable distances and, as early as 1934, had resulted in the world's first specialist infantry landing ship. The 9,000-ton *Shinshu Maru* could discharge up to twenty pre-loaded Daihatsu craft over the stern via a rail transfer system. These could be re-loaded with embarked cargo up to the size of a light tank and, eventually, recovered by the ship's own cranes. A substantial number of floatplanes could also be carried. Up to seven 'follow-ons' were converted from cargo liners. During the Pacific war Japan produced large numbers of specialised landing craft, some of original design, others obviously derived from Western types.

Germany's interest in amphibious warfare was limited originally to major river crossings. Only after Dunkirk, and a realisation that the United Kingdom was not going to seek terms, did the German High Command begin to take seriously an invasion across a stretch of water over which they did not exercise sea control. A further pre-requisite, air superiority, failed with the Battle of Britain, which effectively killed-off the proposed operation.

In April 1940 Germany had demonstrated great boldness and a willingness to take chances in seizing Norway and Denmark. This exercise, however, was a combined operation in that virtually the entire German fleet was mobilised to put military detachments ashore at key points in both countries, but using regular quaysides for the purpose.

Above: In June 1940, as the last British troops were being evacuated from France, the specification was issued for a landing craft capable of delivering tanks on to an open beach. The first LCTs were ready by the end of the year. The Mk4, seen here was the first to have the tank deck above the waterline.

Left: The LST (1) *Thruster* was one of four purpose-built tank landing ships ordered from Harland & Wolff. The bow ramp had a 145 ft extension capable of taking medium tanks. Maximum load was up to 13 medium tanks.

Right: German soldiers land at Oslo in April 1940, beginning a rapid conquest of Norway in which German air power soon compensated for Allied naval superiority.

Shinshu Maru data

Displacement:	9,000 tons standard	Speed:	19 knots
Dimensions:	150 m (492 ft 2 in) x 22 m	Armament:	up to 8 x 76 mm (3 in) AA guns;
	(72 ft 2 in) x 8.16 m (26 ft 9 in)		20 landing craft;
Propulsion:	two turbines delivering 8,000 shp		20 aircraft.

Shinshu Maru was the world's first purpose-built landing ship. Built for the Japanese army and launched in 1935, she carried 20 landing craft which exited through the stern doors. She was sunk by a rogue torpedo fired by a Japanese destroyer during the invasion of Java in March 1942, raised and repaired but sunk again by US aircraft off Formosa in 1945.

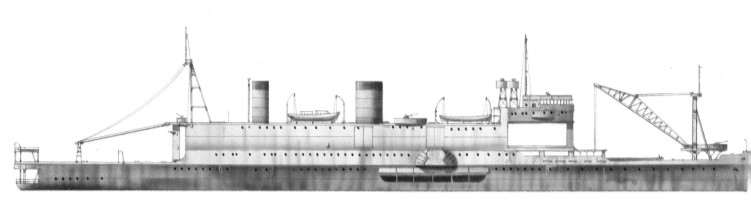

During World War I the Russians had used a combination of military forces and their Black Sea Fleet to good effect along the Anatolian coast. This promising start was terminated by the purges subsequent to the 1917 revolution. The new Soviet Union had internal problems enough and foreign adventures were not on the agenda. Military exercises concentrated on countering incursions from the sea, probably a reaction to remembered Allied amphibious operations during the abortive anti-Bolshevik campaign of 1919. Nonetheless, outflanking movements by seaborne marines became a late feature of Soviet Russian operations during World War II.

British amphibious operations

Prime Minister Churchill moved early to create what he termed the 'apparatus of counter-attack'. A Combined Operation Headquarters was established, initially under the 68-year old, fire-breathing veteran Admiral of the Fleet Sir Roger Keyes. Its intention was to mount a series of raids on continental Europe, to keep its occupiers on their toes and to gain experience against 'The Day'. It was hoped that apprehension would result in over-large enemy garrisons being posted, the resultant inactivity of which would be corrosive to morale.

Ten companies of what were first termed 'Striking Companies', then 'Commandos', were raised from the Royal Marines and the regular army. Selected fast merchantmen were converted for their passage accommodation and to deploy Landing Craft, Assault (LCA) from their davits. Larger examples could also utilise their normal cargo-handling gear to float and to recover Landing Craft, Mechanised (LCM). These craft were the direct descendants of the pre-war ALC 1 and ALC 10 classes. The few available, and highly valuable, ships of this type were termed Landing Ships, Infantry (Large), or LSI (L), the best-known being the three big Glen Line conversions. In contrast, fast ex-cross channel packets became LSIs (Small) or (Medium). While

Right: Developed in 1943, the LSM was an ocean-going tank lighter able to ship 5 medium tanks or up to 9 DUKW amphibians. Over 500 were ordered and they played a key role in US landings in the Pacific 1944-45.

Below: The British built several ungainly 'monitors' during World War I for shore bombardments off Flanders and the Dardanelles. Two new ones were built on the eve of World War II and were used to support landings in Italy and France. *Abercrombie*, seen here, was damaged by a mine off Salerno but sistership *Roberts* saw extensive service from Normandy to Walcheren in 1944-45.

handy and well-endowed with accommodation space, such ships were not designed to load heavy items and sometimes experienced stability problems when fitted with their complement of LCAs.

Operations requiring heavy transport, armour or artillery demanded a different type of carrier. A handful of train ferries and tankers were thus converted to carry numbers of LCMs, transferred to the water by stern chute or heavy gantry. These ships were the antecedents of the Landings Ship, Dock or LSD. But this is to anticipate.

The first raid was mounted on 3 March 1941, its objective was the fish processing complex on the Norwegian Lofoten Islands. Involved were two LSI (M), carrying a dozen LCAs and 500 commandos. For so extended a thrust the Home Fleet provided both close and distant escort. In six hours ashore the raiders demolished their objectives, destroyed seven enemy merchantmen and returned safely with over 200 prisoners and 300 Norwegian volunteers.

A further, and similar, raid against Vaagsö later in the same year convinced the Führer that the ultimate Allied intention was to invade Norway. Large German forces were subsequently deployed to garrison the country, and retained there even at the height of the German manpower crisis later in the war.

During the summer of 1941 British and Commonwealth forces were wresting control of Syria against strong resistance from Vichy French forces. The main thrust, northward up the coast, was aided by an LSI (L) landing a Commando behind the French lines to seize crossings over the Litani river. Although the operation was a classic move by a side enjoying sea control, it succeeded ashore only at a heavy price to both sides.

While the British continued to irritate the enemy with sudden incursions, such as that at St. Nazaire (to put out of action the only drydock on the Atlantic coast capable of stemming the German battleship *Tirpitz*) and at Bruneval (to capture state-of-the-art German radar equipment), something more ambitious was required to gain experience in an opposed assault.

LCI(L) data

Displacement: 246 tons light and 384 tons loaded

Dimensions: 48.9 m (160 ft 4 in) x 7.2 m (23 ft 6 in) x 0.9/1.6 m (2ft 9 in/5 ft 3 in)

Propulsion: two diesels delivering 2,320 bhp to two shafts

Speed: 14 knots

Endurance: 14,822 km (9,210 miles) at 12 knots
Armament: 5 x 20 mm guns.

Crew: 29

The LCI(L) or 'landing craft, infantry (large)' was a British design, built in America and originally intended for commando raids around the European coast. Numbers were allocated up to LCI(L)1139, but about 300 were converted to gunboats or other specialist roles.

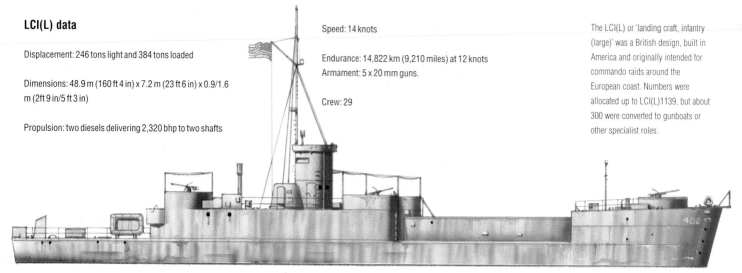

In May 1942, therefore, the large island of Madagascar made a suitable objective. It was occupied by the Vichy French but, with the Japanese now running rampant in the Pacific, it was feared that the French would freely collaborate, as in Indo-China, giving the Japanese a foothold in the Indian Ocean. Operation 'Ironclad', aimed at securing the key areas around the capital, Diego Suarez, stretched the infant skills of the planners to the limit. Some 9,000 miles distant from the

United Kingdom, the operation involved South Africa as the actual springboard. Five LSI (L) were required. They and their supply ships (which also carried transport), tankers and a hospital ship were sailed out incorporated in three separate routine convoys. Naval covering forces were garnered from the Mediterranean, the Eastern Fleet and from smaller units already based on the Cape. Attention to detail showed that the British had learned from an abortive operation in September

1941, which had attempted to put Free French forces ashore at Dakar in Senegal. The Vichy French had successfully resisted the attack. In Madagascar the military side was conducted by only British and Commonwealth forces.

The initial assault was daring: taking place at night in a reef-studded bay, which was surveyed and checked for mines even as the first wave followed. This landing allowed Diego Suarez to be threatened from the rear. At

The LCTs (Landing Craft Tank) were intended to ferry armoured vehicles ashore from LSTs if the latter were unable to beach. They were designed to be 'drive-throughs' so they could serve as an improvised bridge between an LST and the beach.

LCT(7) data

Displacement:	513 tons light and 900 tons loaded
Dimensions:	62 m (203 ft 6 in) x 10.4 m (34 ft) x 1.0/2.1 m (3 ft 5 in/6 ft 10 in)
Propulsion:	two diesels delivering 2,800 bhp to two shafts
Speed:	13 knots
Endurance:	4,030 miles (6,486 km) at 11 knots
Armament:	4 x 40 mm guns and 6 x 20 mm guns.
Crew:	52

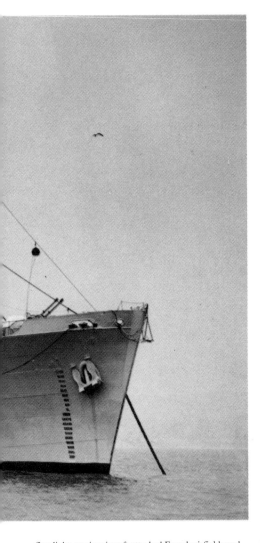

Left: The Glen class LSI(L) *Glenroy.* These carried 24 LCAs (Landing Craft Assault) and 3 LCMs (Landing Craft Medium) with 1,100 infantry. They were armed with six 4 in (101 mm) guns.

Above: The US LST-289 at Dartmouth in April 1944 after an invasion exercise in preparation for the Normandy landings was attacked by German S-boats off Slapton Sands.

first light, carrier aircraft attacked French airfields and shipping. Spearheaded by a Commando, the army took control of the capital by the afternoon of the first day. The naval facility at Antsirane, strongly situated on a small peninsula, held out but capitulated following a bold thrust by a single destroyer, which dodged the fire from shore batteries to land a Marine detachment.

Even in 1940 tanks were developing quickly enough to make the 18-ton load capacity of an LCM look inadequate. As 40-ton vehicles were envisaged the Prime Minister demanded a 'Tank Landing Craft', able to transport three such, and to land them in less than a metre of water. As the Landing Craft, Tank (LCT) this archetypal vessel would graduate from the LCT (1) to the LCT (8) in barely three years, its capacity increasing to eight 50-ton tanks. Endurance at 10 knots also increased from 900 to 2,500 miles. It remained an open-topped craft, however, an absolute pig to steer, with its

shallow draught and blunt lines, and not really suitable for ocean passages. For this purpose, the Landing Ship, Tank, or LST, was developed.

The requirement to ship armoured vehicles 'anywhere' arose as early as November 1940. For designers, the problem was to marry the conflicting requirements of size and capacity with a draught small enough to enable tanks to move directly onto the beach. Somebody recalled that the Shell company used 6,000-ton shallow-draught tankers to shuttle oil from Lake Maracaibo in Venezuela to larger vessels laying in deeper water outside. Three were converted to carry 20 early tanks apiece. For their accommodation the existing centreline trunk was plated topside to the ships' sides, providing two elongated garages. Into their bluff bows was built a watertight door, hinged at its lower edge. Lowered, it permitted extension of a two-part ramp for vehicular access. Conventional cargo gear was added to handle a pair of LCMs. The existing tanker sub-division and pumping arrangements were already effective for the adjustment of fore-and-aft trim for beaching. Their limitations were a nine-knot speed and the vulnerability of the single bow door.

Although ungainly, the 'Maracaibos' included the essential ingredients for a practical LST. These same features were incorporated in three bespoke LSTs built at this time. The Boxer class, or LST (1), were of much the same displacement, but were of much finer sections for a speed of 16 knots. Because of this, their capacity was only 13 tanks. An improved forward arrangement saw the adoption of vertically-hinged doors, meeting on the centreline and backed by an inner, watertight door. Their rather deep forward beaching draught of 1.68 metres required an extendable vehicle ramp some 62 metres in length.

While a successful design, it became obvious that the LST (1) was too complex and expensive to be built in the numbers required. A simplified 3,700-ton design, effectively an enlarged and decked-over LCT was, therefore, discussed with the Americans. Known as the LST (2), this vessel could cross the Atlantic with a 1900-ton embarked load, spread between a lower (tank) deck and an upper (vehicle) deck, which decks were interconnected by a heavy lift.

Like the British, the Americans commenced series production using construction firms rather than conventional shipyards. Timing was fortuitous for they, too, were soon to be plunged into war. Work on British orders commenced early in 1942 but, recognising the value of the LST (2), the Americans retained increasing numbers for their own use. Of over 1000 eventually built, only one in ten became British operated. Because of the resultant shortage, orders for a further-modified version the LST (3), were placed in British and Canadian yards. Major differences in the 61 completed included the substitution of steam reciprocating engines for diesels, a resultant increase of speed to 13 knots, and an increased displacement of nearly 5,000 tons. Both the LST (2) and (3) could stow on the weather deck either LCAs, placed overside by derricks, or a single LCT (6), which was craned aboard but put afloat dramatically by heeling the LST.

From October 1941 the British Combined operation Headquarters were headed by the controversial and flamboyant Lord Louis Mountbatten. He carried equivalent ranks in all services, while being independent of them. Churchill's view of the organisation's importance was emphasised by his giving Mountbatten a seat on the Chiefs of Staff Committee.

Disaster at Dieppe

With the United States entering the war a 'Germany first' policy was agreed, but friction was created when the United Kingdom strongly resisted an American desire to invade continental Europe during 1942. Compromise resulted in the British agreeing to mount an ambitious raid against a defended European objective, in order to gain experience for the eventual full invasion. The selected objective was the French port of Dieppe.

The test was to ascertain whether a medium-sized port could be seized quickly enough to thwart its demolition by the enemy. It was not intended to remain in occupation. 'Attractions' included enemy defences which, while not impregnable, would provide a stiff

The aftermath of the Dieppe raid, 19 August 1942. Supported by 28 early model Churchill tanks and Nos 3 and 4 Commandos, the Canadian 2nd division attempted to seize the port. It was a disaster, with over half the attacking forces killed, wounded or captured.

Left: The Churchill tanks were picked off by German anti-tank guns as they landed. Obstacles blocked their advance from the beach, and 28 tanks were lost.

test. Dieppe's distance from British airfields would permit continuous fighter cover and the prospect of a major showdown with the Luftwaffe.

Originally scheduled for July 1942, the operation was delayed by continuous poor weather. Once postponed, military opinion was for abandonment on grounds of compromised security. At the Prime Minister's insistence, however, it was re-mounted in August 1942.

Dieppe lies in a depression, flanked by high cliffs upon which were enemy batteries. To seize the town quickly, a frontal assault would be necessary, preceded by commando assault to secure the batteries.

Preliminary bombardment was ruled out as politically unacceptable. It would also have had the effect of blocking the streets and alerting the defenders.

Nearly 5,000 troops, mostly Canadian, were involved in the frontal and immediate flanking attacks, with about 1,100 British commandos and a detachment of American Rangers tasked with seizing the batteries. Assault forces crossed directly in new, 37 foot (11.3 metre) Landing Craft, Personnel (Large) or LCP (L)s. Nine assorted LSIs carried the main body, while 24 LCTs took 58 of the new Churchill tanks. Naval forces were minimal.

The eastern flank force ran into an enemy convoy in the pre-dawn darkness, lost cohesion and surprise, and landed most of its troops in the wrong place. In the west the commandos seized their objectives but, in moving inland, found themselves unsupported. The frontal assault on the town was timed for 30 minutes after the flank attacks. It went in against an enemy fully alerted and still able to mount a devastating enfilading fire. Only 27 tanks could be landed, less than half of which could get off the beach. Those that did could not enter the town because of pre-positioned concrete blocks. Unsupported, the infantry were pinned down. Small craft pressed close inshore to assist, but all attempts at smoke cover were defeated by a light offshore breeze.

Even by 0900 it was apparent that a disaster was brewing, yet the agreed time of withdrawal could not be advanced due to rigidly interlocked arrangements for air cover. Communications with the headquarters ship were so poor that situations already hopeless continued to be reinforced.

By 1300 the last man had been taken off, leaving 2,200 men to be taken prisoner and nearly 1,200 already dead. All landed tanks and 33 landing craft including several LCTs were lost. Even in the air things had gone badly, the British losing 106 aircraft, the Germans only 48.

Above: Left dead in the water by a German air attack, the destroyer *Berkeley* is finished off by torpedo as the raiding force retires from Dieppe.

Left: Landing craft heading for Dieppe under cover of a smokescreen laid by destroyers. One reason for the disaster was the strength of the German air attack: the *Luftwaffe* intervened massively, shooting down over 100 Allied aircraft for the loss of 48 of their own.

Right: Landing craft come alongside a destroyer during the withdrawal from Dieppe. This bren gun carrier is one of few vehicles rescued.

Hard lessons learned

Lessons were, indeed, learned. The savage losses - about 68 percent Canadian casualties and 23 percent Commando - dampened American enthusiasm for an early invasion of Europe. The raid proved that there was little future in assaulting around a major port area though, paradoxically, the combination of St. Nazaire and Dieppe convinced the Führer that that was the Allied intention.

Heavy preliminary bombardment, by large-calibre naval guns, was now held to be more important than surprise. Special armoured vehicles would be developed to defeat beach obstacles, while the assault craft themselves would be adequately armed to support their charges. Particularly important would be the creation of a permanent naval force, trained for amphibious warfare and equipped with reliable communications.

The experience of Dieppe spawned a wide range of support landing craft. Gun-armed versions could carry standard tank turrets, ex-naval artillery up to 4.7 inch calibre, high-angle 4 inch or a selection of 20 or 40 mm automatic weapons. The fearsome rocket-armed types were fitted with up to 1,080 projectors, which could ripple-fire 22 tons of explosive in seconds to provide a carpet of shock and destruction immediately ahead of the assault troops. These developments were to prove especially valuable in the Pacific.

There even emerged a Landing Craft, Emergency Repair, or LCE, which salvaged and got moving

Below: The LSI *Prince Baudouin* launches three LCAs during an exercise in England in readiness for D-Day. The Dieppe disaster led to a radical revision of amphibious landing doctrine and to the decision to attack over open beaches rather than try to storm an enemy-held port.

Glen class data

Llangibby Castle was one of many British merchant ships converted for service as an infantry landing ship. Most vessels were used for a specific landing, then returned to trade, rather than swing at anchor, waiting for the next amphibious operation. The Glen class for which data is provided here (see photo p124) were built for the Blue Funnel/Glen/Shire services to the Far East and converted in 1941.

Displacement:	9,800 tons gross
Dimensions:	155.7 m (511 ft) x 20.3 m (66 ft 8 in) x 8.5 m (27 ft 9 in)
Propulsion:	two diesels delivering 12,000 bhp to two shafts
Speed:	18 knots
Endurance:	22,250 km (13,845 miles) at 14 knots
Armament:	3 x twin 4 in (101 mm) guns, up to 8 x 2 pdr AA guns and up to 12 x 20 mm AA guns.
Capacity:	two LCMs, 12 LCAs, 232 landing craft crew and 1,087 soldiers
Crew:	291

Above: American landing craft heading inshore for the Salerno landings, covered by the British Fiji class cruiser *Mauritius*, 9 September 1943. German reaction was fast, reinforcements rushing into the area and Naples was not taken until 1 October.

'drowned' vehicles and damaged assault craft.

Following Dieppe, the British began to build assault forces around a specific army formation, typically a division. For this, the requisite craft were assembled and exercised under a designated senior naval officer. To facilitate close co-ordination and rapid decision-making, the commanders and staffs of all involved services were co-located in a designated Headquarters Ship, usually a small passenger liner with the necessary accommodation and added communications. This concept, too, was borrowed by the Americans, who went on to convert new hulls specifically for the purpose.

The North African landings

In November 1942 the Allies invaded North Africa (Operation 'Torch'). Meticulous planning was essential for, from the United Kingdom alone, six advance and six assault convoys needed to be sailed for landings around Algiers and Oran. From the United States came three convoys for simultaneous landings on the Atlantic

coast, at Lyautey, Fedala and Safi. Groups had varying speeds and distance to travel, yet all had to arrive on time. Secrecy needed to be preserved.

In these pre-LST days the rapid availability of a port was still essential and, at Algiers, Oran and Safi, the ports were rushed by pairs of small warships. At Safi, the Americans were successful and soon had tanks rolling ashore over the quay. British attempts elsewhere met with fierce resistance and failed with great loss of life. The situation was retrieved by support ships targeting forts and batteries, using aerial spotting, as Vichy French resistance stiffened with daylight.

Surf proved a problem, particularly on the Atlantic coast, and coxswains obviously needed better training, both to set down their charges in the correct place and to avoid wrecking their craft in doing so. At Casablanca and Oran French naval units fought back but suffered great loss for little return.

On the Mediterranean coast, rapid hops were subsequently made eastward to seize the ports of Bône and Bougie. These outstripped available air cover and enemy aircraft were able to inflict significant losses on shipping laying offshore.

Amphibious assaults in the Mediterranean

Above: Preparing LCAs for the Salerno landings. The British Eighth Army crossed from Sicily to Calabria on 3 September: the amphibious assault at Salerno was intended to take Naples and prevent the Germans establishing a defensive line in the south of Italy.

Right: Troops and equipment including a 40 mm Bofors AA gun come ashore at Salerno. The landings were conducted by the US 5th Army (US 6th and British 10th Corps) commanded by Lt.General Mark Clark.

As North Africa was being cleared, following 'Torch', the planners had just eight months to prepare for the next assault. This was the obvious step to Sicily (Operation 'Husky') although great efforts were made to convince the enemy that the blow would fall elsewhere. Again, the landings were separated into primarily American and British zones, for where the Allies co-operated, they rarely integrated. The assault, by two British army corps and a Canadian division, and the American 7th Army, respectively east and west of Cape Passero, the island's southerly point, was designed to seize the necessary airfields and east coast ports quickly.

Another small miracle of synchronisation brought together 15 British convoys, originating from points between Malta and the Clyde, and seven American convoys, all from North Africa. A huge difference was made by the availability of over 500 assorted LST, LCT and LCI (L), which made the immediate capture of a port unnecessary.

For fire support, and as a precaution against any foray by the Italian fleet, six battleships and 15 cruisers were available. An active submarine threat was met by over 160 destroyers and escorts, which accounted for a dozen of the enemy. Three years of war had left the waters heavily mined and 40 sweepers were continuously at work.

To guide the final stages of the pre-assault phase, several Royal Navy submarines acted as pre-positioned navigation beacons. The apparently benign weather conditions were offset by a stiff breeze. In the British sector, this disrupted a pre-landing assault by gliders, half of which fell into the sea. A heavy surf caused problems for small craft but, fortunately, resistance was light. Unsuspected sand ridges caused the LSTs to ground too far from the water's edge and unloading proceeded slowly through the use of amphibious vehicles (six-by-six wheelers, designated DUKW, but known universally as 'Ducks').

In the American sector, the pre-landing assault was by parachute and, although well scattered by the wind, it was effective, despite quickly organised enemy counterattacks. The beaches here were exposed to very heavy surf and were also well mined. Close air support was not functioning well and naval gunfire sufficed until artillery and armour were ashore in strength.

The five-week Sicilian campaign was conducted very much along the coasts, so naval support was continuous. A major departure from Pacific experience was that the enemy conducted a skilful, fighting retreat rather than defending to the last man. Finally, covering the Messina Strait by massed batteries, the Germans defied Allied

Above: M4 Sherman tanks await loading aboard LSTs at Bizerte. The Allied landings in the Mediterranean further refined amphibious landing techniques, although vigorous German responses threatened to defeat the landings at Salerno and Anzio.

Left: The South African contingent at Salerno included 1991 Swazi smoke company, seen here awaiting embarkation at Castellammare.

Right: Tracer fire lights up the sky off Salerno as British warships open up on German bombers attacking the beachhead. *Luftwaffe* intervention included Dornier Do-217s which sank the battleship *Roma* with FX.1400 glider bombs.

superiority in spiriting away to Italy over 100,000 troops and 10,000 vehicles. For this the Germans made great use of the ubiquitous Siebel ferries, sectioned, single-deck motorised lighters that could be transported overland and re-assembled for coastal, esturial or riverine activities.

As the long, mountainous peninsula of Italy was a defender's dream, it made sense to the Allies to exploit maritime supremacy by mounting outflanking attacks along the coast. The first such, at Salerno (Operation 'Avalanche'), went in a bare three weeks after Sicily had been secured. Landing craft were still heavily in demand ferrying the British Eighth Army across the Messina Strait, American LSTs were being withdrawn to other theatres and resources were already being assembled for the invasion of northern France, yet nine months away. Hasty preparation also caused confusion through changes of plan.

Above: 'C' company, 2nd battalion, Northants regiment on the quayside at Catania waiting to embark on landing craft for the Salerno landings.

Between Salerno and Paestum the flood plain of the Sele river offered a rare 20 miles of beach perfect for amphibious assault. Its possession would threaten the rear of Axis armies to the south and facilitate the taking of the great port of Naples to the north. These facts, however, were equally obvious to the enemy.

Salerno was a two-corps landing, the British charged with seizing quickly the strategically-important

Montecorvino airfield while the Americans on their right, concentrated on taking the high ground that commanded the plain. While 15 convoys were involved, most could now be more conveniently sailed from North Africa, staging via Sicily to refuel the short-legged assault vessels.

Again, the pre-dawn landings attracted little initial opposition but, as daylight strengthened, so did the enemy's artillery fire. Problems arose in that the very fluid situation ashore prevented forward observers from functioning efficiently. Rather than heavy warships, therefore, it was destroyers, standing well inshore, that were most effective in fire support.

Salerno was also at the limit of fighter cover, and a dearth of fleet carriers saw British CVEs being substituted to provide initial air support. In the very calm conditions, their speed was insufficient to safely operate their high-performance, but very fragile, Supermarine Seafires, whose attrition rate was frightening.

A new menace to offshore shipping arrived in the shape of German radio-controlled glider bombs. The veteran battleship *Warspite* was gravely damaged by one of three aimed at her while, potentially more serious, the British headquarters ship was also identified for attack. She escaped damage, but the incident demonstrated the

hazard of concentrating assets in one hull.

While Salerno was, initially, touch-and-go, the situation stabilised after five days' hard fighting. In a little over a fortnight, Naples was captured. The Germans ascribed the Allied success to air superiority and naval gunfire support.

An interesting counterpoint to these large-scale strategic operations was the occasional use of special forces in tactical moves. Unlike the US Marines, British commandos had no organic artillery, armour or logistic support. Shortly after the Salerno breakout, a formation was landed behind German lines around the port of Termoli on the Adriatic coast. The retreating enemy had

intended to make a stand behind the Bifurno river but, with the Termoli force now in his rear, his retreat continued.

With the onset of winter the Allied advance became bogged down before the so-called 'Gustav line', the enemy, defending from behind the fast-flowing Sangro and Garagliano rivers. To outflank this line a further major landing (Operation 'Shingle') was made near the small port of Anzio, only 30 miles from Rome, in January 1944.

Landing craft were again in very short supply, and even to put two divisions ashore, units had to be assembled from as far away as the Indian Ocean. This

Above: The invasion fleet en route to Salerno, barrage balloons overhead to discourage low level air attack. The operation was timed to coincide with Italy's changing sides, but the German forces in the peninsula anticipated their allies' defection. Although few Italian units offered much resistance, the Germans were able to rush enough troops to the Naples area to halt the Allied advance.

small force was behind about ten enemy divisions, strongly entrenched behind the Garagliano so, not surprisingly, Anzio was for long only an armed pocket, very expensive for the Navy to maintain and build up.

The D-Day landings

News of a rather superfluous assault on the island of Elba and, indeed the taking of Rome itself, was eclipsed in June 1944 by the long-awaited invasion of northern France. Knowing that any major Allied foothold here would, eventually, result in his defeat, the enemy had made much of the defences of the 'Atlantic Wall' and 'Festung Europa' but, in truth, the coastline was too extensive to defend thoroughly at all but the most vulnerable points. Two German armies were thus held back, ready to be hurled at the location of a major assault.

The Allied requirement was to establish a deep beachhead, a massive armed camp from which an eventual breakout would be made. While encouraging the enemy belief that they would require a major port to do so, the Allies quickly constructed the huge concrete and steel elements of a pair of harbours. These, the 'Mulberries', would be towed across the Channel and sunk in position to form temporary ports in both British and American sectors. Complementing these were the 'Gooseberries', expendable ships which would be sailed over and scuttled bow to stern in shallow water to form a virtually indestructible breakwater.

A huge programme of deception was initiated to keep the Germans guessing regarding the place and time of the invasion. Air supremacy, aided by the short distances involved, enabled extensive damage to be caused to the enemy's road and rail communications, aimed at preventing the deployment of his reserve. Efforts were deliberately spread widely to disguise the area of particular interest.

As usual in European assaults, Operation 'Overlord'

Right: American LCMs pass the US LCI-323 and an LCT off the invasion beaches, 6 June 1944. Within 16 hours, over 130,000 Allied troops were landed in Normandy.

Left: The guns that sank the *Bismarck* engage German positions ashore at Normandy, June 1944. *Rodney* had bombarded targets near Oran in 1943, exposing problems with the fuze of the 16 in (406 mm) HE round. Firing the new HE shell, *Rodney*'s guns had a range of 23 miles (38 km).

Right: Battle ensign flying, the Leander class cruiser *Ajax* bombards German gun batteries inland from 'Gold' beach, Normandy. Seven battleships, two monitors and 23 destroyers provided fire support for the assault on 6 June.

involved separate American and British/Commonwealth beaches. Its major difference was one of scale. On 6 June 1944, four corps were to land over some 50 miles of beach. By day 10, 500,000 personnel, 80,000 vehicles and nearly 200,000 tons of stores would be ashore.

Its success did not mean that it ran perfectly. Despite naval support gunfire being available from up to nine battleships and heavy-calibre monitors, 24 cruisers and 76 destroyers, prolonged pre-assault bombardment was not possible due to the need for surprise, and many critical strongpoints were untouched. Enormous numbers of aircraft were on call but the skilled close support developed by Marine aircraft in the Pacific was lacking. Last-minute saturation of beaches by rocket- and gun-armed support craft was, as usual, a tremendous morale-booster but could not destroy either beach obstacles or strongpoints.

'Overlord' was meticulously planned, but lacked the

cohesive force of an experienced team such as the Spruance-Turner-Smith combination in the Pacific. American requests for LVTs were over-ridden in favour of the less-versatile DUKWs, and at the expense of many heavily-laden troops having to wade ashore under fire through choppy, waist-deep water.

As German reserves endeavoured to move forward to the invasion beaches, heavy-calibre naval gunfire, directed by aerial spotting or forward observers, struck them up to 17 miles inland. Enemy reports attest to its shattering and demoralising effects.

As if to demonstrate the puny nature of even the greatest enterprises of man a three-day onshore gale blew from 19 June, 13 days into the operation. The American Mulberry was wrecked, as were 800 various craft. Urgently-needed supplies fell by some 80 percent. With air operations badly affected, enemy ground forces managed to deploy. Had it occurred just a week earlier, 'Overlord' might well have been a costly disaster. As it

Above: British troops examine a German strongpoint knocked out during the D-Day landings. Protected by thick layers of reinforced concrete, this anti-tank gun was intended to destroy landing craft as they approached the beach.

Right: A knocked out *Sturmgeschutz* assault gun in Normandy. Naval gunfire support was often critical in stopping German counter-attacks as well as preparing the ground for the next phase of the Allied advance.

was, by the time that the naval side of the operation was wound down in early July, over a million troops were ashore.

Difficult to justify strategically, but intended to put yet more pressure on a retreating enemy, was the August 1944 landing in southern France (Operation 'Dragoon'). On a smaller scale, but every bit as savage a fight as anything experienced in the Pacific, was the European

theatre's last amphibious operation, that to secure the Dutch island of Walcheren.

The great Belgian port of Antwerp was taken by advancing Allied forces on 4 September 1944 but, while urgently required, was unable to be used as long as its approaches were commanded by the enemy, well entrenched on the islands to the north. Described as saucer-shaped, with dunes ringing a hinterland that lay below water level, Walcheren had been an inaccessible, muddy wilderness since the Royal Air Force breached

its sea defences shortly before. The gap, at Westkapelle, was flanked by German medium-calibre batteries, sited over about one-third of the island's periphery.

A veritable forest of beach obstacles required daylight assault, but this was on a November day so murky as to severely hamper naval and air support, and even that of artillery from across the river. A diversionary attack on Flushing was successful, but too limited in scope. Four commando groups were landed about the gap. They were almost totally reliant upon the support of 27

rocket-and-gun-armed landing craft. These responded magnificently, pressing right in and, when peppered to the point of foundering, were run ashore to continue the fight from the beach. The invaders triumphed at a cost of nearly 8,000 casualties. Of the support craft just seven returned. Walcheren, together with nearly 30,000 prisoners, was secured and the way to Antwerp opened for the minesweepers to clear.

US forces land at Butaritari beach in the Gilbert islands, under cover of naval and air bombardment 20 November 1944. 'Makin taken' was General Smith's succinct signal 72 hours later.

Amphibious operations in the Pacific

Mid-1942 saw the Japanese consolidating their new empire and, at a more circumspect pace, seeking to extend it. They had control over most of the Solomons chain and had put light forces on the island of Tulagi in order to build a flying-boat base. The Americans had, by now, recovered their composure sufficiently to be considering a limited counter-offensive. When they heard that their enemy had commenced construction of an airfield on neighbouring Guadalcanal, their hand was forced. If the Japanese were allowed to establish land-based air cover, the next advance would surely follow.

New construction and combat-ready troops were already being earmarked for the North African landings, still four months away. Operation 'Watchtower', the landing on Guadalcanal, had to be conducted with what was available, and was known to its participants as 'Shoestring'.

Guadalcanal

Three disparate regiments of US Marines, with supporting units, to a total of about 19,000 personnel, were given rapid training and embarked in 19 large transports and four of the useful little fast destroyer transports (APD), converted from veteran 'four-pipers'. Forces rendezvoused from the United States, Australia and New Caledonia. The major element of the covering force was the three-carrier task group commanded by Vice-Admiral F.J. ('Jack') Fletcher, whose name had already been made through the Coral Sea and Midway actions.

As with all Pacific amphibious operations, the Guadalcanal assault on 7 August 1942, was mounted in daylight but, with minimal opposition, most of the preceding bombardment fell on empty jungle. Build-up was slow, the 36-foot Higgins boats and the LCP (R), their ramped derivatives, being complemented by only a

few LCMs. Despite this, congestion on the beach was severe, as personnel had arrived expecting to fight rather than to shift stores. Nonetheless, by nightfall, 11,000 personnel were ashore and their objective, the half-finished airfield, secured.

Over the strait, in neighbouring Tulagi, however, the Americans encountered their first experience of a Japanese garrison's willingness to defend to the end. Of some 1,500 personnel, less than 100 were taken alive. The invaders suffered about 100 dead, a total, which would have been greater but for the very close support of a couple of destroyers which, under local pilotage, repeatedly came inside the encircling reef.

Furious Japanese air attacks developed on the second day but Fletcher's combat air patrols (CAP) covered the transports which, by keeping on the move, lost only one of their number. Fletcher then made the still-controversial decision to withdraw, ostensibly to refuel. At that time a force of enemy cruisers was making for Tulagi at high speed and, although it was spotted by a reconnaissance aircraft, it was mis-identified and no action was taken. In the small hours of 9 August it arrived, catching the Allied support force (of approximately equal size) totally by surprise. In what became known as the Battle of Savo Island the Allies were overwhelmed by gunfire and torpedoes.

Fortunately, the Japanese pulled out as quickly as they had arrived, leaving the transports, their primary objective, untouched. The amphibious force commander, however, now lacking both air and surface support, had no choice but to withdraw, leaving 16,000 marines to consolidate their position and to get the airfield in operational order. In this they succeeded, and

Below: The US landings on Guadalcanal were just in range of Japanese aircraft based at Rabaul. This Mitsubishi G4M 'Betty', seen from the destroyer *Ellet,* was brought down off Tulagi on 8 August.

Right: Japanese attempts to reinforce or supply their troops on Guadalcanal were constantly frustrated by the 'Cactus Air Force' flying from Henderson Field on the island. The *Kinugawa Maru* was beached after a US air attack on 15 November 1942.

Entering service in 1942, the Higgins 78-ft boats were one of the main types of PT boat used by the US Navy in World War II. Over 200 were built, and were heavily involved in the Solomons and Philippines operations.

the six-month struggle for Guadalcanal began.

As far as it had been applied, the manual had worked well, but Fletcher's withdrawal had almost proved fatal. The powerful response of the small Tulagi garrison had convinced the shore commander that future assaults in the teeth of an organised defence should be avoided but this would prove to be difficult on small Pacific islands.

Of critical importance had been the partnership between the amphibious force commander, Rear Admiral Richmond K.Turner, and commander of the V Amphibious Force, Major-General Holland M. Smith. Both robust characters, their relationship always bordered on the explosive, but their joint expertise

would be crucial in the great enterprises that lay ahead.

In competition with other enormous American war programmes, that for amphibious warfare craft seemed, to those involved, to be perilously long in coming on stream. The first ten of the invaluable LSTs entered service at the end of 1942 but, in support of the Allied 'Germany first' policy, were sent to European waters. In the Pacific theatre, a combination of LSTs and LCTs was first used at Rendova, assaulted on 3 June 1943 as the Americans moved back up the Solomons chain.

With tanks deployed in small numbers in the Pacific, LSTs were available to put personnel and stores straight onto the beach, by-passing the risky and time-

consuming trans-shipment from attack transports and cargo ships. In early operations, LSTs took trucks ready-loaded for rapid disembarkation. As this resulted in a low utilisation factor the procedure was changed to loading cargo at the after end of the tank deck, leaving the forward end for pre-loaded trucks, which would then make return trips to discharge the vessel.

The bulldozer proved to be another vital acquisition, creating causeways where a shallow beach gradient caused LSTs to ground too far from the water's edge. Shortly before beaching, an LST would release a kedge anchor from her after end. This would assist in holding her head-on to the beach and, if required, in hauling off.

Yukikaze Data

Displacement:	2,035 tons standard
Dimensions:	118.45 m (388 ft 7 in) x 10.8 m (35 ft 5 in) x 3.76 m (12 ft 3 in)
Propulsion:	two sets of geared steam turbines delivering 52,000 shp to two shafts
Speed:	35 knots
Endurance:	9,250 km (5,748 miles) at 15 knots
Armament:	5 x 127 mm (5 in) guns, 4 x 25 mm AA guns, 8 x 610 mm (24 in) torpedo tubes
Crew:	240

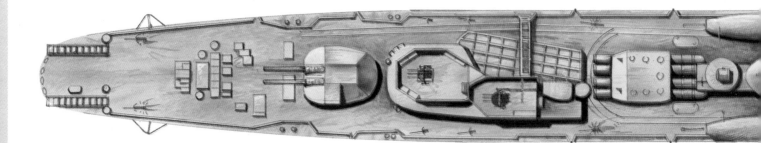

Higgens 78 ft boat Data

Displacement: ....35 tons
Dimensions: ....23.7 m (78 ft) x 6.32 m
(20 ft 9 in) x 1.52 m (5 ft)
Propulsion: ....three petrol engines delivering
4,500 bhp to three shafts
Speed: ....41 knots
Endurance: ....555 km (345 miles) at 41 knots
Armament: ....4 x 533 mm (21 in) torpedoes,
one 40 mm gun and two 20 mm guns
Crew: 17

In the south-west Pacific, commencing with New Guinea, III and VII Amphibious Forces were concerned mainly with shore-to-shore hops. Here, the APD destroyer conversions proved invaluable for the insertion of up to 250 marines, using their LCP (R)s. (Most of the LVTs were reserved for Nimitz 'V Phib' in their trans-Pacific island-hopping campaign).

Following the spearhead came LCTs with light armour and shore party engineers, and LCIs with the infantry. American LCIs were not ramped, using instead personnel gangways, or brows, on either bow.

At the end of 1943, the first Landing Ship Dock (LSD) entered service. A self-propelled, ship-fronted

Above: USS *Helena* fires her last salvo before succumbing to Japanese torpedoes during the action off Kolombangara, 5 July 1943. Landing troops and supplies under cover of darkness gave the Japanese navy ample opportunity to demonstrate its prowess at night-fighting. Only by mid-1943 did superior US radar and new tactics begin to erode the Japanese advantage.

The US amphibious landings in the Solomons triggered a long series of night actions between surface forces. Armed with the best torpedoes in the world, Japanese destroyers were especially dangerous and inflicted several sharp defeats on Allied forces. Illustrated here is the *Yukikaze*, the only one of 18 Kagero class destroyers to survive the war.

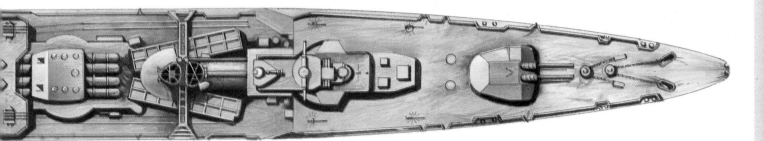

Data (LSD1-8)

Displacement:	4,270 tons standard and 7,950 tons full load		Armament:	1 x 127 mm (5 in) gun (US ships) or 1 x 76 mm (3 in) gun (British) plus up to 6 x twin 40 mm AA and up to 16 x 20 mm AA guns
Dimensions:	139.5 m (457 ft 9 in) x 22 m (72 ft 3 in) x 5.3 m (17 ft 6 in)			
Powerplant:	two sets of reciprocating steam engines delivering 11,000 ihp to two shafts		Capacity:	two LCT(3)s or LCT(4)s or three LCT(5)s or 36 LCMs, landing craft crew and 263 troops
Speed:	17 knots		Crew:	254
Endurance:	14,830 km (9,215 miles) at 15 knots			

floating dock, the LSD was virtually a one-ship assault force, being able to accommodate in its well such combinations as three small or two large pre-loaded LCTs, 14 LCMs or 41 LVTs. Complementary troop transports and cargo ships were, nonetheless, still required.

The island hopping campaign

As the south-west Pacific forces toiled toward their ultimate goal of the Philippines, Nimitz addressed the problem of taking the direct route across the Mandates to Japan. The major island groups had names that would become chillingly familiar, Gilberts, Marshalls, Carolines and Marianas.

Rising barely above the ocean's surface, each group included only one or two islands large enough to be of strategic use. It was Nimitz'ss intention to take only these, bypassing any others that might be occupied, and isolating them to 'wither on the vine'.

In defiance of the Washington agreements, Japan had developed suitable islands to create a network of airfields, lagoon-based flying boat stations and forward fleet facilities. Although Nimitz's resources were not infinite, and operations would necessarily have to be undertaken one at a time, planning overlapped to shorten the timetable. The Gilberts would need to be taken first, as they lay between the Allied-occupied Ellice group and the Marshalls. The only three islands of significance - Tarawa, Makin and Abemama - were over 700 miles from the nearest Allied airfield, and only in October 1943 would sufficient carrier strength be available as a substitute. With a promised seven new fleet carriers and seven assorted auxiliary carriers, Nimitz planned to move in the November. Logistics were formidable, the Gilberts requiring 35,000 assault troops and, just ten weeks later, the Marshalls some 85,000.

Betio, Tarawa's main component, was the objective of the 2nd Marine Division and would be the first major

Below: The US LST-341 beached on Segi Point, New Georgia in December 1943. The superstructure has been camouflaged and netting hung from her midships ventilators.

USS *Belle Grove* was the second vessel of the first
class of American LSDs (Landing Ship Dock). Although
built in large quantities for the US Navy since 1942, the
design was British and the first examples were built by
US yards for the Royal Navy. However, while 7 were
ultimately supplied to the British, the US Navy acquired
20 for itself. Effectively a self-propelled dry dock, the
LSD idea was the inspiration behind the Ro-Ro cargo
vessels of today.

Above: The Gleaves class
destroyer USS *McCalla* the
day before she
commissioned, 26 May 1942.
The camouflage scheme was
widely used by US destroyers
in the Solomons campaign.
McCalla survived the war to
be sold to Turkey in 1949,
serving until 1973.

Left: Some of the 4,500
Japanese naval troops and
construction teams killed on
Tarawa, November 1943.
Their commander, Rear-
Admiral Keiji Shibasaki was
killed on the first day by US
naval gunfire, but resistance
lasted for three days. Only 17
Japanese were taken prisoner.
The US 2nd Marine division
lost 997 dead, 88 missing
and 2,233 wounded.

test for amphibious war theory. A scrawny triangle in shape, it was perhaps two miles (3200 metres) in length and, at its widest point, some 600 yards (550 metres). Powerfully dug-in, in a web of mutually-supportive strongpoints, were about 4500 combatants, commanded by a rear-admiral.

Tidal predictions indicated that, at H-hour, there would be insufficient depth to float LCVPs over the surrounding reefs. Holland Smith relied instead on 120 LVTs, some new, others already well-worn. His intention was for them to land the first wave and then to return to the reef and off-load the next wave from stranded LCVPs. Turner hated the slow-moving amphibians, and only a major showdown with Smith changed his mind.

Above: The heavy cruiser *Minneapolis* lost her bows to a Japanese torpedo during the night action off Tassafaronga in November 1942. She is seen here on passage to Pearl Harbor for repairs. Three of her sisterships were sunk in the disastrous defeat at Savo Island two months earlier.

Left: USS *President Jackson* (AP-37) turns hard to port as Japanese aircraft from Rabaul pounce on American shipping off Guadalcanal, 12 November 1942. On the right, a Japanese aircraft has just crashed into the cruiser *San Francisco*. The next night, Japanese surface forces returned in force, two battlecruisers shelling Henderson field but losing one of their number in a furious close quarter battle with US cruisers and destroyers.

USS Ancon Data

Displacement:	13,910 tons
Dimensions;	132.59 m (435 ft) x 19.2 m (63 ft) x 7.32 m (24 ft)
Powerplant:	steam turbine delivering 6,600 shp to one shaft
Speed:	17 knots
Armament:	2 x 127 mm (5 in) guns, 8 x 40 mm guns, 20 x 20 mm guns
Crew:	507 plus 368 HQ personnel

Below: Attempts to co-ordinate landings from warships had been fraught with communications problems, so dedicated headquarters ships were introduced. USS *Ancon* was a former liner converted to be the navy's amphibious force flagship. She served as the headquarters ship at Salerno, Normandy and Okinawa.

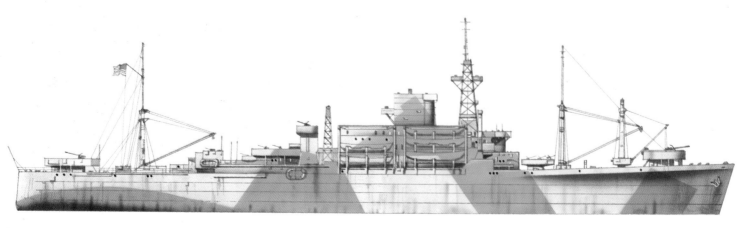

Above: The assault on Iwo
Jima, 19 February 1945.
Iwo became the bloodiest
battle in the history of the
US Marine Corps, the only
one of the Pacific war in
which American forces lost
more men than the
Japanese.

Right: Ashore were 22,000
Japanese commanded with
considerable skill by Lt.Gen
Kuribayashi, a cavalry officer of
the old school, previously
commanding the Imperial Guard.
He and all but 200 of his men
died. US losses were 6,891 killed
and nearly 19,000 wounded.

From 0440 on 20 November 1943, Betio was
subjected to a three-carrier air strike and a 2½ hour
bombardment from three battleships, four cruisers and
several destroyers. Unfortunately, the Pearl Harbor
veteran *Maryland* was headquarters ship, and the heavy
shocks of her salvoes repeatedly disrupted the rather
delicate communications of the force commanders. As a
result, the timetable lacked flexibility.

Organised in three waves, the LVTs had over six miles
to travel to the beaches. Having lost some cohesion,
they arrived about 30 minutes late, allowing the

Left: US commanders in the central Pacific (from the left) Admiral Nimitz, Lt.Gen Emmons, Vice Admiral Fletcher, Vice Admiral Spruance and Lt.Gen Buckner. The latter would become the highest ranking US Army casualty of the war, killed by Japanese artillery fire on Okinawa, 18 June 1945.

Below: Supplies are relayed ashore from landing craft on the beach at Iwo Jima. Massed *kamikaze* attacks on the fleet offshore failed to drive off the invasion forces and B-29s were landing on the island's airfield before the last members of the garrison had been eliminated.

defenders to recover from the bombardment and to concentrate forces at what were the obvious assault points. As they approached the beach, the tractors and their occupants took a terrible beating from barely-damaged strongpoints. Those vehicles not immobilised or destroyed outright were usually too badly holed to return to the reef as planned.

The fourth and fifth waves comprised LCVPs and LCMs, with further personnel, light artillery and armour. Stranded, heavily-laden marines disembarked on the reef and stumbled around in waist-deep water. Falling on the jagged coral, or wounded, they drowned under the weight of their equipment. Ashore, some 1500 survivors desperately sought to get to grips with their enemy, whose strongpoints yielded only to direct onslaught by flame-thrower or satchel charges.

Throughout the day, the issue remained in doubt, the huge offshore armada being unable to assist. Without communications, the force commanders were unable to stop transports from discharging as planned, so that LCMs, with as-yet unwanted cargo, milled around off the reef under fire. By the end of the first agonising day, the force ashore had been built up to about 5,000, but one-third were already casualties.

Betio's three-hundred bloody acres took 72 hours to clear, assisted by artillery landed on a neighbouring island. Over 1,000 Americans died. Ninety LVTs were lost, two-thirds of their crews becoming casualties.

Not since the Civil War had the United States experienced blood-letting on this scale, and a long road still lay ahead. Shocked, and often hostile, public reaction to Tarawa greatly influenced planning for the Marshalls.

In a preliminary move, unoccupied Majuro atoll was taken as a fleet anchorage and the remainder of the group by-passed for the main objectives of Kwajalein and Roi-Namur. Against these, the yet-unblooded 7th

Left: The battleship *Idaho* provides fire support for the Okinawa landings. Here, the Japanese commander did not bother to defend the water's edge, since US supporting fires were so heavy. Instead, the defences were concentrated inland, concealed from US observers.

Below: Landing craft on the beach at Okinawa, below Mount Suribachi. There were about 110,000 Japanese troops on the island and 95 per cent of them were killed, along with 150,000 native Okinawans (one third of the population).

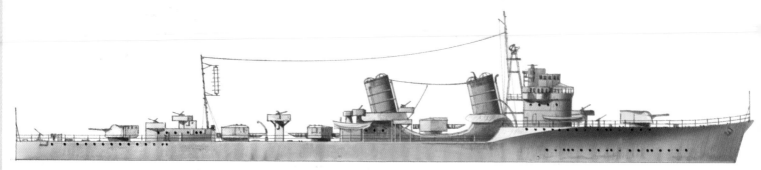

Above: The Japanese Fubuki class destroyers were well represented in the 'Tokyo Express' actions in the Solomons. From 1943 the increasing danger of US air attack led to the landing of the after super-firing 5 in turret in favour of an increased anti-aircraft armament. Up to fourteen 25 mm cannon were added.

Data (as built)

Displacement;	2,090 tons
Dimensions:	118.35 m (388 ft 3 in) x 10.36 m (34 ft) x 3.2 m (10 ft 6 in)
Powerplant:	two sets of geared steam turbines delivering 50,000 shp to two shafts
Speed:	37 knots
Endurance:	8,700 km (5,406 miles) at 15 knots
Armament:	6 x 127 mm (5 in) guns, 9 x 610 mm (24 in) torpedo tubes with 18 torpedoes
Crew:	197

infantry division and 4th Marine division would be deployed. Air reconnaissance from rapidly-established airfields in the Gilberts pinpointed the defensive schemes of the islands' 8,000 defenders. The new objective was to destroy, rather than just neutralise, the fixed defences and, to this end, Admiral Spruance could deploy six fleet and six auxiliary carriers, supported by six new battleships. In addition, seven veteran battleships and eight escort carriers were available for close gun and air support.

Three days of carrier strikes wiped out local enemy airpower; three nights of naval harassing gunfire wore

Above: US Army troops study the wreck of a Kawanishi H8K flying boat (Allied reporting name 'Emily') on Makin atoll. The Japanese established flying boat bases throughout their island empire and planned to use H8Ks for a raid on Oahu. These ten-man aircraft had a defensive armament of five 20 mm cannon and four machine guns and a range of nearly 4,500 miles.

Left: President Roosevelt with General MacArthur and Admiral Nimitz. His commanders pursued two different routes to Japan, which might have been a controversial waste of resources had the US not enjoyed such overwhelming industrial superiority.

Left: Amphibious tractors land on Enwietok in the Marshalls where the US bombardment has reduced the trees to stumps. These amphibians were a major advance, enabling US forces to overrun beach defences and press inland.

Above: US troops step ashore at Massacre Bay, Attu, in the Aleutian islands, 11 May 1943. A rapid advance from two beachheads outflanked the Japanese and overran the island, avoiding carefully-sited defences that covered the more obvious landing sites.

down the defenders. On the day, 1 February 1944, the supporting ships moved in to a range of under a mile, and the assault craft advanced under a howling umbrella of projectiles. Rocket-armed LCIs and air support joined in. Artillery, unobtrusively installed on neighbouring unoccupied islets, maintained a flanking fire. Unlike at Tarawa, the leading waves hit the beach with the defenders still dazed by the cumulative effect of 6,000 tons of explosive. Now-plentiful LVTs included versions with improved protection and turret-mounted cannon.

Roi-Namur was in American hands by the end of the second day, but Kwajalein took nearly a week, the orthodox Army-style way of war not suiting this application as well as the Marines' methods. Over 30 operations were necessary to subdue the whole, well-occupied atoll, but overwhelming firepower and much-improved planning combined to keep American fatalities to below 400. Fighting to the end, the Japanese

Left: Both US and Japanese forces sometimes combined airborne landings with amphibious assaults during the Pacific war. Here US paratroops drop on New Guinea, November 1943.

Left: Both US and Japanese forces sometimes combined airborne landings with amphibious assaults during the Pacific war. Here US paratroops drop on New Guinea, November 1943.

Below: B-25 Mitchell bombers of the 5th US Army Air Force sweep low over a convoy loaded with US Marines heading for Cape Gloucester, December 1943.

lost nearly 8,000 dead, less than 300 surrendering.

In June 1944 the American amphibious juggernaut moved on to the Marianas. Again three main islands needed to be assaulted - Guam in the south, Saipan and Tinian in the north. Of these, Saipan posed the severest test. No coral islet, it was 13 miles long and five miles wide, with a mountainous, forested hinterland. Offshore reefs posed their usual problems. Nearly 30,000 Japanese army and navy personnel garrisoned the island, which already supported a significant Japanese population. Excavation was easy and strongpoints abounded to provide a linked defence in depth.

The extent of the island, and the extensive tree canopy, resulted in a less than thorough aerial reconnaissance. The pre-assault bombardment was too brief, totally missing a shallow valley, running parallel with the landing beaches, which was packed with Japanese mortars and light artillery.

Initial assault was by the 2nd and 4th Marine divisions, but poor positioning left a half-mile gap between them. This was full of Japanese, admirably

Above: In another leapfrog move up the New Guinea coastline, US landing craft cross Humboldt bay en route to Hollandia. MacArthur repeatedly outflanked Japanese strongholds, exploiting US air and naval superiority to carve out new beachheads behind the enemy 'frontline'.

Left: A flame-thrower team passes the body of a Japanese rifleman during the battle for Bougainville in the northern Solomons. Flame-throwers were used extensively in the island-hopping battles, and were one of the few weapons able to deal with Japanese-held bunkers.

placed to enfilade the beaches.

Drivers of LVTs, under withering fire, in some cases refused to take their troops inland as ordered, returning without even waiting to discharge the supplies and ammunitions upon which they depended. Sixty-four LSTs deployed most of the 700 LVTs involved. Two LSDs carried LCMs pre-loaded with armour. For 24 hours, matters hung in the balance. Fire control parties were pinned down, their radios often dowsed in water, so much of the enormous firepower available offshore remained silent.

Once well ashore the invaders made steady progress but Saipan took 23 days to subdue. Hospital ships cut the toll of fatalities, but some 3,400 men were killed or missing and over 13,000 wounded. Nearly 24,000 enemy dead were counted but about 1,800, mostly Koreans, were persuaded to surrender.

Owing to the need to commit reserve forces on Saipan, the assault on Guam had to be delayed. The lesson re-learned, the pre-assault bombardment was so fierce that the equally-large garrison was driven into the hinterland, the island being taken for about one-third the cost.

As Guadalcanal had proved the catalyst for several

Left: US Marine anti-tank companies were equipped with M3 half-tracks armed with a 75 mm gun. By 1945 these were replaced by M7 105 mm self-propelled guns, issued on a scale of four per regiment. There was no danger of Japanese tank attack; what the Marines needed was armoured fire support to take on Japanese strongpoints.

Mogami class Data

Displacement:	12,400 tons standard
Dimensions:	203.9 m (669 ft) x 20.2 m (66 ft 3 in) x 5.8 m (19 ft)
Powerplant:	geared turbines delivering 150,000 shp to four shafts
Armour belt:	100 mm (3.9 in)
Armament:	10 x 203 mm (8 in) guns, 8 x 127 mm (5 in) guns, 8 x 25 mm AA guns, 12 x 610 mm (24 in) torpedo tubes.
Aircraft:	three floatplanes
Crew:	850
Class:	*Mogami, Mikuma, Suzuya, Kumano*

Above: The US 5th Amphibious Corps assaulted Saipan on 15 June 1944. Taking the Marianas would give the USAAF airbases within B-29 range of the Japanese home islands. Saipan fell on 9 July, one of the Japanese leaders to commit suicide there was Admiral Nagumo, commander of the raid on Pearl Harbor in 1941.

Left: Minneapolis, San Francisco and *New Orleans* bombarding Japanese positions on Wake island in October 1943.

significant naval actions, so the Marianas operation resulted in the Battle of the Philippine Sea. The Japanese fleet, with nine carriers and 430 aircraft, flung itself at Spruance's Fifth Fleet. Not only did the Americans have twice the carrier strength, however, but it was shielded behind a 'gun-line', backed by aggressive CAPs and equipped with new, proximity-fused ammunition. In what became known as the 'Marianas Turkey Shoot' the Japanese lost three carriers and about 450 aircraft (including land-based machines). The losses in aircrew could not be made good and, in the face of overwhelming and still-growing American carrier-borne air strength, the Japanese fleet was no longer an effective force.

Although the general trend of Nimitz's and MacArthur's advances convinced the Japanese that the Philippines would be the next major objective, the latter prepared four complex counter-plans to meet eventualities. During the weeks of late September and early October 1944, the American carrier forces scourged the central and northern Philippines, Okinawa and Formosa, claiming the destruction of an incredible 1,800 Japanese aircraft.

Japanese 8 in gun heavy cruisers proved deadly opponents in the Solomons, their powerful torpedo armament coming as a nasty surprise to Allied forces. The Mogami class illustrated here began life as equivalents to the US Brooklyns and shipped fifteen 6 in guns, but their armament was changed to ten 8 in guns in 1939.

Left: After 17 days' naval bombardment and airstrikes, US forces return to Guam on 20 July 1944. Elements of the Japanese garrison vanished into the jungle and were still being encountered after the war had ended. Two soldiers did not surrender until 1960.

Below: US Marines under fire on Guam. The island was secured by 10 August, by which time most of the 20,000 man garrison had been killed or committed suicide. US losses were 1,023 dead and 6,777 wounded.

On 20 October huge assault forces went ashore virtually unopposed on the central Philippines island of Leyte. It was expected that the enemy effectively devoid of local air power, would be forced to commit the remainder of his fleet. And so it proved.

The Japanese plan was to use their virtually aircraftless carriers as bait to lure away the American covering force. In its absence, powerful surface forces would converge simultaneously on Leyte from north and south. It very nearly worked, but resulted in a series of four actions, known collectively as the Battle of Leyte Gulf, in which the Japanese fleet was all but annihilated. Their mistake was to rely on land-based air power to cover their long approaches - apparently unaware that this air power no longer existed.

As the Philippines comprise an extensive and complex territory, much amphibious shipping was retained in the area, encountering two new hazards. One was the onset of the typhoon season. Having to keep the sea, the covering force (Admiral Halsey's Third Fleet) suffered considerably, losing three destroyers and having many ships damaged. Its carriers were so battered that 150 aircraft were shunted beyond repair. A second problem

LSTs 614, 667 and 555 land bulldozers and a crane at Lingayen Gulf, January 1945. Admiral Nimitz commented after the war that had he known how quickly the Navy construction battalions could build airbases, he would not have ordered so many assaults on Japanese-held atolls.

arose when escort carrier (CVE) groups, operating off Samar in support of forces ashore, found themselves being targeted by suicide aircraft. The *kamikaze* had arrived.

To the north, Nimitz moved on remorselessly. Occupation of the Marianas had put Japan just within range of the new Boeing B-29 'Superfortress' heavy bomber. As flights were so long, however, bomb loads were restricted and fighter escort was not possible. Attention thus focused on Iwo Jima, a 4 x 2 mile half-way house in the so-called Volcano Islands.

Left: USS *Cabildo*, seen here in 1960 was one of the second batch of LSDs built during the war, powered by steam turbines instead of reciprocating engines.

Below: Japanese positions at Hollandia, New Guinea are attacked by US aircraft in advance of the US landings, April 1944.

Iwo Jima

Forecasting correctly that the island's two airfields would prove irresistible to the Americans, the Japanese had garrisoned it with 20,000 men. Their orders were to make the place a fortress and to defend it to the last, giving the *Kamikaze* adequate time to destroy the supporting ships laying offshore.

A fortress it was. The volcanic cone of Suribachi brooded over both practical landing beaches, its easily-excavated flanks pocked with prepared positions for all type of artillery, ranging from medium-calibre naval guns to automatic weapons and mortars.

The garrison had honeycombed the island with a mesh of strongpoints, often reaching down to several levels, and interconnected by a labyrinth of passages. Able to resist the invader at the water's edge and in depth, the garrison could also literally 'go deep' to avoid the initial bombardment.

Because of the anticipated *kamikaze* threat, Spruance's Fifth Fleet carriers (eleven fleet and five auxiliary) shipped a larger-than-usual fighter complement. For three days before the assault, strikes were mounted on

Above: Many LCIs were modified to fire rockets, unleashing a massive barrage just before the assault was delivered. This LCI is firing on Morotai in the Moluccas, September 1944.

Below: The US advance across the central Pacific was sustained by underway replenishment on a scale no other navy could match. Here the destroyer *Patterson* fuels from *Makin Island* during the Lingayen Gulf operation, January 1945.

The Minekaze class destroyers were built just after World War I but were retained in service, most falling victim to US submarines during World War II. Several were converted as shown here, carrying up to four *Kaiten* suicide torpedo craft to attack American shipping off the beachheads.

Data (as built)

Displacement:	1,215 tons standard
Dimensions:	102.5 m (336 ft 4 in) x 9 m (29 ft 6 in) x 2.89 m (9 ft 6 in)
Powerplant:	two sets of geared steam turbines delivering 38,500 shp to two shafts
Speed:	39 knots
Endurance:	6,670 km (4,145 miles) at 14 knots
Armament:	4 x 120 mm (4.7 in) guns, 6 x 533 mm (21 in) torpedo tubes
Crew:	148

every Japanese airfield that could possibly intervene. For two days, five support battleships used heavy calibre fire to literally excavate shell-proof concrete gun emplacements from the rock flanks into which they had been constructed. Most, however, escaped detection.

On 19 February, the 3rd, 4th, and 5th Marine divisions went ashore under an unprecedented scale of rolling barrage, supplemented by aircraft armed with rockets and napalm. Covered by support landing craft, the massed LVTs touched down on schedule, only to encounter a natural obstacle in the beach being ridged high with soft, volcanic tufa fragments, which offered no traction. Vehicles bogged down, or concentrated around gaps blown in the obstruction by the pre-assault bombardment.

As the defenders emerged from their deep shelters, the marines came under a murderous fire. Virtually unsupported by their armour, immobilised on the beach as soon as it disembarked, they inched forward under the cover of naval gunfire, destroying the entrenched enemy

with flame throwers, grenades and satchel charges.

In deteriorating weather conditions, one beach became a lee shore, soon littered with broached and wrecked craft of all descriptions, and all still under mortar fire.

Iwo Jima was won yard by yard. It took six weeks and broke all records. Barely 200 of the defenders survived but American dead exceeded 7,000, 14 percent of them naval personnel. The 19,000 wounded created a logistic problem of their own. Even during the closing stages of the battle, however, Seabee battalions were working on the air strips and, on 7 April, the first P-51 Mustang fighters flew from them, supporting B-29 strikes on Japan.

Below: The minelayer *Aaron Ward* (DM-34) was hit by no less than five *kamikaze* suicide aircraft on 5 May 1945.

Right: Injured men are transferred from the *Franklin* after a *kamikaze* aircraft crashed through her flight deck on 19 March 1945.

The Battle of Okinawa

Before undertaking the ultimate and daunting task of invading the Japanese home islands themselves, Nimitz required a forward base, large enough to act as springboard and to offer subsequent support. Formosa, often favoured, was ignored for Okinawa, in the island chain of the Nansei Shoto. While only 340 miles from Japan's most southerly point, Okinawa was still 900 miles from the American-held part of the Philippines, the closest region from which a large force could be staged and supported.

Some 500 square miles in area, Okinawa is mountainous but supports a large population. More importantly, it boasted five airfields. The Japanese would never allow it to be taken cheaply, and a major matter of concern were the 120 airfields within flying range. In view of the need to acquire airfields quickly for defensive purposes, landings were to be adjacent to two of them, on a four-division front, and occupying five miles of coastline. In total, three marine and four infantry divisions would be employed, with one infantry division in reserve. Over 172,000 combatants, with 115,000 service troops, would be mobilised against an estimated 77,000 defenders.

For the assault, on 1 April 1945, eight transport squadrons were required. Each had a nominal strength

Above: Boeing B-29 Superfortresses on the Marianas from where they could reach the Japanese home islands. US strategic bombing knocked out most Japanese industry by summer 1945.

Below: The heavy cruiser *Portland* laying a smokescreen during the US landings at Leyte Gulf, the Philippines, October 1944. The Japanese attempt to stop this assault led to the greatest naval battle in history.

Right: Rockets stream into the sky from an LCI off Okinawa, March 1945. It was firepower like this that persuaded the Japanese to abandon their usual tactic of defending right at the water's edge.

of 15 attack transport (AP), six attack cargo ships (AK), 25 LSTs, ten LSMs and an LSD.

The battle of Iwo Jima had shown that fleet replenishment and support would benefit from a secure anchorage, and a new departure at Okinawa was the prior seizure of the small islands of the Kerama Retto. A bonus here was the capture of 250 suicide boats, not yet integrated into the defence scheme. By 1 April a flying-boat base had been established here by the Americans.

Great use was also made in later landings of Underwater Demolition Teams (UDT). These were 'frogmen', dropped from APDs to reconnoitre beaches, assess defences and demolish obstacles, erect temporary navigational aids and blast gaps in obstructive reefs.

Over the week before, the bombardment groups poured

5,000 heavy-and 35,000 medium-calibre rounds into the island. It remained silent and apparently deserted. The ships were threatened only by *kamikaze*, kept mainly at a distance by CAPs from the Fifth Fleet carriers.

The assault itself met no opposition, the Japanese having established themselves in the high ground - a tacit admission that seaborne landings now came in such strength as to be unstoppable at the water's edge. On

Okinawa, the invaders would be engaged well inland, beyond the effective range of naval support fire. The garrison would hold out for the maximum duration, exposing the ships offshore to weeks of *kamikaze* attack and a final, one-way sacrificial lunge by the rump of the Imperial Japanese Navy. This latter threat commenced with the group sailing on 6 April. Totally swamped by American aircraft, and devoid of its own air cover, it

lost the 'super-battleship' *Yamato* and several smaller units before aborting the mission.

Anticipating a *kamikaze* onslaught, Admiral Turner established a picket ring of 16 radar-equipped destroyers. In issuing early warning and directing CAPs, however, they drew attacks on themselves, several suffering severely.

During the 82 bloody days that it required to subdue the island, the fleet endured ten major *kamikaze* strikes, co-ordinated with torpedo and bombing attacks, in addition to almost daily individual suicide missions. For an expenditure of an estimated 2,800 aircraft, half of them *kamikaze*, the Japanese sank 21 ships and damaged 66, of which two thirds were never repaired. The 5,000 American naval and mercantile fatalities were nearly as numerous as the 7,600 killed ashore.

Only sheer weight of numbers enabled the United States to emerge triumphant and, when Okinawa fell, it acted as a catalyst for peace. Even the most die-hard of the Japanese war leaders now recognised the inevitability of defeat. Given the final warning in the shape of two nuclear bombs, they surrendered unconditionally. The final, apocalyptic landing on the Japanese home islands was, thankfully, never required.

Chapter 5 – Aviation at Sea

Early days

In 1910, the American pilot Eugene Ely became the first person to both take-off and land from a warship's deck in a heavier-than-air machine. A year later the British followed suit. In the early years of the century, aviation was still an exciting new concept and intrepid young men in the major fleets worked to ally aircraft with ship, for purposes yet ill-defined.

The war that soon followed forced the pace. Deeply-involved throughout, the Royal Navy had, by the armistice in 1918, harnessed the potential of aviation in the fields of reconnaissance, attack and defence from ships, and in land-based flying-boat support.

Reconnaissance extended the visual range of the fleet and gave an admiral the edge in decision-making. The primitive means available at the time limited this to seaplanes which, in good conditions, could be both launched and recovered from the sea itself. Despite patchy performance and poor communications, these also proved the possibilities of aircraft spotting for gunfire.

World War I saw the introduction of the first aircraft with folding wings, and the first successful attacks on shipping by air-dropped torpedo and on targets ashore mounted from shipboard. For reconnaissance the Germans relied extensively on Zeppelin airships. These combined long endurance with an emergency rate of climb that could be matched only by a high performance fighter. To counter the airship threat, the British favoured flying-off suitable aircraft from short, forward-mounted platforms and recovering them from the sea, whereon they eventually landed with the aid of auxiliary floatation. A natural extension of the take-off operation was the introduction of the catapult, a device that was more enthusiastically developed by the US Navy.

Recovery of aircraft remained the major problem, and following unsuccessful experiments with ships fitted with a flying-off deck forward and a landing-on deck aft, the British produced the first classic aircraft carrier in the 15,800-ton *Argus*. Her through deck, overlaying a hangar housing specialist aircraft, defined the shape of the carrier familiar today, but she was completed just one month too late to see active service in World War 1.

By April 1918 the Royal Naval Air Service (RNAS) boasted over 55,000 personnel and 3,000 aircraft, spread over nearly 150 separate commands. Unfortunately it

A Nakajima B5N bomber (Allied reporting name 'Kate') falls to the anti-aircraft guns of USS *Yorktown*. Aircraft carriers were to dominate the war in the Pacific, with powerful squadrons of battleships relegated to a supporting role. Japanese carrier aircraft had greater range than their American opponents, but did not have self-sealing fuel tanks or armoured protection.

Above: Seen here off North Africa in late 1942, the *Argus* was converted into a carrier in 1917 and her airgroup was to have been used to attack the German battle fleet in harbour during 1919.

was then integrated with the Royal Flying Corps (RFC) to form the integrated Royal Air Force (RAF). From this point until the late 1930s the Royal Navy therefore differed from the fleets of the United States and France in controlling its aircraft carriers but not their embarked aircraft. It was an arrangement that would have a huge impact on the potential of the Fleet Air Arm during World War 11.

At the armistice the US Naval Flying Corps could muster over 1,400 aircraft and the already-independent US Marine Corps a further 600. Early enthusiasts for flying, the French were not far behind with about 1,250 naval aircraft.

Between the wars

World War I had been fought on an unprecedented scale, and it was followed by an equally record-breaking run-down of military establishments in the 1920s. The RAF was cleansed of residual conflicting loyalties (at considerable saving to the Treasury) by being reduced to a total strength of just a dozen squadrons.

By contrast, the Royal Navy cleared away its wartime carrier conversions, and added the converted battleship *Eagle* of 22,600 tons, and the 10,900 ton *Hermes*, the first warship to be designed as an aircraft carrier from the outset. Together with the still-interim *Furious* the Fleet could thus deploy four carriers, but they were a disparate bunch, with greatly varying capability, capacity and speed. Not for the first time, it would not pay to be leader in a new field.

Despite its large air arm, the US Navy acquired its first true carrier only in 1922. The 11,500-ton *Langley* was converted from a surprisingly unsuitable 14-knot fleet collier. Japan, allied to both the United States and Great Britain during World War I, was assisted by both nations in the formation of a credible naval air service.

Her first carrier, *Hosho*, also dated from 1922, but was an ex-tanker displacing only 7,550 tons. France, despite her interest in naval aviation, had as yet no carrier other than the primitively-modified *Foudre*.Each of the major allied fleets were, at the time of the armistice, embarked on an extensive capital ship construction programme. None wished to relinquish its own, and not to drop behind the remainder was sufficient justification to continue. To effect a mutually face-saving way out of another naval arms race the United States convened the Washington Conference at the end of 1921. Rather than a cull of capital ship tonnage the result was a slaughter. Each signatory agreed future total tonnage limits and the rate and size of replacement hulls.

Inadvertently, the resulting treaty was to have a profound influence on the development of the aircraft carrier (and on the cruiser, but that is another story). The treaty's Article VII allowed the United States and the 'British Empire' each a total of 135,000 tons of carriers, Japan 81,000 tons, and France and Italy 60,000 tons apiece. Article IX limited the size of individual carriers to 27,000 tons but contained an important clause that permitted signatories to convert a pair of incomplete hulls which, otherwise, would have to be scrapped. These ships could each have a standard displacement of up to 33,000 tons. This clause was tailored to the requirements of the US Navy, allowing it to convert two of the planned 43,500 ton Lexington class battle-cruisers. They would, even then, never have been completed within tonnage limitations without involving a further obscure clause (buried at Part 3, Section 1(d) to be precise) that allowed a margin of 3,000 tons to improve protection against bombs or torpedoes. Ships already in service at November 1921 could be classed as 'experimental', and not be counted in the total tonnage ceiling.

Japan planned to rebuild two 40,000-ton Amagi class battle-cruisers, in the same way the USA would convert

the Lexingtons. However, work had scarcely commenced, when the nameship was heavily damage by an earthquake. The incomplete battleship *Kaga* was substituted, but she was shorter and, more significantly, some 3.5 knots slower than her 30-knot running mate. Together, they consumed 56,500 tons of the Japanese allowance.

Great Britain had never advanced its planned '1921 battle-cruisers' sufficiently to use them as bargaining chips in Washington. Under construction the Royal Navy had the *Eagle* and *Hermes* with a combined accountable tonnage of 33,500 tons. Lacking the large incomplete hulls available to the other navies, a the British nominated the Furious' two sisters, *Glorious* and *Courageous*, for conversion. They were not true battle-cruisers, but were capable of between 30 and 32 knots, being shorter and slimmer than the foreign conversions. As hangars created a massive freeboard, and flightdecks needed to be carried high with an easy motion, all of these conversions required a degree of bulging to improve their stability. There were several schools of thought about how best to exhaust boiler fumes, and similar divergence of opinion with respect to an island superstructure. The latter, feared by early fliers, actually proved to be the best compromise in accommodating uptakes and in controlling both the ship and flightdeck operations.

So it was that the US Navy acquired two enormous aircraft carriers almost by accident. They soon demonstrated the advantages of size: where the British and Japanese carriers could stow only 48-50 aircraft of the day, the Lexingtons could accommodate up to 90. Their 34-knot speed could be maintained and, being vastly superior to that of the battle fleet, taught the value of operating independently.

In 1919, with no serious enemy in sight, the British Government had adopted the notorious 'Ten Year Rule', which permitted defence spending to be based 'on the assumption that the British Empire would not be engaged in any great war during the next ten years'. Renewed regularly, the rule allowed the Treasury to become the prime arbiter of defence capability. It went on to inflict public sector pay cuts that caused great hardship, and such resentment in the Fleet as to bring about a mutiny.

Against this background, the Royal Navy strove to recover control of its air element, something the other navies had managed to retain. With the creation of the RAF, most of the Navy's able and enthusiastic pioneers of flying were lost to it. Even the post of Fifth Sea Lord, whose responsibilities were directed toward naval aviation, was abolished. To establish a positive identity for the new, integrated air force, it was given a new primary role in strategic bombing. This not only proved to be too rigid but also moved the service away from the

requirements of the navy and army that had spawned it.

The wasteful duplication resulting from two services specifying and ordering aircraft had been a powerful argument for the creation of a single, unified air force. Rather more wisely, and beyond the urgencies of war, the Americans created a joint board to define the boundaries of interest for each service, and to consider common and separate needs. Its progress was anything but smooth, but it survived. A naval Bureau of Aeronautics (BuAer) was also established to advise the Chief of Naval Operations (CNO) on developments.

The creation of a unified air service in Great Britain had, nonetheless made a considerable impression and, as Congress considered its potential advantages, the Army Air Service made a determined attempt to dominate it from birth. By steamrollering a series of inter-service bombing trials on expendable ex-German and American warships during 1922, Brigadier-General William ('Billy') Mitchell 'proved' that his aircraft could destroy any type of ship. As the bombing was conducted against stationary, unmanned targets, with no damage-control parties aboard, it of course proved very little. Nevertheless, the mere fact that such relatively primitive aircraft were able to sink battleships created a significant impression. One really valuable lesson learned was that the 'mining' effect of a near miss could actually prove more lethal to a ship than a direct hit.

American fleet exercises, including a high-profile 'bombing' of the strategically-sensitive Gatun Locks on the Panama Canal, soon demonstrated the carriers' ability to strike at shore targets without warning. They showed also that a carrier force commander would need tactical freedom with respect to the remainder of the fleet. The obvious possibilities were a great incentive to improve both the endurance and robustness of the aircraft themselves. A further, and very promising,

development was dive-bombing, adopted to compensate for the poor bombsights then available.

Despite the official view that 'the naval security of the Empire will tend to become more and more (dependent) on co-operation with aircraft operating partly from shore but principally from sea-going carriers', the Treasury sought to reduce such carriers from the Navy's permitted seven to only two. Sniped also by an impoverished Royal Air Force, British naval aviation during the 1920s was a sickly child. In addition to endless friction with respect to the provision and training of personnel afloat, the two services also had problems agreeing on aircraft. Due to a carrier's limited accommodation, aircraft were expected to be multi-role; they were defined by the Admiralty in terms of numbers and performance but by the Air Ministry for specification. The latter also oversaw production. For aerial units working from ashore the Air Ministry insisted on having control, except for specific naval operations. In place of the inter-service co-operation for which the Government had hoped, there developed a two-decade wrangle that finally resulted in the obvious conclusion that the Fleet Air Arm (FAA) should be under naval control. Only in May 1939, however, was the transition complete.

The Royal Navy followed the three Courageous-class conversions with only one other carrier in the interwar years. This, the Ark Royal, brought the number of decks to the agreed seven, and aggregate carrier tonnage to the treaty maximum. Even by the outbreak of war, however, the FAA could muster only 340 aircraft, two-thirds of which were carrier-borne.

The British assumed that the battle fleet was still the instrument by which actions would be decided, so the primary roles of the FAA were reconnaissance (to extend the fleet commander's visual range), torpedo

Above: Completed in 1938, *Ark Royal* was the first carrier to join the Royal Navy in nearly a decade. With armoured flight decks and hangars, she was still capable of handling over 60 aircraft although she never embarked her full airgroup.

Below: Laid down in 1929, the *Ryujo* was built as a 10,000 ton carrier to circumvent the Washington Treaty. Sent ahead of the heavy carriers in the battle of the eastern Solomons, 24 August 1942, she was sunk by aircraft from *Enterprise* and *Saratoga*.

Shokaku was built after Japan withdrew from the naval treaties and her design incorporated lessons learned from earlier carriers *Soryu* and *Hiryu*. The *Shokaku* and sistership *Zuikaku* formed the 5th carrier division in 1941 and took part in the Pearl Harbor raid.

Data

Displacement:	32,000 tons full load
Dimensions:	257.5 m (844 ft 9 in) x 26 m (85 ft 4 in) x 8.9 m (29 ft 2 in)
Propulsion:	Steam turbines delivering 160,000 shp to four shafts
Speed:	34 knots
Armour:	215 mm (8.5 in) belt
Armament:	16 x 125 mm (5 in) guns, 36 x 25 mm guns
Aircraft:	72
Crew:	1,660

Class: *Shokaku, Zuikaku*

attack (to slow an opponent sufficiently to enable him to be brought to action), spotting (to improve the accuracy of fleet gunnery) and air cover (to protect the fleet from enemy air attack). To torpedo attack was later added both level and dive-bombing. All the above roles were limited to assisting the battle fleet; it took the Americans and Japanese to demonstrate that carrier-launched air strikes were a weapon in themselves.

The Japanese regarded the reluctantly-accepted limitations of the Washington Treaty as consigning them to second class status. Their allowed total of 81,000 tons of carriers acknowledged Japan's position as the

dominant naval power in the western Pacific, but it rankled. In the course of their campaign in China, the Japanese used aircraft carriers as large transports, in addition to their more orthodox role of supporting military operations ashore. Japanese industry no longer built foreign aircraft under license but had developed its own competent designs, including carrier aircraft. There were already too few decks and, as the *Kaga* and *Akagi* had consumed nearly three-quarters of their allocated ceiling tonnage, the Japanese resorted to the small carrier. The 10,600-ton *Ryujo*, a 29-knotter completed in 1933 showed, however, that such ships were too limited.

World-wide condemnation of Japanese action in China led Japan to withdraw from the League of Nations in February 1933 and to renounce treaty obligations in October 1934. The already-funded 15,900-ton *Soryu* would, in any case, have breached agreed totals and the chance was now taken to increase the displacement of her sister, *Hiryu*, to 17,300 tons. Convinced of the value of carriers, the Japanese Navy had, by December 1941, taken delivery of the two large conversions *Zuiho* and *Shoho*, and the two 26,000-ton Shokaku class.

Continuing American interest in the rigid airship as a naval asset came to a premature end with the crash, in 1933, of the *Akron*. With her crew died Rear Admiral

William A. Moffett, the chief of the BuAer. It had been he who had steered naval aviation through its mauvais quart d'heure but, fortunately, a highly-capable replacement was available in Rear Admiral Ernest J. King, a later CNO, who enjoyed the personal support of a navy-minded President Roosevelt.

Having converted the Lexingtons, the General Board had to decide how to allocate its remaining 69,000 carrier tons. From the outset it disliked the limitations of small designs, typified by the *Hermes* and *Hosho*. The Navy wanted a high aircraft capacity together with a near-impossible 35-knot speed. The Board wanted a standard series so, bearing in mind the treaty-defined limit of 27,000-tons per hull, simple arithmetic dictated three, four or five hulls, each displacing 23,000, 17,250 or 13,800 tons respectively. Design studies showed that aircraft capacity increased rapidly with ship size, and that speed was very expensive. For instance, a 27,000-tonner capable of a still less-than-ideal 32.5 knots could stow 60 aircraft; by reducing her maximum designed speed by five knots she could accommodate 72 aircraft. High speed was deemed essential for guaranteeing adequate wind-over-deck and also to operate independently of the slow (21-knot) battle line.

With the Lexingtons yet to show their full potential,

Above: By 1939 British carriers were cursed with aircraft far inferior to US or Japanese equivalents, a qualitative gap that widened during the war. The Fairey Swordfish torpedo bomber seen here remained in service until 1945.

decisions were difficult but, like the Japanese, the US Navy opted for the maximum number of smaller decks. The next carrier, *Ranger* (CV 4) was, therefore, a nominal 13,800-tonner. Capable of a shade under 30 knots the *Ranger*, although so much smaller than the Lexington, possessed by careful design a similar hangar volume. To reach her designed speed she was very fine, and her 70 aircraft had to compete for limited parking space topside and accommodation below.

A weight-saving measure, which was to become a standard feature on American carriers, was to make the hangar deck the main strength deck, the flight deck being a light structure of wood planking laid on thin plate. This improved stability and allowed large apertures to be worked into the hangar sides which, in turn, permitted aero engines to be warmed-up below decks.

Once commissioned, the Lexingtons quickly emphasised the *Ranger*'s limitations, particularly by operating in high sea states. Too tight, the *Ranger*'s

design incorporated neither protection nor scope for later modification. The Americans thus used their remaining 55,000 allowable tons to build two carriers (*Yorktown* (CV5) and *Enterprise* (CV6)) to a practical 20,000 tons apiece. This was a minimum that allowed a maintainable speed of 32.5 knots, to incorporate an armoured hangar deck (to resist the growing threat of dive-bombing) and to accommodate an air wing of about 80 aircraft. The composition of the air wing varied but usually comprised about 20 percent each of fighters, strike and torpedo bombers, the remainder being scout/divebombers.

With the less than 14,000 tons remaining to them, the Americans produced the *Wasp* (CV7), a Yorktown diminutive. Shorter than the *Ranger*, she had fuller sections and a larger flightdeck area. She introduced the deck-edge elevator, which intruded into the useful space of neither hangar nor flightdeck. The penalty was lack of speed. In nil-wind conditions, aircraft required long take-off runs, reducing effective flight deck area and increasing the time necessary to launch a strike.

Successive updates of Plan Orange emphasised to American planners the critical importance of carrier aviation in a future war across the Pacific. Designs were

prepared for the emergency rebuilding of passenger liners and cruisers as small carriers. Equally air-minded, the Japanese and British were also looking at the same possibilities, the latter with a particular eye to commerce protection. A problem, which was to continue, was the remorseless growth in the size and weight of aircraft.

From 1933 the US Navy prospered from the hawkish support of influential people, including the President. The unlikely National Industrial Recovery Administration and Public Works Administration re-vitalised depressed shipyards with orders for 32 warships, including CV5 and CV6. A 1000-aircraft boost for the Navy and Marine Corps commenced. This was followed in March 1934 by the Vinson-Trammell Act which authorised a five-year fleet replacement programme. This was designed to renew and expand US Navy to the very limit permitted by the treaty which was, in any case, due to lapse and be re-negotiated in 1936.

The Japanese had been building to the limit of the treaty — quite legally — while the western democracies had not. As a result, the strength ratio was nearer to 5:4 than the 5:3 enshrined in the treaty. Although the Americans, too, were acting quite legally, such a large

Above: Victorious launches a Fairey Fulmar in Scapa Flow, March 1942. The Fulmar was a lumbering two-man fighter introduced in 1940 but hopelessly outclassed when it faced Japanese Zeros in 1942.

Right: Clearing ice from the forecastle of *Victorious* during operations in support of the arctic convoy PQ12, March 1942. The following year *Victorious* was in action in the South Pacific as part of a US Navy carrier group.

infusion of funds understandably had a serious effect on what moderate opinion remained in 1930s Japan. Having demanded, and been refused, a common upper limit for the two fleets, the Japanese announced at the end of 1934 that, once the treaty lapsed in 1936, they would no longer be so bound.

In 1938, as the pace quickened, the Americans extended the Vinson-Trammell Act. Work began on the design of what would become the extensive Essex (CV9) class but, as this would take an estimated 15 months, and a further deck was urgently required, a third unit of the Yorktown class was authorised. Completed in October 1941, the *Hornet* (CV8) built in just 25 months.

Below: The German aircraft carrier *Graf Zeppelin* was nearly complete in April 1940 when construction was stopped on Hitler's orders. Her airgroup was to have included 30 Junkers Ju-87 Stukas and a dozen navalized Messerschmitt Bf 109s. Loose in the Atlantic with raiders like the *Bismarck*, she could have posed a serious menace to Allied convoys.

Graf Zeppelin Data

Displacement:	33,550 tons full load
Dimensions:	262.5 m (861 ft) x 36.2 m (119 ft) x 8.5 m (27 ft 10 in)
Propulsion:	Four sets of geared turbines delivering 200,000 shp
Speed:	34 knots
Endurance:	8,000 miles at 19 knots
Armour:	100 mm (4 in) main belt
Armament:	16 x 150 mm (5.9 in) guns, 12 x 105 mm (4.1 in) guns, 22 x 37 mm guns, 28 x 20 mm guns
Aircraft:	42
Crew:	1,760
Class:	*Graf Zeppelin, Peter Strasser*

Faced with the near-inevitability of another war in Europe, the United Kingdom also reacted, laying down the first pair of carriers with protected flightdecks in 1937. The still-building *Ark Royal* had a two-hangar layout which increased aircraft capacity but also freeboard. Although the flightdeck was thus drier, it could not be armoured. Contrary to American practice, the flightdeck was supported by a double hangar wall along either side, and contributed to the strength of the hull girder. The arrangement reduced her practical aircraft capacity to a bare 60.

There arose the powerful argument, however, that her raison d'etre, her aircraft, were virtually unprotected from bombing. This was the reason for the new, 23,000-ton *Illustrious* and *Victorious* having the so-called 'armoured flightdeck'. The extra topweight meant that a second hangar was no longer feasible. Eventually, six generally similar units would be built, but their construction times (37 to 48 months for the first three, and longer for the later, and improved, *Implacable* class) were far longer than equivalent American ones. This almost leisurely building pace for fleet carriers, dictated mainly by a pressing need for A/S escorts, would greatly affect the striking power of the Royal Navy during World War II.

Of the remaining two signatories at Washington, only the French went ahead to build a new aircraft carrier. The only practical candidate for conversion was the incomplete battleship *Béarn*. She was hopelessly slow —capable of a maximum 21.5 knots — and her planned capacity of 40 aircraft was, in practice, nearer 25. With Germany no longer seen as a threat in the 1920s, the French primarily concerned with their traditional rivals, the Italians. The interests of both centred on the Mediterranean and, as each could base aircraft on either shore, there was little incentive to indulge in expensive carriers. In the event, the French would be in no position to rue this ill-judged decision but, for the Italians, it was to prove disastrous.

France reacted too late to the re-emergence of Germany as a blue water naval power in the late 1930s, laying down a pair of 18,000-ton carriers (*Painlévé* and *Joffre*) which had not even approached launching stage by the time of the German invasion in 1940.

The German navy came far closer to operating aircraft carriers. Taking Germany out of the League of Nations in 1934, Hitler repudiated the Versailles Treaty, with its

restrictions on armaments, the following year. To international surprise, Germany obtained British agreement to a 100:35 naval ratio. The German building plan was based on producing a 'balanced fleet' by 1942. It included two 22,000-ton aircraft carriers, of which the keels were laid in 1936. The first, *Graf Zeppelin*, was launched in December 1938. Designed to be capable of 33.5 knots, she was designed to stow a variable mix of 40 navalized Junkers Ju-87 divebombers and Messerschmitt Bf-109 fighters. Fortunately for the British, the 700 aircraft agreed for German naval purposes were obstructed by Hermann Göring, head of the Luftwaffe, who jealously guarded his responsibility for German military aviation. One major reason for the carrier's never commissioning was a lack of suitable aircraft. By the outbreak of war, only half the promised 27 squadrons of maritime co-operation aircraft were available for service.

Land-based air was vital to the operations of all the major navies but, in most cases, its effectiveness was reduced by inter-service rivalries. The Italian fleet was initially dependent upon about 100 aged Cant flying boats which, still under airforce control, shared few common procedures. Eventual Luftwaffe support should have rectified this state of affairs, but the Germans held the Italian fleet in contempt and preferred to use aircraft to support convoys directly. Italian naval activities thus suffered further, and the attempt to convert two passenger liners into aircraft carriers also came to nought.

In the United Kingdom, the Royal Air Force recognised the importance of maritime co-operation through the creation, in 1936, of Coastal Command. By the outbreak of World War II, a disparate range of aircraft was being replaced by American-built Lockheed Hudsons and the medium-ranged Sunderland flying boat. However, the command was still well below strength in September 1939 and lacked credible strike aircraft and torpedo bombers.

Right: France's only inter-war aircraft carrier, *Béarn* was converted from an incomplete Normandie class dreadnought in the 1920s.

Airpower in European and Atlantic waters

Operations here fell into two main categories: fleet support and anti-submarine warfare. (The latter has already been covered in Chapter 2.) In 1939 the Kriegsmarine was plunged into a war for which it was still greatly under strength. It had to avoid major confrontation, playing a subsidiary role as the U-boat offensive took its course.

The first opportunity offered to the Royal Navy was in April 1940, when virtually every German surface unit was mobilised for the invasion of Denmark and Norway. However, this bold and highly risky venture took the British by surprise, and the Allied response was piecemeal. Only one carrier, *Furious*, was in home waters but the *Ark Royal*, which had recently sailed for the Mediterranean, had left behind two squadrons of brand-new Skua dive-bombers. These were in the

Orkneys to bolster the Scapa flow defences but, operating at extreme range, attacked the German light cruiser *Königsberg* in the port of Bergen. Having landed a military force, she was still alongside with machinery problems when she was very neatly 'taken out' by precision dive-bombing that caused minimal collateral damage. It was a promising start for a technique that, somehow, was never to realise its full potential with the Royal Navy.

Militarily, the Allied counter-campaign in Norway was a disaster but the *Furious*, quickly reinforced by *Ark Royal* and *Glorious*, was active not only in supporting operations ashore but in ferrying RAF fighter aircraft to northern airfields. In the course of the inevitable Allied pull-out in June 1940, the *Glorious* became the second British carrier to be lost unnecessarily. Proceeding independently for no good reason, her flight deck was cluttered with RAF fighters which, it was later claimed, prevented her from keeping a Combat Air Patrol (CAP) aloft and an armed strike

Above: Argus and *Eagle* with battleship *Malaya* in the Mediterranean, March 1942, seen from the cruiser *Hermione*. The carriers were used to fly Spitfires to Malta, but it took four sorties to deliver just 31 aircraft as the carriers could not accommodate many fixed wing aircraft.

ranged. It is possible that, had she been following correct procedures, she could have greatly discomfited the prowling *Scharnhorst* and *Gneisenau*. In the event, she was sunk with heavy loss of life.

In this same month the Mediterranean became an active combat zone, as France was lost as an ally and Italy became an opponent. The latter had the fleet and airforce to dominate the theatre and *Ark Royal* was sent to back up the elderly *Eagle*. The 'Ark' was based on Gibraltar where, teamed with a battle-cruiser and supporting ships as Force H, she could operate both in the Mediterranean and the Atlantic.

The standard British torpedo aircraft was the Fairey Swordfish biplane, whose venerable appearance and,

indeed, performance belied the fact that it had entered
FAA squadron service as recently as 1936. Very little
torpedo-dropping practice had been undertaken pre-war,
and this resulting in a poor showing in Norway.
Paradoxically, the Swordfish's first torpedo targets in
the Mediterranean were not Italian but French. The fall
of France left powerful naval squadrons based on Mers-
el-Kebir near Oran in Algeria, and Dakar in Sénégal;
forces whose allegiance remained unknown. Despite
assurances by the French that the ships would never be
allowed to be seized by the Germans, the British could
not risk such an event.

At Oran, British persuasion failed and an ultimatum
was rejected. Force H, suitably reinforced, had the
unpleasant task of firing on its late ally. Air-dropped
magnetic mines failed to stop the battleship *Strasbourg*
breaking out and two half-hearted air strikes by six
torpedo aircraft apiece failed to score. Her sister,
Dunkerque, was beached with heavy-calibre gun
damage. As she was obviously repairable, a further six
Swordfish were despatched. One torpedo hit an armed
trawler laying alongside. As she sank, her complete outfit
of depth-charges detonated, damaging the battleship
further. Two more attempts to destroy the *Dunkerque*
completely were foiled by French fighter aircraft.

At Dakar, Swordfish from the *Hermes* scored a
torpedo hit right aft on the new battleship *Richelieu*.
The damage was beyond the capacity of the port to
repair. Considering the desultory nature of the French
defence, the result at neither location boded well for
future operations.

Despite the Royal Navy's acute shortage of carriers,
the *Argus* was fit only for training and, often in
company with the *Furious*, ferrying RAF fighters to
Malta, or Takoradi, whence they flew overland to Egypt.

Operations toward Malta brought the first contacts
with the Italians, who showed a marked respect for
carrier aircraft, even though their own bombers out-
performed them. The new, eight-gun Fairey Fulmar
proved disappointing as a fighter but was being
supplemented by purchases of the American Grumman

Above: Entering service in late 1938, the Blackburn Skua was the first monoplane operated by the Fleet Air Arm and was intended to double as a fighter. In 1940 Skuas flying to the limit of their range sank the cruiser *Königsberg* in Norway, the first dive-bombing attack to destroy a warship in action. Only 190 Skuas were ordered before the war, and after losses in Norway and France in 1940 the type was relegated to training duties in 1941.

Right: Seen from the bridge of her sistership *Euryalus*, *Cleopatra* makes smoke, during the second battle of Sirte, March 1942. Rear-Admiral Vian earned a knighthood for his brilliant defence of a Malta convoy, firstly against an Italian battle squadron, then against concentrated air attack. *Cleopatra* was hit on the bridge by a 6 in shell and *Euryalus* was to be straddled by 15 in shells from the battleship *Littorio*.

F4F Wildcat (initially called the Martlet in FAA service). These showed the toughness and reliability essential for service afloat, while their outfit of four 0.5 machine guns was more damaging than the British .303s.

HMS Eagle was based at Alexandria, attached to the Mediterranean Fleet. During her periods in port between operations her 18 Swordfish operated from airstrips ashore. As they worked first the North African, then the Red Sea, coasts they became highly proficient.

HMS *Illustrious*, first of the new 'armoured deck' carriers, completed in May 1940. Having worked-up, she joined the *Eagle* in one of the many convoys to Malta. The island's survival was vital to the defeat of Axis forces in North Africa, but its support was a matter of never-ending pain to the Royal Navy. Operations involved not only covering merchantmen from unrelenting land-based air attack and probing for the ever-present hazard of the U-boats, but also taking due precautions against a sortie of the Italian fleet. Italy's six new or modernized capital ships could out-run, out-gun and outnumber Admiral Cunningham's veteran battleships.

To redress this imbalance Cunningham planned a two-carrier strike on the southern Italian base at Taranto. Mishaps and damage reduced this to the *Illustrious* only, which shipped some of *Eagle*'s experienced Swordfish for the occasion. The attack was undertaken on the night of 11/12 November 1940 and involved only 21 aircraft. These struck in two waves, eleven torpedo carriers supported by ten bomb- and flare-droppers. As the latter distracted the defences the others used their low speed to weave at very low altitude around the cables of the many barrage balloons. Four hits, one of which did not explode, were scored on the exposed battleship *Littorio*, one each on the *Cavour* and *Duilio*. The small warheads of the 18-inch aircraft torpedoes and the shallow water saved the Italians from total loss, although the *Cavour* was never fully repaired.

For the loss of just two aircraft the Italians had been reduced to two operational battleships (the *Doria* was completing modernisation). Taranto did not, as has been claimed, inspire the Japanese attack on Pearl Harbor, which had been extensively war-gamed before the British operation. But it certainly emphasised the possibilities.

While the strike was a significant and economic success, the bulk of the enemy fleet had been obligingly lined-up, moored 'Mediterranean-style' and could have been overwhelmed by an air strike in credible numbers. Never was the absence of the *Courageous* and *Glorious* more keenly felt.

Identifying the Royal Navy as the principal threat to the survival of her armies in North Africa, Germany despatched Fliegerkorps X to Sicily in January 1941. This powerful Luftwaffe formation specialised in attacking shipping. Within days a force of its dive-bombers broke through the defences of the *Illustrious* and inflicted seven heavy bomb hits and near-missed once more. Patched up, she had to proceed to the United States for permanent repair.

Probably the worst injuries to be survived by any carrier, they did not prove fatal. *Illustrious* was saved by a combination of generally tough construction and the absence of uncontrollable fire — not by her protected flight deck. Three bombs (one 250 kg and two 500 kg) impacted beyond the hangar box, while no less than three more (two 250 kg and one 500 kg) exploded in or around the after elevator well. The lift itself was not armoured, but its well was isolated from the hangar by armoured screens. The seventh bomb, of 500 kg, was the only one to strike the armoured part of the flight deck, which it penetrated, exploding within the hangar. While the resulting fire was severe enough, it could not feed on the massed ranks of fuelled and armed aircraft usually found in American and Japanese carriers. Alongside at Malta the final hit by a 500 kg bomb penetrated the unarmoured after end of the flightdeck.

Commissioned about six months after the *Illustrious*, her sister *Formidable* was also sent to the Mediterranean. During the evacuation of Crete in May 1941 she, too, absorbed 500 kg bomb hits at either end of the flightdeck. The only permanent damage she suffered was inflicted by the mining effect of near-misses.

During the preceding March, a series of British military convoys had run from Egypt to Greece with no interference from the Italian fleet. Finally, chided by their German ally, it sailed a powerful squadron to a point south of Crete. Alerted by a Malta-based Sunderland flying boat, Admiral Cunningham left Alexandria with his three battleships and the *Formidable*. Finding no convoys but harassed by British light forces, the Italians turned for home. Cunningham's approach was unsuspected but, as the flagship *Vittorio Veneto* had a five-knot speed advantage over the elderly *Queen Elizabeth*, she would have to be slowed to make an engagement possible. A first attempt, with Crete-based Swordfish supporting the *Formidable*'s new Albacore torpedo-bombers, was unsuccessful. A second, of just five aircraft from *Formidable*, was co-ordinated with a high level bombing run by RAF Blenheims. Hit aft, the *Veneto* halted briefly but was soon making 20 knots again. As dusk deepened a final force of ten

Right: Victorious launches a strike of Fairey Albacores against the battleship *Tirpitz*, March 1942. The attack was frustrated by the pitifully slow speed of these obsolete aircraft, struggling to overtake a 30 knot battleship steaming into a head wind.

Above: The incomplete *Graf Zeppelin* lying under camouflage netting at Gotenhafen in 1942. Plans to complete her were dropped in favour of U-boat construction, and she was used as a storeship until 1945.

Albacores found the Italian squadron and, missing the flagship, immobilised the heavy cruiser *Pola*. Left behind, this ship was later joined by two sisters and a destroyer division. This force was discovered by the radar-equipped British force, which annihilated the Italian cruisers in a brief gunnery action which entered the history books as the Battle of Matapan. The *Formidable*'s aircraft were not fitted for nocturnal operations but had succeeded in the Fleet Air Arm objective of bringing an enemy to action.

British naval aircraft succeeded in the same mission just two months later when, breaking out into the Atlantic on a raiding cruise, the new German battleship *Bismarck* encountered and sank the British battle-cruiser *Hood*. Damaged by the *Hood*'s consort, the *Prince of*

Wales, the German turned back. Shadowed by British cruisers, she was closed by the third of the new carriers, *Victorious*. Her Swordfish scored a single torpedo hit which, after a shallow run in heavy seas, impacted on the armour belt, causing negligible damage. Contact with the *Bismarck* was then lost but, working on the assumption that she was making for a French Biscay port, the British re-located her after 31 hours. Ordered up from Gibraltar, Force H was well-placed for an interception and the *Ark Royal* launched a 14-Swordfish strike. In error, this attacked the cruiser *Sheffield*,

Below: 4.5 in (114 mm) ammunition being loaded aboard the British carrier *Victorious*. The development of proximity-fuzed ammunition greatly enhanced the anti-aircraft firepower of Allied warships 1944-45.

Right: Sailors shovel snow from *Victorious*'s 673 ft (205 m) flight deck while supporting convoy PQ12 to Russia. The battleship *King George V* steams ahead. This was to prove the carrier's only chance to engage the *Tirpitz* at sea.

fortunately unsuccessfully, and incidentally revealed that the British magnetic torpedo pistols malfunctioning. Chagrined, the carrier repeated the attack. In marginal weather conditions and fading light, two torpedoes found their mark. One damaged the *Bismarck*'s port propellers and jammed her rudders. Now slowed and steering erratically, the *Bismarck*'s fate was sealed. She was intercepted the following morning by British heavy units and despatched by gunfire and torpedo.

The Kriegsmarine was to offer few more such opportunities during the war. Its heavy units were immured in remote Norwegian fjords, from the security of which they threatened the essential Allied convoy route to North Russia. The British Home Fleet, usually accompanied by a fleet carrier, provided deep cover against such movements.

Below: Seen from the destroyer *Jervis*, an Italian SM.79 torpedo-bomber presses home its attack despite a hail of anti-aircraft fire from British warships as the Malta convoy approaches the island, March 1942.

In March 1942 the *Bismarck*'s sister ship, *Tirpitz*, moved against a point at which two convoys were crossing. Located by the British, she was the objective of a strike by twelve Albacores launched from *Victorious*. In high wind conditions and with the enemy manoeuvring at full speed, the aircraft were discovered to have insufficient power to achieve satisfactory launch positions. That the attack failed was surely an indictment of a system that obliged brave men to be equipped with such outrageously poor aircraft.

Four months later the mere presence at sea of this same ship was enough to order the scattering of convoy PQ17. Although the *Tirpitz* never sighted them, the individual ships were an easy prey for the Luftwaffe's torpedo bombers, which accounted for 14 of the 22 ships lost.

As all of the few British carriers were engaged in a single operation to lift the siege of Malta, the next Arctic convoy was covered by the first of the new escort carriers, *Avenger*. The movement was challenged, not by German heavy surface units but by over 200 aircraft.

To face these, the *Avenger* could deploy just twelve early-model Sea Hurricanes and three Swordfish. The first German attack used a high-level feint to draw the defending fighters out of position, whereupon 40 torpedo aircraft attacked simultaneously. They hit eight ships. Tactics were changed, the *Avenger*, previously integrated with the convoy escort, being allowed to manoeuvre at will. In a series of engagements the attackers accounted for a total of ten ships, but at a cost of 41 aircraft. Of the four Hurricanes lost, three were to the undisciplined anti-aircraft fire of the convoy.

One, possibly two, of the attackers fell to the guns of a Hurricane launched from the merchantman *Empire Morn*. She was one of 35 emergency conversions known as CAM ships, which retained their mercantile status while being fitted with a catapult on the forecastle. This could launch an early Hurricane ('Hurricat') or Fulmar, their primary target being the enemy reconnaissance aircraft that summoned airstrikes and U-boats. Following his flight, a pilot would have to ditch and be rescued if he was too distant from an airfield ashore.

Data (after 1939)

Displacement:	36,080 tons full load
Dimensions:	242 m (794 ft) x 31.1 m (102 ft) x 9.6 m (30 ft 6 in)
Propulsion:	Four shaft geared steam turbines delivering 120,000 shp
Speed:	30 knots
Armour:	main belt 229 mm (9 in)

Armament:	6 x 15 in (381 mm) guns, 20 x 4.5 in (114 mm) DP guns, 28 x 2 pdr pom-poms and 64 x 20 mm guns
Aircraft:	2 x Supermarine Walrus
Crew:	1,200

Class: *Renown, Repulse*

The battlecruiser *Renown* as she appeared in July 1942. She spent most of 1941 in company with the carrier *Ark Royal* based at Gibraltar as the core of Force 'H', operating in both the Mediterranean and Atlantic. Unlike her sister *Repulse*, sunk by Japanese aircraft off Malaya, *Renown* was reconstructed 1936-39 and given twenty 4.5 in (114 mm) anti-aircraft guns.

Above: The Fairey Albacore (dubbed 'applecore' in the fleet) was a modernized Swordfish but although nearly 800 were built, it never fully replaced the famous 'Stringbag'. Like the Swordfish it carried one 18 in torpedo.

German heavy units in Norway continued to threaten the flank of the Arctic convoy route and, in the gloom of the northern winter, carrier operations were still limited. Some relief was gained by the Home Fleet's disposing of the *Scharnhorst* in a pure gun action on Boxing Day, 1943, but the *Tirpitz* remained a problem.

The great battleship had been severely injured by a British midget submarine attack but the damage did not appear externally. During 1944, therefore, the Royal Navy used its increasing carrier resources in a series of determined attacks on the ship. These were notable for their employment of numbers of escort carriers (CVE) and the, by now, general use of American-supplied aircraft - Grumman F6F Hellcats, F4F Wildcats and the superb Vought F4U Corsairs - serving alongside Seafires, Swordfish and the newly-introduced Barracuda divebomber.

Tirpitz's anchorage was surrounded by torpedo nets. Ashore were flak sites and comprehensive smokescreen installations,. Fighter airfields were within easy reach and any final approach by air was limited by the steep terrain. As fleet assets were being assembled prior to the invasion of Normandy, it was possible, in March 1944, to put together a force of two fleet and four escort carriers. They shipped a total of 39 divebombers, twelve torpedo aircraft and 110 fighters, of which the Corsairs

Above: With *Renown* and *Duke of York* astern, *Victorious* prepares to launch 12 Albacores against the *Tirpitz*. Two were shot down by the battleship's anti-aircraft guns during the attack; *Tirpitz* evaded the torpedoes. As it was a single 18 in torpedo hit that doomed *Tirpitz*'s sistership *Bismarck*, it was with some relief that Captain Topp brought the *Tirpitz* into Vestfjord on the afternoon of 9 March 1942.

Left: The *Prince of Wales* was sent to Singapore with the old battlecruiser *Prince of Wales* on Churchill's orders. Both were sunk off Malaya on 10 December 1941 when attacked by Japanese twin-engined bombers flying from Vietnam. Some made level bombing attacks, but it was a strike by nine Mitsubishi G3Ms ('Nells') that inflicted the fatal damage. They scored two or three hits with 450 mm (17.7 in) torpedoes, leaving the battleship listing and without electrical power. A second strike by some half dozen G4s ('Bettys') scored at least three more torpedo hits and *Prince of Wales* capsized. Admiral Philips, Captain Leach and 335 officers and men went down with her.

could carry a 1000 pound bomb and the Hellcats 500 pounders.

The operation was well planned. Gaining complete surprise, the assault was led by low-flying fighters strafing the ship and all shore sites. This inhibited both flak and smoke while detracting the defenders' attention from the dive-bombers, following-up high above. Encountering little return fire these aircraft achieved nine hits and a near miss. An hour later, against a now fully-alert defence, a similar second strike was mounted, scoring five further hits. Unfortunately, despite preliminary exercises, the dive-bomber pilots, in their enthusiasm, released from too low an altitude. Only one large (1,600 pound) bomb therefore penetrated the *Tirpitz*'s horizontal protection, and that did not explode.

Additional operations were staged in July and August 1944 to finish the job, but they encountered strengthened defences, and it became apparent that bombs from carrier aircraft were too small to inflict terminal damage. As torpedoes were not an option the ship was finally despatched in November 1944 by RAF Lancasters dropping 12,000 pound 'Tallboy' bombs.

By 1945, a wealth of assets was seeking out a dearth of

Left: Deck accidents remained a regular hazard of carrier operations. This Grumman F6F Hellcat of No 800 squadron crashed aboard *Ravager* in 1943. The USA supplied nearly 1,200 F6Fs to the Royal Navy, 1943-45.

Right: HMS *Formidable* launches an Albacore. It was her Albacores that hit the Italian battleship *Veneto* and cruiser *Pola*, leading to the destruction of three Italian cruisers at the battle of Cape Matapan in 1941.

targets, and the Fleet Air Arm was able to assist in tightening the grip on the enemy war machine by swamping the long iron-ore route from northern Norway.

Air support for amphibious assaults

For the North African landings, in Morocco and Algeria in November 1942, carriers had to provide cover and close air support until airfields were seized. At this point, American and British aircraft, already concentrated at Gibraltar, flew in and carried on the work, allowing the carrier forces to disperse, the Americans to the Pacific where their need was urgent, the British to maintain guard against the latent threat from the Italian fleet and to break up the numerous air attacks aimed at offshore shipping.

In July 1943 Sicily was invaded but air support could be provided directly from Malta and newly-taken North African airfields. Two fleet carriers again watched for

any move from the Italian fleet. Two months later came the landings at Salerno, at the limit of support from Sicily-based fighters. Four escort carriers and the deck of the repair ship *Unicorn* were thus tasked to provide air support. Unfortunately the ships were equipped almost entirely with Seafire fighters. Conditions were virtually windless and the CVEs slow, resulting in fast approaches, heavy landings and an abnormally high attrition rate. The situation was exacerbated by the unexpectedly long time that it took to secure a key airfield ashore. Four days of intensive flying wrote off most of the force, whose survivors were then landed to work from a temporary airstrip.

The long hop to the South of France in August 1944 again required the services of the CVEs, this time seven British and two American. These could muster a total of about 225 aircraft and, in the absence of substantial opposition from the Luftwaffe (heavily engaged in northern France against the Normandy landings), most acted in the fighter-bomber role against specifically-designated targets.

Left: Eagle steams for Malta with a deckload of Spitfires. Laid down as an improved Iron Duke class battleship for Chile, she was taken over and converted to an aircraft carrier. She was sunk by *U-73* during the Malta convoy 'Operation Pedestal' in August 1942.

Right: British fleet carriers shipped up to six octuple 2 pdr anti-aircraft mountings by 1945. The guns had a rate of fire of up to 115 rounds per minute, firing a 40 mm round to a maximum ceiling of 13,000 ft.

Carrier warfare in the Pacific

Peacetime exercises had shown both Japan and the United States the possibilities of carrier warfare. The awful reality was demonstrated for the first time on 7 December 1941. The Japanese were under no misapprehensions. If the fateful step of hitting Pearl Harbor had to be done, it had to be done in maximum strength. All six of their operational carriers were assembled and exercised under the command of the able Vice-Admiral Nagumo. The bulk of the support group comprised its tankers and supply ships, for the Japanese were not seeking a surface action.

Against the seven American ships berthed in 'Battleship Row' the Japanese launched 40 torpedo bombers and 49 divebombers. For defence suppression, these were accompanied by a further 51 dive-bombers and 43 fighters. The overwhelming power of this strike alone would have achieved all the attackers' objectives, but it was followed by a second, with even more strike aircraft. These would have been better directed at fixed installations ashore, but that is to apply the benefits of hindsight. The Japanese objective had been to destroy the forward-based elements of the American Pacific Fleet. The wreckage of five battleships and 188 aircraft testified to how well that objective had been met. Its cost to the Japanese had been just 29 aircraft.

The course of the great Japanese offensive that followed in the Far East was a ten-week nightmare for the United States and its allies. While the forces that they could muster were considerable, they lacked common procedures and, increasingly, the will to tackle an enemy that appeared to be everywhere, and on whom little intelligence existed. In truth, the Japanese took some fearful risks but found that boldness paid handsomely. Their moves were calculated to be either within the range of land-based air cover or supported by an aircraft carrier. With these at a premium, seaplane carriers were used extensively, their aircraft agile enough to be used circumspectly in strike and defensive roles. Forward seaplane bases were established rapidly for the purposes of support and reconnaissance, moving quickly on to follow the tide of war. Floatplanes from cruisers were used widely, their sighting usually presaging another surface operation. The western Pacific is dotted with islands and the rapid establishment of airfields soon created a network of interlocking air support that defined a zone hazardous for enemy surface forces to penetrate.

Landings on the Malay Peninsula had been carried out simultaneously with the attack on Pearl Harbor. The British capital ships *Repulse* and *Prince of Wales* had been despatched to Singapore by a British Prime Minister anxious to show that he meant business. The Japanese were unimpressed. As the two ships moved against reported landings, unsupported by carrier-or land-based aircraft, their progress was carefully tracked. Flying from bases in Indo-China the Japanese despatched a striking force of 34 bombers and 54 torpedo aircraft, which completely overwhelmed the defences of the two ships. Their loss was a tremendous blow to British prestige, but their deployment had been a political decision that paid no attention to the hard-won experience of Norway and Crete, which showed that the fleet operated at grave risk in waters over which the enemy enjoyed air superiority.

Admiral Nagumo's carriers were a constant source of concern, as they operated in various combinations. Despite attritional losses, they put together 188 aircraft to join 54 Celebes-based bombers in a particularly damaging attack on the forward staging port of Darwin. This massive strike against an Australian target also caused a major invasion scare.

The Americans quickly passed the *Yorktown* through Panama, bringing their Pacific carrier strength to four. Each carrier formed the core element of a self-contained task force. These could be amalgamated as required, as in March 1942, when the *Lexington* and *Yorktown* served notice of things to come by hitting Lae in New Guinea with over 100 aircraft. American inexperience and the still wide dispersal of the Japanese Navy meant that results were meagre.

Also completed at this time and hurried to the Pacific was the *Hornet*. She was loaded secretly with 16 twin-engined Boeing B-25 bombers which, under Colonel Doolittle, precariously left her deck to deliver the famous 'Thirty Seconds over Tokyo' raid, before flying on to China. Little damage was caused but its implications resulted in uproar in Japan and a critical boost to American morale at a particularly difficult time.

With most Japanese objectives realised by April 1942, Nagumo took his carriers into the Indian Ocean to neutralise the still-extant Royal Navy strength based on Ceylon. This included three carriers, of which two, the *Formidable* and *Indomitable* were new. Together with the *Hermes*, the British could muster 37 fighters and 58 torpedo aircraft. The five enemy fleet carriers, in contrast, could put up 105 fighters (all the formidable Mitsubishi 'Zero'), 114 dive-bombers and 123 torpedo aircraft. Operating separately against merchant shipping along the Indian coast of the Bay of Bengal was the smaller *Ryujo*.

The British commander, Admiral Somerville was well aware of enemy intentions and his own limitations. He wisely resorted to a 'fleet-in-being' policy, basing himself on the secret base of Addu Attol, some 600 miles to the Southwest. Keeping well to the west of Ceylon by day, but closing the island by night, his weakness was in not knowing precisely when the Japanese would strike. Several fruitless days of this routine saw the short-legged British force in need of replenishment and, in their absence, on 5 April 1942, Nagumo pounced on Colombo.

The Royal Air Force fighter defence was badly worsted but managed to keep down casualties in the harbour, where only two out of 34 ships were sunk, and to minimise damage to installations ashore. More serious was the sighting of two British heavy cruisers, which were overwhelmed by a secondary strike of 88 aircraft, which numbers could virtually guarantee the destruction of the best of ships.

Right: The USA strikes back: one of Lt Col Doolittle's B-25 Mitchell bombers takes off from USS *Hornet* for the famous '30 seconds over Tokyo' raid, 18 April 1942.

Four days later Nagumo wrong-footed Somerville again and struck at Trincomalee. The port had fortunately received some warning from a British patrol aircraft, giving time for shipping to be dispersed. Eighty-five attackers thus found little in the way of targets but soon discovered the *Hermes* and several smaller ships, all of which were destroyed.

During this disastrous sequence the *Ryujo*'s air group had been ravaging the unconvoyed shipping that thronged the Indian coastal waters. In five days they accounted for 23 merchantmen, aggregating over 100,000 grt.

Nagumo had been supported by a powerful force that included four battleships but, as in the Pearl Harbor raid, these had not been called upon to fire a shot. In a new style of maritime war, the Japanese carriers had seen 20 weeks of non-stop operations, had inflicted tremendous damage but suffered none in return. When they pulled out of the Indian Ocean on 10 April 1942, it was not for maintenance, but to take part in a new strategic operation.

With no answer to an opponent who attacked with scores of aircraft, the Royal Navy accepted the inevitable and pulled its main forces back to East Africa.

Coral Sea: first clash of the carriers

Admiral Yamamoto, Commander-in-Chief of the Japanese Combined Fleet, was imbued with the concept of the 'decisive battle': a modern version of Trafalgar that would knock out an enemy fleet once and for all. Pearl Harbor had not accounted for the American Pacific Fleet, particularly as its carriers had not been affected. The Japanese admiral therefore planned to provoke a full-scale fleet action on his terms. His plan was to seize the island of Midway, sufficiently close to the Hawaiian Group to pose a threat that the Americans

Above: Mitchell's audacious strike by 16 B-25s (carrying four 500 lb bombs each) outraged and humiliated the Japanese high command and provided a timely boost to American morale.

Right: USS *Lexington* was hit by 3-5 torpedoes from a nine-ship formation of Nakajima B5s during the battle of the Coral Sea. Damage control had her operational within 30 minutes, but gasoline fumes built up in a motor room, igniting with explosive force.

could not ignore. Once enticed out, the US fleet would be ambushed by superior forces.

Before this operation could be undertaken, however, the south-eastern corner of the new empire needed to be secured. For this the Solomons and certain outlying island required to be taken, together with the long eastern peninsula of Papua-New Guinea. Already established on the northern coast of the latter, the Japanese needed to take Port Moresby, situated on the southern side. The direct, overland route was a wilderness of jungle-clad mountains. The Japanese therefore decided on a further hop by sea. Typical of the complexity of their planning, they combined it with an operation to seize Tulagi in the southern Solomons. Each invasion force had its own support group, while a third squadron, which included the light carrier *Shoho*, was available to assist either.

Yamamoto appreciated that the scale of this operation would detract from his Midway plan but anticipated it being large enough to attract an American riposte. He added, therefore, yet another force, including two fleet carriers, which would loop around to the east and attack any interfering American squadron from the rear. He went into the Coral Sea with the intention of fighting history's first carrier-on-carrier action, and planned accordingly.

The Japanese were unaware of the extent to which the Americans, assisted by the Australians and the British, had broken their naval signal codes. Strong evidence

pointed to a move against Port Moresby, to be followed by a larger operation in the central Pacific. Admiral Nimitz, CinC Pacific, ordered Rear Admiral Frank ('Jack') Fletcher to the Coral Sea area with the *Lexington* and *Yorktown*. By 1 May, as Fletcher awaited events under the cover of thick frontal cloud, he had the full organisational breakdown of his opponent's groups.

First news came of a Japanese landing on Tulagi. Fletcher, instead of remaining quietly concealed, ordered *Yorktown* to intervene. Three air strikes made little difference to the situation on the ground but effectively blew the American cover. Takagi, the Japanese carrier admiral, used his surface ships' float planes to seek Fletcher in the murk, while Fletcher relied on land-based air. Unfortunately for the Americans, the battlezone straddled two command

zones, and a vital sector along their junction remained unchecked. Early on 7 May each side thought that it had located its opponent's main force. Each was mistaken. The Americans hit the *Shoho* group with 93 aircraft and the Japanese unleashing a full strike against a fleet tanker and its escort. Both strikes were successful, but against the wrong targets!

During the course of the Japanese strike, a floatplane discovered Fletcher himself, but the small, 27-plane, strike that Takagi was able to muster suffered badly at the hands of the American CAP, achieved nothing and experiencing difficulty in regaining its carriers.

It was, therefore, on 8 May when the main clash took place. Learning quickly, both admirals sent up vectored air searches from their own decks, and each was successful. Mixed strikes of 69 Japanese and 82

American aircraft were soon airborne. The *Yorktown* and *Lexington* wings attacked separately. All torpedoes missed, being launched from too great a range, but the *Shokaku* was hit by three bombs.

Fletcher's still inexperienced air controllers allowed the Japanese to approach too closely before interception, and, although about 20 enemy aircraft were shot down, the *Lexington* was torpedoed at least twice, besides being hit by two small bombs. Structurally, she could have survived the damage but Avgas mains (which, with their tanks, were then supported rigidly by the hull) were ruptured. Fuel and explosive vapour caused the first of a series of massive explosions which eventually destroyed the vessel. The more agile *Yorktown* succeeding in evading a number of torpedoes and bombs but, after being shaken by near misses, was

struck by a single large projectile which exploded deep within her. Despite extensive damage, her flight operations were not impaired.

The Battle of the Coral Sea showed the experienced Japanese to have a distinct edge but, though they inflicted the greater material loss, they suffered a strategic defeat. Their objective, the invasion of Port Moresby, was abandoned and not re-attempted. The Americans found that improvement to aircraft performance was required and that an air wing needed to include a higher proportion of fighters. The Japanese required four months for repair of the *Shokaku* and the withdrawal of her undamaged sister, *Zuikaku*, to replace and train losses to her air wing. Their absence was to be crucial in the next, decisive encounter between American and Japanese carriers.

For two hours after the explosion, *Lexington* continued flight operations while damage control parties fought to extinguish the fires below. The engine room had to be evacuated due to the heat, and Captain Sherman gave the order to abandon ship just after 5 pm on 8 May 1942. There were some 2,700 men aboard the giant carrier, but there was time to evacuate all the survivors. The burning wreck was finished off with torpedoes that night. The battle of the Coral Sea became famous as the first naval battle in which the surface forces never saw each other: the damage was inflicted by air power alone.

Above: Yorktown ablaze after Japanese dive bombers put three bombs through her flight deck two hours after her own aircraft sank the *Soryu* at the battle of Midway.

Right: Excellent damage control had *Yorktown* under way, fires out, only an hour later. But ten Nakajima B5s from *Hiryu* made a surprise attack later in the afternoon, hitting her with several torpedoes on the port side. The carrier took on a 26 degree list before Captain Buckmaster gave the order to abandon ship. Part of *Yorktown's* airgroup survived to avenge the ship, flying from the *Enterprise* to sink *Hiryu*. The wreck of the carrier has recently been located by Dr Robert Ballard, discoverer of the *Bismarck* and *Titanic*.

Decision at Midway

Admiral Yamamoto was still about to move on Midway. Its occupation was of little importance in itself, the invasion intended to lure the Americans to action. Preparations involved an enormous volume of radio traffic, only a small proportion of which could be intercepted and deciphered. Piece by piece, however, Nimitz' cryptographers built up a picture of Japanese intentions. One priceless piece of data was that the enemy had given up the idea of taking Port Moresby by sea, intending to advance overland. American carriers could thus be withdrawn for the coming trial of strength.

Frantic efforts were made to patch up the damaged *Yorktown*. As most of the *Lexington*'s aircraft had survived the battle of the Coral Sea, carrier air groups could be increased. Up-graded, folding wing F4Fs offset some of the Zero's advantages but the less than satisfactory Douglas TBD Devastator still formed the bulk of the torpedo aircraft. Only one flight of its replacement, the Grumman TBF Avenger was available.

Once again, Yamamoto's plan involved an element of deception. In addition to a fleet engagement and the occupation of Midway, he proposed to invade the western Aleutians, far to the north. As he still lacked his two largest carriers, he was reduced to four decks for the Midway force but, misled by over-optimistic reports of damage inflicted on the Americans in the earlier encounter, and unaware of American knowledge of his plans, he considered his force adequate. His overall

Above: One of *Yorktown*'s SBDs returns from the most successful carrier airstrike of all time: the sinking of the Japanese fleet carriers *Kaga*, *Akagi* and *Soryu* on the morning of 4 June 1942. The Japanese CAP was drawn to sea level by the initial US torpedo bomber attack, and the carriers, decks lined with fully-fuelled aircraft, were set ablaze one after the other.

Left: A Grumman F4F-4 Wildcat takes off from *Yorktown* on the morning of 4 June. Against the fearsome Zero, the Wildcat was pressed to hold its own, but pilots learned not to dogfight with the 'Zeke', but to exploit their heavier fighter's speed and acceleration.

The fourth Japanese carrier at Midway escaped the initial holocaust as she was some 20 miles north of the main force. Rear-Admiral Yamaguchi elected to continue the battle, launching a strike that sank the *Yorktown*. He had another strike assembling on deck by the time the final US attack of the day arrived. *Hiryu* was set on fire by several direct hits and, although the carrier stayed afloat for another seven hours, she was abandoned shortly after 3 am on 5 June. The Admiral, the captain and some 416 men went down with her.

strength was greatly superior but, by dividing it for an over-complex plan of action, he laid it open to being attacked in detail. The attack on the Aleutians, which were not held by the Americans to be of strategic importance, and was ignored by Nimitz as a feint, involved the services of three smaller Japanese carriers, whose 90 aircraft would probably have been decisive to the outcome of the ensuing battle of Midway.

Admiral Nagumo was known to be planning to strike Midway from the north west. The American carriers, *Enterprise* and *Hornet* under Rear Admiral Fletcher, were accordingly stationed to the north east.

Early on 4 June 1942 Nagumo, some 200 miles west of Fletcher, launched a 108 aircraft strike to soften up the island's defences. Although the 25 defending fighters lost 19 of their number, they prevented the Japanese from inflicting sufficient damage. Unaware of the presence of the three American carriers, Nagumo ordered a second wave, already armed for use against ships, to be re-armed for hitting Midway again. This process was itself slowed by piecemeal air attack from the island, which mobilised every aircraft available.

It was shortly after 0700, and Spruance's two-carrier strike was already aloft. At 0728 the US carriers were sighted by a Japanese floatplane, but the sighting report

Left: Shore-based aircraft from Midway attacked the Japanese fleet as it approached. *Hiryu* is seen here turning hard to avoid a stick of bombs from a B-17 Flying Fortresses. Sixteen of these heavy bombers attacked from 20,000 ft, straddling the *Hiryu* but scoring no hits.

Below: Hiryu listing and on fire after the last US strike on 4 June. Admiral Yamamoto relieved Admiral Nagumo of his command that night, demanding a night surface action with the US fleet.

The US landings in the Solomons led to a succession of night surface actions as the Japanese attempted to reinforce their garrison on Guadalcanal. Northampton class heavy cruisers were involved in many of these, *Northampton* herself being sunk by torpedoes at the battle of Tassafaronga on 1 December 1942.

only hinted at a carrier. Nagumo, now uncertain, suspended the re-arming of his aircraft and awaited confirmation. He was still at this stage when he needed to accept his returning strike aircraft. It was now about 0900, and following Spruance's 97 aircraft were now 35 from the *Yorktown*.

The first American formations became uncoordinated and, with insufficient fighter cover, their lumbering torpedo aircraft were massacred by the Japanese fighters. However, their attack brought the Japanese CAP down to low level, and caused Nagumo's tight formation to lose cohesion as the carriers manoeuvred to avoid torpedoes. The Japanese carriers unable to launch additional fighters. Their attention drawn to the American torpedo aircraft, the Japanese failed to spot the arrival of the dive-bombers, high above. Most of these had overshot and were, in any case, approaching from an unexpected direction.

At 1020 three squadrons began their dives against the three Japanese carriers that were in sight. Within a space of four minutes, the *Kaga*, *Akagi* and *Soryu* were flaming wrecks, hit three, four and three times respectively. Within minutes, however, the surviving *Hiryu* launched 18 dive-bombers with fighter escort. Although the Americans themselves now had most of their aircraft committed, the *Hiryu*'s strike was heavily

mauled. Nonetheless, it succeeded in putting three bombs into the *Yorktown*. The carrier stopped temporarily, well on fire, then managed to get under weigh again. But the vengeful *Hiryu* had launched a last-gasp strike of ten torpedo aircraft and six fighters. Two torpedoes found their mark. Listing heavily and without power, *Yorktown* was abandoned. Nevertheless, the doomed carrier had already launched a scouting mission, which found and pinpointed the *Hiryu*. Twenty-four dive-bombers, for which no fighter escort could be provided, sped from the *Enterprise*. Despite the enemy carrier's fast steaming another brilliantly executed attack put four bombs into her. As with her colleagues, she burned out of control but, despite attempts to destroy her by her escort's torpedoes, she took 17 hours to founder.

Likewise, the *Yorktown* hung on and, belatedly was re-boarded. Taken in tow, she remained an easy target and was sunk by submarine torpedo on 7 June.

Information that there had been three large American carriers present, and that only one had been put out of action, came late to Yamamoto, who ordered his scattered forces to concentrate, attack the 'fleeing enemy' and take Midway. Only slowly did the magnitude of the disaster become apparent, by which time the two still-lively carriers of Admiral Spruance

USS Northampton Data

Displacement:	12,350 tons full load
Dimensions:	183 m (600 ft) x 20.1 m (66 ft 3 in) x 4.95 m (16 ft 3 in)
Propulsion:	Geared turbines delivering 107,000 shp to four shafts
Speed:	32.5 knots
Endurance:	10,000 miles at 15 knots
Armour:	main belt 76 mm (3 in)
Armament:	9 x 8 in (203 mm) guns, 8 x 5 in (127 mm) guns, 6 x 21 in torpedo tubes
Aircraft:	4
Crew:	1,200

Class: *Northampton, Chester, Louisville, Chicago, Houston, Augusta*

had sunk a heavy cruiser and disabled another.

Even more than Coral Sea, the battle of Midway typified the new-style fleet action, with the primary weapon, aircraft, deployed in hundreds and expended in scores. Their major objective, in either case, was to destroy their opponent's carriers. The powerful surface combatants involved did not seek battle with their peers but closed the carriers to protect them.

Left: The heavy cruiser *Mikuma* collided with the *Mogami* as they executed an emergency turn in the early hours of 5 June (lookouts had seen the periscope of the US submarine *Tambor*). Airstrikes from Midway and the US carriers finished off the *Mikuma*

America strikes back: the Solomons campaign

Buoyed by success the Americans went on to invade Guadalcanal and Tulagi just two months after Midway. The landings were a further morale booster, but were immediately offset by the disastrous Battle of Savo Island. On 9 August 1942, after Admiral Fletcher's precipitate withdrawal of carrier cover, a Japanese cruiser force virtually wiped out an Allied squadron covering the landing area.

Admiral Yamamoto moved quickly to reclaim Guadalcanal. Giving little forewarning, he tried to run in 1500 troops, with a main cover given by a force containing the two Shokaku class carriers. The smaller carrier *Ryujo* was charged with the neutralisation of Henderson Field, the now-operational Guadalcanal airstrip, and a fourth carrier, *Taiyo*, ferried replacement aircraft. For reconnaissance, much store was set on the continuing use of cruiser floatplanes, supplemented by more from the specialist carrier *Chitose*.

The Americans had three carriers in the area — *Saratoga*, now Fletcher's flagship, *Enterprise* and *Wasp*.

Each was the focus of its own group, which now included an anti-aircraft (A/A) cruiser. Unfortunately, the *Wasp* group had to be detached to replenish just before the Japanese attacked, and missed the ensuing action, known as the Battle of the Eastern Solomons.

Throughout 23 August 1942 each side probed to establish the position, strength and intentions of the other. Odd sightings of the very fragmented Japanese forces, combined with very poor radio reception gave Fletcher a confused tactical picture. The *Ryujo*'s attack on Henderson, however, was clear enough on the following day, the *Saratoga* launching 30 dive-bombers and eight torpedo bombers in response at 1345 hours. These were only 30 minutes into their flight when a further reconnaissance report established that Nagumo's two big carrier were just 60 miles further on. Fletcher,

aware that he himself had already been seen by enemy 'snoopers', and unable to re-direct the strike, readied every available fighter for his groups' defence.

At about 1550 the *Ryujo* was caught by the American strike. Most of her aircraft were still over Guadalcanal. Launching her nine remaining fighters too late she was destroyed by four bomb hits and a torpedo.

Nagumo, meanwhile, had put up 27 dive-bombers, covered by ten fighters. Fletcher met these with 53 fighters but, so badly were these directed, the enemy was able to concentrate on the *Enterprise*. Ringed by her destroyers, and trailed closely by the battleship *North Carolina*, she and the group put up a fierce A/A barrage. Nevertheless, the Japanese pressed home their attack and hit *Enterprise* with three bombs. Her situation was bad, despite heroic efforts from her

Below: A Douglas SBD Dauntless lands on USS *Ranger* in 1942. Just under 6,000 SBDs were built, and they were responsible for sinking the majority of Japanese major warships lost in battle 1942-3.

Right: The *Ryuho* was a 15,000 ton submarine tender converted to an aircraft carrier during 1942. Too slow for service with the fleet carriers, she was used for training until damaged by a US airstrike at Kure in March 1945.

damage-control parties. At this point, with the CAP in disorder and low on fuel, the Americans' radar screens revealed the approach of Nagumo's follow-up strike. The situation for the *Enterprise* was critical, but the ship survived because the Japanese failed to find her.

Although the *Wasp* group was heading back to the scene, Fletcher's priority was to save the *Enterprise* and he steered eastwards to disengage. Nagumo had lost too many aircraft to persist. The reinforcement convoy went on until the following day but, in the face of increasing attention and losses from attack by land-based aircraft, including four-engined Boeing B-17s, it finally turned back.

In repulsing the Japanese the Americans again won a tactical victory but at the cost of the *Enterprise* requiring two months of repair. An already critical shortage of carriers was then exacerbated when, on 31 August, the *Saratoga* took a single torpedo from a Japanese submarine, putting her in dockyard hands for six weeks.

Worse was to come. With available decks reduced to those of the *Wasp* and *Hornet*, the Americans needed to keep one in the Guadalcanal area in order to maintain local air superiority by day. Attrition of Marine aircraft at Henderson field also required regular re-supply runs. On 15 September both carriers were engaged in covering the movement of six transports, ferrying in a Marine regiment. Apparently secure and screened, the *Wasp* was just turning to commence air operations when she was struck by three submarine torpedoes. With much larger warheads than air-dropped weapons, these caused immense shock damage. Ruptured Avgas mains fed uncontrollable fires and she was lost. Later criticism pointed out that the carriers had been tied to a restricted operating 'box' for nearly four days, so that their position had become known, and that they were cruising at comparatively low speed to conserve the fuel of their escorting destroyers.

During October 1942 the Japanese made a supreme

effort to recapture Guadalcanal. It coincided with Nimitz replacing the Vice Admiral Ghormley as Commander-in-Chief, South Pacific(ComSoPac) with the over-aggressive Admiral Halsey. The carrier Admiral Fletcher, whose actions were sometimes difficult to explain, was replaced by Rear Admiral Thomas C Kinkaid.

As the Japanese Army tried, and failed, to take Henderson, the Imperial fleet supported operations ashore with battleship-based, surface action groups. Their opportunistic nocturnal bombardments threatened to reduce the airfield to total ruin. Again, the Japanese anticipated that this would trigger an intervention by the US Navy so, once more, Admiral Nagumo was laying back as distant cover, with both his large carriers and the smaller *Zuiho*. Their supposition was correct, as Kinkaid was watching developments very closely but, although having both his available carriers present, he was substantially outnumbered.

Above: Saratoga seen in 1942 after her 8 in (203 mm) guns were replaced by 5 in (127 mm) dual purpose weapons. *Saratoga* survived a submarine torpedo hit during the battle of the Eastern Solomons and severe damage from a *kamikaze* bomber off Iwo Jima in 1945.

Right: A Japanese destroyer under attack by US aircraft off Bougainville, September 1942. The Japanese 'Tokyo Express' missions had to clear Guadalcanal well before dawn to be beyond the reach of the Cactus air force the following day.

By early on 26 October Nagumo was low on fuel and Kinkaid's ceaseless air searches had caused significant attrition to his airgroups. The US force was sighted by a Japanese cruiser floatplane before 0700 and, within the hour, 62 aircraft were on their way, followed at intervals by three more groups, of 24, 20 and 29 aircraft respectively (the last group from a fourth carrier, *Junyo*, supporting the bombardment groups). Nagumo had also been detected and, in the opposite direction, were winging three groups of American aircraft - 29, 19 and 25 strong. Both sides, expecting the worst, had powerful CAPs aloft.

Nagumo's day had started badly, as two bomb-armed Enterprise reconnaissance aircraft found the *Zuiho* and, undetected to the last momment, made a surprise attack. Their bombs tore up her flight deck so that she could no longer recover aircraft.

With the opposing carrier groups only about 200 miles apart, and with so many formations airborne, the Americans experienced problems with fighter control. The *Hornet* was caught with her CAP too close and too low. In ten short minutes the ship was reduced to a wreck by two torpedoes, four bombs and two Japanese aircraft that crashed straight into her. *Hornet*'s aircraft, however, found the *Shokaku* and put her out of the war for nine months with four, possibly six, bomb hits. She only survived because the Japanese had tightened their procedures after the ease with which their carriers burned at Midway.

Yet unscathed, the *Enterprise*, *Zuikaku* and *Junyo* were readying their second strikes, while a Japanese surface action group, learning of the disabled *Hornet*, headed fast in her direction.

At 1100 USS *Enterprise*, her CAP weakened and attention diverted by a submarine's torpedoing one of the destroyers screening her, was hit by the Japanese second wave. The carrier weaved desperately, the new battleship *South Dakota* close astern putting up a fearsome AAA barrage. Their combined fire knocked down a probable two dozen attackers, but 23 bombs were released, hitting the carrier twice and near-missing her once. Fortunately, all torpedoes were evaded for, shortly afterward, the ship had to recover both her own and the *Hornet*'s aircraft. As two uninjured Japanese carriers were still in the area, the *Enterprise* was ordered out.

USS *Hornet* was not so lucky. Under tow, she stayed stubbornly afloat despite mounting damage from further attacks by aircraft from the *Junyo*. Finally, with no hope of getting her clear of the closing enemy surface-action group, her escorts were instructed to finish her off. Nine torpedo hits and over 400 rounds of 5-inch later, the blazing carrier had to be left to her fate. It was then about 2200. Just thirty minutes later the Japanese arrived and themselves attempted to take the wreck in tow. Only when this failed did they sink her with four more torpedoes.

This action, the Battle of Santa Cruz, left the Americans with no serviceable carriers in the Pacific, and an appeal to the British for the loan of a deck could not be met. The most favourable aspect had been the considerable attrition of the Japanese navy's veteran aircrews. In the Southwest Pacific, however, the Japanese now held the advantage, and their failure to immediately capitalise on it was a measure of their general disappointment over their failure to take Guadalcanal. It had the important consequence that Nagumo, the most able Japanese carrier admiral, was replaced.

This would be the last spell during which the Japanese held the upper hand for, on the last day of 1942, the nameship of the extensive new Essex class commissioned followed, just a fortnight later, by the first Independence-class CVL, built on fast, cruiser hulls. From this point the commissioning of new decks

Below: USS *Enterprise* during the battle of Santa Cruz, 26 October 1942. Her reputation as a lucky ship was confirmed as a rainstorm obscured her from the Japanese airstrike that would sink the *Hornet*.

Right: A Nakajima B5 from the *Zuikaku*'s airgroup passes astern of a US cruiser during its torpedo run against the *Hornet*. Hit by two torpedoes and three bombs, the carrier was left dead in the water.

was a regular event backed, equally importantly, by a massive expansion in aircrew training. However tenaciously the enemy fought, the issue could no longer be in doubt.

The months of 1943 were to pass as a sort of carrier war holiday, as the US Navy worked-up its new units. Both attack carriers (CV) and light fleet carriers (CVL) were equipped with new types of aircraft. The F4F Wildcat was replaced by the F6F Hellcat and the F4U Corsair, while the SBD Dauntless divebomber made way for the SB2C Helldiver. Lacking the Americans' industrial base, the Japanese stuck to the improvement of existing types, the result being a widening qualitative gap.

Before all this, the last months of the drawn-out agony of Guadalcanal were marked by the Japanese continuing to control things by night, bombarding US positions and running in reinforcements via the 'Tokyo Express'. By

Above: The Gleaves class destroyer USS *Ellyson* seen from the carrier *Wasp* during operations off the Solomons. Ironically, the *Ellyson* was transferred to the Japanese navy in 1954.

Below: The 13,000 liner *Argentina Maru* was converted into an escort carrier at Nagasaki during 1943. Commissioned as the *Kaiyo* she carried only 24 aircraft, and was used for transportation duties and aircrew training.

Right: A Grumman F6F Hellcat of VF-5 lands aboard the *Yorktown* (CV10) in mid-1943. Bigger and faster than the F4F, the Hellcat was designed using data from a captured Zero. Its speed and climb rate were far superior to the Japanese fighter.

day, the area was dominated by American air power from Henderson, the 'Cactus air force'. This was reinforced by the air group of Kinkaid's battered *Enterprise* which, with an army of repair men aboard, was stationed safely, well to the south.

Until mid-November 1942 the Japanese had succeeded in building-up their military forces on Guadalcanal faster than the Americans. But they eventually accepted that victory on the island would come at too high a cost. The month saw two furious nocturnal surface actions, the Americans taking the honours at the Second Night Battle of Guadalcanal and the Japanese a fortnight later at Tassafaronga.

The Americans were heartened by the return of the *Saratoga* at the end of November, followed by a pair of the big Sangamon-class CVEs, released after their involvement in the North African landings.

Early in February 1943 the Japanese evacuated Guadalcanal but, typically, set about reinforcing what they already held. American intelligence discovered that a whole division of infantry was to be moved in to buttress strongholds in Eastern New Guinea. Travelling in eight transports, covered by as many destroyers and an air umbrella, they were attacked by American and Australian land-based aircraft. About 130 Allied fighters

engaged the attention of the top cover, while 200 high- and low-level bombers took on the ships. American B-25s used for the first time a technique known as 'skip-bombing', approaching at very low level to lob a 500 pound bomb straight through a ship's side. From 37

Above: To help protect the carriers against air attack, the US Navy began to attach fast battleships, bristling with anti-aircraft guns. Here *Saratoga* steams abreast of a North Carolina class battleship, mid-1943.

'decisive battle', in no way matched Yamamoto's abilities.

In the four great carrier battles up to Santa Cruz, Japanese carriers had lost over 500 aircraft, the majority with their aircrew. To make matters worse, a further 170 aircraft were transferred ashore to fight in the Solomons. By contrast, US force levels were increasing rapidly. From mid-March 1943 'MacArthur's Navy' was re-titled the Seventh Fleet and Halsey's South Pacific Force the Third Fleet. Three new CVs and three CVLs arrived in the theatre by the July. During September and October these were used in the new technique of scourging every Japanese airfield in range of the Gilberts, to break the back of aerial defence prior to the first of the great amphibious assaults. Submarines and amphibians were also now employed for the speedy rescue of downed American aircrew. Admiral Nimitz could now plan boldly, knowing that he would shortly have ten CVs and CVLs and seven CVEs, together with support forces of five new battleships, twelve cruisers and over 60 destroyers.

While the glamorous new arrivals began to steal the limelight in covering the big amphibious operations, the much-repaired *Saratoga* found useful employment with

such attacks, 28 hits were claimed. By any standard, it was a disaster for the Japanese, who lost all the transports and four destroyers. Of 6,900 troops embarked, only 2,400 survived. Known as the Battle of the Bismarck Sea, it equated to a major American military victory.

It was land-based aircraft that were the major means of interdicting the famed and feared 'Tokyo Express'. Interception by surface forces at night resulted in confused and bloody skirmishes but, if the Japanese

destroyers were delayed in their rapid turn round, aircraft could sometimes overhaul them at first light, before they escaped out of range.

Land-based aircraft also produced a major coup when intelligence learned of a planned inspection visit to the central Solomons of Admiral Yamamoto himself. With full knowledge of his timetable and itinerary, American Lockheed P-38 Lightning long-range fighters intercepted and shot down his aircraft. His successor, Admiral Koga, while maintaining the belief in the

Above left: CV10, the second unit of the Essex class was to have been USS *Bon Homme Richard* but was re-named *Yorktown* after the latter's loss in 1942. Seventeen Essex class carriers were commissioned by the end of the war: a production effort Japan had no hope of matching.

Below: On 22 May 1943 *U-569* was sunk in mid-Atlantic by aircraft from the USS *Bogue*: this was the first 'kill' achieved by a US escort carrier. *Bogue*'s aircraft sank two more U-boats that year, and three in 1944, using radar-equipped TBMs able to drop sonobuoys.

Above: The flight deck of the escort carrier *Monterey* seen in 1943. One of the converted cruisers, she took part in many major actions, her airgroups supporting the landings at Makin, Kwajalein, Hollandia, Saipan and Tinian. She was part of TF58 at the battle of the Philippine Sea in 1944.

Right: Another Essex class carrier to carry on the name of a famous flatop, *Lexington* (CV16) is seen here off the Marshalls from the escort carrier *Cowpens*. Like many of her class, the *Lexington* had a long career after the war, remaining in service for nearly 50 years.

the Seventh Fleet. Early in November 1943 Admiral Koga reinforced the Japanese base at Rabaul, New Britain with no less than seven of his formidable heavy cruisers, supported by lighter units. His intention was to counter American progress up the Solomons chain. This powerful squadron represented a major threat to operations in the Solomons Sea, so USS *Saratoga* and CVL *Princeton* were directed to make a strike against them. The two ran in at 27 knots and, putting up 97 aircraft in an all-out effort, required a land-based CAP for their protection. Caught flat-footed, the Japanese had four of their cruisers heavily damaged for the loss of ten attacking aircraft.

As Rabaul had to be reduced as a naval base, a further strike was mounted six days later, when three of the new carriers sent in over 180 aircraft. There was little

left in the harbour for their attention but the resultant air battle took a heavy toll of the defenders. More were lost in a vain attempt to get at the American carriers, which adopted a tight, mutually-supportive formation. Over successive weeks land-based air took up the strain, reducing Rabaul as a fleet base. However, its substantial military garrison remained and the port was by-passed rather than taken by ground assault.

As the Fifth Fleet supported the Gilberts landings, informed Japanese must have already acknowledged the hopelessness of their cause, for the US forces included six CVs and five CVLs, together capable of deploying over 700 aircraft. Supported by a largely-new surface group built around five fast battleships, they already represented a near-unbeatable force, and yet more were to come.

The expanded carrier force allowed greater risks could be taken and, within the space of a fortnight, one Essex and one CVL were put into dock by aerial torpedoes, while the CVE *Liscomb Bay* was sunk by submarine torpedo. In the latter case, the C3 hulls from which the majority of CVEs were converted were shown to be too small to offer much protection to the large quantities of Avgas and ammunition carried: *Liscomb Bay* disintegrated in a series of massive explosions.

At the beginning of 1944 the Fifth Fleet carriers, under Vice Admiral Marc A. Mitscher, spent a week working over Japanese airfields ahead of the Marshalls landings. These went ahead in the virtual absence of enemy aerial activity. With aircraft replenished by dedicated CVEs, and supported by a comprehensive fleet train, the fast carrier force could now guarantee local air superiority for each stage of Nimitz's island-hopping campaign. Between events, it operated also against the enemy's fleet bases, such as Truk and Yap, forcing the Japanese fleet to drop back to the more distant Palaus.

Termed Task Force (TF) 58, Mitscher's carriers were organised into four Task Groups (TG), numbered TG8.1 to TG8.4. Each, at this stage, was built around three carriers, a mix of CVs and CVLs. Each had its own dedicated cruiser/destroyer screen while, in overall support, were now six new battleships, including the first two Iowa class.

The strike against the Japanese fleet base at Truk was particularly impressive. Strafing fighters neutralised much of the defences before the bombers arrived. These came in ripple attacks that never allowed the Japanese to catch breath. They included the first carrier-based night strikes and spilled over into a second day. Running out of 'live' targets, aircraft re-directed their attentions to installations. For some 1,250 sorties and 25

Left: Vice-Admiral Marc A Mitscher aboard his flagship *Lexington*, 8 July 1944. TF58's airgroups supported US troops at Saipan after the battle of the Philippine Sea. Resistance ashore was almost over: the Pearl Harbor raid commander Admiral Nagumo had shot himself two days earlier.

Above: The Japanese naval base at Truk atoll under attack from Mitscher's TF58, February 1944. The Combined Fleet had left the anchorage, but US airstrikes accounted for two cruisers, four destroyers and 34 merchantmen.

Running short of carriers, carrier aircraft and trained aircrew, the Japanese formed the so-called First Air Fleet. This force was designed to exploit the network of island airfields, moving around as required to meet American threats. This formation was deficient in both quality and quantity; pilots were inadequately trained due to lack of time and fuel, the most promising fliers being skimmed off to serve aboard the remaining carriers.

Increasing numbers of CVEs meant that 'MacArthur's Navy' could also acquire a credible air component. Task Force TF78 comprised TG78.1, with three of the Sangamon-class tanker-based conversions operating 31 aircraft apiece, and TG78.2, with three of the more common C3 conversions, each accommodating 26 aircraft. Mitscher's Fifth Fleet carriers were thus required only in the first instance, as prior to the long hop to Hollandia on the northern coast of New Guinea

aircraft lost, the attackers destroyed about a dozen small or auxiliary warships. Equally importantly, at a time when available shipping was disappearing fast due to the US submarine campaign, the aircraft also sank about two dozen merchantmen, aggregating over 130,000 grt. Of 300 Japanese aircraft based on Truk at least 250 were destroyed.

Chuyo Data

Displacement:	17,830 tons
Dimensions:	180.1 m (590 ft 11 in) x 22.5 m (73 ft 10 in) x 8 m (26 ft 3 in)
Propulsion:	Geared steam turbines delivering 25,200 shp to two shafts
Speed:	21 knots
Armament:	8 x 127 mm (5 in) guns (120 mm in *Taiyo*), 8 (later 22) x 25 mm guns
Aircraft:	27
Crew:	800

Class: *Taiyo, Unyo, Chuyo*

Below: Capable of only 21 knots and without arrester gear or catapults, the Japanese Taiyo class escort carriers were intended for ferrying aircraft to distant bases. All three were sunk by US submarines.

in April 1944. Support following the landings was then rendered by TF78.

In June 1944, the American assault on Saipan in the Marianas appeared to Admiral Koga to offer an opportunity for the 'decisive battle' that he still sought. The bulk of the Imperial Japanese Navy was now re-organised as the 'First Mobile Fleet' under Vice Admiral Ozawa. It followed American practice in being divided into three groups, each equivalent to a task group. Two were primarily carrier groups, with cruiser/destroyer support. The third was a powerful surface action group, which included three light carriers. Still with only nine decks to his opponent's 15, Ozawa depended upon land-based air support.

Mitscher was placed west of Saipan, in the direction from which Ozawa was most to likely come. Beyond Saipan were the Japanese-held islands of Guam, Rota and Yap. Ozawa's plan was to keep his carriers well to the west, out of Mitscher's range. His aircraft could then strike at the American force and carry on to the island airfields to replenish and hit Mitscher a second time on the way back. As Ozawa had only 470 aircraft against 960, his plan would virtually offset his disadvantage — if it worked.

The reluctance of Japanese officers to admit losses to higher authorities served Ozawa ill. His subordinates did not inform him that the First Air Fleet had just undergone a week of battering from TF58, losing possibly up to 200 aircraft in the Marianas and Iwo Jima to the north. The coming battle would again be decided by carriers.

Left: A Nakajima B6N bomber (Allied reporting name 'Jill') launched from Truk falls to the guns of USS *Yorktown* during operations in the Carolines, April 1944.

Right: The SB2C Helldiver was supposed to replace the SBD Dauntless during 1943, but 'the big tailed beast' had a troubled introduction to service and it was mid-1944 before large numbers of them were at sea. These 'Beasts' are from *Yorktown*'s airgroup, seen after attacking Iwo Jima in July 1944.

Below: Another Japanese aircraft crashes into the sea. By 1944 Japanese aircrew training programs were so short that many pilots were barely capable of tactical flying, merely following their experienced leaders to the US fleet and making what was often their first and last attack.

Left: Sister of the *Shoho* sunk at the Coral Sea in 1942, *Zuiho* survived to take part in the battle of Leyte Gulf, helping to draw Halsey's fast carriers away from the Philippines and the battleship squadrons committed there by the Imperial Navy. Seen here under attack by US aircraft, *Zuiho* was sunk on the afternoon of 25 October 1944.

Below: One of the most devastating attacks made by shore-based airplanes in the Pacific occurred on 2 February 1944. A Japanese convoy bringing 6,000 troops to reinforce New Guinea was attacked in the Bismarck Sea by USAAF B-25s. Using their new 'skip bombing' tactics, the bombers sank eight transports and four destroyers. Here, a Japanese merchant ship is machine-gunned by a US aircraft.

Admiral Spruance, the Fifth Fleet commander, was fully fuelled and replenished when sighted by a Japanese reconnaissance aircraft late on 18 June. As Ozawa waited for dawn on the 19th, Spruance was aware of his presence but not his position.

Early on the 19th, a perfect day, Spruance ordered a pre-emptive strike at Guam but this hurried back on hearing of a Japanese formation approaching its carriers. 69 aircraft, mostly bomb-armed had been launched from the three small Japanese lead carriers at about 0830. They were not only tracked by American radar but also eavesdropped by a specialist radio intelligence section, which monitored the flight-leader's instructions. Hellcat fighters were stacked to meet them, the Japanese inexperience now showing as the formation had to regroup before attacking, with its escorting fighters over-concerned for their tails rather than protecting their charges. An astonishing 42 were shot down for the loss of one Hellcat. Their achievement was a single bomb hit on the battleship *South Dakota*.

Vice Admiral Willis A. Lee's TG58.7 was built around seven new battleships, well-equipped with radar-laid weaponry, firing proximity-fused ammunition. Positioned adjacent to the zones covered by CAPs, it looked a most attractive target to any enemy pilot who missed the carriers, but the relationship was as a sundew to a passing insect, for it was a gun trap.

One hundred miles, and a half hour, behind the first Japanese strike came the second, this time from Ozawa's trailing main group. Its 128 aircraft were detected by American radar at a comfortable 115 miles.

Hellcat patrols, working from a pool of 450 fighters, were positioned in good time. Fighters and A/A barrage slaughtered the attackers, of whom just 31 survived to fly on to Guam as planned, only to find American intruder patrols over their airfields. Spruance's TF58 had incurred no damage.

Ozawa, however, had seen his new carrier *Taiho* torpedoed by an American submarine, one of 25 in the area. She maintained speed but slowly filled with fumes from ruptured fuel lines. About six hours later, she

erupted and was destroyed along with 80 percent of her ship's company.

With the often demonstrated Japanese inability to contemplate bad news, Ozawa appeared to be under the impression that all his missing aircraft had flown on to Guam and were, as planned, hitting Spruance as they returned. Soon after 1000, therefore, a third strike was despatched. Its 47 aircraft, through being poorly targeted, missed Lee's gun trap and attacked unexpectedly from the north. Its lacklustre approach

Above: Enterprise seen in May 1944 with TBF Avengers and F6F Hellcats on deck. She took part in almost every major carrier battle in the Pacific, ending the war specializing in night fighter operations.

Above: The US Navy's first purpose-built carrier, *Ranger* seen in 1944 by which time she was used for training purposes. She took part in the Allied landings in North Africa and raids on Norway in 1943.

was matched by a fatigued American defence, which downed only seven enemy aircraft.

An hour's lull followed, during which American search aircraft made a determined, but again fruitless, attempt to find Ozawa. The latter flew off a fourth, and last, strike at about 1100. Again mis-directed, its 82 aircraft attacked without co-ordination or, missing the objective, flew straight on to Guam. Either way they ran into fresh groups of Mitscher's rolling Hellcat defence. Of the 81 that set out, 73 were shot down or crash-

landed on the island.

Ozawa's problems continued when, at 1220, his Pearl Harbor veteran *Shokaku* staggered under the weight of three, possibly four, torpedoes from another American submarine. She foundered some three hours later.

Although only about 100 of his aircraft had so far returned, the Japanese admiral was led to believe that, having inflicted significant damage on Spruance, the bulk of the force was intact, and on Guam. As yet untouched himself, he therefore commenced refuelling

with the intention of resuming the action.

The air battle of 19 June, dubbed thereafter as 'The Great Marianas Turkey Shoot' had accounted for about 300 Japanese aircraft. A fatigued reaction set in on the American side, and Mitscher made no urgent effort to find the still-invisible Ozawa. Almost by accident, a search aircraft finally sighted the Japanese at 1540 on the 20th. As Spruance had expected, he was steering about north westward. It was late in the day and the distance was considerable but, by 1630, TF58 had 77 divebombers, 54 torpedo bombers and 85 fighters away, with a second wave being prepared.

Encountering Ozawa at 1840, already sunset, the attackers wasted no time. In a 20-minute assault they torpedoed the big auxiliary carrier *Hiyo* twice (she sank two hours later), heavily damaged the *Zuikaku* with bombs, the *Hiyo*'s sister, *Junyo*, less so. Three accompanying tankers were destroyed and various other ships damaged. Twenty US aircraft were shot down, but the escorting Hellcats claimed two-thirds of Ozawa's CAP. At this point, the remaining Japanese carriers had just 35 aircraft between them.

The surviving American aircraft arrived back at their carriers in deep darkness, guided by Mitscher's legendary instruction to illuminate the ships. Having flown near 600 miles and fought an action, all were critical on fuel and while orbiting, awaiting a clear deck, 80 aircraft had to ditch, losing 49 aircrew in the process.

Mitscher exhorted Spruance to continue the battle on the 21st but the latter's first priority was to cover Saipan and he refused to be drawn. The Battle of the Philippine Sea marked a watershed for the maritime balance in the Pacific. Six carriers remained to the Japanese, but virtually no trained aircrew. There was no shortage of surface firepower but, in the face of TF58, this would have small hope of survival. It was estimated that it would take a year to recoup such losses but, as such a spell would not be granted her, Japan's best response was the Kamikaze.

The British Pacific Fleet

After nearly five years of war, the British Eastern Fleet was built up to a respectable strength without the continual need to rob it of assets essential to operations elsewhere. By mid-1944 Admiral Somerville could field three new fleet carriers to reclaim the Bay of Bengal. This force which, just two years earlier, would have made such an impact in European waters, was now effectively too late, for the eastern foe, albeit with plenty of fight still in him, was already beaten. Political pressure allowed the Royal Navy to operate alongside the Americans in the Pacific, but the unpalatable fact was that it was neither welcome nor needed. Like a once-great actor making a cameo appearance near the end of his career, the imposingly-named British Pacific

Right: The doomed *Gambier Bay* seen from another Sprague's light carriers during their epic battle off Samar. A Japanese salvo has landed just 'over'. Visible on the horizon just right of the splashes is one of Admiral Kurita's heavy cruisers.

Below: The view from *White Plains*, CVE-66 during the action off Samar. Three US destroyers were sunk as they tried to protect the vulnerable carriers from Kurita's battle squadron. Survivors spent two nights in the shark-infested waters before they were rescued.

217

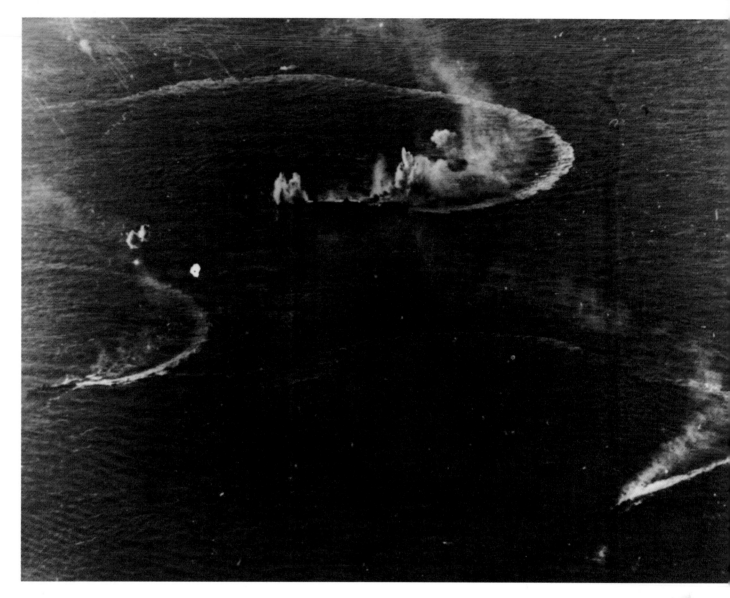

Above: With much less effective anti-aircraft weapons than their opponents, the Japanese carriers were reduced to frantic circling at high speed when under attack. Here *Zuikaku* is straddled by bomb explosions during the battle of the Philippine Sea, 20 June 1944. She survived this attack, but would be sunk off Cape Engano in October.

Fleet equated barely to one American Task Group. Its ships were ill-suited to the protracted operations that the theatre demanded and, as its fleet train was inadequate, it relied on the Americans for support and, indeed, for replacement when it was not on station.

The loss of Saipan was blamed by the Japanese on the navy, for losing the 'decisive battle'. A crisis of confidence brought about the resignation of the cabinet but, although a new realism set in now American heavy bombers were within range of the home islands, any first moves to end hostilities had to overcome a huge military inertia.

Japan awaited the next major American move. As this could be directed at Formosa, the Ryukyu islands or the Philippines, The Japanese fleet CinC, Admiral Toyoda (who had succeeded Koga), had developed plans to counter each. He knew that, in the absence of powerful

Left: After the Midway disaster, the Japanese converted the battleships *Ise* and *Hyuga* to carry 22 seaplanes in a hangar that replaced two of their 14 in gun turrets. Part of Ozawa's decoy force at Leyte Gulf, both survived, but would be sunk at Kure in July 1945.

Above: Kamikaze attacks began in earnest during the battle of Leyte Gulf. Here the escort carrier *St. Lo* lies blazing after a Japanese bomber dived into her on 23 October 1944. Crew members are leaping from the flightdeck as her list rapidly increases.

carrier support, he would require total commitment from his fleet, and that total commitment would certainly bring about a second decisive action. Of its outcome, he entertained few illusions.

American operations were now on so vast a scale that Nimitz adopted a new strategy in using either Spruance or Halsey as fleet commander. With one at sea, the other and his staff were ashore planning the next move. From September 1944 this led to regular, and confusing, changes of fleet designators. Operations were based around the Fifth Fleet under Spruance and the Third under Halsey; Mitscher's carrier force was variously designated TF58 and TF38.

Well aware that any major operations on the part of the Japanese fleet would depend upon land-based air cover, Halsey used no less than 17 carriers, in four groups, to flay enemy airfields over a wide area. This kept the Japanese guessing as to the next American move and cost them an estimated 600 aircraft. The attackers themselves lost 90, but the major difference was that these were immediately replaced.

Japanese doubts were resolved when, on 20 October 1944, the Americans landed on the island of Leyte in the central Philippines. Their plans for a counter-attack were, as usual, highly complex.

The invasion beaches, in the Leyte Gulf, could be approached from both the north (via the San Bernardino Strait) and the south (via the Surigao Strait). As the full strength of the US Third Fleet lay to seaward, the Japanese planned to exploit Halsey's known impetuousness by using Admiral Ozawa's virtually plane-less carrier force as a lure. Once Halsey had been drawn off to the northward, powerful Japanese surface action groups, covered by land-based aircraft, would issue simultaneously from the two straits and destroy the US amphibious fleet in a classic pincer movement.

Timing was critical, as four separate groups were

Seen from one of *Enterprise*'s aircraft, *Yamashiro* fights her way into the Surigao strait on the morning of 24 October 1944. Her 14 in guns are fully elevated as even the main armament was brought to bear on the US airplanes. She survived this attack only to run into Admiral Lee's battleships that night.

Admiral Kurita's northern force fought its way across the Sibuyan Sea during the same day. Here one of the Yamato class super-battleships turns hard while under US air attack. One of the giants, *Musashi*, foundered after 19 torpedo and perhaps 20 bomb hits.

Camouflage schemes like these were widely used by US destroyers during the Solomons campaign when surface actions were common. The first Fletcher class destroyers were launched in February 1942 and 175 had been completed by September 1944.

involved. Ozawa was required to sail from Japan to a point well to the north-east of the Philippines, where he would advertise his presence. Vice Admiral Shima would also leave Japan and, proceeding to the west of the islands, link with Vice Admiral Nishimura, coming up from Brunei. Together, they would form the southern attack group. Vice Admiral Kurita's northern attack group would sail from Singapore, again via Brunei. Due to the desperate fuel shortage, these forces could be sailed only at the very last minute, at which point the Second Air Fleet, of about 400 aircraft, would be deployed to Philippines airfields.

As American reconnaissance coverage to the west of the islands was still very patchy, Kurita's force, by far the most powerful, might have moved unseen but it ran into American submarines in the Palawan passage. These sighted the Japanese on 23 October, sinking two heavy cruisers and disabling a third. One, the *Atago*, was Kurita's flagship, obliging him to make an inauspicious start to the operation by transferring to the super-battleship *Yamato*.

Admiral Halsey's response to the sighting of Kurita

Fletcher

Displacement:	2,050 tons
Dimensions:	114.76 m (375 ft 6 in) x 12.04 m (39 ft 6 in) x 5.41 m (17 ft 9 in)
Propulsion:	two sets of geared steam turbines delivering 60,000 shp
Speed:	37 knots
Endurance:	6,500 nm at 15 knots
Armour:	side 19 mm (0.75 in)
Armament:	5 x 5 in (127 mm) guns, 3 x twin 40 mm guns, 4 x 20 mm guns, 10 x 21 in (533 mm) torpedo tubes
Crew:	295

was to move three of Mitscher's carrier groups close to the eastern Philippines to maximise their striking range, and to order the fourth, TG38.1 to replenish. Search aircraft first contacted Kurita at 0815 on 24 October but, even before a follow-up strike could be launched, Rear Admiral Frederick A. Sherman's TG38.3, the nearest group, was targeted by the enemy's Second Air Fleet. Ozawa, desirous of being noticed, chipped in with 76 of his 116 available aircraft. At considerable cost, the attackers put a large bomb into the CVL *Princeton*. This detonated, with fatal results, in a hangar filled with fuelled and armed aircraft. The Americans were too

busy to notice that some of their attackers were carrier aircraft, and Ozawa's presence remained unremarked.

With the Japanese concentrating on Sherman, the other two American groups were allowed free rein. Most of what should have been Kurita's rolling CAP had been diverted to hammer TG38.3, so few defending fighters were available to distract from the overwhelming US airstrikes that followed. The giant battleship *Musashi* was finally sunk after numerous bomb and torpedo hits. With damage to other units mounting, Kurita forced his way across the Sibuyan Sea. Slowed by relays of attackers, he eventually (at

Above: Japan's defeats in the Philippine Sea and Leyte Gulf left the US Navy supreme in the Pacific. Seen here at Ulithi in December 1944 are the carriers *Wasp, Yorktown, Hornet, Hancock, Ticonderoga* and *Lexington.*

Left: The US Navy's mastery of replenishment at sea enabled it to conduct operations over distances no other fleet could attempt. Here the *Merrimack* (AO-37) refuels an Essex class carrier off Japan, July 1945.

Right: USS *Essex* hoists in a vast supply of 'Lucky Strike' cigarettes from USS *Mercury* (AK-42) during operations off Okinawa in April 1945.

1500) reversed course. This reversal was spotted and reported to Halsey, but not the resumption of course some 75 minutes later. These manoeuvrings were to have important repercussions but, for the moment, Kurita was on course for the San Bernardino, yet already too late for his planned dawn rendezvous with Nishimura and Shima off Leyte.

The latter two commanders, although forming the Japanese southern strike force, never managed to link up, Shima trailing by some 40 miles. Even if they had combined, their group would have included two battleships and three heavy cruisers, almost insignificant compared with the five capital ships and ten cruisers with which Kurita had started.

Nishimura and Shima were sighted by a TG38.4 search aircraft early on the 24th, as they approached the strait between Negros and Mindanao. Suffering superficial bomb damage from an air strike at 0920, they bore on. Except for continuous air reconnaissance, they then remained undisturbed as the American carrier groups concentrated on Kurita. To Admiral Kinkaid, CinC of the Seventh Fleet, supporting the landings, it was apparent that the Japanese southern force would need to make a night transit of the Surigao Strait, between Leyte and neighbouring Dinagat. Attached to the Seventh Fleet was Rear Admiral Jesse B. Oldendorf's bombardment group of six elderly battleships, five of them Pearl Harbor veterans.

Despite their being loaded with the wrong ammunition for a surface action, the US battleships were ordered to plug the Strait. Destroyers and PT boats harried the Japanese the length of the waterway, delivering them finally to a scything hail of heavy-calibre projectiles and near annihilation in the small hours of the 25th. It was the last of the great battleship gun actions, unaffected by air power.

Only at 1540 on the 24th did Ozawa finally get himself noticed. By this time, his four carriers and two hybrid battleship/aircraft carriers had expended all but a handful of their aircraft. Halsey, previously critical of Spruance for allowing the Japanese to withdraw after the Philippine Sea battle, was determined to grant the Japanese no second chance. His latest information, coloured by his aircrews' over-ambitious claims, was that Kurita's heavily-damaged squadron had turned back. That he then took off after Ozawa is understandable but what will, for ever, remain incomprehensible is that he took the entire Third Fleet with him, even TG 38.1, returning from replenishment.

The Japanese plan had worked brilliantly. At midnight on 24th/25 October, the San Bernardino was being watched by not so much as a single US destroyer. As Nishimura approached his nemesis to the south, Kurita moved unopposed through the strait, albeit suspecting a trap. At 0540, with gathering daylight, he turned southward for the Gulf, just three hours' steaming.

Between Kurita and his objective, unsuspected and unsuspecting, lay 16 little CVEs of Rear Admiral Thomas L. Sprague's TG77.4. These, with their light screens, were organised in three task units, and their duties as Seventh Fleet ships were primarily to support forces ashore. Although a dawn search had been ordered by Admiral Kinkaid, it was about 0700 before it was airborne: a delay that nearly proved fatal. Fortunately,

Franklin (CV-13) was one of 16 carriers in TF58 taking part in air raids against the Japanese home islands prior to the Okinawa landings in 1945. On 18 March two Yokosuka D4Y divebombers attacked at low level, hitting her with two bombs just as she was preparing to launch aircraft. Here, firefighters run for safety as explosions hurl debris across the flightdeck. A terrible fire ensued and toxic fumes entered the ventilation system, 724 men were killed and 265 wounded. *Franklin* returned to the New York Navy Yard under her own power, but was never returned to full commission.

an aircraft on anti-submarine patrol ran across a large group of ships which the pilot assumed to be from the Third Fleet. But he came under fire as he approached them. Reporting this, he was ordered by Sprague to check their identification. The admiral need not have bothered, for his own lookouts soon spotted them visually. Any doubts were allayed as the orange flashes of the first enemy salvoes stabbed the northern horizon.

Fortunately, only one of Sprague's units was in sight of Kurita. As its ships made smoke and worked up to full speed, the whole task group was ordered to get every aircraft they had airborne. With Kurita present in overwhelming force, Sprague's position appeared desperate but, from the other side of the hill, the situation was not so clear-cut. The Japanese commander believed that he had run into one of Mitscher's groups and, with no air cover of his own, expected to be assailed rapidly from all sides. His only hope was to try to stop the carriers turning into the wind to launch their strikes. The course he steered thus favoured Sprague's escape and, as speed was of the essence, Kurita

Left: A TBM Avenger in the markings of a training unit seen on the catapult of an escort carrier during 1945. General Motors built 4,664 TBMs, bringing total production of the Avenger to 9,836. By comparison, Japan built just over 1,000 each of its main naval torpedo bomber types, the Nakajima B5 (Allied name: 'Kate') and B6 ('Jill').

Right: The war ended for the *Enterprise* on 14 May 1945 when a kamikaze attack caused severe damage that required her to return to the USA for repairs.

signalled 'General Chase'. Each ship thus moved independently and his formation quickly lost cohesion. Japanese shooting, opened at 36,000 yards, deteriorated rapidly and his most fearsome weapons, torpedoes, could not easily be used.

Sprague's calls for assistance were repeated by Kinkaid to Halsey but, for the moment, he was alone. He escorts laid continuous smoke and attacked valiantly, often singly. Aircraft sortied with anything to hand, even harrying the enemy with nothing at all.

As the US aircraft began to mount more organised attacks, Kurita became indecisive. He had several ships damaged, one seriously. He had come through a couple of days of attack already and, psychologically bad, he knew of the Japanese disaster in the Surigao Strait. When, at about 0900, he came in sight of a second Sprague unit, he assumed his position to be hopeless. Although he knew that he was hitting the enemy carriers (two were sunk) he was now feeling the weight of their 350-odd aircraft. What he did not know was that most

Left: Converted on the stocks from a liner, the carrier *Junyo* took part in the invasion of the Aleutians and her airgroup damaged the *South Dakota* and *Hornet* at the battle of Santa Cruz. Forming carrier division 2 with her sistership *Hiyo* at the Philippine Sea, she was damaged and *Hiyo* sunk. Torpedoed by a submarine in December 1944, she was decommissioned at Sasebo in the summer of 1945. She is seen here in September 1945.

Right: SB2C-3 Helldivers bank above the *Hornet* during TF58's raid into the China Sea in early 1945.

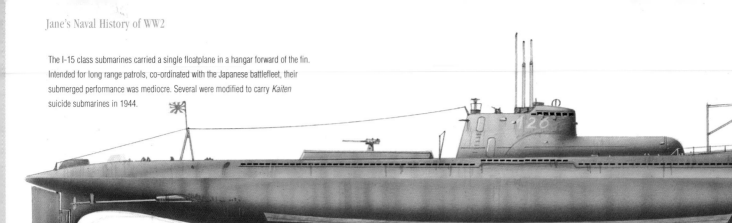

The I-15 class submarines carried a single floatplane in a hangar forward of the fin. Intended for long range patrols, co-ordinated with the Japanese battlefleet, their submerged performance was mediocre. Several were modified to carry *Kaiten* suicide submarines in 1944.

of his heavy armour-piercing projectiles were passing clear through the lightly-built CVEs without exploding! At 0911 Kurita ordered a withdrawal to re-group.

Sprague's carriers, already in mortal danger, had also been fighting off a new threat. From about 0740, Japanese aircraft appeared in ones and twos but, instead of attacking conventionally, they dived steeply into their targets, strafing as they came. Bomb-armed, they exploded with tremendous effect. The kamikaze had arrived.

As the desperate action off Samar progressed, the air thickened with radio traffic from sources up to Nimitz

Below: By 1944 the Mitsubishi G4M (Allied name 'Betty') was too slow to evade enemy fighters and still lacked self-sealing fuel tanks. Nevertheless, they were used to attack US naval forces until the end of the war, some carrying *Ohka* suicide jets. Here another G4M falls to US AA fire.

I-15 Data

Displacement:	2,590 tons surfaced and 3,655 tons
Dimensions:	108.6 m (356 ft 4 in) x 9.3 m (30 ft 6 in) x 5.1 m (16 ft 9 in)
Propulsion:	diesels delivering 12,400 bhp and electric motors delivering 2,000 hp to two shafts
Speed:	23.5 knots surfaced and 8 knots dived
Endurance:	16,155 miles at 16 knots surfaced or 115 miles at 3 knots dived
Armament:	1 x 140 mm (5.5 in) gun, 2 x 25 mm guns, 6 x 533 mm (21 in) torpedo tubes with 17 torpedoes
Aircraft:	one Yokosuka E14Y1 floatplane (Allied name 'Glen')
Crew:	100

himself. Where was Halsey and the Third Fleet? How did Kurita get where he was? Halsey, in fact was well to the north, in contact with Ozawa. Even as his carriers launched the strikes that would destroy four of their now near-defenceless opponents, the radio was becoming insistent. At 0848 he reluctantly detached TG38.1 to tackle Kurita. Then, following a direct query

from CINCPAC, he sent TG38.2 and the bulk of his fast battleships. By then it was 1115 and, 14 hours' steaming from the San Bernardino, so these fine ships were wasted as far as this action was concerned.

Kurita, meanwhile, steamed around apparently aimlessly, for about three hours, finally ordering a complete withdrawal at 1236. Sprague gratefully

Below: HMS *Formidable* seen after a kamikaze aircraft dropped a bomb on to the flight deck just before it crashed. Splinters punctured several steam pipes, but the damage was repaired and the carrier operational again within a few hours.

Right: Gripped by the same death cult as the army, the Imperial navy despatched its great battleship *Yamato* on a suicide mission to Okinawa. Seen here with her bows already low in the water, the battleship was overwhelmed by US airstrikes on 7 April 1945.

disengaged. If the Japanese admiral had really believed himself to be in the presence of the whole Third Fleet, why had he not withdrawn smartly? If he did not, why did he not annihilate Sprague? Kurita's actions were those of an unnerved man. At 1300 his retiring force was found by TG38.1's first strike, reaching to an extreme 330 miles and lightly armed as a consequence. It caused insignificant damage, as did a second two hours later.

The Japanese transited the strait at about 2140 but, during the following day, their progress was punctuated by a series of attacks from Halsey's vengeful carrier groups, which had to remain in the open sea. Curiously, they were able to sink only a light cruiser, Kurita withdrawing with the bulk of his force intact.

Thus petered out the great series of actions that, collectively, came to be called the Battle for Leyte Gulf, a final affirmation that, however powerful, a fleet that was obliged to operate in an area where the enemy enjoyed air supremacy was doomed to fail. Leyte Gulf ensured the loss of the Philippines and that, in turn, cut Japan's access to the very raw materials that were instrumental in her first going to war.

A major reason for the Japanese failure was that their limited available land-based air power was expended in attacking American carriers rather than in covering their own ships. (An analogy would be to use frigates to hunt submarines that were causing damage, at the expense of escorting convoys where the damage was being caused). That the Japanese never grasped this essential fact was

demonstrated in early April 1945 when the rump of the Imperial Navy was grouped around the surviving giant Yamato for a final, one-way lunge at American forces operating around Okinawa. In a virtual re-run of the Repulse/Prince of Wales disaster the Japanese, with no air cover, tried vainly to survive the attentions of 280 aircraft from two American carrier groups. Again, a gridiron of torpedoes proved fatal. Three thousand of the Yamato's crew perished with her, a further 1,200 in her escorts. The Americans lost just ten aircraft.

All that the Japanese had left was the kamikaze and the 'Okha' suicide flying-bomb. A series of massive raids on American naval forces supporting the Okinawa landings sank 30 ships of varying sizes. Although these, and the 4,900 personnel who were killed in them, were comparable to losses in a major naval action (cf. 5,672 British fatalities at Jutland), the kamikaze was never more than a weapon of desperation. Its main contribution to the course of air war at sea was to hasten the introduction of the surface-to-air guided missile, due to the need to disintegrate an attacking aircraft at a safe range rather than just to shoot it down.

As almost a postscript to this sequence of actions, whose outcome was decided by ever-larger masses of aircraft, one of the very last seemed a reversion to earlier days.

One of the few Japanese major warships left operational by May 1945 was the heavy cruiser Haguro. With a single destroyer, she was tasked with evacuating the Japanese garrison of the Andaman Islands. As these

Above: The British Formidable class had armoured hangars intended to keep out 6 in gunfire, and small airgroups as a consequence. This vertical protection was never tested but *Victorious* seen here, survived two kamikaze hits.

Right: Victorious and the British Pacific Fleet formed TF57, under operational control of the US 5th Fleet. The British carriers attacked Japanese airbases between Okinawa and Formosa, mounting over 8,000 sorties in two months.

were in the Indian Ocean, it was a British responsibility to deal with her. Four CVEs accompanied the British force but their Hellcats were out of range and their nine Avengers were not equipped for torpedoes. As a three-plane bombing sortie caused no damage, it was left to five destroyers to execute a classic, but rarely-used night torpedo attack. Despite all that had gone before, British carriers were still used as a means to bring an enemy to surface action, not as a weapon in themselves.

Below: Victim of the last destroyer attack of the war, the Japanese heavy cruiser *Haguro* as she appeared during her fatal sortie in 1945. Having fought at the battles of the Java Sea, Sunda Strait and Samar, she was sunk in a classic night operation by British destroyers after air attacks failed to stop her.

Haguro Data

Displacement:	13,380 tons
Dimensions:	201.7 m (661 ft 9 in) x 20.7 m (68 ft) x 6.3 m (20 ft 9 in)
Propulsion:	geared turbines delivering 130,000 shp to four shafts
Speed:	33.5 knots
Armour:	belt 100 mm (3.9 in)
Armament:	10 x 8 in (203 mm) guns, 8 x 5 in (127 mm) guns, 8 x 25 mm guns, 16 x 24 in (610 mm) torpedoes
Aircraft:	3 floatplanes
Crew:	780
Class:	*Myoko, Nachi, Haguro, Ashigara*

Chapter 6 – Last Days of the Battleship

Up to and including World War I any major confrontation at sea would, by default, be resolved by big-gunned capital ships. Only they had both the armament and survivability to influence the outcome of what had come to be known as the 'decisive battle'. By 1914, the long reign of the gun had been challenged by a usurper, the torpedo. Through its ability to bypass a battleship's protection and strike, literally, below the belt, it posed a mortal threat. However, the means that delivered it were subject to severe limitations. Torpedo boats and destroyers could be swatted by battleships' secondary armaments far beyond the range of their weapons. Submarines, then virtually static thanks to low underwater speeds and limited endurance, relied on the slim chance that a target might make itself available. While capital ships might, from time to time, be lost to such means, the final showdown of battleline on battleline would still be the means to decide a naval battle and, by extension, a maritime war.

Although aircraft had made an appearance, the naval establishment (the British in particular) viewed it primarily as a means of observation. Aerial reconnaissance would give an admiral an edge in accurate decision-making; aerial spotting would get his guns more quickly on target. By 1918 the latest battleships still had little to fear except from their peers.

Treaties signed in the wake of World War I forestalled another arms race between the major naval powers in the 1920s. Most capital ships completed before 1914 were scrapped, while later units were modernized. HMS *Malaya*, was refitted from 1927-29 and again 1934-36. Improvements included extra deck armour, new anti-aircraft weapons and anti-torpedo bulges. *Malaya* is seen here leaving New York in 1941, where she was repaired after a torpedo hit from *U-106*. From the German point of view, this made a mockery of the USA's neutrality.

Above: The old and the new: the battlecruiser *Renown* seen from the flightdeck of *Victorious*. The British regarded aircraft as a means to bring the enemy to surface action, rather than as weapons in their own right. Whether this was the cause or the effect of having inferior naval aircraft is an enduring controversy.

Tosa

Displacement:	39,930 tons full load
Dimensions:	181.6 m (715 ft) x 30.5 m (100 ft) x 9.4 m (30 ft 9 in)
Propulsion:	four turbines delivering 91,000 shp
Speed:	26.5 knots
Armour:	main belt 280 mm (11 in)
Armament:	10 x 406 mm (16 in) guns
	20 x 140 mm (5.5 in) guns
	4 x 76 mm (3 in) guns
	8 x 610 mm (24 in) torpedoes
Class:	*Kaga, Tosa*

Hard-earned battle experience was being distilled into the monstrous battleships being built by all the wartime allies, each of which was unwilling to terminate its hugely expensive construction programme unilaterally. Without interruption, the capital ship would quickly have gone to approach natural limits, for size would eventually have been governed by depths of water and dimensions of docks, while guns could be enlarged little more without defying basic physical and engineering laws.

Below: The long-bodied 2,048 lb (929 kg) APC round fired by *Rodney*'s 16 in (406 mm) guns caused excessive muzzle wear, but quickly reduced the *Bismarck* to a blazing wreck.

In the event, battleships never did reach their 'natural' limits. Post-World War I construction programmes were all interrupted by the 1921-2 Washington Naval Treaties. These swept away huge swathes of older, but still serviceable, capital ship tonnage together with the new generation of battleships, as yet uncompleted. The latest and best extant battleships survived; but not only were these relatively few in number, they could not be replaced for a period that effectively skipped a battleship generation, and even then only by ships of an arbitrarily chosen maximum size. With the abandonment of new ships which incorporated the improvements dictated by the hard-won experience of war, the battleships that remained as front-line units - the Queen Elizabeths, the Marylands, the Bretagnes, Dorias and

Below: The Japanese battleship *Tosa* as she would have appeared on completion in the mid-1920s. Launched in 1921, *Tosa* and sistership *Kaga* were intended to be larger and faster than the Nagato class battleships that preceded them. The Washington treaties halted their construction, and effectively froze battleship design for 15 years. *Tosa*'s hull was used for research into the performance of guns and torpedoes before being expended as a target in 1925. *Kaga* was converted to an aircraft carrier.

Right: Gun crews inside the turrets of the *Duke of York*. The KGV class battleships had persistent problems with their main armament: *Duke of York* experiencing repeated stoppages during her battle with the Scharnhorst.

Below: Japan's four Kongo class battlecruisers were launched before World War I but were the most active Japanese capital ships in World War II. Two were sunk off Guadalcanal. *Haruna*, seen here survived until 1945 when she was destroyed by US aircraft.

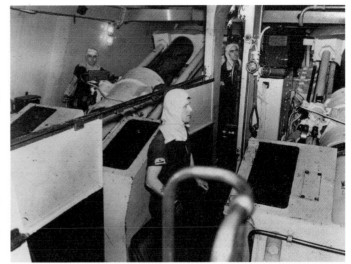

Mutsus - were all of pre-war design. They had been built and, in some cases, were still being built, to varying degrees of obsolescence. The big hulls that would have corrected their deficiencies were scrapped, expended as targets, or converted into aircraft carriers, which last option effectively used the battleship to develop the means of her own redundancy. There is little doubt that, in the absence of the Washington agreements, the reign of the big-gun capital ship would have been extended, and World War II at sea less influenced by aircraft.

Because new construction was prohibited until the agreements were due to lapse in 1936 — except in special cases — most fleets modernised their existing tonnage. Enormous weight and space savings could be achieved through the installation of new machinery and boilers. In the case of the latter, just eight compact units could output greater energy than 20 of earlier design. The Italians for instance, doubled power in the Doria class, reduced shafts from four to two, lengthened the hulls with a new forward section and increased speed by a remarkable 5 1/2 knots.

Further weight saving was achieved by the removal of casemated secondary batteries, usually of about 6 inch calibre, and their replacement with turreted, high-angle dual-purpose guns. Margins were thus created to permit the addition of further horizontal protection, to improve resistance to bombs and long-range shellfire. Bulges were commonly added to reduce the effects of torpedo hits but, as these usually incorporated liquid-filled spaces and/or a considerable quantity of steelwork, they added less buoyancy than might be assumed.

A further major task was to re-engineer the main

Left: Malaya ploughs her way through the Atlantic towards Norway in May 1943, as part of a diversionary operation intended to draw German reinforcements north, away from the Mediterranean.

Right: The KGVs were notoriously wet forward, the result of the Admiralty's insistence on both forward turrets being able to fire directly ahead. *King George V* is seen here in early 1942.

Below: King George V with *Prince of Wales* astern during gunnery exercises in September 1941.

battery to increase gun elevation and, thus, effective range. Again, the Italians went furthest, removing an amidships turret and increasing the gun calibre in the remainder.

Dual-purpose secondary armament, better horizontal protection, and increasing numbers of small-calibre automatic weapons gave the illusion that the growing threat from the air was well contained. Gunnery exercises, however, were conducted against towed aerial targets or single, radio-controlled aircraft which moved in straight lines, giving no idea of what it would be like to defend against scores of aircraft attacking simultaneously and determinedly. On the other hand, there had been no shortage of modern ships to expend

as targets, to gauge the destructive effects of bomb and torpedo. As these were well understood, it was axiomatic that avoidance was the best policy, an aim easier in theory than in practice.

Any hopes by the democracies that the terms of the Washington agreements might be renewed in 1936 were dashed by the behaviour of the German, Italian and Japanese dictatorships. In rearming, however, the democratic powers still wished to adhere to the 35,000 ton limit originally imposed in 1921. On this displacement the armament favoured by the British was of only 14 inch calibre. The Japanese, no longer party to formal agreements, were thought to favour 16 inch guns. It was hoped to persuade them to down-grade this

Below: During 1938-9 the Soviet Union laid down three 'super battleships' along the same lines as the Japanese Yamato class. Two were almost ready for launch in 1941 but work was suspended owing to the German invasion. This is *Sovietsky Soyuz* as she would have appeared by the mid-1940s. The prototype of her main gun saw action on the Leningrad front 1941-44. The hull was launched to clear the slip in 1949 and used for missile tests until 1956.

The world's largest and most powerful battleship, *Yamato* completing builder's trials in October 1941. Both *Yamato* and sistership *Musashi* would eventually succumb to air attack, but it required hundreds of sorties and over a dozen torpedo hits to inflict serious damage.

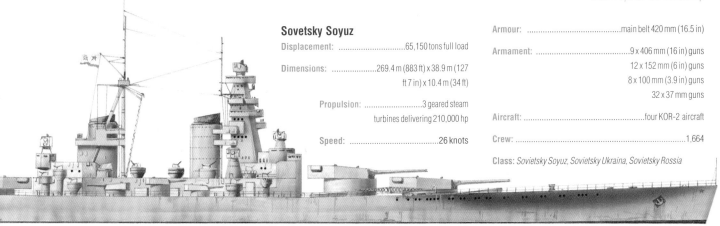

Sovetsky Soyuz

Displacement:	............................65,150 tons full load
Dimensions:	..................269.4 m (883 ft) x 38.9 m (127 ft 7 in) x 10.4 m (34 ft)
Propulsion:	.........................3 geared steam turbines delivering 210,000 hp
Speed:	....................................26 knots

Armour:	..........................main belt 420 mm (16.5 in)
Armament:	.........................9 x 406 mm (16 in) guns
	12 x 152 mm (6 in) guns
	8 x 100 mm (3.9 in) guns
	32 x 37 mm guns
Aircraft:	...................................four KOR-2 aircraft
Crew:	1,664

Class: *Sovietsky Soyuz, Sovietsky Ukraina, Sovietsky Rossia*

Below: Perhaps the most famous battleship engagement of the war: *Bismarck* seen from her accompanying cruiser *Prinz Eugen* fires on HMS *Hood*, 24 May 1941. The unmodernized battlecruiser was caught in the zone at which she was most vulnerable, her weak horizontal protection exposed to plunging fire from *Bismarck*'s main battery. *Bismarck* herself had only three more days afloat.

Bismarck at Bergen on the eve of her ill-fated sortie into the Atlantic. She embarked an admiral and his staff because the operation was also supposed to involve the battleships *Scharnhorst* and *Gneisenau*, then lying at Brest.

Warspite (as modernized)

Displacement:	36,450 tons full load
Dimensions:	195 m (640 ft) x 31.7 m (104 ft) x 9.3 m (30 ft 9 in)
Propulsion:	geared steam turbines delivering 80,000 shp to four shafts
Speed:	23.5 knots
Armour:	main belt 330 mm (13 in)
Armament:	8 x 15 in (381 mm) guns
	8 x 6 in (152 mm) guns
	8 x 4 in (102 mm) guns
	32 x 2-pdr pom-poms and
	15 x 12.7 mm machine guns
Aircraft:	two Fairey Swordfish floatplanes

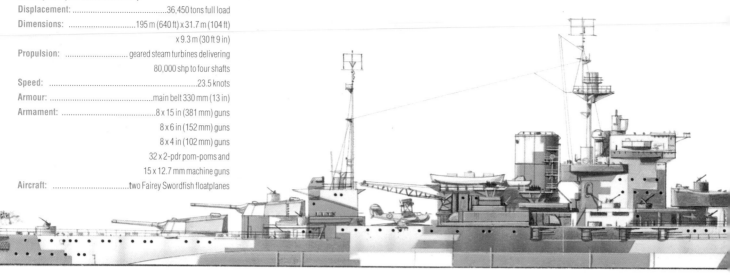

but, as the deadline for such an agreement came and went, the Americans opted 16 inch guns (on displacements that only officially adhered to the treaty limit). Faced with the obsolescence of their existing tonnage, the British had already been obliged to move. The result was that their 14 inch armed King George Vs, although of a good design, were out-gunned by their contemporaries. New French and Italian battleships received 15 inch guns, while the Americans went to 16 inch and the Japanese adopted 18 inch guns.

For capital ships, World War II proved to be totally different to World War I. Battleships retained much of their importance in the European theatre; Germany and Italy had no aircraft carriers, and the British had very few available at any one time. As we have seen above, German heavy units were regularly employed against Allied convoys, so that older British battleships

accompanied Atlantic convoys, with the Home Fleet's more modern units covering those to the Arctic. However, even in European waters, airborne weapons proved increasingly deadly to battleships, their impact muted only through their lack of numbers. At Taranto, despite her modernisation (particularly the inclusion of the patent Pugliese cylindrical protection system), the *Cavour* was put on the bottom by just one small-calibre, air-dropped torpedo. Three more bottomed the brand-new *Littorio*, constructed to the latest standards. Three years later her sister, *Roma*, was to be destroyed by her late German allies. Steaming to be handed over to the Allies, following the Italian armistice, she was attacked by the Luftwaffe and hit by two guided bombs. The first of these early air-to-surface missiles passed vertically through the ship, exploding beneath her keel (an experience shared by the British battleship *Warspite* just

Below: Rodney wore this green camouflage scheme during her service in the Indian Ocean in June 1942. Combining nine 16 in guns and heavy protection on a treaty-limited displacement led to the unique turret layout, but *Rodney* and *Nelson* were among the most powerful battleships in the world in 1939.

Seen here as flagship of the Mediterranean fleet in 1940, *Warspite* had survived heavy damage at Jutland and was modernized in the 1930s. She saw action at Narvik and Cape Matapan, but was damaged off Crete and sent to Seattle for repairs, serving with the Eastern fleet before returning to Europe in 1943.

Left: Warspite was struck by an FX1400 glider bomb off Salerno in September 1943 and never fully repaired. She is seen here bombarding German positions in France, June 1944; note 'X' turret is inoperable and there is a tug in attendance. *Warspite* struck a mine off the invasion beaches and had to be assisted into position for bombardments of Brest, Le Havre and Walcheren.

Right: 6 in (152 mm) shells for *Rodney's* secondary armament are taken below. The main armament is near its full elevation of 40 degrees.

Nelson

Displacement:	18,400 tons full load
Dimensions:	216.4 m (710 ft) x 32.3 m (106 ft) x 8.5 m (28 ft)
Propulsion:	geared steam turbines delivering 45,000 shp to two shafts
Speed:	23 knots
Armour:	main belt 14 in (356 mm)
Armament:	9 x 16 in (406 mm) guns 12 x 6 in (152 mm) guns 6 x 4.7 in (120 mm) guns 16 x 2-pdr pom-poms
Aircraft:	none
Crew:	1,314

Class: *Rodney, Nelson*

a week later off Salerno). The second exploded within the ship, fatally detonating a magazine. In both cases the mother aircraft, high above, went unnoticed and unscathed.

The *Warspite* had already spent a period being repaired in the United States, following a heavy bomb hit incurred during the campaign in Crete. Six months after this, in November 1941, her unmodernised sister, *Barham*, blew up after being hit by a salvo of three submarine-launched torpedoes. In all these cases, neither heavy armament nor massive protection defeated the attacking weapons.

Also in 1941, the *Bismarck* episode might be taken to demonstrate that in the absence of significant air power, heavy-calibre gunfire was necessary to complete the job. But these guns would never have come remotely within range had it not been for the modest-sized, carrier-based air strike which had disabled the fugitive ship.

In the case of her sister ship, *Tirpitz*, the reverse was true. Immobilised by naval action in her landgirt Norwegian anchorage, air power was necessary to complete her destruction. When 1000 pound, then 1500 pound, bombs failed to inflict terminal damage, heavy bombers were deployed, using five ton weapons. Although this was a unique case, her heavy guns which had barely seen action, remained important.

Towards the end of the war, all modern British battleships had been transferred to the Far East. A handful of older units operated, almost purely in the bombardment role, in European waters, but the

Above: *Scharnhorst* and *Gneisenau* escaped back to Germany from Brest after repeated attacks by the RAF prevented further Atlantic sorties. *Gneisenau* seen here was soon crippled by another Bomber Command raid, but her sistership survived until the end of 1943.

Left: The men that sank the *Scharnhorst*. Admiral Sir Bruce Fraser and his captains aboard *Duke of York*. Note the blistering on the gun barrels. The only man aboard privy to 'Ultra', Fraser had to conceal his knowledge of the enemy's movements from his own staff.

Right: 1,803 men went down with the *Scharnhorst* when she was sunk off North Cape. As Admiral Bey and all his officers were lost, details of her final movements remain uncertain. These are some of the 30 men rescued by the British.

Above: Drifter men cheer as *Duke of York* returns to Scapa Flow after the battle of North Cape, the very last capital ship action fought by the Royal Navy.

remainder had already been reduced to reserve status, their most valuable asset being their large crews, now drafted to more useful types of ship.

In the Pacific, the disaster of Pearl Harbor had put on the bottom what was popularly considered to be the pride of the US Navy. National honour demanded, where practicable, the salvaging and re-commissioning of these ships. However, once re-constructed, they did not serve as front-line battleships (replacement keels had been laid long before) but as heavy fire support ships in amphibious landings.

Between April 1941 and June 1944 the United States commissioned ten final-generation battleships with

Below: The French navy built some magnificent battleships in the inter-war period, but the outbreak of war prevented the construction of the *Gascogne*, fourth unit of the Richelieu class. Unlike her sisterships, and the earlier Dunkerque class, the *Gascogne* was to revert to a conventional layout for her main armament, and two additional units were planned to follow.

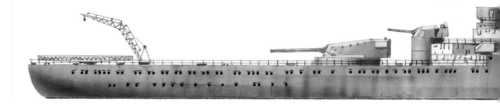

uniform 16 inch main batteries. A generation earlier, these would have been deployed as the core of the battlefleet, but priorities had changed with the style of naval warfare. What would have been a Fleet was now categorised a Task Force, subdivided flexibly into Task Groups. The Japanese adopted much the same system. Battleships 'might' form the nucleus of a surface-action group, but this would be tasked less with operating against its enemy peers as covering friendly carrier forces. On occasion, a single battleship would steam

close aboard a carrier under conditions of heavy air attack, to add the weight of her anti-aircraft fire. Either way, the role had become essentially defensive, with ever-lessening chance of meeting the enemy in a classic gun duel.

Gun actions could still occur, albeit involving few units, when circumstances or nocturnal conditions precluded the interference of land-or carrier-based air power. Notable examples include those of the USS *Massachusetts* disabling the yet-incomplete French

Above: Gun crews of the victorious *Duke of York* assemble forward of A turret, still wearing their fire retardant hoods and gloves. The battleship required over 1,400 men to crew her.

battleship *Jean Bart* at Casablanca, the *Duke of York* sinking the *Scharnhorst*, the *Kirishima*'s destruction by USS *Washington*, and the unfortunate sister ships *Fuso* and *Yamashiro* by Oldendorf's gun line in the Surigao Strait.

Gascogne

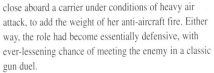

Displacement:	40,900 tons
Dimensions:	247.8 m (813 ft) x 33.1 m (108 ft 7 in) x 10.7 m (35 ft 1 in)
Propulsion:	geared turbines delivering 150,000 shp to four shafts
Speed:	33 knots
Armour:	main belt 345 mm (13.6 in)
Armament:	8 x 381 mm (15 in) guns
	9 x 152 mm (6 in) guns
	16 x 100 mm (3.9 in) guns
	20 x 37 mm guns
	36 x 13.2 mm guns
Aircraft:	unknown
Crew:	c.1,750
Class:	*Gascogne* + 3 (cancelled)

USS *Washington* with the *Enterprise* in the background, seen in 1945. Of the ten American battleships completed between 1941 and 1944, *Washington* was the only one to engage and sink an enemy capital ship. On the night of 13-14 November 1942 she sank the battlecruiser *Kirishima* off Guadalcanal. Built to take on the giant Japanese super-dreadnoughts, the US fast battleships spent most of their war as escorts for the carrier groups.

Above: The battleship *Indiana* bombarding Kamaishi, 250 miles north of Tokyo in July 1945. This was the first naval bombardment of the enemy home islands, and signified the total defeat of the Imperial Navy.

Right: Built during World War I, *Maryland* was damaged at Pearl Harbor but returned to service and was part of Admiral Oldendorf's squadron at Surigao strait. She fired 48 rounds from her 16 in guns in history's last battleship fight.

A proven need for heavy saturation bombardment prior to an amphibious landing ensured that American battleships were all fully employed to the end. But, as in European waters, this was still a support function. In the Pacific, tiny coral islets were reduced to powder but, off Italian and Normandy beaches veteran capital ships could still intervene in military operations 20 miles and more inland.

Any doubt that the big-gunned ship had yielded its leading position to the aircraft and the submarine is surely dismissed by the following table. It summarises the percentage losses of major warships (aircraft carriers, battleships and cruisers) to each of the main agencies.

Agency	Royal Navy	US Navy	Japanese Navy
Surface Ship	22.7	21.5	16.9
Submarine	37.5	20.2	32.1
Carrier aircraft	6.2	45.1	47.1
Land based aircraft	27.8	13.2	0.1
Other	5.8	0	3.8

A handful of battleships lingered on in several navies during the decade following World War II but, in a world now polarised between East and West, they were increasingly anachronistic, outdated by a tide of technology.

The publishers would like to thank the following organizations and individuals for providing photographs

10: IWM/IWM. 12: IWM. 13: IWM. 14: US National Archives/IWM/IWM. 16: IWM (two). 18: IWM. 19: IWM (two). 20: IWM. 21: IWM (two). 22: US National Archives. 23: IWM/US Naval Historical Center. 24: IWM. 25: US Naval Historical Center. 26: Aldo Fraccaroli/IWM. 27: IWM. 28: IWM. 29: US National Archives. 30: US Naval Historical Center. 32: IWM. 33: IWM. 34: IWM. 35: US National Archives. 36: US Naval Historical Center. 37: IWM. 38: IWM. 39: IWM. 40: US Naval Historical Center. 43: US Naval Historical Center. 44: US Naval Historical Center. 45: US Naval Historical Center. 46: US National Archives. 47: US Naval Historical Center. 48: US Naval Historical Center. 49: IWM. 50: IWM. 51-3: IWM. 54: US Naval Historical Center/IWM. 55-61: IWM. 63: US National Archives. 64: US Navy. 65: IWM. 66: US Naval Historical Center/IWM. 67-73: IWM. 74-5: US Naval Historical Center. 76: US Navy. 78: US Navy. 79: IWM/US Naval Historical Center. 80-81: US Navy. 82-4: IWM. 85: US Naval Historical Center (three). 86: US Navy. 87: US Naval Historical Center. 88-91: US Navy. 92: US Navy. 93: US Navy. 94: US Naval Historical Center. 95: US Naval Historical Center (two). 96: US Naval Historical Center. 97: US Naval Historical Center (two). 98: IWM. 99: US Navy. 101: US Naval Historical Center. 102: US National Archives. 103: US Naval Historical Center. 104-110: US Naval Historical Center. 111: IWM/ US Naval Historical Center. 112: US Army. 113-22: IWM. 123: US Naval Historical Center. 124-31: IWM. 132: US Naval Historical Center. 134-5: IWM. 136: US Naval Historical Center. 139: US Navy. 140: US Navy. 141: US Naval Historical Center. 142-58: US Naval Historical Center. 159: IWM. 160-62: IWM. 163: US Naval Historical Center. 164-71: IWM. 172: Bunbury Collection. 172: US Naval Historical Center/IWM. 173-79: IWM. 181: US Naval Historical Center. 182: US Naval Historical Center/US Navy. 184-90: US Navy. 191: US Naval Historical Center (two). 192-9: US Navy. 200: US Naval Historical Center. 201: US Naval Historical Center. 202: US Naval Historical Center (two). 204-7: US Navy. 208: US Naval Historical Center (two). 209: US Navy. 210-11: US Naval Historical Center. 212-8: US Naval Historical Center. 219: US Navy/IWM. 220: IWM. 221: IWM. 232-7: IWM 238: US National Archives. 240: IWM. 241-47: IWM. 248: US Naval Historical Center. 250: US National Archives. 251: US Naval Historical Center.